Diablo's Vengeance

Horsemen of Wrath MC # 1

Ciara St James

Copyright

ISBN: 978-1-955751-70-4

Printed in the United States of America
Editing by Mary Kern @ Ms. K Edits
Book cover by Kiwi Kreations

Warning

This book is intended for adult readers. It explores some topics that may not be to everyone's taste. Subjects considered taboo by some will be explored. It contains foul language and adult situations and includes things such as assault, torture, kidnapping, and murder, which may trigger some readers. Sexual situations are graphic. If these themes aren't what you like to read or you find them upsetting, this book isn't for you. There is no cheating or cliffhangers, and it has a HEA. This is a second chance at love, age-gap MC romance.

Dedication

This book is dedicated to several people. First, I have to thank my husband Tony, aka Trident, to many of you. He gave me the central idea of the first chapter scene two years ago, and I've been sitting on it until I found the right hero to star in it. Diablo is that man. Next, this book is dedicated to all my readers. You keep me going and inspire me to write more. A special shout-out to one particular reader: Jauhnna Hober. I told her that I loved her name, especially how it was spelled, and that I intended to use it one day as a character's first name. Well, as you can see, I did it.

And a final shout-out to my friend Brea. She's been asking me to write Diablo's story for over two years. I had to promise her I'd do it this year or else, . Brea, here's Diablo. All you other readers who may want to claim him as yours, Brea said to tell you all he's already hers. (Psst, I think she licked him.)

Pronunciation:
Jauhnna is pronounced Jawn-nah, the same as the most traditional spelling, Johnna

Horsemen of Wrath MC:

Victor Tate (Diablo)- President w/ Jauhnna
Kendrick Brady (Scorpion)- VP w/ TBD
Ryker Davila (Thunder)- Secretary w/ TBD
Madden DeLoche (Butcher)- Enforcer w/ TBD
Legend Belanger (wolverine)- Medic w/ TBD
Jagger Manning (Micro)- Treasurer/hacker w/ TBD
Aryek Sharpe (Crash)- Road Captain w/ TBD
Gray Cashman (Lucky)- Member w/ TBD
Cole DeMarco (Punk)- Member w/ TBD
Zander Brashears (Cowboy)- Member w/ TBD
Giovanni Vicenti (Turbo)- Member w/ TBD
Zax (Zaxton) Rizzo- Prospect
Liam Mosley- Prospect

Reading Order

For Dublin Falls Archangel's Warriors MC (DFAW), Hunters Creek Archangel's Warriors MC (HCAW), Iron Punishers MC (IPMC), Dark Patriots (DP), Pagan Souls of Cherokee MC (PSCMC), & Horsemen of Wrath MC (HOW)

Terror's Temptress DFAW 1
Savage's Princess DFAW 2
Steel & Hammer's Hellcat DFAW 3
Menace's Siren DFAW 4
Ranger's Enchantress DFAW 5
Ghost's Beauty DFAW 6
Viper's Vixen DFAW 7
Devil Dog's Precious DFAW 8
Blaze's Spitfire DFAW 9
Smoke's Tigress DFAW 10
Hawk's Huntress DFAW 11
Bull's Duchess HCAW 1
Storm's Flame DFAW 12
Rebel's Firecracker HCAW 2
Ajax's Nymph HCAW 3
Razor's Wildcat DFAW 13
Capone's Wild Thing DFAW 14
Falcon's She-Devil DFAW 15
Demon's Hellion HCAW 4
Torch's Tornado DFAW 16

Voodoo's Sorceress DFAW 17
Reaper's Banshee IPMC 1
Bear's Beloved HCAW 5
Outlaw's Jewel HVAW 6
Undertaker's Resurrection DP 1
Agony's Medicine Woman PSCMC 1
Ink's Whirlwind IP 2
Payne's Goddess HCAW 7
Maverick's Kitten HCAW 8
Tiger & Thorn's Tempest DFAW 18
Dare's Doll PSC 2
Maniac's Imp IP 3
Tank's Treasure HCAW 9
Blade's Boo DFAW 19
Law's Valkyrie DFAW 20
Gabriel's Retaliation DP 2
Knight's Bright Eyes PSC 3
Joker's Queen HCAW 10
Bandit & Coyote's Passion DFAW 21
Sniper's Dynamo & Gunner's Diamond DFAW 22
Slash's Dove HCAW 11
Lash's Hurricane IP 4
Spawn's She-Wolf IP 5
Griffin's Revelation DP 3
Twisted's Storm PSC 4
Diablo's Vengeance HOW 1

For Ares Infidels MC

Sin's Enticement AIMC 1
Executioner's Enthrallment AIMC 2
Pitbull's Enslavement AIMC 3
Omen's Entrapment AIMC 4
Cuffs' Enchainment AIMC 5

Rampage's Enchantment AIMC 6
Wrecker's Ensnarement AIMC 7
Trident's Enjoyment AIMC 8
Fang's Enlightenment AIMC 9
Talon's Enamorment AIMC 10
Ares Infidels in NY AIMC 11
Phantom's Emblazonment AIMC 12
Saint's Enrapturement AIMC 13
Phalanx & Bullet's Entwinement AIMC 14
Torpedo's Entrancement AIMC 15
Boomer's Embroilment AIMC 16
Daredevil's Engulfment AIMC 17
Vicious, Ashes & Dragon's Entrenchment AIMC 18

For O'Sheerans Mafia

Darragh's Dilemma
Cian's Complication
Aidan's Ardor
Aisling's Craving

House of Lustz

Mikhail's Playhouse

Please follow Ciara on Facebook. For information on new releases & to catch up with Ciara, go to www.ciara-st-james.com or www.facebook.com/ciara.stjames.1 or https://www.facebook.com/groups/342893626927134 (Ciara St James Angels) or https://www.facebook.com/groups/923322252903958 (House of Lustz by Ciara St James) or https://www.facebook.com/groups/140489416021085 1 (O'Sheeran Mafia by Ciara St James)

Blurb:

Diablo's love and happiness had been ripped away from him years ago. He's left with a broken heart and his daughter. Since that day, he's done everything he could to keep her, his sister, and his club safe. Many call him cold, distrustful, and overprotective, but he doesn't care. He'll do anything to protect what is left of his family. The one thing he never seeks is another special woman. He's content with the fleeting encounters with the women who come to the club.

Another wedding of a biker friend has left him restless and questioning how he's lived his life for the past twenty-plus years. His best friend notes it and calls him on it. As he struggles to name what the cause is, a spur-of-the-moment ride with his club leads him to rescue a woman. One he and his club believe is a victim of more than kidnapping.

As the mystery and danger surrounding Jauhnna are revealed, Diablo is forced to acknowledge this woman has awakened things in him he thought long dead and buried with his wife. Jauhnna's story isn't pretty, and she's not free to do whatever she wants, no matter how much she wants Diablo.

Diablo is determined to free her, and as they grow to know each other and plan the steps to free her, Diablo finds he's still able to love and his heart isn't made of ice. Jauhnna discovers that there are men you can trust and that intimacy doesn't have to equate to pain and humiliation.

However, before they can be free and together, they have to eliminate her husband, the men who harmed her, and so much more in order for her to get her happily ever after with Diablo. And Diablo has to show her the whole Diablo and let her see how he got his name. Will it be too much for her? Will she walk once she knows the devil he has inside him? The devil is revealed when Diablo claims vengeance for Jauhnna. She's the second woman he's loved that he's had to release his devil fully to gain retribution.

There's danger, passion, misery, surprises, and miracles in this second chance at love for these two deserving people. See how the first of the Horsemen of Wrath falls. Everyone knows in these clubs that once the first succumbs, it's not long until the rest fall like dominoes. It has the other Horsemen wondering, who's next?

Diablo: Chapter 1

Pacing the house at loose ends, I tried to decide what to do. It was unusual for me not to be able to fill my time. If I wasn't doing my president's work for the club, I oversaw stuff at Wrath's Prep & Restore, the club's preparation and restoration business. Being in Florida, we did a lot of that, especially where it pertained to hurricanes. I'd never understand why some people waited until we were battened down for one to hit before they decided to call us, frantic to have shutters and other work done to their homes and businesses. Although, with this business, we benefited either way, so it was no skin off our noses.

That wasn't to say we used their desperation or misfortune to line our pockets beyond what was reasonable for our work because we didn't. We started our own business, offering our services several years ago, because of those who did that underhanded stuff. We were tired of hearing and seeing so many people being taken advantage of. At first, many potential customers were scared to trust an MC, but after a few did and began to rave about our work and prices, more and more people began to reach out to us. We had gained an excellent reputation and had more work than we could handle a lot of the time.

I was kept busy with my job as club president and as Prep & Restore's manager. Still, I was lucky to have several brothers who managed our other businesses expertly, so the responsibility for them didn't all fall on me, too. Of course, after being in the club in one way or another since birth, I knew the ins and outs of everything. It was an advantage to being what they called a legacy, someone whose close family member had been a club member. My father, Fiend, had joined once he got out of the service after Vietnam. He needed a way to wrap his head around what he'd seen and done. Not having a bunch of bullshit rules and the freedom to set your own boundaries appealed to him. He eventually worked his way up to enforcer.

He'd been lucky to find a woman who understood him, let him be himself, and was willing to stick with him in this lifestyle. Mom had been an ideal old lady. Growing up, I knew I wanted someone like her when I was ready to settle down. She was tough, fair, loving, and simultaneously a badass you didn't relish messing with. Just like that, I was traveling down memory lane to my wife, Amy.

We'd been so damn young when we met and fell in love. Most people would've said we were too young and would never last. They had said it when they noted I was a biker while she was the sweet, good daughter of a middle-class family. I was nineteen to her seventeen. We knew if her parents found out about us, they'd find a way to separate us, so we hid it and snuck around until she was eighteen. By then, when she ran off to be with me, she was three months pregnant with our daughter, Brooklyn. We married a week later, and I'd like to think if she hadn't been murdered, we'd still be together. I hadn't met any woman who made me want to have one around permanently since her.

Maybe last weekend brought on my restlessness and thoughts of Amy. We'd traveled to Cherokee, North Carolina, for a wedding. Since Brooklyn married Torch and became part of the Archangel's Warriors MC in Dublin Falls, Tennessee, my club has become friends and allies with them, their other chapters, and their allied clubs. One of those, the Pagans Souls of Cherokee, had invited us to their latest wedding. Twisted and his old lady, Zahirah, had tied the knot.

It was a good time, and we relaxed and enjoyed spending time with everyone even if there had been a bit of work thrown in, but they refused to let it interfere. I spent time with Brooklyn and my two grandsons, Thane, who was two-and-a-half, and Jai, who was seven months. It was good to have small children around. The utter joy they felt in almost everything and their innocence was damn refreshing to me. I tormented Torch that it would've been perfect if I didn't have to put up with him. I grumbled and bitched about how he'd ruined my life by taking my baby girl away from me and then denying me my grandchildren. Threats were made to kill him and bury his ass in the mountains of Cherokee. There were a ton of places in the thick woods to do it.

Unfortunately, after being with her for over three years, he knew I was full of it, mostly. She loved him so much, and I knew he loved her. He would do anything to make sure she and their kids were happy and safe. He reminded me a lot of me with Amy, although I didn't tell him that. It was good to keep him on his toes. He knew if he ever hurt her or those kids, whether it was emotionally or physically, I'd take them away and punish him tenfold.

When it was time to leave and return home, I hated to part with them. Torch and Brooklyn promised to bring themselves and the kids to visit me in Florida soon. I hoped so. My house was too quiet and empty. More and more, I wondered if I should downsize. I'd built a bigger house right after Torch claimed Brooklyn. I'd hoped they'd be here more often and wanted plenty of room for them and any grandchildren. She'd teased me that I was getting ready to find another woman and settle down to have her some brothers and sisters. I told her that wasn't happening. Recalling the conversation made me reflect on it.

"Dad, it's good to see you make changes," Brooklyn said with a smile.

"What do you mean? It's just a different house." I waved nonchalantly.

"Yes, a new, bigger one. You're finally going to do it, aren't you? I'm so glad."

"Do what, Brookie? You're not making any sense."

"You're going to find someone special and settle down again. You'll have someone to grow old with. Maybe give me those siblings I've wanted all my life. You deserve it."

"Stop right there. This house is for you and your family. I want room for all of you and however many kiddos you have when you come to visit. I have no plans to find someone. I don't need or want a woman. I had my chance, and I lost her. I'm just happy I had her for the time I did, and I got you."

She gave me a sad look. "Dad, you're so young. You're only forty-four, with years ahead of you. A whole second family is more than possible. You love kids. I don't think Mom would begrudge you finding happiness. She wouldn't want you to be alone. Don't tell me you don't get lonely. And before you say it, because I don't want to think about it, those women you hook up with at the clubhouse or around the area aren't what I mean. Most of them are just chasing a patch and a man to take care of them. You need a good, loving, strong woman, not those sluts."

I chose not to touch on the subject of me and sex. There were things you didn't want to talk to your kid about, even if she was an adult. I didn't want to speak about her and Torch having it, either. The baby she was pregnant with was immaculately conceived, was what I told myself.

"It's not happening, so forget it. The house is for your family, and now that you've brought all these other clubs into our lives, I'll have more places for others to stay if they visit."

She tried to talk me into at least trying to find someone, but I refused. She finally gave up. She mentioned it a few times since then, wanting to know if I was seeing anyone, and I told her no every time.

So why was I dwelling on it so much after this last visit? I'd been to numerous weddings over the past three years and had seen countless happy couples. The other MCs seemed to have a knack for finding and knowing someone was their match almost immediately. I was glad for them. I wished them long, happy lives, but my mind hadn't changed. Except, could I still say that? This time, I found myself checking out the women there to see if there was anyone single I might want to get to know, though it wouldn't be ideal when living so far away.

All this week, as I went to and from work and about town running errands and other stuff, I'd found myself paying attention to the women I passed and ran into. There wasn't a lack of them, not in Florida. And even though I was forty-seven, I still got more than my share of looks and come-ons.

I hadn't paid a good, honest woman attention since Amy. I hadn't wanted to risk leading one on. To have her think there was a chance for something more than a casual fling. I loved sex as much as the next man, and I got my needs taken care of, but I'd always been careful not to do it where Brooklyn could see me. She was taught early on never to be at the clubhouse after a particular time, especially on the weekends. The guys mainly were single even then, and they liked to party and get wild. Even with that rule, I'd been cautious never to engage in sex of any kind out in the public areas of the clubhouse. I always took the woman to my crash room in the back. My house was off-limits, too. Even now that she was out of the house, none of them were brought home with me.

These days, those encounters were less often, but not because I wanted sex less or was becoming unable to perform. Every morning, my morning wood attested to the fact that I could still get it up. When I did have sex, I could get it up more than once and go for a long time. No, it was due to finding the whole process of being with club sluts or hangers-on unappealing. They bored me. It was the same woman, with a different body, face, and agenda.

What the fuck is wrong with me? Get out of your head, Diablo. You don't need a woman or anyone other than your daughter, her family, and your club.

A loud thumping on my front door got my attention. Wondering who it was, I went to answer it. I opened the door without looking out to see who stood there. There was no need. My house was inside the club's property, surrounded by fencing. You had to be either let in one of the gates or have the access code to open those gates to enter. Someone thinking they could jump it would have a difficult time getting over it without tearing their asses up. The ten-foot chain link fence had anti-climb mesh and fence extensions to prevent scaling.

In addition, at the top, we had the coiled wire, which most people call razor wire, to give it extra security and make it nearly impenetrable. Micro, our IT wizard, had CCTV security cameras, alarms, and motion sensors to alert us to unauthorized access. It looked like a military installation. Some might think that was going overboard, but if they had lost someone the way I had, they wouldn't. After Amy was murdered, I moved Brooklyn inside the fence and, over the years, fortified it. As the door swung open, my gaze landed on Butcher, our enforcer. He was wearing a sober expression. He gave me a chin lift.

"Butcher, come in," I said as I stepped back to let him inside. He stepped inside but didn't go to the living room, which was what he typically would do. He stopped to face me.

"Pres, we need to talk."

"Okay, do you wanna sit or stand here and do it?" I had no idea why he was acting this way.

"We can sit. I know this might not be my place, but I need to say something."

"Then let's have a seat. If you want a drink, help yourself."

He chose not to go to the kitchen, so I didn't either. After we sat, he launched right into it without waiting for me to say a word. I liked to get straight to the point. Some would say I was too direct, but to me, it eliminated confusion and wasted time.

"Something has been eating at you. It's been under the radar for a while, but it's become more noticeable since last weekend. Talk to me. This is me, your friend Butcher, talking to my friend, not my president. You've been restless and spending more time alone. The others are noticing and talking about it. I've waited for you to talk to me, but you haven't, so here I am."

Butcher was the next oldest in the club after me. I was five years older than him. We'd been in the club the longest. Others had come and gone, leaving us the elders. Christ, that made me feel old, an elder at my age. Maybe I should've gotten a drink after all. We'd come up through the ranks together, although I started five years ahead of him and moved slightly faster. He began prospecting at eighteen, the same as I had. I considered him my best friend.

I didn't answer him right away. Not because his bluntness surprised or offended me, but because I didn't have an answer. I considered what he said and what I'd been thinking before he arrived. It was as if he had read my mind. A minute later, I knew I had to say something. I sighed.

"Butch, I have no goddamn clue what's wrong with me. You're right. I am restless, feel unsatisfied, and I'm trying to figure out why."

"It's been coming on for a long time. What happened this past weekend? I thought you enjoyed yourself and loved seeing Brooklyn and the family. Did something happen between you two that I don't know about? Did you have a fight?"

I was shaking my head before he even finished. "No, nothing happened. I did love it. Thane and Jai are growing so fast. I admit seeing them and knowing I miss out on so much due to the distance sucks. We do web chats and calls, but they're not the same."

"If she didn't love Torch so much, I'd say let's go steal them back, but she'd be miserable and kick our asses, and he'd come down with his whole club to rescue them. The man is crazy for them, which is damn lucky for him," he muttered.

Butcher was like an uncle to Brooklyn. He'd been one of the ones who stepped up to help me raise her after Amy died. There were a few old ladies in the club back then. The ones to the older guys had helped a ton, too, but they had their own families, and I never wanted to take advantage of them. The sight of us learning to braid hair or put it in ponytails and pick out girly clothing and gifts had been hilarious to the others and stressful as hell for us. I thought she turned out pretty damn well. The newer members of the club claim they were her brothers versus her uncles. When she settled in Tennessee, there had been a lot of grumbling.

"He's a damn good father and old man," I agreed.

"So if it's not Brooklyn, then what is it? Are you no longer loving the club? Don't tell me you want to step down or get out altogether?"

"Hell no, I don't want to step down or leave! This club has been a part of me my whole life. I'll leave when I either can no longer ride, and I'm kicked to the curb, or I die. Now, if I can no longer effectively serve as your president, I'll step back and let someone else lead, but that's it."

"Whew, okay, it's not that. You had me worried for a minute or two that you might be losing your mind and contemplating doing one of those. I'd hate to have to beat sense into you, but I would," he told me, sporting a big grin.

"Listen, fucker, don't forget who the enforcer was before you. My ass isn't so easy to whip. You're welcome to try, but don't get upset when I beat yours." I smirked. He chuckled. but didn't deny it.

"Come on, you have to have some idea of the cause. You spend less time at the clubhouse. You barely look at any of the sluts or hangers-on, let alone accept their offers. As far as I know, you're not fucking anyone in town."

I threw up my hands. He was like a dog with a bone. He wouldn't stop until I gave him something. "I'm not sure, damn it! I was thinking about it before you showed up. You're right. The women don't interest me, and before you ask if I can get it up, I can—no little blue pills needed here. I'm tired of the same old thing. They're interchangeable—same conversation, and the majority are scheming patch chasers."

"You're lonely, and one of those women won't do. You need an old lady," he said decisively. I opened my mouth to deny it, but he cut me off before I could utter a word.

"Uh, don't say it. You see the same thing I do. Most of our friends in other clubs are settling down, and they're thrilled about it. I believe you want that because I do. I'm forty-two, Diablo. I've spread my wild oats and had a bunch of fun doing it, but I want more. I want someone to come home to every night. I want a family and love."

"And you should get it, Butch. In my case, I already had it."

"Don't take my head off, but Amy has been gone for over twenty years. I know you loved her. You can still honor your two's love and her memory and still love another woman. It's not betrayal or a sin. I won't nag you about it, but I need you to promise to consider it. I've always believed you would find another woman and your life would be even better. Okay, I've said my piece for now. On to the other reason I came over." He paused. The asshole always made me ask.

"Yeah, why's that?"

"The guys are at the clubhouse. It's a great day out—sunny and hot. They want to go for a ride. We were up to Cherokee last weekend, but let's get out and blow away the cobwebs again. Crash has a route plotted out."

His suggestion was one I could get behind. Any excuse to be on my bike with the wind in my face was a yes. I stood up. "Why the hell didn't you start with that? What're you waiting for? Get your ass moving. I'll meet you guys at the clubhouse. Give me about ten minutes."

He rose to his feet, chuckling. Giving me a fist bump, he strode to the door and opened it. "See you in ten," he called out before closing it.

As I got my stuff together and went to get my bike out of the garage, I tried not to dwell on what he'd said or the impact his words had on me. I might reexamine them later, but it was time to ride for now.

Pulling out of the garage a few minutes later, I revved the engine and headed to the clubhouse, which wasn't far from my place. I wanted to be close to it in case I was needed, but far enough away not to hear all the noise when the guys were partying. I wasn't the only one who had a house. All the officers and Crash had built one over the past few years. The others were talking about doing it one day. I thought we might get one or two sooner rather than later. There was plenty of room in the clubhouse, but it got old.

As I made my way toward the clubhouse, the sound of motorcycle engines grew louder. God, there was nothing like the throaty rumble of a bike. When Brooklyn was a baby and toddler and had a hard time sleeping, I'd lull her to sleep by turning on my bike. She'd go out like a light.

Today, I rode my Harley Road King rather than my Indian bike. I stopped in front of the clubhouse, where there was a designated area for bike parking and regular vehicle parking on the opposite side. A quick scan told me the entire club was going on the ride. Good. Zax and Liam, our two current prospects, had the crash truck and trailer out and ready to go. We took them along in case any of us broke down. We'd either be able to haul our bike back or fix it with the parts and tools we carried in the truck if it was minor enough.

Liam had joined us three months ago, and Zax two months before him. The two prior prospects hadn't been able to cut it, so they were let go. Suffice it to say, neither was happy with our decision. So far, I was pleased with what I saw from these two. Unless they majorly screwed up between now and when it was time to take a vote, they should patch in with no problem.

Unlike other clubs, who made their prospects do a year or less before deciding whether to patch them or not, in ours, it was two years. I'd implemented that rule a few years back when we had a run of issues with guys gutting it out for the year, only to end up disappointments after they got their patch. They were subsequently shown the door or made to see they weren't a fit. They were lucky. If it had been back in my dad's day or my early years, they would've been made to bleed, and, in some cases, that meant death. It depended on the reason they were no longer a part of us.

Hands were raised, and chins lifted in greeting as I weaved my bike to the head of the pack. I rode at the front, with the officers behind me and the regular members behind them. The prospects brought up the rear. If we didn't have them, the road captain often brought up the rear to ensure everyone stayed with the group. Once I noted they were all in their usual spots, I raised my hand and made a fist. The roar got louder as we made our way to the front gate. We had two of them, but this was the one we used most of the time.

Easing out onto our road, which wound through the heavily wooded area around us, we headed for County Rd 214. Our compound was outside the city of St. Augustine, near Cowan Swamp. As we got to the 214, I noticed a car sitting alongside the road. I didn't see anyone nearby. Probably someone who ran out of gas and had to call for help or, worse, hoof it to a gas station. Some people never learned.

We kept heading west, passing over Interstate 95. Once we got out further, we broke off onto more minor roads. We rode for a couple of hours. It was as great as I knew it would be. If we'd started earlier, we would've gone longer, but since we hadn't, and it was Saturday and I knew the guys would want to be back to party, we kept it shorter.

It was late afternoon when we came zooming back, headed for our turnoff. As we got close, I saw that the abandoned car was still there. Hmm, I wondered why it hadn't been either towed or recovered. The business-minded part of me knew we might be able to gain a customer. One of our main businesses was our garage, Horsemen's Repair, which offered a mobile mechanic service if you were willing to pay and the problem could be fixed without a lot of specialized equipment and tools. You'd be surprised how many times that was the case. The majority of people seemed unable or unwilling to do the most straightforward maintenance or repairs these days. I had no complaints. It made us a lot of money.

Raising my arm, I signaled I was pulling off. When I did, the others followed. It looked like it would be a club affair. Shutting off our bikes, I swung off mine. I stretched my back out for several moments before walking the rest of the way to the car. Hopefully, it wasn't locked, and I could get inside to hunt for the registration. With a name and address, Micro would have no problem finding a number to call. Lacking that, we'd get the license plate number so he could run it to get the information. Sure, it would be easier to have one of us jot it down and be done with it, but we weren't in a hurry.

Walking up to the passenger door, I checked out the car. It was a newer dark sedan with dark-tinted windows. There didn't appear to be any damage to it, to explain why it was here. Tugging on the handle, I was pleased to find it unlocked. The door swung open. Leaning inside, I discovered it was sweltering hot. Christ, why didn't whoever it belonged to at least open the window? If you left it sealed up enough times, your windows might crack.

I opened the glove box. I was taken aback to find only the owner's manual in it. Looking around, I saw no other places where the registration could be. Well, shit, so much for that idea. The guys were all talking and joking. Ignoring them, I went to the rear of the car to get the license plate number. There wasn't one on the front. A piece of cloth caught my attention as I glanced at the plate. It was hanging out of the trunk. Peering at it closer, I saw it was a semi-sheer blue material.

Immediately, every crime show I ever watched flashed through my mind, and there were a ton of them. All I thought was, what if a body was in the trunk? I gave a loud, piercing whistle to get the others' attention. They quieted down instantly and started toward me.

"What's wrong, Diablo?" Scorpion, my VP, asked.

"Someone pull the trunk release. I wanna check something out."

Thunder opened the driver's door and pulled it. As the trunk unlatched, my guys gathered around me in a semicircle. Slowly, I reached out and shoved the trunk lid up. As it fully lifted, I blinked. Hisses and muttering broke out as we took in the sight before us. Lying curled up in the fetal position, covered from head to chest in blood, was a body.

It was clear it was the body of a woman. Long jet-black hair was sticking in the blood covering her face. Around her wrists and ankles were ropes. The fabric I'd seen belonged to a long, gauzy skirt she had on. My gut clenched. Jesus Christ, no wonder whoever was driving abandoned it. They'd killed someone and were transporting the body. God knew we had enough woods and swamp land to dispose of one. We'd done it ourselves more than a few times.

Shit, we needed to think about how to handle this. If we called the cops, most likely, they'd think we had something to do with it and throw all our asses in jail. As I debated what to do about it, Wolverine moved closer and touched her neck. He was our medic. He'd done a few years in the Navy as a corpsman. As he pressed into the side of her bloody neck to check for a pulse, we were all startled to hear a soft, pitiful moan come out of her.

"Fuck, she's alive! Someone call 911, and one of you go get my kit," Wolverine snapped, taking charge.

I heard footsteps running away. I had no idea who they belonged to because I was too busy staring at the woman.

"We need to get her out of there. It's sweltering. She no doubt has heatstroke," Wolverine muttered angrily.

"I'll lift her out. You get your equipment out to check her over," I told him. I wasn't sure why. It was as if this overwhelming urge to do it overcame me. He didn't argue. He just moved back.

I had no idea if she could hear me. Other than that single moan, she hadn't made another sound or even moved. "Honey, I hope you can hear me. I'm gonna pick you up. I'll try to make it hurt as little as possible. We're here to help you, not hurt you. My brother, Wolverine, is a medic. He wants to check you out."

After lifting her out, I cradled her close. I took a few steps and then went to crouch down to lay her on the ground. I stopped. "Someone throw a blanket or something on the ground. She doesn't need any dirt in her wounds," I barked.

Liam popped up carrying Wolverine's kit, and he

had a blanket, too. He didn't waste time handing the kit over and spreading the blanket out. I squatted and placed her on it as soon as it was down. I stayed there and watched as Wolverine got to work. He got out his stethoscope and blood pressure cuff first.

"How long until the ambulance gets here?" he hollered after he checked her blood pressure. He had a worried frown on his face. That didn't bode well.

"They said twenty minutes. There was a big wreck in town," Lucky answered back.

"Son of a bitch," he snarled. He was listening to her chest.

"What is it?" I asked.

"Her pressure is low. She's burning up. She's suffering from heatstroke from being in the trunk for God knows how long. I've got to get her body temp down now. If I don't, she might die or at least have permanent damage to her brain and organs."

It took me mere seconds to decide. "Load her into the crash truck, and we'll take her to the clubhouse. You can work on her there. Lucky, call the ambulance back and tell them where to come. Let's roll," I shouted.

There was a flurry as they went for their bikes. Zax ran to bring the truck closer to us. When he got it there, I was the one to carry her to it. As I placed her in the back, Wolverine told Liam to ride his bike back, followed by the obligatory threat of death if he put a mark on it, and then he climbed in with her. I almost protested, then stopped myself. He was the logical one to ride with her. I wouldn't have a clue what to do. Shutting the door, I ran to my bike, and we were off. The short ride to the compound was filled with me wondering who she was and why she'd been in the trunk.

Diablo: Chapter 2

Anxiety seemed to be swirling in my gut as I carried the woman into the clubhouse and to the room set aside for Wolverine to do his medical work. He called it the sick bay. It was what they called it in the Navy. After seeing what they had set up in Dublin Falls and Hunters Creek, he'd become envious and insisted we needed something similar. I wasn't about to argue with him, so we conferred with Zara, Demon's old lady and wife in Hunters Creek, on what was essential. Being a doctor and having a clinic, she was the expert. The other old ladies, who were medically trained, helped as well.

I thought we had a more-than-decent setup. Occasionally, he'd come to church to ask for something new. He only did that when it was a big-budget item. He had a set budget we gave him each month to buy other needed supplies. We'd hear him out and then vote on whether to purchase it. We didn't have that many medical needs, but it paid to be prepared. Sometimes, it wouldn't be wise to go to the hospital for treatment unless necessary.

"Put her here," he told me, pointing to the exam table. I placed her down as gently as possible. I was worried. He'd told me she hadn't made a sound or moved the whole ride here. I slipped my fingers up to feel for a pulse. Relief flooded me, feeling it was there, although not as strong as I thought it should be.

Wolverine was at the sink, running water into a basin. He'd closed the door to the room, so it was just us and her. I stood there, not knowing what to do, but I couldn't leave either. He came to the table with the basin and several washcloths.

"I need to cool her down. Could you ask someone to run and get as much ice as possible? And tell them to knock when they come back. Don't just barge in," he instructed.

"Sure thing."

Moving to the door, I cracked it. The hall was full of guys. They cast me quizzical looks. "We need ice, as much as you can get. Knock, don't come in." I saw Liam dart off. I addressed Scorpion.

"Is someone at the gate waiting for the ambulance?"

"Lucky and Zax are, but I don't know how soon they'll arrive. When Lucky called them back, they had no idea how soon they'd get here. I guess the wreck was huge and had so many casualties they had to call for help. She might be here for a while."

"Shit! Alright, let me talk to Wolverine. Maybe she isn't as bad as we think, and we can just cancel them since they're not doing us much good anyway. If she needs to be moved, we might be better off taking her ourselves," I muttered before shutting the door.

When I turned, I found Wolverine had her top off and was working on her skirt. The sight of her exposed to him, even though she had on underwear and a bra, bothered me.

"What're you doing?" I asked, even though it was plain to see what he was doing.

"I've got to get these off so I can place cool cloths all over her body. I'll leave her underclothes on. I don't want her to wake up and freak out that she's naked with strange men."

"Scorpion said the ambulances are tied up and have no idea when they can reach her. Do you think it's severe enough that we should just take her to the hospital, or can you take care of her here?" I wanted to be beside her but stayed near the door to get the ice.

"Goddamn it, just our luck. I can't be sure, Pres. If she doesn't start to react, wake up, or cool down soon, I think she needs more help than I can give her." He was placing wet cloths on her head, wrists, ankles, and underneath her neck and armpits.

"Why those spots?"

"Those are where you have pulse points, and the blood comes closest to the surface. Placing them there will cool her faster. Ah, hell, forget these. I need a sheet. Where's the damn ice!" He raised his voice.

I swung around to open the door to yell for it. I had my hand on the handle when there was a knock. Cracking it again, I reached out to snag the big bowl of ice Liam held.

"I can run and get more if you need it," he said.

"Gather what you can, then hang onto it, in case we do. See what everybody has at their houses. Scorpion, tell Lucky to call the ambulance back and tell them to cancel the call out if they can't be here in the next ten minutes. We'll bring her in if she needs to go," I ordered.

"Got it. Let us know what else you need," he responded before walking off.

"Thanks," I said to Liam as I shut the door and

rushed the ice to Wolverine. He took it and dumped it into the sink with the water he'd run into it. Next, he dunked a bedsheet into the iced water, soaking it. Wanting to be helpful, I took one end of the sheet and helped him to wring it out when it was thoroughly wet. We carried it to the table and spread it out over her. Once it was in place, he picked up one of the washcloths and handed it to me, along with a pair of gloves.

"Will you wipe the blood off her face while I examine her? I need to know where she's injured and how badly. With all that on her, I have no clue."

"Sure."

I wrestled the gloves on. I hated when I had to use them. Admittedly, it was never to help someone. They were necessary when getting my hands dirty for other reasons. After I got them on, I re-wetted the cloth and began to wipe at the hair sticking to the blood on her face. I pretended she was a baby. I recalled how it was to wash Brooklyn when she was small, and I'd been afraid I'd hurt her.

It took some work, but eventually, I got her hair out of the way and was able to tackle the blood. As her skin became visible, I couldn't help but notice things about her other than her injury. She was young, maybe a few years older than Brooklyn. Her skin was so pale but based on what I saw of the rest of her, this was her natural skin tone. It contrasted with her jet-black hair, which was long, thick, and straight. Her nose was straight and delicate. It matched with the rest of her face. I was tempted to take off my gloves and run my fingers over her skin to see if it was as soft as it looked. The only blemish I saw, and it was almost unnoticeable, was a thin white scar above her left eyebrow. When I got to her hairline, I discovered the source of the blood or at least one of them. There was a cut there. I stayed away from it, not wanting to cause it to start bleeding again.

"She's got a cut along her hairline," I told him. He was cleansing and examining her upper chest, listening to her breathing with his stethoscope, and re-checking her blood pressure.

"So far, I haven't found any others. It could very well be this is all from her head wound. They bleed copiously. I need to check the back of her head. Will you hold her up so I can?"

"I can. You wanna do it now?"

"Yeah, let's. In fact, we need to roll her over. I'll examine her backside and put down a wet sheet underneath her. Give me a minute to get one," he said, before walking to the cabinet where he kept bedding and other supplies. He pulled out another sheet and took it to the sink. Within no time, he was back. I hesitated to touch her. What if I hurt her? He appeared sure of his touch, so I followed his lead.

He told me where to place my hands and when to roll her. She ended up pressed to me. He spread out the sheet and then began running his hands over the back of her head. He hissed and scowled harder.

"What?"

"She's got a big knot back here and a cut. I think it's a pretty good bet whoever put her in that trunk ambushed her, knocked her out, and then stuffed her in there. I'm not sure how she got the cut on the front of her head. She might have a concussion. Let me finish checking her back and stuff."

He quickly ran his eyes and hands down the rest of her. Again, I was struck by the need to tell him not to touch her. What the hell was up with that? I didn't know her. Why care about anyone touching her, as long as it wasn't to harm her?

"Okay, you can let her rest back. I'm done. There's some bruising and scrapes along with her head injuries. Let me take a closer look at the rest of her front," Wolverine said. I eased her back.

He removed the wet sheet and tossed it back into the cold water. I took notice of her body this time. Was it the time or place? No, but then again, I was a healthy male, and an attractive woman was hard to ignore for long. As he continued to prod and poke her, I scanned her from head to toe. Even still bloody and in less-than-ideal shape, there was no denying she was a tempting woman. Her body was what I called shapely. She had curves and meat on her bones. Her breasts filled out the bra more than adequately. Her waist was slightly curved inward before swelling wider, revealing she had hips. No one would see her from a distance and mistake her for a boy. Her legs were toned, and her thighs were thick, but not in a bad way. When he had me holding her on her side, I noticed she had an ass on her, too. Jesus, I had no right to be thinking any of this. She was my daughter's age. Talk about a dirty old man.

Of course, the club sluts and hangers-on tended to be young as well, but they were different. Whoever this woman was, I doubted she'd appreciate a man ogling her and cataloging all her attributes while she was unconscious. I needed to concentrate on getting her the help she needed, not fantasizing about her body and how sexy I found her. I was shaken from my perusal by Wolverine's next remarks.

"Whoever did this, she fought back. See her

knuckles? I wonder who she is and why someone felt the need to take her?" As he considered it, he was back to wringing out the sheet again. I hurried over to help him. I felt relief when she was covered again. He got out a small light. I knew it was used to check her pupils. I leaned close to watch.

When he lifted her eyelid, I was struck. She had the greenest eyes I'd ever seen. They didn't look real. Before I thought of it, a comment slipped out.

"Damn, those are some green contacts."

"They're not. Those are all hers, and you're right. They are an unusual green. Her pupils are a bit sluggish. She might have a concussion. We need to see if we can get her to wake up. Give me a second, and I'll grab the smelling salts. Be ready. If she does wake up, she'll likely be confused and terrified. We can't let her hurt herself more," he warned, as he went to one of the drawers and then returned.

I stood still as he broke the white capsule and waved it under her nose. She jerked, and her head moved slightly away from the noxious scent. He did it again. She scrunched her brow this time, and then her eyelids fluttered slightly. He leaned closer to her.

"Sweetheart, we need you to wake up so we know if you're alright. Come on. You can do it. Show us those gorgeous green eyes. Tell us your name. We want to help you, honey," he softly crooned to her. Hearing him talk to her like that made my hackles rise. I had to force myself not to snap at him.

Her head shifted from side to side a couple of times. I held my breath. Moments later, her eyelids fluttered again, but this time, she opened them. When she saw us, surprise and then fear entered them. She gasped and tried to move away from us. I placed my hand on her shoulder. Her body was shaking. She flinched when I touched her.

"Honey, it's okay. No one here will hurt you. We brought you here to help you," I told her.

For several seconds, she shifted her gaze between the two of us, as if trying to determine if I was lying. Finally, she opened her mouth.

"W-who are you? Where am I?" she whispered hoarsely.

"I'm Diablo, and this is Wolverine. You're in our clubhouse just outside of St. Augustine, Florida. Can you tell us your name? Do you live in St. Aug?" I asked.

"Clubhouse?" she asked in confusion.

I watched as her eyes scanned us. She noted the tattoos she could see and our leather cuts. I turned far enough to allow her to see the back of my cut to answer her unspoken next question. Her eyes widened, and instead of reassuring her, it terrified her more. Suddenly, she was lashing out with a fist and trying to get up at the same time. Both of us reached out to subdue her.

"Whoa, that's not necessary. We're not harming you. You need to lie still. You've been through an ordeal. I don't know if you have other serious injuries," Wolverine explained as he prevented her from getting up. I had both of my hands holding her shoulders. I made my grip as gentle as possible.

"Please, let me go. I won't tell. Please," she pleaded. Hearing those words and seeing her terror, tore at my heart.

"Honey, we can't. Not until we know you'll be alright. Just calm down. Yes, we're bikers, but you have nothing to fear. We don't hurt women and kids. I'm the president. I can promise you, you won't be harmed by anyone here. Will you tell us your name, please?"

I eased off my hold on her as I talked. I don't know if it was that combined with my smile and calm tone, but she seemed to relax a bit more. I waited patiently for her answer.

"My name is Jauhnna. You said I'm in St. Augustine, Florida?"

"It's nice to meet you, Jauhnna, although I wish it had been under better circumstances. Yes, St. Aug, Florida. We're outside the city limits. My club has property, and you're in the clubhouse. We found you along the road in the trunk of a car. Can you tell us what happened?" I asked. I wanted to know who the fuck did this to her.

"Wait, sorry, Pres, but first I need to ask her a few questions to check out her memory," Wolverine interjected before she could answer me.

"You're right. Go ahead and ask whatever you want. I'll wait."

Her gaze went from me to him.

"Thanks. Jauhnna, can you tell me your full name, where you live, and how old you are? I need to assess if your memory is impaired. You have a big knot on the back of your head and cuts in front and back. We suspect you were hit at least twice," he explained kindly.

"My name is Jauhnna Carter. I live in Savannah, Georgia. I'm thirty-two."

Savannah wasn't far, just under two hundred miles north of us. I wondered why her kidnappers were bringing her to Florida. As I thought that, her age pushed into my head more. Damn, she was only six years older than my daughter. Disappointment filled me at the thought, though I had no clue why. What did it matter? Wolverine was asking her more questions. I chose to focus on those.

"Do you hurt anywhere? I need you to be honest. I can't help you if I don't know."

"My head is pounding, and my arms and legs feel stiff and achy. I'm so thirsty."

"I put in an IV to hydrate you in the truck, but you're alert enough to drink. Stay right there and let me get you some water."

He went to the small fridge he had in here and took out a bottle of water. He brought it to her. She tried to sit up but slumped back down. Finding the latch on the table, I raised the head of it for her. She gave me a faint, grateful smile. I noticed her hand shook when she took the bottle from him to take a drink. Without thinking, I put my hand on the bottom and held it for her.

"Take it slow. Take little sips until we know if you can keep it down. If you have a concussion, it can make you nauseated," Wolverine warned her. He was closely watching her.

She did as he said. When I thought she'd taken enough for her first time, I eased the bottle away.

"Thank you," she muttered.

"Can you tell us what happened? Who did this to you? Do you know why they'd bring you to Florida?" I asked, impatient to have something to go on.

She grimaced and was silent for a few moments before she began her tale. Emotion was evident immediately.

"I wish I could tell you who did this to me, but

I didn't know any of the men who took me. They were strangers."

"Okay, where were you taken from? What did they say to you? Did they say anything to indicate if you were a random person they grabbed or if they were after you specifically? There's a huge human trafficking trade all over the world, and Florida is a prime spot for it. They seem able to get people in and out of the country more easily from here," I explained.

She shifted on the table before continuing. "They were waiting for me when I left my house for work. I think it was this morning. A man approached me. He said he was looking for his dog, which had run away. I asked him what kind it was and its name. When he hesitated over it, I got suspicious. I tried to escape him by saying I would go in one direction while he went in the other.

"I planned to either get to my car or back to the house. He knew he was busted, though, and he came at me. I tried to fight him and would've gotten away if it wasn't for the fact that he had a partner hiding nearby. When I resisted, he came out of the shadows and hit me on the back of the head. I remember everything getting woozy after he did it.

"They picked me up and took me to their car. It was parked not far away. When we got to it, I started fighting again. I hit the front of my head when I was slammed into the bumper of the car and then was shoved into the trunk and restrained. After that, it was just endless driving until I lost consciousness. What day is it, and what time?"

She shivered as she came to a halt in her explanation. I didn't want to badger her, but the more details we had, the better.

"It's Saturday, the third, and it's six ten in the evening," Wolverine supplied as he came to her with a thermometer. It was one of those you ran across the forehead. It beeped quickly. He glanced at the reading and nodded.

"Your temperature is coming down. That's good. We were afraid you'd suffered heatstroke in that trunk. It can be deadly."

His remark made the wet sheets and her state of undress register. She glanced down at her body, and then her cheeks reddened. She wouldn't make eye contact with either of us. I thought it was cute. When was the last time I saw a woman blush? I couldn't recall. She crossed her arms over her chest, even though it was technically covered.

"Jauhnna, I swear you were treated with respect. I wouldn't have removed your clothes if it wasn't for the heatstroke. Your temperature was a hundred and two. It's one hundred now. As soon as it returns to normal, you can get dressed," he promised.

"Did they say anything after they captured you? Like, why they did it?" I asked again.

"They argued after they put me in the trunk. The one who said he was looking for his dog was telling the other they had to get me to the pickup spot or the boss was going to be pissed. He had plans for me, and failure wasn't an option," she whispered as she stared down at her hands, now clenched on her lap.

"Jauhnna, I need you to look at me," I demanded.

She slowly raised her eyes to me. God, that green was mesmerizing. I fought not to get lost and drown in it. When I had her whole attention, I continued. My gut told me there was more to this, and she held something back.

"I need the truth. We can't help you if we don't know everything. Do you know where they were taking you or to whom?"

She sat there mutely. I was about to demand she speak when she did. "I can't say for sure it was him, but I suspect I know who their boss is. I have no idea where they were taking me. He was never in Florida before." She paused, swallowed, and then finished. "I think they were hired to find me by my husband. I doubt very much he's happy that I left him."

Anger and crushing disappointment hit me. She was married and running from her husband. Hearing this conflicted me. On the one hand, that itch was growing inside of me—the one where I let the demon or maybe the devil inside of me out. There was a reason my road name was Diablo. I was my daddy's son. One sure way to be the target of my rage was to harm someone. After what happened to Amy and Brooklyn, anything to do with hurting children and women set me off.

On the other, I detested knowing she had a husband, even though she didn't want him. Unless they'd fought, she'd run off in a tizzy to prove a point and to teach him some kind of lesson. I had to know.

"Why did you leave him? How long have you been hiding from him?" I snapped. She jumped and gave me a wide-eyed look.

"W-why does it matter? I don't want to be with him. I just want to be left alone to live my life in peace."

"If you want our help, tell me why and how long. Is this just a lover's quarrel that got out of hand?"

Her expression changed to a fierce one as she

straightened on the table. Her fists were clenched at her sides now. "Does being beaten and degraded for years until you can't take it anymore and you decide you either escape him one way or the other sound like a lover's quarrel? I've been hiding from him for three years! I got complacent and thought he'd stopped looking, and even if he were, he'd never find me. I must've screwed up somehow. I will never go back to him. Do you hear me? If he gets his hands on me for good, I'll take my other escape option," she snarled. There was a fire in her that, truthfully, I liked seeing.

My gut churned at the conviction in her voice. I homed in on her last remark. I prayed I was wrong. "What is your other escape option?" I asked gruffly.

"I'll die before I let that man touch me or dictate my life again. He was never my choice, and I won't be his whipping girl and prisoner again."

"You're talking suicide," I stated.

"Yes, I'm talking about suicide. You'd be surprised at the many ways you can accomplish it. He's a monster."

The fury was building in me the more I heard. The thought of her ending her life to escape him floored me. There was no way I'd allow it. Protecting those weaker and in danger was what we did whenever we had the chance. How could we turn our back on her? We needed more information, of course, but she wasn't going to be left to deal with this alone.

Wolverine gave me a chin lift. He knew what I was contemplating. The club wouldn't be shocked at all when I told them we were going to go hunting. That's assuming she was speaking the truth and wasn't someone who hurt others and was as evil as her husband sounded. I doubted she was, but we had to make sure. Over the years, I'd encountered a few women who were worse than some men and deserved to be put down so they could never hurt anyone else. A thorough background check would confirm whether her story was true. I'd get Micro on it first thing.

"There will be no hurting yourself, you hear me? You leave him to us. I need more information," I told her.

"What kind of information? What can you do? Believe me, you don't want to be on his radar. If he finds out you helped me, assuming it was him, he'll retaliate. I can't let you get hurt because you were nice enough to help me," she stated firmly.

"If he comes looking for my club, he'll get the surprise of his life. Trust me. This kind of situation is right up our alley. I need to know his name and where he can be found. Another club member, our brother, Micro, will want to talk to you. He's our research guy."

She shook her head. I waited to see what else she'd say, but as long as she was legit, it wouldn't matter. We wouldn't leave her to the wolves. It went against everything we believed in. To turn our back on a woman in need would require me to hang up my cut—no goddamn way.

Jauhnna: Chapter 3

"Diablo, you don't know him. He's evil. He's killed people—destroyed lives. You don't want him to target you. I thank you all for helping me. I appreciate it more than you know, but the best course of action is to let me go. I'll find a way to get my emergency stash and hide again. No matter how long it's been, I won't let my guard down this time."

I was terrified at the determination I saw on his face. He was serious about going head-to-head with Galway. No one in their right mind would ever do that. Why risk everything for a stranger? He didn't owe me anything. It was the reverse. I owed his club for saving my life. I didn't doubt if it wasn't for them, I would've died before someone found me. I needed to run before it was too late. If those men left me, they had to have thought I was already dead. It was the only explanation for not taking me with them. I gasped at the idea.

"Wait. Think about it. If they were ordered to capture me and take me to him and they left me, they must've thought I was dead. Why else leave me there?"

"I could see how they might think that. You were covered in so much blood and not moving. Hell, it was hard to see if you were breathing. If they saw you and were worried about being caught by a passerby, they might not have checked you thoroughly, assumed you were dead, and ran," Wolverine agreed.

"So that means there's no reason for you to do anything. Well, maybe one thing if you would. I'd appreciate it if you'd help me get to my stash of money and documents. I know it's a lot to ask, but I can pay you for your time and inconvenience once I get it. I'll just disappear again, except this time, I'll go further and remain vigilant," I explained as my mind began formulating my next steps.

"No, by God, you won't! You're staying here where you're safe. There's no need to run and hide. I'm getting Micro to work on this. You rest and do whatever Wolverine tells you," Diablo commanded.

Before I was able to argue, he turned and walked to the door, and then he was gone. My mouth fell open. It was Wolverine's chuckle that got me to look back at him. He smirked.

"What's so funny? Does he just throw out commands and expect people to comply?" I fumed. As I began to feel better, my normal personality was surfacing. The days of me being some man's property with no say in my life were over. Never again would I do that. It would be better to live my life alone or dead than submit to that kind of hell. Living it once was more than enough.

"Yeah, pretty much. He is the president. It's his job to command and control things. It's bred into him. It might irritate you, but he's right."

I gasped and glared at Wolverine. "Oh, really. Do you think it's okay for him to control someone like a puppet? For them to be expected just to shut up and do as they're told, like a good little slave. Take what is dished out, even if it hurts you, degrades you, or destroys your soul. Hell, no. I won't do it. It makes him the same as what I ran from. I appreciate your help, but I'm out of here." I tossed off the wet sheet.

I was too upset to be embarrassed that I was in nothing but damp underwear and a bra, which made them practically see-through. I threw my legs off the far side of the table and stood. Or I tried, but my legs wouldn't hold me, and I went down on my ass. A cry of shock burst forth as I fell.

I heard Wolverine swear, then the quick approach of his boots. At the same time, the door to the room flew open, banging into the wall, and Diablo charged in. He was scowling. Directly behind him was another man. Great, just my luck. Three hot, sexy bikers were witnesses to my humiliation of falling on my ass almost naked. Why couldn't the floor open up and swallow me?

Refusing to lie there and be humiliated further, I leaned to the side so I could use my arms to push myself up. I gave a small scream when I was lifted off the floor and held against a broad, hard chest. A chest I swear I'd felt before, although how, I had no idea. It must be the head injury. I kicked my legs and tried to squirm. It did no good. His arms were like steel bars, although he wasn't exactly hurting me.

"Put me down!" I demanded.

"Not until you stop fighting. What the fuck is going on in here?" Diablo thundered. Glancing up, I saw he was glaring at Wolverine. As for him, he was calmly looking back at Diablo.

"It seems she takes exception to being treated like a slave, and she's determined to leave. I was trying to explain that your dictating wasn't meant the way she took it, but boom, she tried to stand up and went down. I was coming to pick her up when you charged in."

"Slave? You're not a slave," he said incredulously. He was back to staring at me. I had to fight not to look away or fidget.

"Should I have used the word prisoner or puppet? Do you prefer those?" I snapped back. Probably not the smartest thing to do with men I didn't know or trust, but what was the worst they could do to me? Beat me? That wouldn't be new. Rape me? Ditto. Kill me? It would be a solution.

His face registered his surprise, which quickly morphed into anger. "It sounds like we need to clear some things up," he growled.

I shivered. Seeing it, he must've thought I was cold based on his frown. His expression made me recall I was practically naked in front of three guys, and my underclothing didn't cover much. He remembered it, too, because he barked out to Wolverine, "Give me a blanket."

Then he turned his attention to the other man. "Turn your goddamn head." The man did as he was told. Within moments, I was covered with a blanket but still in Diablo's arms.

"Would you mind putting me down?" I asked, knowing it wasn't wise to remain in his arms. I discovered I liked it more than I should, which wasn't like me. Having any man touch me wasn't something I allowed.

"I might if you promise to keep your sweet ass where I put it. No more trying to get up and leave. You were half dead less than an hour ago," he reminded me.

"I make no promises," was my snappy comeback.

As soon as I said it, I knew I should've agreed, even if it was a lie. What it earned me wasn't a slap or other punishment but him walking over to a chair and sitting down with me still in his arms.

"Put me on the table. There's no need to hold me. It's not like I could escape even if I tried. There's three of you and one of me. I can't win a fight."

"Christ, woman, why would there be a fight? We're not here to hurt you. We rescued you, remember?" Diablo muttered.

"Since when does that mean anything? You're a dictator. Maybe the reason you helped me was so you could use me for your gain. You mentioned human trafficking and how easy it is to ship to and from Florida. How do you know that? Are you in that business yourselves? Was your offer to help with Galway just a ploy to get me to drop my guard? I promise you, whether it's you, Galway, or someone else, I won't be a prisoner or slave. That isn't a life, and I refuse to live it again."

His face became redder. Here it comes.

"Pres, she mentioned being a slave to me and asked if you expected her to let you control her like one. She asked if she was expected to take it even if it hurt, degraded, or destroyed her and that if you did, it made you the same as what she ran from," Wolverine blabbed. He didn't appear happy.

Risking a glance at the unknown guy, he was watching us, and he wore a pissed look. *Crap. You should've kept your mouth shut, Jauhnna.*

"We're gonna clear the air about some things. I want you to sit here and listen. Don't interrupt. You'll get your chance to speak when I'm done. And yes, that's me dictating," Diablo commanded.

I folded my arms over my chest and raised a brow

at him. I made no verbal promise. Let him think what he will. I'd come to understand I needed to play along until they felt they had me cowed enough to obey. My only chance was to get them to believe it and then wait for the opportunity to escape when they let their guard down. It would gall me to do it, but if it earned me my freedom, so be it. I'd endured worse.

The other man came closer and sat on the edge of the table I'd been on. Wolverine leaned against the wall nearby. The stranger was studying me closely. I lowered my eyes, pretending to be intimidated.

"This is Scorpion. He's the club's vice president and my right hand," Diablo said unexpectedly. I didn't look up. I just nodded. I was channeling the old me. It aggravated me that I had to.

"Hello, Jauhnna, it's nice to meet you. I want you to know we're here to help. Trust Diablo. Yeah, he's bossy as hell, but he has his heart in the right place."

His assurance did make me look up. He was smiling. I wasn't falling for his charm or words, but I had to admit, he was believable and damn good-looking. I gave him a faint smile in return. Hopefully, they'd see it as me softening toward them.

"I'm not bossy. I just know what needs to happen. Enough side chatting. I gave our guy Micro your name and where you lived. He's working to see what he can find. I want to know your husband's full name and where we can find him. I originally wanted it so we could determine if he was behind this. Now, after those comments, I don't care if he is or not. He's still getting paid a visit. Tell me a story." He paused.

I had no choice but to look at him. He was staring so intently at me that it felt like he saw inside my heart and soul. I fought back a quiver. "What story?"

"Tell me why you ran from him in the first place. Why do you trust no one and make the comments you have? Only someone who has been repeatedly hurt would say those things. Tell me what he did to you."

Instantly, I began to add more bricks to the wall inside of me. No way was I sharing anything with him. No one needed to know my horrors or shame. I'd said more than enough as it was. I pressed my lips together and shook my head. He gave me a disapproving look.

"Why don't we tell you a little about us and let you ask us questions first?" Scorpion suggested.

"Okay," was all I said back.

"I've been with the club since I was eighteen. I'm thirty-five. When I patched in, Diablo had just become president. The only other one here then, who still is, besides Diablo and me, is Butcher. He's our enforcer. The rest have come along over the years." He stopped after giving me that tidbit.

"I've been with them for six years. I came after I got out of the Navy. I was a corpsman while there. That's why I was the one working on you. I'm the club's medic. I'm twenty-eight," Wolverine added.

"I've been a part of this club since I was born. My dad was a member, and I joined when I got old enough. We've done a bunch of things over the years, and I won't lie and say they were all legal or what some may call moral, but there have been a few things we've never done. We've never been men who abuse or hurt innocent men, women, or children. That was never tolerated. If my dad had ever thought to do that, my mom would've not only left his ass, but she would've also beat it. They raised me to be the same. I don't know what you know or have heard about motorcycle clubs, but it's probably not good if you've watched TV or read books.

"Are we angels? No, but we're not evil, either. Some clubs are, I hate to admit. We don't associate with them. In fact, until a few years ago, we didn't truly associate with any other clubs. Since then, we've been very selective of who we've allowed into our lives. None of them tolerate hurting the innocent, either. In fact, they do a lot to help them, and we pitch in when needed," Diablo unexpectedly explained.

I knew it could all be lies, and likely there was a bunch they weren't telling me, but they sounded so sincere as they shared. I found myself half believing them.

"We've been known to help some of those in need in whatever way they require. Some need to escape, and others require more intensive help. We've done it all," Scorpion added.

"We're a smaller club of twelve members and two prospects at the moment, but that's more due to us being selective than not having guys wanting to join. We have a variety of businesses. I think that should give you an idea about us. You can ask questions if you want," Diablo offered.

I scrambled to think of what to ask. A few popped into my head as they talked. I organized them and then asked the first one. "You mentioned being patched in. What does that mean?"

"It means to get this cut with the club's name on it and our road name. My road name is Diablo," he said, pointing to the leather vest. I was glad because I had no clue it was called a cut. I didn't watch television shows or read books about motorcycle clubs.

"Those are chosen for us by someone in the club who's a member. In this one, I often come up with a road name, and the others agree. Sometimes, one of the other members suggests it. Other times, if the guy was in the military and had one, we adopted it. You're not automatically voted in. You have to prospect for a designated time. With us these days, it's two years," Diablo explained.

"What does prospecting include? How do they prove they should be in your club? Do they have to steal something or kill someone to prove it? If so, why so long to decide whether they get in? Or do they have to do those things repeatedly until you know they can keep doing them?" My frank questions earned me swearing from all three.

"Son of a bitch," Scorpion uttered.

"Fuck," came out of Wolverine.

"What the hell?" Diablo snapped.

I shrank back at the anger in them, only to jerk as I recalled I was still on Diablo's lap. "Can I please sit alone?"

He didn't answer me at first, then he stood, placed me in the chair we'd been sharing, and stepped back to stand beside me.

"Jauhnna, I've gotta ask. Why would you think we steal and kill to get into this club? Do we project that, or is it because of all the shit you've read and seen on television? Christ, it gets old that people think those things of every club," Scorpion muttered.

"I don't watch shows about motorcycle clubs, nor do I read about them. I assumed you did them because isn't that what most gangs require of their initiates?

I didn't mean to offend you. No more questions," I hurried to assure them. The less I knew, the better.

"Honey, don't do that. If you have questions, we'd rather you ask them than assume you know the truth. We're not angry at you. We're upset that so many people think the same thing you do. First, let me be clear. We're not a gang. We're a club. Yes, there are things prospects do to get in, but we don't ask them to steal, beat, or kill innocent people. Most of the time, they're gophers who show they're willing and able to complete any task asked of them, not just for a short period of time. We take time to get to know them and let them know us. The last thing we want is to get someone who isn't a fit, or we can't trust. Even with all we do, a few have found a way in, and it causes nothing but grief." The way Diablo said it made me think it hadn't been a good experience.

I was hesitant to ask more, but they were piquing my interest. "You mentioned having businesses. What kind? If you can't say, that's okay," I tacked on the end.

"If that's your way of figuring out if they're illegal, the answer is they're not. In the past, when I was growing up and even in the early days of being a brother, we did deal in illegal stuff. It was how we made our money. But even then, there were things we never dealt in, such as prostitution, selling drugs, or people," Diablo added.

"These days, we're just regular Joes. I oversee our garage, which offers mobile mechanic services," Scorpion interjected.

"I oversee our fishing charter and bait shop business. We have others, too," Wolverine added.

"And you? What do you oversee?" I asked Diablo.

"I oversee the whole club, but as for a specific

business, it's our Prep and Restore business. We do a lot of work on homes and businesses to prepare for or repair after hurricanes and tropical storms. On top of the three we just mentioned, we have a thrift shop, beach rental property, a repossession business, and a seafood restaurant. It helps that we catch much of our seafood with the fishing charters."

I wasn't expecting that. They all were ordinary businesses. Deciding to ask another question, I asked, "What does brother mean? You mentioned being a brother. Are you all related somehow?"

Wolverine chuckled. "Not by blood, but we consider each other brothers and refer to ourselves as such."

I smiled at the idea, but then it slid away. Being someone's brother didn't make them loving or your ally.

"Stop right there. Why did you smile and then let it melt away? You thought something to make it happen. What was it?" Diablo demanded.

The way he was studying me, I knew if I didn't answer him, he would continue to ask until I did. It wouldn't hurt for me to tell a partial truth. "I thought it was great to think of someone as your brother. Then I recalled that even blood siblings don't always support or love their brothers or sisters. It's good that you seem to be good ones who do."

"How did your brother betray or not support you? Or was it a sister?" Diablo pounced on my statement. Damn.

Ignoring him, I asked the last question I had. "You said a few years ago that you opened up to being allies or friends with other clubs. Why? What changed your minds?"

Bossman, the nickname that popped into my head for Diablo, raised an eyebrow at my evasion but didn't call me on it. Instead, he answered my question. "My daughter went to Tennessee to help out my brother-in-law, Sam, and sister, Julie. He broke his leg and wasn't able to work. While there, she met and fell for a biker in a club up there called the Archangel's Warriors. When I couldn't persuade her to leave his ass and come home, I found I had to let them into our world. In doing so, they brought others with them. They're all like-minded to us, so it's worked. If I don't have assurances that a club is, we don't associate with them."

"Daughter?" I asked, dumbfounded.

He didn't look old enough to have an adult daughter. What was he, twelve, when she was born? Chuckles made me realize I'd said the last part out loud. I blushed.

"No, darlin', I wasn't twelve, though thank you for the compliment. I was legal, I promise. Brooklyn is twenty-six. I'm forty-seven. I have two grandsons as well, Thane and Jai. Thane is two-and-a-half and Jai is seven months."

"You're a grandfather! He's joking, isn't he?" I asked the other two. I'd place him in his late thirties, not fifteen years older than myself.

They both chuckled and shook their heads. The next thing I knew, Diablo handed me his open wallet. Inside, I saw his driver's license. Right there, along with his real name, *Victor Tate*, his stats of *brown hair*, *brown eyes*, and height of *six foot three* was his birth date. A quick calculation told me he hadn't lied. He was forty-seven. I handed it back to him.

"Sorry, you just don't look your age. I thought you were closer to my age."

"Like I said, thank you. Yes, technically, I'm old enough to be your dad. Did you have any other questions?" he asked with a slight smirk. I pretended not to know how it made me feel. Nothing would come of finding him attractive and intriguing.

"Just one more. You said you tried to persuade her to leave him and couldn't. Why did you try? Is he mean to her, unloving, abusive? If so, the way you spoke of how your club doesn't like that, why would she stay with him? Or your club bother to associate with his club?"

"He's not a bit mean or abusive, or he'd be dead. He loves her to death. Torch adores her and their kids. That man protects her like I have. I never wanted her to be that far away from me. I've always wanted her near to ensure she was happy and safe. Despite the fact the bastard stole my daughter and has my grandkids hours away from me, Torch takes care of them," he grumbled.

His evident love for his daughter came through loud and clear. It made me wistful to experience that for once in my life. No one could say my father was loving while he was alive. The silence lasted a good minute or more before he began his interrogation. That was the only word for it. He showed me he was serious about getting answers, whether I wanted to give them or not.

"You said you've been hiding from your husband for three years. Why? What did he do to make you leave him? Why not just divorce him and be done with it? Where are you from originally? How did you meet him? Do you have children? Is there someone we should contact now about finding you so they know you're safe? What's your husband's name? Tell me about your birth family. Why didn't you go to them for help? Are they dead?"

He fired them out so fast I couldn't keep up with them. He made my head spin, which I suspected was his intention. He wanted me confused so I'd blurt out stuff.

"Did he cheat on you? Lie? Hurt you?" Scorpion fired off as soon as Diablo finished.

"You said you were taken while going to work. Where is that? Won't your friends and coworkers be worried? They'll call the cops, won't they?" Wolverine added.

I began to panic as I fought to keep everything they were asking straight and formulate answers. I was starting to feel hunted. It was triggering the fight-or-flight instinct within me. In the past, I would've run without a thought. These days, I usually would fight. My head was pounding, and the urge to vomit was increasing. What the hell? I'd conquered these tendencies. Why were they coming back?

"Jauhnna, we can't help you unless we know what we're protecting you from. You have to help us," Scorpion said softly.

"Come on, tell us," Wolverine cajoled.

A loud slamming sound made me jump. Diablo had brought his fist down onto the table. "What are you hiding? If you need help, why all this evasion? Or are you a liar, and this whole thing was a lie?" he snarled.

All the questions, his anger, and the rest all accumulated and peaked as I barely leaned over in time to vomit on the floor and not myself. I heard swearing, but I couldn't concentrate on it. My head was hurting worse, and there were spots in front of my eyes. I felt myself slump.

"Christ, what the fuck are we doing? She has a concussion, and we're badgering her like she's a criminal. Here, you need to lie down," a kind voice said. Vaguely, it registered it was Wolverine, but I didn't let his tone fool me. He was no better than Diablo. None of them were. When hands touched my arms, I slapped at them and tried to move away. My vision was gone.

"Don't touch me, any of you. You're all bastards," I mumbled. That was the last thing I remembered saying or doing.

Diablo: Chapter 4

It was a stress-filled night for all of us, especially for me. I'd only drifted off a couple of times. Every time I did, I would jerk awake and check to be sure she was still there and breathing. After the disastrous questioning of her yesterday, I'd been a ball of anxiety. Not only had we made her sick enough to puke, but she passed out on us. When she slumped over in her chair, unresponsive, for a moment, I thought she was dead. My heart almost stopped.

I beat Wolverine to her and got her on the table. He swiftly examined her, then informed me and Scorpion she'd only passed out. From that point onward, I kept watch over her. She'd surface but only long enough to mumble, then go back to sleep. While she slept, she was having nightmares. There was no other explanation for her crying out and pleading not to hurt her in her sleep. My torment was the question, was her tormentor her husband or me?

There's only been a handful of times in my life I ever felt regret for how I treated people. She was one of those, and it ate at me. Deep down, I knew she was an innocent. Whatever prevented her from telling us the facts we asked for wasn't subterfuge. I'd begun questioning her like I would an enemy I had in our swamp box, the place we took those needing questioning, a beating, or worse. It sickened me that I subjected her to it. If she were planning to tell me what I needed to know, she probably wouldn't anymore. We'd be lucky if she didn't run as soon as she fully woke up.

I was worried about how much she was sleeping and asked Wolverine if we should take her to the hospital. It was the last thing I wanted to do, but if it would help her recover, I'd do it. He assured me her vitals were good, and she quickly woke up when he prodded her. He thought she was physically and emotionally exhausted.

The night passed slowly. It was morning now. I eased to my feet and stretched. She seemed to be peacefully sleeping. I needed to piss and take a quick shower. Slipping out of the room, I nodded to Zax. He'd been given night duty to stand outside the room. It was in case I needed to leave or wanted something. There was no way I would risk leaving her alone. She might try to leave or hurt herself.

"I'm gonna grab a shower. I'm sending Wolverine to check on her. Liam should be here soon to relieve you," I informed him.

"Not a problem, Pres. Liam is due to come spell me soon but I can stay as long as you need me. Is she still asleep?"

"She is. Try to keep it down. She had a restless night. Call me if she wakes up. I'll be using my room here."

"Will do."

Giving him a chin lift in acknowledgment, I headed down the hall. Even though I had a house, I still had a set of rooms in the clubhouse. It was in case I needed to crash here, and it had my work office connected. I worked out of it mainly, although I had one at home and at Wrath's Prep & Restore. The one at the business was where I only dealt with Prep & Restore clients' work details. The one at the clubhouse was for the club as a whole. At home, my office was used when I wanted to work in total peace.

Pausing outside Wolverine's door, I knocked. "Come in," he yelled.

Opening the door, I looked for him. He came out of the bathroom in his underwear. Neither of us paid his almost-naked self any mind. It was typical for guys to do it. Hell, I think I'd seen everyone's junk at one time or another and vice versa.

"How is she?" he asked, pulling on his socks and jeans.

"She's still asleep. She finally stopped tossing and whimpering in her sleep. I'm gonna take a shower. Will you check on her? Zax is waiting on Liam to spell him."

"That's where I'm headed. Take your time. I've got this. If anything changes, I'll call you at the house."

"I'm showering in my room here. Just call or send someone to get me. I won't be long." I turned to reopen the door.

"You can trust me to take care of her, Pres. You can relax or do whatever. There's no need for you to stay with her all the time. I would've stayed with her last night."

There was a hint of something in his voice I couldn't quite figure out. Was he trying to indicate he was into her, or was it something else? I whipped back around. He was watching me closely.

"I decide where I'm needed or not. I know you would've stayed. You offered. I felt it was my responsibility. After all, I was the one to make her collapse and get sick."

"You weren't the only one asking her questions. I don't think she vomited due to our questions. It was her head injury. We were only trying to help her."

"By badgering her? We totally forgot her injuries and went at her like she was an enemy we were interrogating. We'll be lucky if she tells us anything. Which reminds me, I need to speak to Micro and see what he found out. Maybe he can answer some of those questions. Gotta go. Talk to you later."

I didn't give him time to say more before I went out the door and to my room. Unlocking my door, I let myself inside. None of us left our rooms unlocked. You didn't know who might slip into it and snoop or wait for you. I wasted no time getting into the bathroom with the shower on. As the water heated, I stripped. I sighed when the hot spray hit my tense, sore muscles. It had been a while since I'd slept in a chair. Fuck, was I too old for this? I mean, most days, I didn't feel old, but the truth was, I was fast approaching fifty.

Thinking of my age made me think of Jauhnna. Finding out she was close to my daughter's age had bothered me. The only conclusion I came to was that I found her attractive. After only a day of knowing her, she drew me in more than any woman I recalled except for Amy. She'd grabbed my attention the first time I saw her, too. Despite finding out she was underage, which in Florida, the legal age of consent was eighteen, I kept seeing her. I won't lie. We broke the law while she was still seventeen. It was apparent when she was eighteen and already pregnant. No matter the risk, I'd fallen for her, and there was no way I could deny my feelings for her, and she felt the same.

I had no idea why I remembered that at a time like this. Even if I was attracted to Jauhnna, it wasn't going anywhere. She was someone we'd hopefully be able to help so she could get on with her life free of fear and hiding. The most it could be on my end was a few nights together, and she didn't strike me as the kind of woman who would go for that. Shoving any other thoughts of her away, I rushed through my shower. In no time, I was out taking care of the other things I needed to do to be ready for the day. Thankfully, I kept spare clothes and personal items here, just in case. Feeling better when I was done, I locked up and headed back to the sick bay.

Getting there, I saw no one outside. I wonder where the prospects were. Maybe Wolverine sent one of them to get something. Knocking swiftly to announce I was coming in, I swung the door open and came to a screeching halt mere steps inside. Wolverine was sitting on the bed we'd placed her on last night. It was more comfortable than the exam table. What made me stop was the sight of her in his arms and him with his head lowered to hers. Straightaway, anger filled me. I slammed the door. He glanced up, and I saw her jerk as if startled.

"What the fuck is going on in here?" I demanded.

She gave me a scared peek over his shoulder. Most of her face was hidden. He appeared unruffled by my question or my loud voice. "What do you mean? What's going on?"

"Why the hell is she in your arms with your heads together? She should be resting, not being mauled."

He scowled. "I wasn't mauling her. I was comforting her."

"Oh, is that what you call it? Mind if I ask why you

were comforting her?"

I knew I was making a fool of myself, but I wasn't able to stop. The thought of him holding her and the possibility they'd been kissing pissed me off. I stomped to stand next to them. When I did, that's when I noticed she'd been crying. The wet tears were still on her cheeks. My ire began to fade as concern took over. Why was she crying? Without a thought, I leaned over, took her out of his arms, and cradled her in mine. I walked to the chair I held her in yesterday and sat.

"Darlin', why are you crying? Did you have more bad dreams?" I asked as I smoothed her hair away from her wet face. Those tears offended me. I wiped at them with my thumb. She was giving me an astonished look. Yeah, I knew I'd switched gears abruptly, but I had to know. I'd question Wolverine later about what he'd done to comfort her and if he had some kind of feelings developing for her.

"I'm fine. There's no need to make a fuss. I'd like to change if I may and maybe take a shower. Then, if you're still willing to help, I'd like someone to take me to my stash. I need to get on the road. The longer I wait, the more likely it is I might be found if they're even looking for me. Hopefully, after yesterday, they think I'm dead. Assuming it was Galway who sent them, he might not be satisfied that I am without proof. Do you have someone here I can borrow clothes from? I'll pay her back when we get my money," she babbled.

"You're in no condition to go anywhere. No one knows you're here. We had the car we found you in towed to our garage. No one knows you're at the compound. Take time and heal. We have plenty of room for you," I told her.

"I can't. You don't understand. If it was Galway's men, there's a chance he'd want to see my body. It would be something he'd do to make sure I was dead. It would feel like he achieved a goal or prize. I can't risk it."

"Which is it? Either you can leave because it's safe due to them thinking you're dead, or it's too dangerous to stay because they'll want to see your body even if they suspect you're dead," I asked.

She wiggled to sit up further in my lap. I bit back the moan that it almost caused to come out. Her ass was rubbing across my cock, and I was trying not to let myself grow hard. Pretending I was helping her up, I shifted her so she wasn't sitting directly on it. I knew I could let her have the chair or put her back on the bed, but I didn't want to. I was enjoying holding her, and I didn't desire Wolverine to be close to her. He was watching us attentively.

"It's both. I have no way of knowing which it is, so I have to hedge my bets. The longer I stay, the likelier someone might see me leaving town. You won't want his attention on you. How can you be positive no one knows you took the car? Undoubtedly, somebody saw it being towed and would know it was your garage. If they trace it to there, they'll come asking about it. Their suspicion will be raised if you or your people claim not to have found a body in the trunk. Don't you see? Me leaving is what's best for all parties concerned."

She was becoming agitated. I wasn't risking her having another vomiting-and-passing-out episode. "Jauhnna, I need you to calm down. Take deep breaths and relax. You're going to cause yourself to relapse. We don't want another incident like last night," I cautioned her.

"I won't. That was a fluke. I feel fine," she protested.

"Honey, you said you still had a headache when I came in. Let me recheck your blood pressure," Wolverine told her with a smile as he got to his feet.

He grabbed his equipment from the table beside the bed and approached us. I refused to make eye contact while he did it. I was watching how he touched her arm. He was gentle, but I thought his touch lingered longer than it should on her skin. I bit my tongue to keep from calling him out. He pumped up the cuff and listened.

"It's slightly higher than it was. I think you should come back and lie on the bed. You'll be more comfortable." He held out a hand to her. I almost didn't let go so she could stand, but I knew I had to. She seemed steady on her feet as she went to the bed, but he held on to her. I detested it. She was dressed in a thin hospital gown he'd put over her underclothing after she passed out. We'd tried to clean most of the blood off her, but there was still some in her hair.

Wanting to divert her, I made a suggestion. "You said you wanted to have a shower. Why don't you do that? You look steady on your feet, but in case you become unsteady, you can use the one in my room. It has a seat built into it. It'll make you comfier."

"She shouldn't be alone, just in case she passes out. I can help her get cleaned up," Wolverine stated.

I opened my mouth to tell him over my dead body was he showering with her, but she beat me to it. "I can shower alone. I don't need help. I'll be fine as long as I can sit down if I need to. I'm not dizzy. If I begin to feel like I am, I'll call out. I'd love a shower. This blood is itchy and stinks." She wrinkled up her nose at the word stink. The face she made I thought was precious.

I stood up. Wolverine was scowling. "Then come with me. It's not far. Do you need me to carry you? I don't want you to exhaust yourself while walking and not have the energy to wash. You know what, never mind."

She'd risen off the bed. Taking a couple of steps, I reached her and swept an arm under her legs as the other one cradled her back. She gasped and clutched my chest. "Diablo, I can walk!"

"Nope. This is best. Just enjoy being pampered. Get the door, will ya?" I directed to Wolverine, although I didn't bother looking at him.

He stomped around us and wrenched it open. As I passed him, I felt the heat of his gaze on me. He and I would be talking very soon. No way was I allowing one of my guys to play games with her. Carrying her down the hallway, I was surprised no one was out and about, although I was glad. They didn't need to see her in this flimsy gown.

At my door, I hated having to set her down to get to my key. Unlocking it, I swung the door open and waved for her to go ahead of me. She tentatively entered. I saw her scanning the room. I wasn't a slob, and the room was neat since I rarely used it. The dirty clothes from earlier were in the hamper, and I planned to take them to the house with me later. I closed and locked the door, then walked her to the bathroom. I flipped on the light. She hesitated to enter.

"Let me show you where everything is. I'll stay out here in case you need anything. I'll get you some clean clothes. The towels and washcloths are in here.

I'm sorry, I don't have any pretty-smelling soap or shampoo. You'll have to use mine. There are extra toothbrushes and razors in this drawer. If you need anything else, just holler. Here, let me get the water started." I opened the shower door and turned on the water. I set it to where it wouldn't be too hot. With that done, there wasn't any reason for me to stay, so I backed out and let her shut the door.

"In case I need to get in, don't lock the door. I promise you're safe."

She didn't reply, but the lock didn't engage. To keep myself from thinking about her naked in the water, I went to my dresser. Now, to find her something to wear. We had no old ladies or female family members at the compound. The only women who came here were the sluts and hangers-on. While there was a good chance some of them had left clothing behind, no way would I have her put on anything they wore. I was hoping to find something Brooklyn left, and barring that, I'd give her one of my t-shirts and figure out her bottoms.

Rummaging in my drawers, I came up empty. Going to my closet, I went through the few things hanging up. Nope. I was about to take a shirt off a hanger when a box at the top of the closet caught my eye. Bingo. I recalled it was one Brooklyn had meant to take with her the last time they were here, and she had forgotten. I offered to mail it, but she told me to hang on to it and that she'd get it next time. I'd shoved it up in the closet and forgotten about it. Taking it down, I put it on the bed and opened it. Inside were a few tank tops, a couple of pairs of shorts, a pair of stretchy leggings, and a bra.

Jauhnna was more filled out than Brooklyn, but the clothes were stretchy. They should fit her well enough. The bra wouldn't fit her, though. She was more sizable in the tits department. I groaned. *Stop thinking about her tits*, I admonished myself. Images of them and what they'd look like bare were crowding into my head, and my cock was taking notice and swelling. Snatching a tank top and a pair of shorts out of the box, I put the lid back on and laid the clothes on the chair. I kicked back on the bed and turned on the television to forget about my misbehaving body. I found a building show and decided to watch it. I still kept an ear out for her to call for help.

I'd been watching the show for about five minutes when there was a knock on my bedroom door. Wondering who it was, I got up to see. If it were Wolverine, his ass would be mine. I unlatched it. Standing there was Micro.

"Morning, Pres, Wolverine said you were here. I thought you might want an update on what I found. He says she's showering. Do you wanna come to my house when you're done or should I meet you in your office here later?"

I was torn. While I wanted to hear what he found, I wasn't leaving her to shower without someone nearby. If I waited until after her shower, it would leave her alone with Wolverine. As I mulled it over, I was struck with an idea.

"Why don't you come to the house and we can talk? I'll send you a text when I'm ready. It shouldn't be too long. Does that work for you?"

"Works fine. I'll see you in a bit." He gave me a chin lift and then walked off. Closing the door, I went back to the bed.

I barely sat back down when I heard the water turn off. I bounded to my feet. I knocked on the bathroom door.

"Yes?" she called out, sounding cautious.

"I found you some clothes. If you crack the door, I'll pass them through to you. They were my daughter's. That's all I could find unless you want a shirt of mine. There's a few more of hers in a box you can go through."

"I'm sure they're fine. Thank you. Give me a minute."

I went to get the clothes I set out and tried not to imagine her drying off. I waited outside the door. The door cracked open, and her hand came out. I slipped them into her. She quickly drew back and shut the door after saying thank you. Turning off the television, since I wasn't able to concentrate anyway, I smoothed out the bed's covers and paced the room. I don't know how long it was before the door opened and she came out.

Her hair was wet, but she'd fashioned it into a long braid. I could see all of her face now. She was gorgeous, but what made me almost swallow my tongue was seeing her in those clothes. Her lush figure filled them out in a way that made them way sexier than plain shorts and a tank should be. Her tits were straining against the fabric. Since she had no bra on, her nipples were poking against the material. My mouth went dry at the thought of pulling her top down and sucking them into my mouth. I wondered what color they'd be and how big her nipples were. Fuck! I had to stop this. She'd run screaming from the room if she guessed what I was thinking.

One thing I knew for sure... there was no way

in hell I was letting any of my guys see her like this, especially Wolverine. She gave me a tentative smile. "I hope it's alright that I borrowed the hair tie I found in the drawer. Not sure who it belongs to, but I had to find a way to get all this out of the way." She gestured to her hair.

I had no clue who the tie belonged to. "Anything you need, you're welcome to it. You know, it's probably a little cool out this morning. Let me get you one of my shirts to wear, too. There's the box I told you about." I pointed to it.

She went to check it out as I went to the closet and grabbed the shirt I planned to give her earlier. When I handed it to her, she smiled.

"Thank you. For everything. Are you sure your daughter won't mind me wearing her things?"

"She won't mind. She's left them here for months and hasn't demanded they be sent to her. Believe me, she has plenty of clothes. That's one thing she never lacked. How was your shower?"

She sighed contentedly. "It was wonderful. I could've stayed there for hours. I feel much better."

"Good. Are you hungry? You haven't had anything to eat since yesterday morning, have you?"

As I asked, her stomach let out a loud growl. Her cheeks turned pink as we both laughed. "I guess that answers your question," she replied.

Holding my arm so she could take it, I gestured to the bedroom door. "Then let's go get some food. I want to show you something anyway. Do you think you can walk or should I get one of the prospects to bring a car to us?"

"A car? Where are we going? I thought I wasn't

allowed to leave."

"You aren't. We'll stay within the compound."

"As long as you don't want me to walk miles, I should be fine."

"I promise, it's not miles. Come." I led her to the door and then out. I paused long enough to lock it up, then I took her out the side door. It was the closest to my house. She swiveled her head around, taking in the outside. When she noticed the houses, she blinked.

"Oh, I had no idea you had houses here. I thought all of you lived in the clubhouse."

"About half of us do, and the rest have houses. This one is mine. We can fix breakfast. I've got all the fixings. The clubhouse might not. The guys eat like locusts, so I never presume there's food to cook there. Besides, my coffee is better than what they drink there. I get the good stuff." I grinned.

"Well, what are you waiting for? Take me to the java. I'm dying for a cup."

As we got closer to my place, she spoke again. "Your house is lovely, Diablo. It's so big. You live there alone?"

"I do. I built it a few years ago after Brooklyn and Torch got together. I wanted room for when they visited."

"So this isn't the house she grew up in."

"No, it's on the other side of the clubhouse. We have it in case we need a guesthouse."

"Who lives in these other ones?"

Pointing at them, I named them off. "That one belongs to Scorpion. The two down from him are Micro and Crash. These two belong to Butcher and Thunder."

Reaching the door, I opened it and took her inside.

"You don't lock your front door?"

"There's no need inside the fence."

"But you did back at the clubhouse."

I wasn't up to explaining about club sluts and hangers-on to her, so I left it vague. "There are other people in and out of there but not our homes. It's a precaution."

"Oh, okay. Well, I must tell you that the inside is beautiful, too, even just from seeing your living room and kitchen. Did you decorate it yourself or did your daughter help?"

"You crush me. You don't think a guy can decorate on his own?" I pretended to be hurt and put my hand on my chest.

"No, I mean yes, of course, a guy can. I'm sorry," she said quickly.

I laughed. "Darlin', there's no need to apologize. I'm teasing you. If left to me, the walls would be white, and everything would be gray and black. When I said I was building a new house, Brooklyn told me she would decorate it and that I had to let her help me pick out the carpet, tiles, and everything else. She recalled how the old house was until she got old enough to demand something more than white."

She threw back her head and laughed along with me. "She's a smart woman. Some men supposedly can do it, but I've never met one. Well, she did a lovely job. This kitchen is amazing." She admired the counters and the appliances. I got into the fridge and took out the bacon and eggs. I searched for pancake mix in the pantry, but it seemed I was out.

"Damn it," I muttered.

"What's wrong?"

"I thought I had pancake mix, but I don't. I guess we'll have to settle for eggs and bacon."

"I can make them from scratch if you have the ingredients. It's not hard."

"You'd do that?"

"Sure, show me where you keep your flour and baking ingredients," she said as she came to stand by me.

I took her into the pantry and pointed to the section where I kept my baking ingredients. While she went through them, I went back into the kitchen and got to work on the bacon. I decided to cheat since we were starving. One year, Brooklyn had gotten me one of those trays you put bacon on and microwave it so it would get crispy. It was quicker than frying or baking it for one person. I put several slices in the slots, then popped it into the microwave. While it cooked, I got her a bowl, measuring cups, spoons, and a whisk.

She came out with the items she needed and began putting them together. I watched her. She wasn't following a recipe, but the sure way she did it told me she made the batter often. The microwave beeped, and I changed out the cooked bacon for more raw slices. She saw me.

"What's that?" she asked curiously.

I explained how it worked.

"I've never seen one of those. I need to get me one. It's a pain to cook bacon for one person. It never fails when I fry it that it pops and burns me no matter what I do."

"I hate that too."

We worked effortlessly together. After putting in the second tray, I got to work on the coffee. I got out the milk. "I don't have any creamer, but there's milk and sugar."

"Milk and sugar will do. God, that smells good. I have a cup every morning. Yesterday, I was running late, so I didn't get one. I planned to drink a cup at work. We know that didn't happen."

"Well, you can have two today to make up for it. Although, I warn you, this is strong. It'll put hair on your chest."

She giggled. "Just what every woman wants, hair on her chest."

I winked at her, which made her laugh harder. As soon as it was done brewing, I poured us both a cup and let her add the milk and sugar to hers. I took mine black. Her moan after the first swallow made me uncomfortable. Her eyes widened.

"What kind is this? It's wonderful."

"It's called Death Wish. I get it online. It's been out three years, I think. It's pricier than others, but I like it."

"It would be worth it. I'll get another job to pay for it if I have to. God, this is perfect." She sighed.

As we finished making breakfast, we chatted about our favorite foods. I found we had a lot in common. When it was done, we filled our plates and sat at the kitchen counter. We dug in. The only noise was our forks scraping the plates. I tried to get her to eat seconds, but she insisted she was full.

We'd barely finished cleaning our plates when there was a loud pounding on the door. "I'll be back," I told her before going to see who it was.

Most of the time, the guys would walk in unless they knew I had company, but no one knew she was there. As I opened it, I came face-to-face with an irate-looking Wolverine. I pulled the door shut behind me and stood on the porch.

"What?" I asked.

"Why the fuck didn't you tell me you were bringing her to your house? I've been going crazy wondering where she ran off to."

"The last time I checked, I don't have to tell you shit. You knew she was with me. I was making sure she was okay. She showered and hadn't eaten since yesterday morning. She was starved, so I brought her here to have breakfast, not that it's any of your business. She's fine."

"What's your angle, Diablo? You're not interested in her, other than to warm your cock for a night or two. And anyone can tell she's not that kind of woman."

I pushed up to him and got into his face. "I'd watch your mouth, boy. You have no right to say shit to me. I'm not doing anything but helping her out. I could remind you of the same thing. She's not a club slut or hanger-on. Last I heard, that's all you go for."

"Well, maybe I've changed my mind! She's a good woman. We don't get those around here. It's a nice change of pace."

His answer angered me. I was about to challenge him to explain precisely what he meant by that, but we were interrupted by Scorpion walking up. His house was on the backside of mine. He came from that direction. He was frowning at us when he joined us.

"What's gotten into you two? I could hear you yelling over at my house."

"He's trying to put moves on Jauhnna, and we all know he's not interested in a permanent woman in his life," Wolverine told him.

"And he's trying to stake some kind of claim when we all know he's not into anything for more than a night or two," I argued back.

"If neither of you are serious about pursuing something more, then you both need to leave her be. It'll leave the way clear for another brother to see if she might be the one for him. I think it's time we started to do things differently in this club."

This remark caught both our attention and turned us on him. "Who? Has someone said something?" I snapped.

"Do you want a chance with her?" Wolverine demanded.

"What if I do?"

My fury was mounting. I wanted to plant them facers and tell them to stay the fuck away from her. They were bickering with each other. I was about to order them to leave when I caught a glimpse of her passing along the side of the house. She was headed toward the clubhouse. I shoved them out of the way and took off after her. I caught up to her not far from my house. When I latched onto her arm and twirled her around to face me, the furious look on her face floored me.

"Where are you going?" I asked because I didn't know what else to say.

"Somewhere I don't have to listen to grown men arguing over who wants to fuck me. Newsflash, I won't be screwing any of you. I guess I know what the payment for your help is," she said acidly. Her assertion stunned me. I was left speechless, and so were Scorpion and Wolverine since she yelled it loud enough for them to hear her.

Jauhnna: Chapter 5

I was so upset, I could barely keep from shaking. My enjoyment of the morning changed to anger as I stood inside Diablo's house and heard some of what they were arguing about. Did they think I was someone who would just have sex with a man, one I didn't know, at the drop of a hat? Or was it that they intended to extract payment for their help by insisting I sleep with one of them regardless of whether I was willing or not? Or possibly all of them? The thought filled me with anger and horror. Hoping I could sneak past the house to get to the clubhouse and find my way out of this place, I took off out the back door once I discovered it.

Unfortunately, Diablo saw me, and now I was face-to-face with him. My answer to his question about where I was going clearly stunned him. He was standing there gaping at me. The other two had gotten quiet. Shaking my arm to get him to let go, I jerked on it when he didn't. He gripped it tighter and tugged me closer to him. I put up my hands to keep some distance between us, which meant my palms were on his hard chest.

"You think we'd demand sex as payment for helping you?" he asked incredulously.

"Why not? Isn't that what all men want? Who cares if it's freely given? If the woman says no, just take it. After all, she's nothing but a woman. What rights does she have?" I spit out. My stomach rolled. I wanted to kick myself. I'd been letting down my walls with him. Breakfast was fun and lighthearted, something I'd never had with a man. See where it got me? This time, when I yanked on my arm, he let go.

Scorpion and Wolverine were coming toward us. I backed away from them. There was no way I could fight all three. Not waiting for them to reach us, I took off running. I had no idea where to hide, but I had to do something. I heard them yelling my name and telling me to stop, but I kept running. My heart pounded so loudly in my ears that I had no idea anyone was close to me until I was picked up off the ground. As those massive arms encircled me, I screamed and began to kick and struggle to get away.

"Jauhnna, please, you've got to listen. No one is going to hurt you or force you to have sex with them. Stop!" Diablo shouted next to my ear.

I kept fighting. I didn't believe a word any of them said. The other two were now in front of me. They were trying to get me to settle down, too.

"Honey, God, you can't think that. Surely not," Wolverine was saying. He appeared troubled.

"Jesus, babe, you've got this all wrong. I swear to you. No one plans to touch you against your will. You heard what we told you last night," Scorpion argued.

I was drumming my heels off Diablo's legs. He must've gotten tired of it because the next thing I knew, he wrapped a leg around mine to capture and hold them trapped between his. My arms were useless, the way he had them pinned at my sides, so I tried using my head. I groaned as the cut and knot on the back of my head made contact with his upper chest when I slammed it back, hoping to catch his face or at least his jaw.

"Stop. You're hurting yourself," he ordered gruffly.

"Go to hell! You're not touching me. I won't be violated," I shouted.

As I was yelling, I saw more guys coming toward us. My panic hit new highs. Oh my God, I'd never survive this. I began to hyperventilate.

"Shit, she's freaking out. Please, you've got to slow your breathing, Jauhnna. No one is here to violate you," Wolverine said louder.

As the other men approached us, dark spots started to dot my vision. Along with them, a flood of memories hit me. I let out another useless scream and then choked. Everything became a jumbled mess of blurred images and loud voices. Suddenly, one of the voices came through loud and clear.

"Jauhnna, Galway isn't here. He can't hurt you anymore, and neither can his men. You're safe. We're your guardians. We'll protect you. You're safe," a strange voice shouted. I tried to believe him, but I couldn't. I wasn't able to get air into my lungs. I gasped and struggled, but it was no use. As it all quickly faded to black, I sent up a prayer. *Don't let me wake up. Let me die.*

Diablo:

I wanted to roar to the heavens while, at the same time, I wanted to hurl up my guts. She was so terrified she was like a blind animal in a trap. She wouldn't or couldn't hear a word we said. She was struggling so hard to breathe she was gasping. When Micro ran up and started saying shit about Galway, I didn't pay attention to him. She was my only concern. When she went completely limp in my arms, I was terrified. Without thinking about it, I turned and ran for my house. They all followed me to the front door, then right on inside. I took her to the couch in the living room and laid her down. I checked her carotid pulse with shaking fingers.

"Let me check her," Wolverine barked as he pushed past the others. I came to my feet. I was relieved to feel her strong pulse, but I didn't want him touching her.

"You keep your goddamn hands off her. It's your fault she's like this. You had to come to the house, running your mouth about shit you know nothing about," I snarled.

"My fault? You were the one playing some game with her," he snapped back.

I lunged at him, but Scorpion and Butcher got between us.

"Move," I ordered them.

"I can't do that. You both need to cool off. I believe

you should listen to what Micro has to say," Butcher said calmly.

"Butch, if you don't move, I'm putting you on your ass," I warned him.

"You can try. I haven't had a good tussle in a while. It might be fun. Instead, I believe the two of you need to calm the fuck down. Tell us what started this?" Butcher demanded.

I was about to blast him when Micro got my attention. "Pres, I don't mean to piss you off more, but you've got to hear what I found out. It's important. Is she okay as she is, or should we try and wake her up?" he asked Wolverine.

"I think she probably passed out from hyperventilating, but I can't be sure unless he lets me check her," he sneered slightly at me.

"She's fine. Her pulse is good. Micro, tell me what you think is so damn important," I ordered as I dismissed Wolverine.

Micro hesitated a couple of seconds, then got to it. I think my death glare convinced him to spill it or meet my fist. I was barely holding on to my temper. When it was let loose, it wasn't a pretty sight. Inner Diablo came out like the demon he was. I didn't want to release him on my brothers, but I might if pushed too far.

"I told you I'd discovered some things I thought you should know about Jauhnna. Well, while I waited for you to text me that it was fine to come over to talk, I kept digging. I found more, way more. Christ, it's not good. First, I know who her husband is. The name Galway isn't exactly common here in the States. She's right to be afraid of him. His name is Galway Radigan. He's the head of a small, deadly, driven criminal family in Nevada. She told the truth. She ran away from him three years ago, and he's been searching for her since. I'd bet money that those men who took her work for him, even if indirectly. There's been an open reward, bounty, whatever you want to call it, for bringing her back." He paused.

"A fucking bounty! Are you kidding me? What, like the old West, dead or alive bullshit?" Scorpion chimed in, sounding disbelieving. I was right there with him. What the fuck could she have done to warrant a bounty on her head?

Micro nodded. "An honest to God bounty. The only good thing is in order to get paid, she has to be brought to him alive. Whoever took her must be shitting themselves at the thought they had all that money in sight and lost it. If they or anyone else has a clue she's not dead, they'll be sniffing after her in a heartbeat. I don't know how she evaded them this long."

"How much is he promising?" I asked gruffly.

"It's two million dollars. He's got the backing and financial help to pay it from his brother-in-law, her brother." He dropped his next bomb.

"Her fucking brother is helping him! Jesus Christ, why? What did she do? You said he's the head honcho of some crime family. How big? Are we talking about the Mafia? What about her brother?" I asked.

Everyone knew the Mafia was thick in Vegas and other parts of the country. Hell, we even had one of the alleged top Irish Mafia families right here in St. Augustine, the O'Sheerans. We'd never had trouble with them, although we'd heard they had cleaned up their act over the last few decades. Bull and his club in Hunters Creek had some slight connection to them through

Maverick's old lady, Rylan—something to do with a lawyer.

"The Radigans are a small gang with ideas of grandeur. I'm still getting information on how well they're connected. The same goes for her brother. As for what she did, I don't know, but whatever it was, he's determined to get her back."

"Over my fucking dead, cold body, is he taking her! There's no telling what he'll do to her. She stays, and we figure out how to make her safe," I commanded. I wasn't taking it to the table for a vote. It was happening. Anyone wanting to argue could meet me in the ring.

"No one can make me safe. The only way that happens is if he and my brother and their top guys are dead or I am. I think we know the most feasible option," a husky voice whispered from the couch.

Wheeling around, I saw her green eyes watching us. There was distrust there, plain as day. She was curled on her side, fists clenched. She shifted and stiffened when Wolverine moved toward her. He halted.

"Jauhnna, we need to talk. You've got us all wrong, but I can understand how intimidating it is to be faced with all of us at once. Let me get rid of these guys, and then we'll work this out," I told her gently.

I hadn't had to find the gentle side of me outside of my daughter and grandkids in ages. Usually, I was a more abrasive guy who didn't care who liked me. In her case, I wanted, no, it was critical, that she like and trust me. I wasn't so sure why.

She shook her head. "There's nothing to talk about. If you're telling the truth and have no plans to hurt me, you won't have a problem letting me go. I hate to ask for money, but it won't be much. Just enough to get what I need, and then I'll repay you. You can forget you ever saw me."

"We can't do that," Scorpion said.

The rest of my guys nodded in agreement and murmured the same words. Wolverine was staring extra hard at her. Wanting to divert her argument for at least a few minutes, I hurried to speak.

"I think before they go, you should be introduced to everyone. They're a motley bunch, but they're good guys. You've met Scorpion and Wolverine. This is Micro, if you haven't guessed. He's the one I told you about yesterday. He's our resident IT wizard and the club's treasurer." Micro gave her a chin lift and smile.

I pointed to his left. "This is Butcher. He's our enforcer. It's his job to maintain order during our meetings and activities. He ensures members adhere to the rules and our bylaws and defends the club's members, property, and territory." I watched her pale and shrink further into the cushions.

"Ahh, honey, there's no need to be afraid. I'm only a menace to our enemies. You're not one of those," he told her with a wink. She untensed a tad.

I hurried to the next person. "Thunder is our secretary, and this is Crash. He's our road captain. He plans our riding routes when we go out as a club, to a rally, or on a run." Each smiled, nodded, or gave her salutes to ease her tension. I wasn't sure it was working.

"These four are Cowboy, Lucky, Punk, and Turbo. They round out our dozen members. The only ones missing are our prospects, Liam and Zax. You'll meet them later. Now that we've got introductions over, you guys head back to wherever. I need to talk to Jauhnna, and then I'll update you later. Micro, I need you to stay for a while."

I noted Wolverine was opening his mouth to argue. I gave him a quelling look. Butcher shook his head at him. He subsided, but he was unhappy about it. Too bad.

"It's nice to meet you."

"We're here to help."

"No worries, we've got you."

Those remarks and more came from my guys as they streamed out of my house. Wolverine was next to last to leave. Butcher stood there as if a sentry. Wolverine walked out in a huff. Before he left, Butcher had one comment.

"We're all here to help her, Diablo. Remember, we're on the same team. As for you, honey, tell him everything. It's hard to trust, I get it, but you can trust us. We won't let you get hurt." He walked out as soon as he finished saying his spiel. The door closed firmly behind him. As I faced her, I saw she was still curled in a protective ball on the couch. It wouldn't do.

"Who would like a drink? I know I would. It's too early for liquor, so it's soda, tea, coffee, or water."

"If you're offering some of your precious coffee, then yes," Micro said.

"Don't get used to it. You bastards would drink me dry if I let you. You know, you can order this, too," I grumbled, waiting to hear what she wanted.

"Yeah, but if I order it, I pay. It tastes better if someone else does," was his smartass comeback.

I gave him the middle finger. A soft giggle made me glance back at her. She watched us with an amused expression, and her body wasn't as tightly wound. I pointed to her. "Hey, none of that, missy, or you won't get a second cup. I saw how much you loved it. You're gonna be like this one, I can tell."

My teasing remark made her smile. "You should've never shared it with me. It's addictive. Yes, please, I'd love another, if I may."

I grinned at her as I bowed. "You may. Micro, get your ass to the kitchen. I'm not waiting on you. She gets VIP treatment. You don't."

He pretended to pout as he dragged himself to the kitchen. When he tried to get a huge travel mug for his cup, I smacked him in the back of the head. He grinned at me. A second giggle came from the living room. He and I bickered back and forth as we prepared the coffee. We all had a hot cup of java within no time. It was time to get down to business. The amusement slid off her face. She was back to looking apprehensive.

I asked her, "Where would you like to start?" She glanced at Micro and then back at me but didn't reply.

"Why don't you tell him your name?" Micro suggested.

"Your name?" Of course, I should've known it wasn't her real one. How else would she have been able to hide for so long? I detested the idea of calling her something else. Jauhnna suited her.

She took a deep breath and then spoke up. "Jauhnna Carter isn't my real name. If it were, there would be no way I would've remained hidden for so long. My real name is Joanne Radigan, née Vierra. I'm from Las Vegas."

Joanne seemed too ordinary for her, but I offered, "Would you prefer we call you Joanne?"

She vigorously shook her head. "No! Please, I don't want to hear that name again, ever. In my heart,

I'm Jauhnna. It was the name my mom tried to give me, but my father said no. It feels more me than the name I had for the first twenty-nine years of my life."

"Okay, we can do that. Mind if I ask where Carter comes from?" I asked next. I wanted to ease her into the more complicated questions. The ones I had no doubt would trigger things she might rather forget.

"That was chosen by the man who made up my fake identity. I thought it was solid since no one found me for so long, but if Micro easily found the truth, it's a miracle they hadn't been at my door long ago."

"Sweetheart, the cover was damn good. I only got suspicious because we knew you were on the run, and I knew what tiny anomalies to look for. When I found one, I unraveled it, and that's how I found your real name and who your husband is," Micro assured her.

"Don't call him that. Galway has never been a husband, not in the sense that I understand the word. If I had my way, he'd have zero connection to me, and I'd never hear his name or see him again," she said vehemently.

"We know it's not easy to talk about him. Why don't you tell us about your brother? The one helping with the reward to find you. Why would he help Galway? Does he not know he treated you horribly?" I was guessing on the horrible part, but I was convinced it was a fact. The way she reacted to any mention of him and the mere fact she ran and hid told the truth. I was steeling myself to hear the details.

"My brother Janus is as evil as Galway, and our father wasn't any better. When Father died, Janus assumed his position as head of the family. He's pushed the boundaries to go further than even our father did.

He won't want anything to upset his rise to more power, influence, or money, just as Galway won't."

"Don't take this wrong, but why are you so significant to them obtaining or keeping those things that are so important to them?" Micro asked.

She cast her eyes down and stared at her cup. It was glaringly obvious she didn't want to answer—the why of it was what was nagging at me. The silence stretched until she set her cup on the coffee table and met our eyes. There was determination staring back at us. She straightened her spine.

"A couple of reasons. Initially, it was to create a tie between our families. That would be achieved not only by our marriage but also by our children. I was a disappointment in that department. No matter how many times he tried to get me pregnant, I never conceived. I'm barren. He was furious about it."

"So if all he wanted was a child, why not divorce you and marry someone else who could give him children? Shit that sounds cold. I don't mean to diminish your inability to have kids," Micro added.

"I want them very much, but it's not to be. However, I'm thrilled I never had one with him. No way would I ever want that man to be the father of any child, especially mine. As for why he didn't just get rid of me and get another woman who could, it's complicated. He was never faithful. I never cared if he was. I loved when he gave his attention to his whores and mistresses. It meant he was giving me a break. One reason he didn't divorce me was there's money involved. See, my mother was quite wealthy in her own right. She found a way to protect her wealth from my father. When she bore him a son and a daughter, she knew Janus would be raised in my father's image, so she ensured the majority of her wealth would come to me. As his wife, Galway hoped to have access to it."

"And?" I prodded when she hesitated. I knew there was more.

"And two, Galway doesn't like to lose or give up anything that belongs to him, even if he doesn't want it. He'd rather destroy it than give his possessions to someone else."

Her casual reference to herself as a possession, as if she was an inanimate object, pissed me off. I came to my feet. I paced to try and let the anger seep away. There was more to it. The way she said one of her first statements was troubling me.

"You said no matter how many times he tried to get you pregnant, it always failed. What does that mean? Tried?"

Her hands clenched into fists for a moment, and then she visibly forced them to relax. Tension was mounting in the air. When she met my gaze, fire and pain mixed in her eyes.

"It means every time he raped me and forced his seed inside of me, attempting to impregnate me, it failed. No matter how brutal he was or how he did it, his seed never took. He was furious and would punish me for my inadequacy as a woman. Every time I saw a negative pregnancy test, I was both relieved and heartbroken. He's a monster."

Hearing her confess to being raped repeatedly for God knows how long sent my rage skyrocketing. I let out a roar and, seeking a target, swept the tchotchkes on the mantel to the floor. Hearing some of them shatter filled me with satisfaction. I could always get more knickknacks. I tried to imagine it was her husband's face I was shattering. It was her cry of alarm that made me rein it back in. I panted as I fought to subdue my fury.

"I'm sorry. I'm alright. I won't hurt you, Jauhnna. I'm just so fucking angry with that bastard. He deserves to be put down like the animal he is. How can your brother help him? You're his sister."

"Because Janus is made of the same cloth. He doesn't care who he uses, hurts, or kills to gain what he wants. I have no doubt he's backing Galway because Galway has promised him something he needs or wants in return. What it is, I have no idea. That's why when I escaped, I didn't go to him. He would've hand-delivered me right back to my prison."

"May I ask why you married him?" Micro asked softly. I'd almost forgotten we weren't alone.

She gave a humorless snort. "You think I was given a choice? That's laughable. My father forced me to marry him. I detested the idea and tried to talk him out of it, but he didn't care. I was marched down the aisle, and threats were made. There were rumors about Galway and how he treated others, especially women. I was sacrificed for the good of the family. Only I wasn't included in the family." Her bitterness was audible.

I asked hoarsely, "How long were you with him before you ran? How did you get away?"

"I was forced to wed him when I was twenty. I ran at twenty-nine—nine years of utter hell. How I got away was rather simple. I made a friend without him knowing it. It was through a woman I met at the library. That was one place he let me go without guards stuck up my ass every second. They'd wait outside. I think it was because the thought of books scared them. Who knows if they could even read? They were morons. They were all about brawn, not brains. One day, I got talking to a fellow reader about our book choices. Over time, the conversations grew personal. She saw my guards always waiting on me and how they treated me. She asked about them, and I was so desperate for a friend that eventually, I confessed.

"That's when she revealed she worked with an underground organization that helped women, children, and even some men to get away from their abusers. She assured me she could get me to safety and I'd have a new identity. It took a while for me to believe her. Finally, after a particularly fierce and brutal night, I told her to do it. It took a few weeks to get everything in place, but when it was, she got people to help smuggle me out of the library under their noses. I wish I could've seen their faces when they realized I was gone. She took me to a safe house, and from there, I was issued a new identity and coached in it. Over several weeks, I was moved from safe house to safe house until I ended up in Georgia. I started over there, and I was there until yesterday."

I knew she was probably downplaying what she went through. If he raped her over and over, God only knew what else he subjected her to. What had finally broken her? She said it was a fierce and brutal night. I burned to ask what happened, but she was slumping. She'd had enough, and I knew we had sufficient information to track down and eliminate not only her bastard of a husband but her brother, too. It would take time and finesse. We'd have to ask for outside help on this. I typically wouldn't, but I'd take it if it meant success. Walking over to the couch, I crouched in front of her.

"Darlin', you're one courageous woman. I know you have no reason to trust us. I hope as time passes, you'll see we're trustworthy. Just know we're here to protect and help you. Can you give us a chance to prove it?"

She studied me for several tense minutes before slowly nodding. I held out my hand. She took it, and we shook on it. The deal was sealed. Now, to start the hunt. My inner devil couldn't wait.

Jauhnna: Chapter 6

The past three weeks I'd been at the Horsemen's compound had been somewhat surreal. As much as I tried not to trust them, it was becoming harder and harder not to. So far, they'd kept to their word on everything they promised. After the emotional download of my past to Micro and Diablo, I'd been wiped out. Instead of returning to the sick bay at the clubhouse or his room there, Diablo insisted I lie down at his house and rest. He claimed it would keep me from being disturbed. I hadn't fought him. Micro promised he'd keep working on getting information, and they would contact their friends to see what kind of help they could give.

I was curious about those friends. Were they the ones Diablo mentioned they gained from his daughter's marriage? Or were they someone else? I thought to ask, then decided maybe I shouldn't.

When I woke up later that day, Diablo had another surprise. It seemed he thought the clubhouse was too noisy for me to heal, so he brought the box of his daughter's things to his house and put it in one of his guest bedrooms. He informed me it would be best if I stayed there. I tried to argue. I didn't want to encroach on his privacy. He and his club were doing more than enough for me. He'd waved it away and said it was done.

A part of me wondered if he insisted because of

Wolverine. As the days passed, there was this tension between them. I hated it, but there was nothing I could do about it. I was confused about the cause. If they weren't out to force me to have sex with them as payment, why were they upset with each other?

Wolverine did get his way when he insisted on examining me to ensure I was recovering and not likely to relapse. While he checked me out, Diablo refused to leave the room. He stood there with his arms crossed over his massive chest and watched every move Wolverine made like a hawk.

As more days passed, I settled into a routine as Micro and others I knew nothing about worked to find Galway and formulate a plan. The Horsemen wouldn't tell me what that was. All I heard was that when the time came, I'd know. It kind of frustrated me. Besides not being allowed off the compound and not having much to do, things were good—well, good in one way and bad in another.

Besides trying to gain my equilibrium being around so many strangers who were men, I was attempting to battle something more. It was this insane attraction I felt for Diablo. No matter how much I tried to limit my time with him, it didn't seem to matter. Even if he was out of sight, he wasn't out of mind. I'd find myself thinking about him randomly and frequently. My dreams were beginning to star him. Those were becoming rather graphic, though why, I had no idea. When it came to sex, I never experienced anything close to pleasurable. What I knew about that kind of sex was from books. I had no clue what kind of lover he'd be, but my imagination told me I'd enjoy it.

I might've been free of Galway for three years, but

I never found a man I wanted to hook up with to see if sex was tolerable. Diablo made me wish I had. Maybe if I had, I'd have enough nerve to see if he'd be willing to let me taste the forbidden at least once. I knew it wouldn't be more than that. If it were, it wouldn't be more than casual. I heard the guys talking at the clubhouse the other day. They didn't know I was nearby. They were talking about the upcoming weekend and debating who would be there. That's when I heard them mention hangers-on and club sluts. My curiosity was piqued. Rather than ask any of them who they were, I did my version of research.

I went online, searched, and then downloaded some MC romances. To help keep me entertained, Diablo came home with an e-reader one day and told me he'd set up an account for me and that I could download whatever I wanted to read. I'd been speechless. In the end, all I was able to do was thank him. Those books opened my eyes to a lot of things, and not all of them were good. They educated me on two main types of women who came to the club, and they weren't old ladies.

Learning about them now had me envisioning them with Diablo. The thought depressed me and made me angry and sick all at once. I needed to stop. He was nothing to me. Heck, there was nothing in his behavior to indicate he found me the least bit attractive. He was kind and helpful. He never touched me in an inappropriate way. I wish I could be unaffected by him the way he was with me.

He was a hugely built man, but it was all muscle and, in my opinion, mouthwatering. He was tall. His brown hair was flecked with silver and cut into a buzz cut like some military guys wore. His beard and mustache were kept trimmed, close to his face, and it had the ever-slightest silver in it, too. He was tanned from all the time in the Florida sun. His dark brown eyes seemed bottomless. His chest was broad, his arms massive, and his trapezius muscles were enormous. I had no doubt he could lift an unimaginable amount of weight. Add to it his tattoos, which ran down his arms, and I was often aroused.

Tonight, I was anxious for a whole different reason. I was about to infiltrate the inner domain of the club. They had no idea of my plan. They were there partying, no doubt. Diablo had left a while ago, explaining he'd be back late and not to wait up. He didn't tell me what he was doing, but I knew. He'd been spending more time at the clubhouse the past week. Maybe he was tired of having a houseguest. If I cramped his sex life, no wonder. He was undoubtedly using his room there to have sex with lord knows how many faceless women.

Nausea rose in the back of my throat at the thought. *You need to stop this ridiculousness. He's not yours. He can do whatever or whoever he wants. Go see for yourself, then put this foolishness aside,* I lectured myself. I'd been doing a lot of that, but it hadn't helped so far.

Another thing Diablo insisted on was that I go online and buy clothes. He asserted there was no way I could go without more clothing, and he knew I needed underthings. Eventually, he grew tired of me refusing to tell him what I needed. I caught him on his computer with an open cart in an online store. When I confronted him, he said his daughter loved it, and he began throwing things into it. I grew alarmed at the amount he was choosing. That was what made me do it myself. I shifted most of it out, but he wasn't to be foiled. He returned later, added them to the cart again, and then paid for them without my knowledge. I got a shock when boxes kept coming. When I demanded that he send the bulk of them back, he shook his head and walked off—frustrating man.

Tonight, though, I was glad I had the clothes. A few of the outfits were more along the line of what I thought a biker babe would wear. They weren't slutty, but they did make me feel attractive and sexy. Something I hadn't felt in years. The last time was before I was forced to marry Galway. They boosted my confidence, but I feared I'd chicken out of wearing them. I didn't plan to be seen, but what would the guys think of them if I was?

The one thing I didn't think they'd do was fall on me like wolves. I was almost sure they wouldn't ever approach me sexually. Even Wolverine made sure to stay away from me for the most part. I believed they didn't quite know what to do with me or what to say. The argument he and Diablo had that day at the house must've convinced them I wasn't someone they wanted, not even for a night. Taking one last look in the mirror to ensure I was presentable, just in case I was noticed, I sucked in courage and then headed for the door.

It was dark outside, but the walk to the clubhouse wasn't far, and they had outdoor lighting to illuminate the area surrounding the clubhouse. I came up to the side entrance and eased the door open. It was left unlocked. No way was I going in the front door. The goal was to remain unseen. The music and voices were loud. I heard laughter. It sounded as if they were having a good time. It was almost midnight, so they should be well into the fun. Closing it behind me, I made my way down the hallway toward the main room.

The main room was dimly lit, the same as the hallway, which worked in my favor as I hung back in the shadows of the hall. As I scanned the room, I saw the Horsemen and a bevy of scantily dressed women all over the place. They were sitting on laps, hanging on the guys, or standing close to them. As I took them in, I gulped. Being here wasn't such a good idea.

For one thing, seeing the women made it clear they were not in the same league as I was. My earlier confidence did a nosedive. They were way skinnier. Many of them had these perfect bodies with huge boobs. I wondered how many were fake. None had to worry about what they ate or hated to get on the scale. They were letting everything hang out, without a care in the world. While they had their faces painted with more makeup than I'd ever considered wearing, it made them appear gorgeous. It was tastefully done. On top of their looks and bodies, it was clear they were several years younger than me overall. I was an old woman compared to them.

I was about to ease further into the shadows and head back to the house. I'd seen enough, or so I thought until one of them dropped to her knees and unzipped Lucky's pants. Oh my God, was she about to do what I thought? Right there in front of everyone! I gulped and turned my head away. As I did, my gaze landed on another sight. I froze.

Sitting at a table, with a few other members was Diablo. Just the sight of him was enough to make me pause every time, but this time, it was more than for his masculine beauty. It was due to the woman who was hanging over his back. She had her boobs pressed into his back and was rubbing his shoulders as she said something in his ear. Instantly, I felt on the verge of puking. There, I had it. Confirmation he was enjoying his time at the clubhouse. I now knew what he had done all those nights he had come here to hang with the guys. Yeah, right, hanging with the guys, my ass.

Holding back stupid tears, I whirled and took off down the hall. I had to get out of here before I was seen. It would be humiliating to have them see me and know I was upset. The hall was much darker, and I bumped accidentally into the wall. I righted myself and came around a corner. I ran smack dab into a hard object. By the feel of it, I knew it was a body, a man's. I glanced up to see who it was that was witness to my spying. Maybe I could get him to keep it to himself. I gulped when I noticed a face I didn't recognize. The man was staring down at me with a smile on his face. As he breathed out, I smelled the beer on his breath. His hands came up, and they rested on my hips.

"Well, hello, where did you come from? I haven't seen you tonight. This must be my lucky night. Since you're not busy and I'm not busy, why don't you come with me? We can have a drink, get to know each other, and then have some fun of our own, beautiful. Damn, how hasn't someone snapped you up?" he muttered. His hands tightened a tiny bit more.

Panic welled up inside of me. I didn't know him. That meant he wasn't safe. Trying not to lose it, I went for logic.

"I'm sorry. You have me confused with someone

else. I was just leaving. Excuse me." I moved away from him, but he kept a hold of me and moved with me.

"Hey, don't run off. You're exactly who I'm looking for. What's your name, sweetheart? Mine is Gio." He smiled.

"Listen, I'm not what you think I am. I'm not one of those women out there. I shouldn't be here." Again, I tried to get away. This time, he tugged me against him.

"And just who are you then? The only ones here tonight are me, my friend, the club, and the entertainment. What's wrong? Did you get cold feet? Is this your first time here? Come on, you and I'll sit and talk for a bit. I bet I can get you past this nervousness." He smiled bigger, then his hands slid down to grab my ass. That was it. I was done.

Lashing out with an elbow, I took him in the ribs. As he flinched, I raised my hand and went for his nose. A heel strike to the nose would break it and make his eyes water. It would allow me to escape. The only problem was he blocked it. The next thing I knew, I was twirled around, with one arm pinned behind my back, and an arm was placed across my chest like a steel band.

"What the fuck was that?" he growled in my ear.

He sounded pissed. Forgetting about being sneaky, I opened my mouth and screamed at the top of my voice. I didn't care who heard me as long as one of the Horsemen came to help me. I'd been an idiot to come here.

"Christ, stop. There's no need to caterwaul like that," he growled. His hold didn't lessen.

I screamed again. His hand came up to cover my mouth. At this point, blind panic was closing in on me. He could drag me into any of these rooms and do anything he wanted to me. *You're so stupid, Jauhnna.* I tried to fight him. I struggled as much as I could. He was saying something, but I didn't care to hear what. I attempted to stomp on his foot, but I connected with a hard boot. It hurt my foot.

The thunder of voices getting closer, accompanied by pounding footsteps, made me sag in relief. The lights flared to life in the hallway, and then I was faced with a wall of men. Men who went from puzzled to angry within two seconds. A loud bellow cut through the din of voices. They were shoved out of the way as Diablo came barreling through them. His face was contorted in rage.

"Why the fuck do you have your hands on Jauhnna? I'll fucking kill you!" he snarled.

His fists came up, and he threw a punch over my head. The guy holding me, Gio, abruptly let go of me. I no longer felt him pressed to my back, and my arms were both free. I was too stunned to move. Someone yanked me out from between them. I found myself being held by Butcher. He was closely watching Diablo as he tried to reassure me.

"Don't worry, honey. Diablo will take care of this. I never thought a Dark Patriot would hurt a woman," Butcher muttered. I was too distracted by the yelled conversation between Diablo and Gio to reply. The stranger was holding up his hands in a pleading manner.

"Diablo, calm the fuck down! I didn't hurt her. I'm sorry. I didn't know who she was. She didn't tell me her name. I didn't know she was Jauhnna. If I had, I would've never touched her or propositioned her. I thought she was one of the hangers-on or maybe a bunny."

"You did what?" Diablo roared louder. He lunged at him. His fist connected with Gio's face, even though he tried to block it.

As it did, I heard Micro, I think it was, mutter, "Well, there goes the Dark Patriots helping us to solve the Galway problem. I hope Pres has another idea."

Horror filled me as I realized this man was one of the friends they had mentioned who was going to help them with my shitshow of a life. Remorse filled me. Had I overreacted? What had he actually done other than hold me and grab my ass? It wasn't until I went after him that he got more physical. I moaned.

Shoving out of Butcher's arms, I darted over to stop them before it was too late. Only I wasn't paying attention. I walked between them as Diablo threw another punch. It was aimed at Gio's stomach, so it took me in the lower chest when it landed. I flew back and slammed into Gio. All air left my body, and I couldn't get any in. Terror filled me as I gaped like a fish out of water. Horrified exclamations came from all of them. I slid to the floor, landing hard on my ass. As my vision wavered, Diablo dropped down to his knees in front of me. He appeared stricken. His hands came out to touch my cheek.

"Baby, take a breath, please. Oh shit, I didn't mean to hit you. I tried to pull it, but it was too late. Jesus Christ, why did you get between us? You never get between men when they're fighting. He deserves those punches and more. The fucker touched you. Why didn't you let me beat his goddamn ass?" he asked.

I tried to answer, but it was impossible when I had no oxygen entering my body. My chest was on fire.

I tried to reach up and grasp his arm, but my arm fell useless to my side. The next thing I knew, I was scooped up in his arms, and he was rushing down the hall. I recognized the door he kicked open. It was the sick bay. I was placed on the familiar exam table. The babble of voices was overwhelming. Diablo was yelling for Wolverine. Things were fading in and out as my brain reacted to the lack of oxygen.

"Do something! She can't fucking breathe," he hollered at Wolverine, who was bending over me now.

"I need the rest of you out. I need to see her chest," Wolverine shouted.

Pushing and shoving as fast and hard as he could, Diablo got everyone out of the room, then slammed and locked the door. He rushed back to the side of the table, anxiety written all over his face.

My top was yanked up and then off. Diablo growled. Wolverine ignored him and assessed my upper chest. I wondered what he saw, but I couldn't move my head to look. Abruptly, his hand was on my chest, rubbing in circles.

"What the hell are you doing?" Diablo snarled.

"I'm trying to ease the spasm to her chest muscles. They're seized up, and that's why she can't breathe. Get your head out of your ass. I'm not feeling her up," he snapped.

"Let me do it. You see what else you can do. She's turning blue." There was panic in Diablo's voice. His hand pushed Wolverine's out of the way and took over the rubbing.

As inappropriate as it was, in the middle of me possibly dying from asphyxiation, Diablo's touch affected me. I pressed into it. He was staring into my eyes, begging me repeatedly to breathe. Wolverine was checking my pulse and muttering. Then, just like a miracle, the muscles eased, and I was able to draw in a tiny amount of air. I inhaled greedily.

"That's it. Nice and slow. Good, baby," Diablo crooned as he kept rubbing.

I fought to take in more and to make them deeper ones. As more oxygen made its way through my body, other sensations came to the surface. My nipples hardened in my bra, and the feeling of his work-roughened hands touching my skin filled me with heat.

"Pres, I think you can stop rubbing her. She's breathing now," came Wolverine's amusement-filled voice.

Diablo's hand lifted away reluctantly. I wanted to beg him to put it back, but I caught myself in time to prevent further humiliation. I had enough to be embarrassed about after my freakout with Gio.

"Do you think I cracked or broke anything?" he anxiously asked Wolverine.

"I don't know. Let me check." He hip-checked Diablo out of the way and laid his hand on my chest. His touch did nothing to me. He pressed around. Diablo was making these funny, growly sounds.

Wolverine smiled at me and then winked. "Tell me if it hurts anywhere."

I had to force myself to concentrate. It hurt as he moved around in a wider circle, but nothing more than it already had. "It hurts, and it's sore, but not worse in any spot over another. I think I'm fine," I said. My voice came out hoarse.

He stopped pressing but left his hand in place. "I think she's good. You'll have a helluva bruise and be sore for a while, but that's it."

"Thank you. Do you mind if I sit up? Oh, and can I have my top?" I croaked.

I was becoming self-conscious with so much of me bare, especially after seeing those women. He lifted his hand away while using the other to lift under my back, bringing me up into a sitting position. Instantly, Diablo was there holding my top. He scowled at Wolverine as he slipped it over my head and helped me put my arms through the armholes. My cheeks were burning with mortification. I was dreading what they'd have to say about my screwup. Why hadn't I kept my ass at the house? It wasn't as if seeing those women made me feel better or helped me get over my infatuation with Diablo. They only succeeded in making me want to cry. I knew I had to answer for my behavior, but I couldn't face it now. Tears filled my eyes.

"Can I just stay here and rest for a while?" I whispered in misery.

"Sure," Wolverine said.

"I'll stay with you," Diablo added.

I shook my head. "No, please, I want to sleep. If someone is in here with me, I won't. I just need to rest. I won't take long."

"Darlin', are you sure you're not in pain? Your eyes are full of tears," Diablo asked in concern.

I shook my head. "I'm just suddenly tired. Will you turn out the lights? They're too bright."

"Are you sure you should be alone?" Diablo asked. When I gave him what passed for a smile and waved him off, I watched as they slowly left, turning off the lights and closing the door behind them. As it latched closed, I let the tears fall. What an absolute moron I was.

Diablo:

It didn't sit right with me to leave her alone, but she kept insisting, and I had something needing my attention. While I wanted to question her about why she was at the clubhouse, the desire to confront Gio again as to why he had his hands all over her was a more persistent urge at the moment. His admission earlier to having propositioned her made me see red. Coming around that corner to find her wrapped in his arms, with his hand over her mouth, had made me lose it. All I wanted to do was kill him. Hearing her screams moments before had scared me. I knew it was her as soon as I heard them.

"Diablo, why don't you take a few minutes to collect yourself?" Butcher asked. He was waiting in the hallway. Wolverine kept walking toward the common area after casting me another amused look.

"Where is he?" I snapped.

"I'm not telling you until you calm down. You've already punched him a few times. He's sorry. He didn't know who she was. Did she say why she was even in the clubhouse?" Butcher continued.

"No, and I didn't ask her. She's in there hurting, exhausted, and about to cry, but she wants to rest, so I have a choice. I can disregard her request and stay with her, or I can let her have what she needs and make sure he never touches her or another woman against their will again. He scared the shit out of her. You saw it. She's been doing so goddamn good, and he just might've set her back. What if she can't regain that ground?"

"Come with me," he said. I didn't want to, but he had that look I knew well. He wouldn't take no for an answer. Fighting my frustration, I went with him. He led me to his room. Inside, behind the closed door, he swung around to face me but didn't say a word.

"Out with it. I've got shit to do," I informed him.

"I know, but first, I've got to know. Are you worried she won't regain the trust we've built with her as a club or the trust you've built with her individually?"

"It's the same thing."

"Like hell it is. Do you think I'm blind and stupid? You like her. You've been so damn careful not to spook her. Tell me you don't want to see if there might be something there. Tell me you see her as nothing but a victim needing our help. That you're not affected physically by her," he demanded.

I wasn't ready to confess anything, but my feelings were tying me in knots. Confused, I blurted out what I thought I should say. "She's only someone in need of our help. She's not anything special to me." It hurt to even say it.

He studied me for several intense moments, and then he nodded. "Okay, that's all I need to know. I won't need to worry then." He turned to open the door.

"You don't have to worry about what?" I asked in confusion.

He glanced back at me. "That you'll come after me when I start courting her to see if she and I can make something happen between us. I thought you were jealous of Wolverine before, but I guess I was wrong."

A loud, wild howl came tearing out of me as I lunged at him. I was back to seeing red. As I reached him, he swung around to face me, throwing a punch that took me in the gut. Air rushed out of me. He shoved me until I stumbled back.

"That's it. Show me. Show me how much you don't care. How you're not affected and couldn't care less if one of your brothers ends up making love to her and having her as part of his life for years. That it doesn't make you sick and furious to imagine another man touching her, taking her, loving her!" he thundered.

"You stay away from her!" I ordered.

"No! You don't want her. I might as well see if she'll have me. As soon as we deal with her husband, she'll be a free woman, although he won't prevent me from claiming her if that's how it ends up."

"If you touch her, I'll kill you, friend or not," I warned him. My anger went from red-hot to ice-cold. I said it without a bit of heat.

He straightened and then pointed at me. "There it is. The devil I know. The one who only goes ice cold when something he cares deeply about is in danger. Now, tell me you don't want her. That it's nothing more than fleeting lust that you feel for her," he goaded.

The urge to fight and bash in his face melted away. I dropped my fists. Wearily, I moved to sit on the chair by the bed. I let my head drop into my hands.

"I don't fucking know if I'm coming or going, Butch. She's got me tied in so many knots. I can't let her stay anywhere but with me, but being so close to her is driving me insane. I want her so goddamn much. I have to leave the house so I don't pounce on her. She's been raped and abused for years. I don't know if she's ever been with someone she desired. Hell, she might hate the thought of any man touching her. I'm trying to give her time and feel her out, but it's killing me. Then, to see Gio with his hands on her and to hear how he propositioned her. Wolverine has been eyeing her since she came, and now you say you want her. Fuck!"

"Diablo, I don't want her. I was trying to get you to admit your feelings. That doesn't mean Wolverine isn't attracted to her or Gio, but you can't blame them. She's a striking woman. As your friend, I need you to hear me. If you want a real chance with her, you have to tell her what you want. Put it out there and let her decide. Suppressing your feelings isn't working. You've been moody for weeks. You come to the clubhouse almost every night, sit here alone mostly, or go to your office and work. You're miserable. You just said you don't know if she wants you or any man. So if that's true, you're no worse than you are now by talking to her. Is there anything else bothering you?"

I was quiet for a stretch, trying to formulate the words. He was patient with me. Finally, I spit it out. He was my best friend. I knew he wouldn't go running his mouth to anyone.

"I haven't done more than have meaningless sex since Amy died. What if I can't love someone else? What if I'm wrong and this is just intense lust?"

"Then you need to walk away if you don't believe you can have true feelings for her. She deserves a man who will love, protect, and cherish her. A man who'll make her the center of his life. If you can't do it or are too afraid to do it, let someone else make her happy," he quietly replied.

The way my head, heart, and soul all screamed, no, in unison decided it for me. I knew I'd never be able to live with myself if I let her go without trying. The truth was, deep down, I knew I could love her. I feared it would be more profound than I loved Amy, which I never thought would happen in a million years. How could I even think that after knowing Jauhnna for less than a month? Sure, I had been immediately attracted to Amy, but love grew between us over several months.

I lifted my head. "I can't. I can't let someone else have her. She's mine."

"Then it's settled. Let's see what Gio has to say. You keep yourself under wraps. He's torn up over what happened. Once we deal with him, you can get back to her and see if she'll tell you why she was here. Make her admit it."

"Admit what? Do you know why she was?"

"I have an idea, but I'll let you figure it out," he said with a smirk.

"Fucker, I hate you," I grumbled as I stood up to follow him out the door. He laughed.

"No, you don't. You love me, and who can blame you? I'm great."

His laughter floated down the hallway ahead of us. Goddamn him, he was right. I did love the bastard, but I'd never admit it. He was conceited enough as it was.

Diablo: Chapter 7

I followed Butcher into church, not to the common room as I expected. Gathered around the table were all of my brothers, plus Gio and Aryan. Gio came to his feet as soon as he saw me.

"Diablo, man, I'm sorry. I had no idea she was Jauhnna. If I had, I wouldn't have said a word to her. I swear to God I wasn't trying to hurt her. She wouldn't stop screaming, and I was trying to quiet her so she could hear me. I was trying to tell her she wasn't in danger. I've never had a woman react that way. The only reason I had her restrained like that is she jabbed me in the ribs and then tried to break my damn nose. It was to protect myself."

"She did what?" I asked, stunned.

He quickly told us what he said, what she did, and how they both reacted. While I could see how it would evolve the way it did, it still didn't sit well with me. He'd manhandled the woman I hoped might end up mine. No matter what woman it happened to, I'd be upset, but the fact she held my interest and no one had in over twenty years made it worse.

"Gio, I hear what you're saying, but you have to see it from my perspective."

"I know. She's the woman your club has promised to help, and from what I heard, she had it rough. We're after her no-good piece-of-shit husband and brother. I understand. I do."

"No, you don't. Jauhnna is more than just someone we're helping." I paused. Damn, was I about to do this in front of everyone? My guys had perked up. Wolverine didn't look happy.

"She is?" Gio asked.

"She is. Her abuse at the hands of her husband was terrible. And that's just what we know. I've been trying to gain her trust to see if she'd consider taking a chance on a man, on me. So you see, you touched the woman I'm pretty certain could be mine. You're lucky you still have a head. If she hadn't gotten between us, you likely wouldn't."

He groaned and then dropped into the chair behind him. "Fuck, tell me I'm having a nightmare. Tell me you didn't just tell me I came onto and mildly touched your soon-to-be woman, Diablo," he pleaded. It was rather pitiful, although sincere. My anger ebbed away more.

"I can't tell you that," I told him.

"God, Undertaker and the guys are gonna kill me," he muttered. "I don't know who's worse, you or Undertaker when it comes to torturing and killing," he added.

Aryan slapped his hand down on Gio's shoulder. "Don't worry. I'm sure Cassidy, Sloan, Gemma, and Hadley will mourn you and put flowers on your grave."

The flowers' remark set the rest of us off in an explosion of laughter. Now that I'd calmed down and knew he hadn't intended harm, I could see some humor in it. I joined in. When we finished laughing, I got serious again.

"You've got to find a way to apologize to her and

put her back at ease. Getting her as comfortable as she has been with us has taken a lot. She has no reason to trust men," I added.

"I will. Do you mind if I ask what's up with the husband and brother? The bosses said we were tracking them, to keep them under surveillance, and to report anything unusual or if they or their known associates start to move this way. They told us they were bastards who deserved to be cleansed," Gio said. He appeared grim.

"Simply put, and this isn't to be discussed among others at headquarters other than Sean, Griffin, Gabe, and Undertaker. She was forced to marry him and was his to abuse for nine years until she got free of him. We don't know all the details, but she has shared that their sexual relations were forced on her. He's angry she didn't give him children, but according to her, he's unwilling to let her go. She's nothing but a possession to further his quest for power and wealth," I snarled.

Both his and Aryan's faces turned red as anger built. It was plain to see. He stood back up. "I don't care when or where, if you need help with this fucker, you call me. I won't do it as a Patriot. I'll help take the bastard out for free," he snarled.

"Me too. What the hell is wrong with people? What makes them so fucked in the head that they do things like that to people? What's the story about the brother? We're watching him too. Surely, he's not part of this. He can't know what her husband has been doing to his sister," Aryan declared.

His question caused a flurry of muttering from my guys.

"You'd think, wouldn't you? The father forced her

to marry him. We doubt the brother is clueless about what she's suffered. He's the same kind of man as the husband," I explained.

My club brothers and I were all cursed out. We'd done more than our share over the past three weeks. It was frustrating, remaining in a holding pattern while dirt was dug up on the sick fuckers, and the case was made for their elimination. There were choice swear words, though, from Aryan and Gio.

In some cases, the Patriots and even the other clubs found ways to send the bad guys to prison. In Radigan's and Vierra's cases, they would die. I would not let them remain in the world. She would never feel safe, and I would never feel she was. I'd been clear with the Patriots when I asked for their help about the outcome. They agreed readily enough once they knew what we knew.

"Your help is appreciated. I hate to cut this short, but I gotta go check on her. She's resting, but I think it's best if she comes home to do it rather than here in the clubhouse. Sorry for interrupting your night. Have fun. I'll see you in the morning," I told the whole room.

Tonight was supposed to be a chance to unwind and get to know Aryan and Gio better. We'd met a couple of times but hadn't gotten to know them as well as the other Patriots, such as Benedict, Beau, and Heath. I hoped the rest of the club continued to get to know them. Barring this misunderstanding, I found the crew at the Patriots to be a great group of people.

"Yeah, go. We'll see you later. Tell her I'm sorry. I'll do it too, but I don't want it to wait until morning," Gio stated.

"I will. She was much calmer once we got her to

breathe. Later." I gave them a final goodbye, and then I was up and hurrying to the door. I was anxious to see her. I hated leaving her alone, but she seemed so wrecked that I hoped she napped. I'd take her home and get her in her bed. Although thinking of doing it, I imagined myself putting her in my bed. *Shit, this isn't the time for this. You need to tell her, but not this exact minute.*

I was almost to the sick bay door when footsteps behind me caught my attention. I glanced back to find Wolverine following me. I halted and faced him. What the hell was he up to?

"Is there a reason you're dogging my steps? I don't need your help to get her home and into bed."

"Are you sure about this?" Wolverine asked.

"Sure about what?"

"That you're not just twisting your loneliness into more? Jauhnna is a beautiful woman. Any hot-blooded straight man would be attracted to her. In all the time I've been here, you've never been exclusive with any woman. You have sex when the urge strikes, but you don't go back for more. The women are interchangeable. Everyone knows you love your wife, even if she's gone. Can you tell me that Jauhnna can replace Amy in your heart?"

His question was one I was struggling with, but I wasn't telling him that. The niggling fear that love was developing and that my developing feelings for her would far exceed my love for Amy was still there. I did give him a partial answer, though.

"You're right about Jauhnna. Any man would be lucky to have her return his interest. She attracts me unlike any other. As for not loving her like I did

Amy, you're right. It'll never be like our love. However, everyone keeps telling me that Amy would want me to move on and not die alone. I'm not getting any younger, as you guys enjoy reminding me. Why all the concern?" I knew it was more than out of concern for me.

"Because she's different, and I was hoping there might be a chance she and I might click and make something out of it. You're not the only one looking for someone. In my case, though, I plan to love and worship the woman I eventually claim. She would never doubt my love or her place in my heart and life. I don't want to see Jauhnna hurt when you can't give that to her."

My ire began to rise again. Who the fuck was he to lecture me? He had no idea what I felt for her or would feel. I was about to blast him when the door swung open, and Jauhnna came out. I knew as soon as I saw her face, she'd heard us, or at least some of it. Her face was expressionless. She stopped and crossed her arms over her chest. She looked me in the eye.

"I'd like to go to bed."

"Okay, I was coming to get you. Let's go home." I held out my hand. It would be better to be alone for our talk. Her head shake made my heart sink.

"No, I don't want to go to your house. I know your arguments about why it's not ideal for me to stay in the clubhouse, but I came up with an alternative."

"What?" I asked.

"The guesthouse. You said it was there for visitors to use. I'm a visitor. I need to have privacy, and you need the same. If it's alright, I'd like to grab a change of clothes from your house, and then I'll go spend the night there. Tomorrow, I'll get the rest of my stuff moved over. Hopefully, things will start to move along, and I'll be out of your hair soon."

"Darlin', no one wants you to leave, and moving to the guesthouse is unnecessary. You're fine where you're at. Besides, we need to talk," I told her.

"Diablo, I'm tired. I don't want to talk. If I can't move, then take me to the house so I can sleep. I can't take much more." She appeared so beaten I pushed my desire to clear the air and find out her thoughts until tomorrow, but only until then. There was no way I'd be able to last longer.

I nodded. She seemed to sag in relief. Glancing over at Wolverine, I caught him studying her. I frowned. "We'll continue our talk later."

"Yes, sir," he responded.

I reached over, tucked her hand through my arm to rest on my forearm, and then moved us down the hall. It was an awkward walk to the house due to the silence, but I had no idea what to say. Talking about feelings and fears didn't come easily to me. We barely cleared the front door before she was rushing away from me. Over her shoulder, she called out a swift, "Goodnight," and then she was gone.

Suffice it to say, I got ready for bed thinking of her. It took me a long time to drift off as I tried to figure out how the talk we were slated to have would go. Lord, don't let me fuck this up.

I tossed all night. It was barely dawn when I called it quits and got out of bed. I went to the kitchen to make coffee. I'd wait a little longer, then make us breakfast. Once we ate and had our coffee, we'd talk. Now that I'd decided to tell her what she did to me and how I hoped she felt something for me and was willing to pursue it, I didn't want to delay.

To keep busy, I went to my office to work on some paperwork I hadn't addressed. It related to some investment Micro wanted to do with the club's money. He was a genius with computers and had a knack for choosing investments that gave us the best return without risking it all.

I read through his notes on it and what he projected we'd make from putting money into a CD for a year versus two or three years. Logic would say invest in the longer ones, but he stated that the one-year was paying more interest than the longer ones. I was good to sign off on it. I trusted his counsel. I sent him a quick email telling him to proceed. Then I went to the next item. Before I knew it, it was eight o'clock. That was it. No more waiting.

Standing, I stretched my tight muscles and directed my feet to her room. Knocking softly on her door, I waited to see if she answered. When she didn't, I did it again, only harder. Still nothing. After a third one, which was hard and loud, unease filled me. Was she alright?

"Jauhnna, I'm coming in if you don't answer me!"

Dead silence greeted my mild threat. Turning the handle, I found it was unlocked. Good. I would've hated to kick it in, but I would've. As the door swung open and I eased inside, I noticed her bed was empty. The bedding was neatly made. I swiveled my eyes to glance at the bathroom. The open door and the darkness inside the bathroom struck me. Still, just in case, I went and peeked inside. Nope. Empty. Where could she be? I didn't hear her leave while I was in my office. Was she elsewhere in the house? The need to find her right away overcame me. I rushed out of her room. I went from room to room, calling her name and checking inside every one of them. She wasn't there. By the time I'd gone through the whole house, I was mildly panicked. Had she moved to the guesthouse during the night?

I ran back to her room and checked her closet and dresser. It seemed some of her things might be gone. It was hard to tell. If they were, why not take all of them? Angrily, I put on my cut and boots, then went outside to trek to my old house. I swear when I found her, I might paddle her ass.

Reaching the front door, I tried to recall how long it had been since I was inside. I rarely came here other than to occasionally check that it was holding up. Brooklyn always visited it when they came home. She said she loved the new house, but the old one had a special place in her heart. She begged me never to tear it down. I promised I wouldn't. It was the only home she remembered. The one we lived in when Amy was killed had been on the other end of town. We rented it. After her murder, the owner tore it down and built a new one. No one wanted to live in a house where someone had been murdered. Shaking off those depressing thoughts, I knocked hard on the door and then walked right in. The house was still. There wasn't a sound in there.

"Jauhnna, are you here?"

Nothing.

"Jauhnna, if you're here and not talking, I'm not happy. Why the hell did you leave the house and not tell me? We need to talk, darlin'."

Still nothing. Working my way through this house, which took much less time, I came up empty a second time. She wasn't here, and there was no sign that she had ever been here. Dread was creeping in. She didn't find a way to leave, did she? Surely, she knew better than to put herself at risk by doing that. What if Radigan and Vierra had people watching, waiting for a chance to snatch her?

I didn't waste time getting out of the guesthouse. I practically ran to the clubhouse. When I burst through the main door, more than a couple of heads snapped up, and my brothers went on alert. A few came to their feet.

"What's wrong?" Scorpion asked. He was on his feet. It looked like he had been at the bar drinking coffee.

"I can't find Jauhnna. She's not at the house or the guesthouse. Has anyone seen her this morning?" I tried to keep the fear out of my voice. Heads were shaking, and they were frowning.

"I've been here a good hour or more, and I haven't seen her. Let's check the sick bay. If she's not there, then we'll divide up and see if she's in one of the other rooms. Maybe she found one open and took it," Scorpion rationalized. He was keeping a level head. Good, at least one of us was.

The rest of them rose to their feet. When I got to the sick bay, I had an entourage. The door was shut, so I barely stopped long enough to rap my knuckles on it before throwing it open. It was empty. Facing the others, I issued orders.

"We'll divide up. Punk and Turbo, check the other rooms that aren't bedrooms on the west side. Thunder, you and Liam do the ones on the east. Make sure to check everywhere. Scorpion and I will do the bedrooms. If you find her, text."

I got nods and chin lifts acknowledging my

orders, and then they broke off. I took the right side, and Scorpion took the left. I didn't skip the rooms where a brother was probably sleeping, either. When Butcher's door flew open at my knock, he was there in his underwear, and his hair was a mess.

"Is there a reason you're pounding on my door?" he asked gruffly.

I swiftly explained. His irritation changed to concern. "I haven't seen her. Give me five minutes to dress, and then I'll help search."

"Thanks. Sorry for waking you up."

"Not a problem. You should've gotten me up as soon as you knew she was missing," he gently admonished me.

I didn't bother to defend myself. I let him close his door, and I was off to the next one. Time seemed to drag by as we inspected every room. When I got to my old room, I sent out a prayer that she was in it. Finding the door locked didn't deter me. I took out my master key and unlocked it. Ducking inside while Scorpion and Butcher continued to the next rooms, I examined it. Unfortunately, it was the same as it was yesterday. Slamming the door closed, I swore. Where the fuck was she? We were almost out of rooms.

The sound of boots running had me swinging around. A breathless Liam almost ran me over in his haste. "I found her. She's outside, stables," he panted.

The stables? Hell, I couldn't recall if I'd ever told her about them. I'd been so caught up in taking care of those two bastards haunting her every step and keeping my distance that I'd totally blanked on them. She'd been shown the clubhouse, the outside near it, and the houses, but not the whole property. The stables had slipped my mind.

Yeah, some would say it made no sense for bikers who rode steel horses to have actual living ones. In our case, it was all thanks to Cowboy. I'd learned to ride when I was a kid. I never thought about doing it as an adult. When Cowboy came to prospect, he'd mentioned his horses. Since he'd be here so much, the time needed to run back and forth to where they were boarded wasn't realistic. He was agonizing about selling them off when I offered to allow him to keep them here. I liked what I saw in him, so I took a chance. With some help from all of us, we put up a temporary shelter for them. After he patched in, a real stable was built. He challenged those who had never ridden to try. None of us were as crazy about horses as he was, hence his road name, but I enjoyed a ride every now and again.

Clapping Liam on the back as I passed him, I took off for the outdoors. I made it into the parking lot before I saw her coming toward me. Walking alongside her were Gio and Aryan, of all people. I came to a standstill. My guys gathered behind and to the sides of me. We were all staring at them. A puzzled expression took over her face when she noted us all standing there watching them.

Aryan and Gio appeared more apprehensive to be the focus of our attention. So much so that as they got closer, Gio began to explain. "We ran into each other at the stables of all places. Last night, one of the guys mentioned you had horses. I ain't been near horses in years. I had to see them. I grew up with them, and I miss them. I dragged Aryan with me. Imagine our surprise to see Jauhnna there. We were just escorting her back. She said she hadn't told anyone where she was going.

We told her never to do that, even within the fence," Gio explained.

"Diablo, please tell me you're all not out here because of me," she called out.

I crossed my arms and stared harder at her. Her face flushed.

"Damn, you are. I'm sorry. I only meant to take a short stroll. It was barely daylight, and everyone was asleep. I like the early dawn and how peaceful it is. I came across the stable by accident and had to stop and admire the horses. God, they're magnificent. I got caught up in petting them. Time got away from me. Please forgive me for disturbing your rest on your day off. It was never my intention. I've got to ask something, though. Do you all ride?"

Her eyes did have this sparkle to them. It was good to see. I moved until I was right in front of her. Our guests had stepped back.

"Darlin', you scared the hell outta me. I searched everywhere with help from my brothers. I thought you'd left. You have to promise not to do that again. I was about to order most of us to ride out to find you," I lectured her.

She grimaced. "Again, I'm so sorry. Please. Let's go inside. I'll make breakfast to soften you all up to forgive me," she told them, sounding hopeful.

This got her smiles and lighthearted grumbles about messing up their beauty sleep, which made her laugh. As she went to pass me, I had to touch her. I turned with her and wrapped my arm around her upper back. She gave me a surprised look, but she didn't pull away. A win in my book. I followed her inside. Breakfast sounded good, but she wasn't slaving to do it all herself.

They'd pitch in, or else.

She went straight to the kitchen. Lucky for us, it was made to accommodate a big crowd. It was industrial-sized, which allowed a large number of people in there at the same time without everyone falling all over or getting in each other's way. The chatter was loud as they all talked about what they wanted to eat. All of us ended up doing something, even if it was fetching bowls and other tools. As we prepped, I found Gio standing next to me.

Quietly, he murmured to me, "She seemed upset and didn't say much at first. Something is bothering her. She's covering it well now, but it's still there. By the way, I offered her my apology and to let her kick my ass. I hoped if she did it then she would forgive me. Thankfully, she said it wasn't necessary. She told me she overreacted, and she was as much to blame as I was. Just wanted you to know."

"Good, except I still believe it was your fault."

He smirked at me. We all pitched in, and several of us helped her cook. As the pace slowed down, the closer we got to eating, the more settled I felt. After breakfast, I'd take her home, and we'd have a long overdue conversation. God, let me do this right. Screwing it up would be devastating. I refused to think she would turn me down and tell me she wasn't attracted to me. I didn't believe I was being conceited. There had been a few fleeting looks, which made me think she was.

Platters and bowls were filled with food and carried out to the common area so everyone could sit and eat. Liam and Zax were busy filling drink orders. She'd even made orange juice to go along with the coffee she made. The coffee smelled damn good, even if it wasn't mine. She'd diced up potatoes and made breakfast potatoes and waffles. I think this was the first time the waffle maker had been used since Brooklyn left. In addition, there was bacon, sausage, and a casserole made of sausage, eggs, and cheese. She rounded those out with a bowl of mixed fruit and lemon muffins.

Before they could fall on the food like starved animals in the wild, I made her sit and ensured she got her plate filled first. She gave me a shocked look. I knew it was the first time a man had put her needs before his own. I would make sure to always see to her needs, no matter when, where, or how. Shoving the sexual thoughts this caused to the back of my head, I diverted my attention to the food. The food was delicious, and it was devoured in record time.

Jauhnna: Chapter 8

My offer to make everyone breakfast served two purposes. One was to make up for worrying them and as a small thanks for what they were doing to rid me of Janus and Galway, although I still had no idea how they hoped to do it. The second more significant reason was to postpone the talk with Diablo. I'd dreaded it all night after hearing him and Wolverine in the hall outside the sick bay. I hadn't been able to catch it all since their voices kept going from loud to soft, but I heard enough to know that Diablo didn't find me repulsive, but he wasn't seeking anything long-lasting, either.

Hearing Wolverine say he thought he and I might click was a surprise. Then, hearing him say Diablo was still in love with his wife even though she was gone gutted me. Especially when Diablo agreed a relationship would never be the same between us as it was with them. I had no idea why he let her go if he was still in love with her. Or why she'd leave a man like him unless he had hidden dark qualities or couldn't remain faithful.

What I did know was no matter how bewitched I was with him, I couldn't allow myself to be with him. If there was a real possibility of me finding happiness and a partner for the rest of my life, I would've risked it, even with my fear of sexual acts. Without that possibility, there was no way I'd do it, which meant I had to stay away from him until it was safe to leave. The walk this morning was to clear my head and help me begin to work on my next step. I needed to make a couple of phone calls. Time to get my new identity in the works.

Breakfast was over faster than I hoped, and with the guys helping, the mess was cleared away too quickly. A hand on my lower back startled me, but I knew who it was. It was crazy that I knew his touch and scent. I steeled myself for what was coming.

"Jauhnna, come with me. You and I need to talk. It's killing me, all this waiting. We have to talk now." His deep, gruff voice made me want to moan and ask him to growl in my ear. I didn't care what he said, just as long as he kept it like that. It made my body tighten all over and lower in my pelvis.

Sighing, I let him guide me down the hall and out the side door. We walked to his house without saying a word. The day was a gorgeous sunny October day. It would still reach the mid-eighties. While most of the country was well into fall temps, Florida was still supplying the sunshine. I should've thought about moving here long ago. I detested the cold. I'd give anything to stay out in the sunshine and forget this painful conversation.

When we got into the house, I thought he'd take us to the living room. I was wrong. Instead, he brought me to my favorite spot in the house. I'd been stunned when he showed me around after I moved in. At the back of the house, he had what some called a solarium, or in this state, the Florida room. It was nothing but windows on three sides, and even the roof was solid glass interspersed with wood beams. It was incredible. It had comfortable and welcoming furniture. I pictured what it would be like if it was filled with plants. It would be a wild retreat. I sat in one of the oversized chairs and curled my legs up partially underneath me. I was trying to brace myself for what he'd say and what I'd be forced to say in return.

"Stay here, and I'll go get us a drink. I won't be long," he said before he popped out.

Lord, why didn't he just get this over with? My stomach was churning. He was true to his word and was back in a matter of minutes. He handed me ice water but with an addition. When I mentioned I didn't like the taste of water and the only way I drank it was if I added flavored drops, the next day, he'd gotten a variety of different flavors and presented them to me. Anything I mentioned, no matter how minor or barely in passing, I found I soon had it. I'd gotten careful of voicing anything. He didn't need to give me anything more. Well, he himself would be nice, but that wasn't happening. A sip told me it was my favorite mixed berry one. He sat across from me on the loveseat. I pretended to be admiring the pattern of sunlight on the cushions.

"Jauhnna, are you gonna look at me or the pillow? Talk to me. I know last night you heard some things which I need to clarify." He paused.

Fortifying my spine, I glanced at him. He was staring intently at me. "I did overhear some things, but I don't think it warrants us having an in-depth discussion. I know I wasn't meant to hear you and Wolverine, and in no way do I want you to feel pressured to say or do something you don't want. We can leave it as a fleeting curiosity. Besides, I'll be leaving soon anyway. It would be foolish to complicate things."

He was slightly scowling when I was done. Oops,

what did I say wrong? He should be relieved I wouldn't be attempting to make something out of nothing. He was sexually drawn to plenty of women and vice versa, as evidenced by the one hanging on him last night. He hadn't been pushing her away. For all I knew, after he escorted me to the house for the night, he might've returned to take her up on her blatant offer. I swallowed the big knot in my throat. *Stop thinking about her and the others.*

"What do you mean you'll soon be leaving? We haven't solidified the plan to get your brother and Galway out of your life and to eliminate any other risks to you. Who knows, once the threats are gone, you might very well want to remain here. I'd think it would be doubly true if you were in a relationship."

"I thought a lot on my walk and time at the stables this morning. I believe I need to put the steps in place to have a new identity created for me. There's no guarantee you and your friends will be able to remove the threats. If that's the case, I'll need to have a new one and move. I'm going to reach out to the group who helped me last time. I still have their information, and they'll help formulate it all. Depending on what's happening, they might be able to have me in a safe house in a matter of days. I can just as easily stay in one of those while my new identity is built. I don't know why I didn't tell you to leave things be and let me do that from the start. I hate the fact I wasted your valuable time these past few weeks. I wasn't thinking clearly."

His incredulous expression swiftly morphed into an upset one. He moved to the edge of his seat and leaned toward me. "What the fuck is this about, Jauhnna? Cut the bullshit. Tell the truth. If you're not interested in me or Wolverine, then say it. No one will hold it against you. Our desire for you doesn't mean we can't control ourselves. You have nothing to fear from us. We'd never hurt you. I thought by now you'd know this. You don't need to leave."

The undertone to his words suggested he was hurt. It was one of the last things I wanted. I rushed to reassure him that wasn't the case. "Diablo, I swear, I don't fear you hurting me. I do know it isn't something you or your men would do. Please, don't think that."

"Then you're not interested in either of us and are uncomfortable telling us? If so, and you don't fear our reaction, then why run?"

"I'm not running away!"

"The hell you're not. You've been vocal about most stuff while here. Just tell me. Why can't you say, 'Diablo, I'm not sexually drawn to you.'"

"Because it would be a lie!" I blurted out, and then, as my brain registered what I'd done, I slapped my hands over my mouth like that would cover up my confession.

God, mortification washed over me. How could I explain that away? While I was scrambling internally to find a viable explanation, he was up on his feet, over to me, and then down in front of me in a crouch. His hand came up to grasp my hands. He tugged them down and then cupped my jaw so I wasn't capable of turning my head away from him. His dark eyes bore into me like a laser.

"What did you just say?" he asked gruffly.

"That came out wrong. You made me mix up my words. I meant..." My mind drew a blank, so my words petered off.

"Meant what? Hmm? Did you mean to say you are interested in Wolverine? Or has one of my other brothers caught your attention?" There was tension in his fingers. They didn't exactly hurt me, but I felt them.

"It doesn't matter if I'm attracted to anyone here or not. There's no chance of it being more than sex a few times then done."

"Really? Why's that? Do you think none of us are capable of more?"

"Capable? Certainly, if you desired it. I don't see why you'd want it."

His surprise was evident. He let go of my jaw and rose. Good. He accepted my answer. Maybe I'd get out of this without spilling my guts after all. A squeak came bursting out of me when he abruptly bent over and whisked me out of the chair and into his arms. He took a few steps back to the loveseat he'd been sitting on. He placed me on the other end before sitting back down.

"Explain what you mean by that?" he ordered.

"There's nothing to explain. Why would you want more? Why would any of you want more with any woman, let alone with me?"

His eyes flared with something I couldn't identify. He snatched up my hand. "What the hell do you mean by that? Start talking. We're not leaving here until I understand what's going through that head of yours. If we have to sit here all day and night, we will," he proclaimed.

By the determined set of his jaw, I knew he was telling the truth. The man could be stubborn. I'd found that out. Wanting to get it over with as fast as possible so I could go hide in my room, I launched my explanation.

"It's simple. Last night, I saw the women who came here, those club sluts and hangers-on. You know, the ones whose main goal is to sleep with as many bikers as they can. They're here to be wild. You guys have an unending supply of variety. They're young and gorgeous. Many are stunning, sexy, and have perfect bodies, and I bet they're willing to do anything you want sexually. Don't sit there and tell me any of you willingly want to give all of them up to settle for one woman. And before you say who said anything about exclusivity, no one but me. I'm someone who would never consider being just one of many."

When I finished, it felt like he didn't respond for a solid minute. I was squirming inside. When he did speak, it wasn't what I thought he'd say. "I'll address all those assertions you just made in a second. However, first, I want to ask you a question, and I need an honest answer. Why were you at the clubhouse last night?"

Shit, one of the things I hoped he wouldn't ask. Well, there was no getting around it. "I wanted to see those women, see if you guys were like the men in the books I'm reading and if they were like the women. I knew they would be there last night."

"How did you know they would be? And what goddamn books are you reading?"

"I overheard some of the guys talking about it. As for what books, I've been reading some about MCs. All of them have club bunnies, whores, sluts, whatever you call them, and then casual women like the hangers-on. I assumed your club had them, too. I'm not sure why I haven't seen the sluts around since you undoubtedly pay for their upkeep. You'd have to in order to have them available to you day and night. I was curious." I shrugged as if it wasn't a big deal.

A deep growl came rumbling out of him. He leaned into my personal space. I had nowhere to go to get away unless I stood up, and something told me he wouldn't allow it.

"I want to see some of those books you're reading, but they can wait. Right now, I need to clear up some things. Let's start with your remarks about those women. You referred to them as variety, young, gorgeous, stunning, sexy, and having perfect bodies. Oh, and they're willing to do anything sexually. The way you said all that made it sound as if you think you're lacking in some way compared to them."

I let out a humorless laugh. "Come on, Diablo, I'm not unrealistic about myself. I can't compete with them, even if one of you does find me slightly sexually attractive. And monogamy would be an absolute must for me. So you see, there's no future here for me. And before you say it doesn't have to be more than casual and brief, I'm sorry, but it would have to be more for me."

He was shaking his head. "That son of a bitch did a number on you, didn't he? He beat you down for so long that you actually believe you have barely anything a man would want. Well, I'll tell you this. All those things you said they are, you are in spades. You're young, beautiful, beyond sexy, have a body that makes a man dream and walk around hard, and a shit load more. You're smart, funny, sassy, and strong, to name a few more. As for willingness to do anything a man wants, that's based on trust and comfort. If there were things a man wanted that you were unsure of, it would be his job to either show you it's okay to try it, or you'd mutually take it off the table." He paused for a heartbeat or two before he continued.

"I've got to ask this since we're having this talk, and I believe it impacts the whole situation. You said you were forced to accept Radigan. That he kept trying to get you pregnant. I know you mean he raped you multiple times. I can't tell you how much it disgusts and infuriates me to know you endured it. What I want to ask is, was it ever consensual between you? Tell me you weren't always raped and that you experienced pleasure at times. If not with him, then at least since you left him."

I gulped. This was getting way deeper than I had ever imagined or wanted it to go. Would he know all my secrets and insecurities? I tried to think how to make him stop, but his expression still said there was no way out. This settled it. I'd get out of here as fast as I could. I'd have no choice after sharing it all with him.

"It was rape every single time from our wedding night when he took my virginity until the last time. No, I never got pleasure from it."

"What about with other men? You had to have dated, had boyfriends since you left him."

"No, I haven't."

His jaw dropped. "Baby, are you saying he's the only man you've ever been with, and it was always rape?" he asked gutturally.

I had to glance away as I answered him. "It was always rape, but he's not the only man I've had sex with," I whispered.

My hand was dropped, and he came to his feet. He stomped away from the loveseat. He went to stare outside with his back to me. Confessing it, I knew he'd read between the lines, and it made me sick and I felt so dirty. Knowing I was used by more than one man had to disgust him. Any degree of desire for me would be killed by this news. I was surprised he and Wolverine had any for me after knowing about Galway. There were men who couldn't handle it and blamed the woman rather than the one who raped her.

He had his fists clenched at his sides, and his loud breathing was evident in the silent room. The tension was too much. I rose to my feet. His head snapped around to look at me.

"You stay right there. Don't move."

"I believe enough has been said. You know why there's nothing for me here. I'd like to go make a few phone calls," I said with as much dignity as I was capable of. I was fighting not to cry.

He charged toward me. I flinched and stumbled back, hitting the back of my knees on the edge of the loveseat. I was unbalanced and fell on my ass on the seat. He immediately slowed and finished approaching cautiously. He sat down next to me.

"Darlin', I'm not gonna hurt you. I didn't mean to scare you. I'm pissed, but not at you. I want to kill that cocksucker and anyone else who hurt you. Who else touched you, Jauhnna? His friends? Family? Who?" He had made it to me and sat beside me.

"It doesn't matter, Diablo. The resulting damage is done. Leave it."

"I can't. What resulting damage?"

"That men will see me as unclean and blame me for allowing it to happen! That it's doubtful I can stand to have sex with any man. That I'm fated to spend the rest of my life alone!" I shouted. The tears spilled, despite how hard I tried to hold them in.

I was startled by him tugging me against his chest. His arms held me tightly as he rocked me and whispered words I couldn't focus on as he rubbed my back. I let myself cry. It felt so good to be held. I let myself pretend it would be okay.

I wasn't sure how long I'd been crying before I pulled myself together and pressed on him so he'd let me move away. He allowed a small amount of space between us, but he didn't let go. He stared down into my eyes.

"Any man who thinks you're unclean and to blame needs his fucking heart torn out. That's utter nonsense. As for you not being able to have sex with a man, that's not true. I know several women who've been through rape, and they've not only been claimed and are very happy, but they have great sexual relationships with their men. You're not fated to be alone. What you need is a man who knows your history, takes time to make you comfortable, and whom you trust. Now, I don't want to set you off again, but I've gotta know. Who else?"

Lowering my eyes, I told him. I was becoming numb to the pain. I just wanted this over with. "After several years of no success getting me pregnant, he forced me to see a doctor to see what was wrong with me. The doctor did a bunch of tests. He ended up telling us that I was barren. I don't produce eggs for some reason. Galway was beyond furious. He accused my father of knowing I wasn't a real woman. He insisted on them paying him for his loss. Since he was seen as my family's way into his criminal circle, they did.

"Not long after that, he got angry again when I

didn't get pregnant. He refused to stop trying, despite knowing it was impossible. I hoped he'd leave me alone after he found out I was barren, but he didn't. Instead, he punished me for it. When he became agitated at something he thought I did wrong, he found a new way to punish me. He began giving me to some of his men. He knew I hated it, which made him happy."

His entire body shook. His fingers tightened on my back. "I want to know how many and their names. Every last one of them will share his fate," he hissed.

"You can't prove they raped me. It'll be my word against theirs. They won't go to prison for it any more than he will."

"Who said anything about prison? Baby, we're not planning to have them arrested. They're going to die. And before they do, we'll make sure they suffer. When they're gone, we have to make sure none of their criminal organizations remains a threat to you or anyone else. This includes not only Radigan but your brother. I need those names so they receive their well-deserved punishment."

I was stunned. I hadn't thought they'd take it to that extreme. "You can't do that!"

He scowled. "Why not? Don't tell me you think they have the right to live after what they've done to you."

"It's not that. I hate them, and that includes Janus, but you'll get caught. I don't want any of you or your friends to go to prison for ridding the world of scum like them. They're not worth your freedom."

His scowl eased into a slight smirk. "Babe, don't you worry about us or our friends. We have our ways, and I assure you, covering our tracks is a huge part of it. Even if someone suspected us of having a hand in it, they'll never be able to prove it. It goes without saying, you can't tell anyone this. Our lives and freedom are in your hands," he warned.

"I would never say anything to anyone. I promise."

"Good. I expect you to give those names to me by the end of today, but enough about that. There's one more thing I've got to know."

"What?" I asked warily.

"Do you find that I or anyone else in the club has piqued your interest in a romantic way? You said you're sexually drawn to me. What about more?"

We were back to that. My mouth went dry. I swallowed. The way he was studying me and the things he said made me want to hope there was a slight chance. "Yes, there's one," I whispered.

"Who?"

"Diablo, I—."

"Who?" he demanded harder.

"You," I mumbled.

I gasped right after I said it because he moved me gently forward, and his mouth landed on mine. His lips were firm and molded to mine. He pressed them together first, then began to move his lips, causing mine to follow his movements. From there, it jumped to his tongue easing into my open mouth. He caressed my tongue with his. A whimper escaped me as heat and tingling shot throughout my body.

His hand came up to angle my head slightly to the left. The pressure on my mouth increased. Suddenly, I was falling forward. He inclined back, bringing me with him. I was half lying on top of his body as we continued to kiss. I would've gladly continued forever, but too soon, in my opinion, he broke our kiss. I whimpered and tried to kiss him. He chuckled.

"Jauhnna, baby, there's nothing I'd love more than to kiss you all day, but my heart can only take so much. We keep this up, and I'll explode."

I wrinkled my forehead. Explode?

He saw it, and he showed me what he meant by sliding me down slightly and then pressing up into me. I gasped as I felt something hard pressing between my legs. He was rock hard from our kiss.

"You make me want you so much. And before you go back to all that stuff about those women at the clubhouse and not being able to be exclusive, I can be that. I just haven't desired it in a long time until now." His words reminded me of the other reason we shouldn't get involved. I eased away from him. He let me.

"If those were the only things to consider, then I'd be so tempted to say let's find out, but it's not."

We were both back to sitting up. He frowned. "What else is there?"

"I can't risk my heart on a man who's still in love with his wife. I'm sorry. No." I stood up. I needed air. He snagged my hand and pulled me toward him. I fought him. I wasn't capable of listening to him right now.

"Let go," I ordered.

He shook his head. "Not until you let me explain."

"What's to explain? You're still in love with your ex-wife, Amy. I heard Wolverine say that. What woman in her right mind goes into a relationship knowing the man she's with will always love someone else and she'll never be as good as her predecessor? A fool, that's who. I'm done being one of those. Whatever happened between you two, maybe it's not too late to get her back." I yanked my hand free and moved toward the door. His following words froze me in my tracks.

"She's dead. There's no getting her back."

My stomach dropped. God, there was no way to compete with a ghost and win. "I'm sorry, but that makes it an even worse idea. I can't win against a ghost. Listen, I have a headache. I think I'll go lie down." I began walking again. The sound of him moving broke my control. I made a mad dash to get away.

"Jauhnna, stop!" he yelled. I ignored him.

I was almost to the stairs when he caught me. He lifted me off the ground. I wiggled. As I did, he spoke into my ear. "You're gonna listen to me. Come on." I thought he'd take me back to the Florida room, but he didn't. Instead, I was carried up the stairs and then to his room. I shook my head as he stepped inside it.

"No, not in here."

"Yes. Nothing is happening in here that you don't want. I swear on the life of my daughter and grandsons."

I went limp in his arms. Last night and today had been such a roller coaster of emotions. I was done for. I needed to sleep. Maybe I'd wake up to find out it was a dream, and I hadn't gone to the clubhouse last night, caused a scene, and exposed my secret yearning.

Diablo: Chapter 9

When she didn't mention Amy at the beginning of this drawn-out discussion, I was thankful Jauhnna hadn't heard that part of Wolverine and my conversation. Well, I was obviously grateful too soon. I was worn out by the back and forth between us, but it had been necessary, just like this next part was.

That kiss had been better than I ever thought it would be. The best of my life, which made me feel a tad guilty because that included the ones I had with Amy. We'd been very sexually active together. She'd been a virgin. I wasn't. Over time, we discovered what brought us both the most pleasure. She wasn't the most adventurous woman I had ever been with, but it had been good, and I was satisfied. Since then, all my sexual encounters have satisfied my physical urges, but nothing more. There was no emotional connection involved. That one kiss with Jauhnna proved to me that emotions were already involved and would only grow stronger. I was so close to having her say yes to giving us a chance. There was no way I'd let my past with Amy ruin it. I prayed I could explain it adequately to her when it was confusing to me.

I took her into my bedroom and shut the door before taking her to sit on the small bench at the foot of the bed. I sat with her on my lap. I wanted to be sure she wouldn't run. She had a tendency to do that. I now knew when things got too emotional or uncomfortable for her, it triggered her to scurry away. I'd keep that in mind for us in the future, assuming we had one.

She wasn't looking at me. I let it go for the moment and launched into my explanation. Nothing was clearer to me than the fact that in order to have this woman, I'd have to bare myself to her. The same way she'd bared herself to me not long ago.

"I met my wife Amy when she was seventeen, and I was nineteen. We were immediately attracted to each other, and we fell in love over the span of a few months. Despite knowing she was underage and having sex with her would land my ass in jail if her parents or anyone complained, we did it anyway. We were careful to sneak around. The age thing wasn't the only reason we did. The bigger reason was her parents. They hated me. Early on, not long after we met, I saw her on the street. I stopped to talk to her. They happened along and hustled her off as fast as they could, after telling me to stay away from her, or they'd have me arrested.

"They said they knew who my father was, all about my motorcycle gang, and their daughter wasn't going to be used by a man like me. They had plans for her to go to college and marry a man they approved of who would be able to give her a respectable and comfortable life. I found that part out later from Amy. It's what they told her when they got her home that day. Anyway, we snuck around for nine months. I kept her away from the club, too. I didn't want her to be exposed to it until I was able to claim her fully. In those books you're reading, do they talk about old ladies and property patches?"

She nodded her head but didn't say anything.

At least she was listening and not fighting to get away from me. I continued, "The day after she turned eighteen, she packed her things and told them she was leaving to be with me. They threw a fit and tried to lock her in the house. If they'd had the opportunity to do it, they would've sent her away. I knew she planned to tell them, and I was prepared for them to resist. I showed up at their door with my club. We surrounded it, and I went in. She let me inside.

"They argued, made threats, and did everything they could to make her stay. It didn't work. After an hour of going in circles, we were done. As we walked out, she informed them she was three months pregnant. They lost it and flung vile words after her. Called her a whore and told her never to speak to them again. From that day forward, she was dead to them. It hurt her so much, but I was determined she'd never regret being mine. We went to stay at a hotel that night. The next day, I took her to the clubhouse to introduce her to everyone. They knew about her and the reason for our secrecy. I had to tell them when I asked a few weeks prior for them to vote her in as my old lady.

"Some of them had tried to convince me I was too young to settle down. They told me I should sow my wild oats first. Dad just wanted to know if I genuinely thought it through and knew she was the one. Lucky for me, the club was cool about it, and other than some cynical comments, in the end, the majority of them voted yes to claiming her. I had her property cut made. When I brought her to the clubhouse that first time, I presented it to her.

"Over the months until Brooklyn was born, we settled into our life. I had a room at the clubhouse like other members did. It wasn't where I wanted her or our baby to be living. Dad and Mom had a house. They insisted we live with them until we got on our feet. They wanted us to save money for the baby and not jump into renting and the expense of a home right away. We agreed. I liked having her with Mom when we weren't home. It was safer, and my mom knew what to do if things got dangerous. She was great at helping to teach Amy about club life. Remember, Scorpion and I told you the club used to be into illegal stuff? Well, it was still that way when she and I got together."

I paused for a moment. The next part would soon get into the hard part. She was absently rubbing a finger on my arm, outlining my tats. Both of my arms were full sleeves. I found her touch soothing.

"After Brooklyn was born, we waited until she was six months old before we moved out and into our own small place. It was a tiny house on the edge of town. Dad knew the guy who owned it. He gave us a good deal on the rent. Everything wasn't perfect. She had to learn to be an old lady and a mom. I had to learn to be her old man and a father. We did marry not long before Brooklyn was born. Her parents stayed out of our lives. If they happened to run into us in town, they'd turn up their noses and ignore us.

"Brookie was two years old when Dad decided to step down as the enforcer for the club. He claimed he was getting too old for it and wanted to just be a regular member. To my surprise, I was voted to take his place. I was only twenty-three and the third highest-ranking member of the club. With it came a pay increase, which was nice. I believe my dad was tired because of the work we had to put in to clean up the club. It was around that time we got into the full swing of reforming it. Too many brothers and even prospects either died or went to prison due to the things we were involved in. We wanted to live and ride, not war all the damn time.

"So how did she die? Did she get sick or was she in an accident?" she asked softly.

"No. Over the next two years, things were hard, but we were making progress. No more war, or so we thought. Unbeknownst to us, another MC saw us as a rival, despite us not being into the same stuff they were anymore. In addition, one of their members, Piranha, had seen Amy and became obsessed with her. He was determined she was meant to be his. We had no clue. One night, when our daughter was four, Dad and I were gone on a run with the club. Amy and Brooklyn stayed at our house, and Mom was at my parents' house. Piranha and a few of his men broke into our home."

She gasped and straightened to look me in the eye, her eyes full of horror.

"Amy had enough time to hide Brookie in a safe room but not to get in there herself. She stopped to try and call the clubhouse for help. A few prospects had remained behind. Piranha and his guys grabbed her. I'm not sure what exactly happened, but I do know my daughter witnessed her mother being raped and then killed by Piranha when she refused to go with him. She told him she would never accept him. He flew into a rage and began to beat her, ending up killing her. We think they got spooked and left afterward. I came home to a murdered wife and a child who wouldn't speak a word for the next six months. We had no clue who did it."

Tears glistened in her eyes. She surprised me

when she wrapped her arms around my neck and hugged me tightly. I clutched her to me. I was misty-eyed. "How did you figure out who did it? What happened?" she asked.

"Well, I was a walking time bomb. I tried to hold it together for Brooklyn, but it was so fucking hard. We were trying our best to figure out who did it without success. When she finally spoke again, she told us enough so we knew who the club was based on the club's logo she described. We figured out it was Piranha based on her description of the scar on his face. They were known to us, just not anyone we thought we had to worry about since we were no longer into the illegal shit. We weren't their competitors anymore, or so we thought.

"As for what happened, we hunted them down, and together as a club, we tortured and killed every single member and prospect in that diseased club. Even though not all of them were there that night, we discovered they all knew what he had planned. No one tried to stop him or warn us, even though they were against what he was planning to do. The sick fucker was delusional and thought she wanted him, and he was rescuing her. When she shattered his delusion, he snapped. Their end was bloody, and I let them see why I earned the road name Diablo. Afterward, I went home to my daughter, able to reassure her the men who hurt her mommy would never hurt her. Luckily, she was too young then to understand what rape was, not that it wasn't bad enough for her. That came when she got older. After Amy's death, I buried the woman I loved, and I carried on living for my club and my child and nothing more."

"Diablo, I'm so sorry you had that happen. I can tell you truly loved her and losing her devastated you. Please, say no more. I understand why you still love and miss her. She was the love of your life. She was a fortunate woman to have a man who loved her so much that the love survived even death. However, I hope you can now see why this can't work between us. If there's a chance a man might feel about me a tenth of what you feel for her, then I owe it to myself to wait for him. I can't settle. Thank you for sharing your pain with me. I understand now." She placed a tender, brief kiss on my lips when she finished. I fought not to plaster her to me and devour her, but I wasn't done yet.

When she tried to move away, I shook my head. "I'm not done. Yes, I love Amy. For the past twenty-two years, no one has ever been a momentary consideration to take her place. I've had sex with numerous women, but it was just sex. No one was a threat to my heart or had a chance at becoming my old lady."

"I get it. Truly, I do."

"But you aren't getting it. Because all that began to shift and change when I learned my heart wasn't dead like I thought it was. That I still had the ability to meet someone and have a long-term, meaningful relationship with her. It all started when I opened the trunk of an abandoned car and found a woman covered in blood inside. I was wrong. My ultimate love story hasn't been fully written yet."

Her brow wrinkled. "So you think there's a chance you might be able to have feelings for me one day? It won't be love, not the kind you have for her or to that degree, but you could care for me? Is that what you're saying?"

"No, I'm saying I'm ninety-nine percent sure I can love you, not just care for you, and it won't be to the degree it was with Amy."

She opened her mouth to say more, but I cut her off before she had the chance.

"There's been this thing I've been wrestling with these past three weeks. The reason I've been going to the clubhouse so much isn't because I was there fooling around with those women like I know you think. It was to keep myself from touching you and scaring the hell out of you. I was trying to give you time to trust me. What has been scaring me is my growing conviction that not only can I love you, but it's already started, and when it's done developing, it'll exceed what I felt for Amy. Yes, there will always be a piece of me that loves her. She was the mother of my child. She gave me several good years. But that love doesn't mean the love I'll have for you is diminished. I've come to realize we're not given a finite amount of love to divide between people. It's limitless. I promise you, you won't be competing with her, Jauhnna."

She stared at me for so long, not saying a word, that I grew more nervous. Suddenly, she gave a loud cry, and she kissed me. Our mutual desire and stress of the conversations from today combined and exploded into a glorious outpouring of passion. Our mouths couldn't seem to get enough of each other. My hands were itching to slide under her clothes and feel every naked inch of her, then strip her bare and feast on her body before sinking my aching, throbbing cock deep inside of her, but I knew it was too soon. The kissing would have to do until she was ready for more. I hadn't forgotten her fear of not being able to stand to have sex. I was confident that with time, I could prove her wrong.

We gave each other deep, drugging kisses. I had no idea how long we'd been at it before we parted. We sat there panting and watching each other through passion-filled hazes. My cock was so hard and swollen it was trying to bust through my zipper to get to her. She was unconsciously rubbing back and forth over my bulge. I could feel the precum leaking from my cock into my underwear. She flexed her hips. I groaned, then grabbed her hips to hold her still.

"Darlin', you've got to stop before I blow my load in my pants. I'm only a man. I'm not made of stone. Fuck, that was amazing. Please tell me that kiss is the start of us. That it means you're willing to give us a chance. If you're not, kill me now."

She giggled and then massaged the back of my head. "Yes, it means if you're sure, then I want to give us a chance, Diablo."

Joy filled me. I knew there was one thing we had to get straight right now. To some, it might not seem like a big deal, but I needed it.

"Baby, my ravishing Serenity, I need you to do one thing for me from this moment forward."

"Anything."

"When it's us, especially when we're intimate, don't call me Diablo. The rest of the world calls me that. I want you to call me by my actual name. Call me Victor."

Her smile was blinding, and she made my day even better as she agreed. "I'd love to call you Victor. Thank you."

"No, thank you." Unable to resist, I gave her a quick peck on her swollen lips.

The remainder of yesterday was spent relaxing and spending time with Jauhnna. Now that we'd made the commitment to see where this would go between us, I stopped avoiding her. I never wanted to in the first place, but I did it to prevent myself from slipping up and saying or doing something that might spook her. With her knowing I wanted her, it wasn't necessary anymore. Later in the day, we went to the clubhouse and spent a bit of time with Aryan and Gio before they headed out today.

It was later, after we were back at the house for the evening, that I brought up the names again. She was uncomfortable, but there was no way I could allow those who had touched her to go unpunished. She wrote them down and handed them to me. I didn't read it in front of her. Instead, I put it in my pocket and then diverted her attention to watching a movie with me. It took a good twenty minutes or more for her to relax. We ended up watching a comedy. I felt we both needed a laugh.

It was hard to say goodnight at her bedroom door and leave it at a kiss, but I found the strength not to push for more. Although I knew it was too soon for us to progress to actual sex, I would've loved to have her in my bed, so I was able to hold her at least. Breaking that kiss had been damn hard. She had me so turned on, I had to take care of myself in the shower so I was able to fall asleep.

Being it was Monday today, I knew I had to go into Prep & Restore for part of the day. I wished Jauhnna could come with me, but it was better to keep her out of sight at the compound. I promised I'd be back as soon as I was done. She assured me she'd find something to do. I hurried through the work I had to do on-site, then rushed home to work the rest of the day from my office there. She came in and spent time with me. I enjoyed spending time with her, no matter if it was sitting together and not talking.

It was evening, and she was sitting in the common room with Zax and Liam while we had church. I brought her to the clubhouse because I hated the thought of her sitting at the house alone. The prospects promised to keep her entertained. I went to explain to her what church was before coming to the clubhouse, but she surprised me by telling me she knew. When she said it was from her books, I made another mental note to read what she was to see how accurate they were, as well as what they were like. She confessed they were romances. I was curious to see what she liked.

All the guys were gathered around the table. I loved church. It shouted Horsemen of Wrath everywhere you looked. To start, the long rectangular wooden table we used had the club's logo burned into the center of it. In addition, on the wall behind where I sat, was a vast flag depicting the same logo in our colors of red, yellow, and black. When the club was formed, the guys who started it were influenced by the old coat of arms, thus the resemblance to a standard. I thought it was a cool-ass design.

On the walls around the room were pictures of past and current members, and they were from a variety of events. At the head of the table was my chair, and I smiled every time I saw it. Several years back, the brothers thought it would be a good idea to get me a custom chair. It was a large, rather ornate one made of wood to match the table, with carved devil horns coming up off the back. To complete the picture, they got me a gavel to use to bring meetings to order and to an end. It was made to look like a large bone. Noting everyone was here, and in their seats, I took mine and then pounded my bone gavel on the table. All murmuring came to a halt, and all eyes were turned to me.

"Alright, you filthy animals, you'd better not have anything to complain about this week, or it's off with your heads," I told them with a scowl.

They all smirked. It was my standard greeting and how I started every meeting just about. This week, we were getting an update on anything new or causing problems at the various club businesses, and then it would be open to new issues. I planned to bring up the list of names with them. I'd already shared it with Micro but told him to keep quiet.

We had seven businesses to run through. Scorpion started first, and then it would run around the table. He oversaw Horsemen's Repair, our garage with the mobile mechanics and towing. Turbo worked there as a mechanic along with several citizens. Micro oversaw Vintage Rummages, our thrift store. Thunder managed Serenity Shores, our beach vacation rentals, and Punk helped him with upkeep and anything else the properties needed.

Butcher ran our repo business, called Wrath's Repo. All the club members pitched in to help when necessary, plus there were regular guys working there, too. It could be a dangerous business, so having the enforcer in charge was a no-brainer. Hook & Reel Charters was managed by Wolverine, and Cowboy assisted him. It was our fishing charter business, along with a bait and supply store. Lucky grew up in a family that had been in the restaurant business, so he'd been a natural to oversee Shipwrecked, our seafood restaurant. I was the last to go to update them on Prep & Restore. Crash worked there with me.

We were lucky. No one had anything significant happening, so the reports went quickly. Once those were done, it was on to new business. I'd let anyone else who had some go first, and then we'd talk about Vierra, Radigan, and the latest information I had. We'd been debating on and off whether to possibly add another business at some point. We just weren't sure what it should be. I wondered if anyone would bring a new idea to the table tonight. They had been doing so lately when an idea came to them. So far, we haven't made a move to do any of them.

"Okay, on to new business. Does anyone have anything new to bring to the table?" I called out.

Thunder's hand shot in the air. Seeing no one else had raised theirs, I nodded at him. "The floor is yours, Thunder."

"Thanks, Pres. I think I know what we should do for our next business. Check this out," he said, laying out his arm on the table. He pointed to a tattoo. It was a new one, still covered in clear plastic. As one, we got up and crowded around him. It was a fantastic eagle. One so realistic it looked like it was about to fly off his skin. I whistled. It was beautiful and made me itch to get a new tattoo. We were all ink addicts, and finding a great ink slinger was always a challenge.

"Where the hell did you get that?" Punk asked in awe.

"I heard about this guy at that tattoo place down off Saratoga and Sevilla. It was a guy who came in to pay for his rental for next summer who told me about him. He was bragging about the ink he'd just gotten when he saw mine. His was fucking awesome, so I asked him who did it. He said that place had a new guy, and he did it. I got his name and then called to see if I could get an appointment. His name is Darian. I consulted with him two weeks ago and told him what I wanted. I didn't say anything because I wanted to see what he could do. I went back this morning. It's why I took the day off. He showed me what he'd drawn, and I said hell yeah, without a single change. It was like he read my mind. We'd blocked out the time to be able to do it in one session. He's fast."

"Alright, that's great, and no doubt we'll all be after him to do some work on all of us, but what does that have to do with a new business?" Scorpion asked.

"I'm getting there. Anyway, while I was there today, I found out the owner is getting ready to put the place up for sale. He said he's had enough and wants to retire. No one at the shop can afford to buy it. They're nervous about what'll happen if a new owner takes over and decides to clean house or bring in their own people. I asked the current owner to give me a few days to see if we might be interested in it before he goes public with the for-sale notice. He said he was planning to post it in six weeks, at the beginning of December, with the hopes that by the end of the first quarter of next year, it would be sold. He plans to move to Southern Florida to live closer to his kids and grandkids. I don't know anything about the other ink slingers' work, but Darian alone is worth it."

"We have been looking for a new business to add to our portfolio, and a tattoo shop has been brought up before. We just had no idea which one to buy. If we go with an established one, we hopefully keep the clientele and the staff that comes with it. Assuming they're good, we'd keep them. What do the rest of you think? Should we do a preliminary check into the P&L on this place?" I asked.

Unlike others who had to rely on sellers being honest about their earnings on a business, we had Micro, who did his thing and got access to their profit-and-loss statements and anything else we wanted. I didn't ask how many laws he broke to do it. I just appreciated his work.

"Hell yeah, if the others who work there are even half as good as this Darian, then we'd make money. If we brought in a portion of the biker crowd, as long as they behaved, and add in tourists and regular folks, we'd make bank," Butcher said.

"It's a good location. It's in what's considered the downtown but not the historic district. Lots of foot traffic and businesses there. There were a ton of people walking by while I was there. I think we're not out anything by digging into it," Thunder added.

There were several minutes of murmuring and admiring his new artwork before I called it. "Micro, do your thing. Let us know if you believe it's worth pursuing. Send me the prelims you get."

"Sure thing, Pres."

"Does anyone else have new business to discuss?" I asked, impatient to get to mine. They all shook their heads, thank God.

"Good, then I do. I know we're still working to get

all the dirt on Vierra and Radigan so we can get Jauhnna free of them, but there's more."

"What do you mean, more?" Crash asked.

"More. Yesterday, Jauhnna and I had a very involved discussion. As part of it, she revealed something that led to me supplying Micro with six more names. I want to know every detail he can find on them. They will be included in the ultimate punishment with the other two."

"Why?"

"Who are they?"

"What did she tell you?" These questions came from around the table.

"They're men who work for Radigan," was all I said as a lead-in.

I knew when she found out I'd shared the details with the brothers, she'd likely be upset, but they needed to know. I would never just tell them we had to torture and kill people without an explanation. This club, for the most part, was a democracy. I didn't make the decisions and they had to follow them blindly.

"Does this mean she knows they have greater roles in the businesses?" Turbo asked.

"I don't know if they do or not, but regardless, they will go down hard," I told him.

Puzzled glances were exchanged. Leaving them in suspense for much longer would result in them muttering for hours, so I supplied the rest after a warning.

"What I'm about to tell you, it doesn't leave this room. You're not to mention it to her. No one is to say or do anything differently than you've been doing. Understood?"

"Understood. Now tell us," Scorpion said.

"It seems after Radigan couldn't get her pregnant after several years, he made her get checked by a doctor. They discovered she was incapable of having kids. Despite knowing that, he continued to try, and whenever she didn't get pregnant or she upset him, he began to punish her more severely. He would give her to some of his men. Those six are the ones who've raped her."

The room erupted. Profanities poured out. Fists were pounded on the table. A few came to their feet to pace. Wolverine was one of those. I let them vent for a couple of minutes before I called them back to order. They reluctantly settled.

"They're dead men," Butcher hissed.

"Yes, they are. She has no idea I'm telling all of you. She knows I planned to give the names to Micro, which I did. She'll be uncomfortable with you knowing. Her life has been hell. When the time comes, I'll be taking the lead on Radigan and her brother. As for the other six, I'll want to spend some one-on-one time with them, too."

"You know we all want to help her. There's no need for you to do it all," Wolverine said.

I guess it was time for one more piece of news. "I appreciate all the help I'll get from you and the Dark Patriots. However, in this instance, it'll be more my responsibility to take care of them than any of yours."

"How do you figure that?" Lucky asked.

"Well, it generally falls to a woman's old man to do it. I'm just following biker code," I said offhandedly.

I had to fight to keep the smirk off my face as I dropped that bomb on them. Some might think I was jumping the gun with the old man remark, but short of her coming back and telling me she wanted nothing to do with me, I was determined she would be my old lady. Christ, that would take getting used to, but I was excited.

Utter silence fell as mouths dropped open and astonished looks were thrown at me. Well, from most of them. Wolverine and Butcher weren't surprised, although Wolverine still didn't act thrilled.

"Thank fuck you got your head out of your ass. Don't you blow it with her. She's exactly what you need," my best friend said, breaking the silence. This led to them talking over each other. I whistled to bring them to order.

"I'm not telling you more just now. All you need to know is she's off-limits and has agreed to see where this goes between the two of us. She needs time to truly believe not all men abuse you or only think of themselves. There's a lot of trust to be built. We've got to show her she can depend on us and our friends."

"And we will," Scorpion added.

There were a few more minutes of murmuring before I decided to call it a night. They'd want a drink, and I wanted to see how my Serenity was doing. God, that name was exactly how she made me feel when she wasn't arousing me or driving me crazy, that is. Walking out of that room, I had to smile.

Jauhnna: Chapter 10

I was about to lose my mind. Diablo would have to cart me off to the looney bin soon. There were a couple of things contributing to my insanity. To start, it was the waiting. This sitting here as the club, the Dark Patriots, and who knows who else worked on getting whatever information they needed in order to go after Galway, Janus, and the others, was maddening.

Now that I'd come around to the idea they would be able to remove them from the picture in a permanent way without it affecting the club or others in negative ways, I wanted them gone. I was allowing my inner hatred of them to surface. In the past, I worked to contain it because there was no way to do anything about it. Even if I'd found a way to send them to prison, they would just find ways to make my life hell from behind bars. This solution lets those emotions come out. It was cathartic in a way. I wanted them purged.

Diablo kept telling me the time it was taking wasn't an indication they weren't able to do the job. They liked to have everything laid out with no surprises. Since they had done this before, I trusted them to know what they were doing. It was just the waiting. It meant I had to stay inside the compound, and as much as I loved to read, I was bored to tears. There were no women around for me to talk to. It took nothing to keep the house clean and laundry done, though he tried to tell me not to do it. I would cook dinner most nights to have something to do. It wasn't enough. I was used to working all day.

The one thing I'd begun to do was spend time with the horses every day and learn from Cowboy how to care for them. It reminded me of my job at the animal shelter in Georgia. I found the animals gave me comfort and a sense of peace. I identified with them. They were in need of love, and so was I. I missed them and wondered who my employer got to replace me and if they were good to them.

I'd also been stressing about my apartment and possessions. I didn't want everything to be thrown out. When I mentioned it to Diablo, he informed me my apartment was okay, and so was my stuff. Then he revealed he was paying the rent and had contacted the landlord with the excuse that I had to leave without warning to care for a sick family member. He informed him I had no idea how long I would be gone. I was touched that Diablo thought of it, but I hated him spending more money on me. Recalling that discussion, I smiled.

We were sitting in the living room, and I'd been telling him about the horses. That led to me mentioning the shelter and my apartment in Savannah and, subsequently, his revelation.

"Victor, please know I appreciate you thinking of doing something like that. It's so sweet, but I can't have you continue to pay for it unless you agree to let me pay you back once I'm back to work. The same goes for the clothing and other things you've bought since I've been here."

"Darlin', you can't stop me from paying for it. As for you paying me back for rent or anything else, the answer is

no. I won't take your money."

I gasped. "Yes, you will! I have money. You know, why don't we take a trip? I'll go to where I have my secret emergency stash. I can get it, repay you, and continue my rent payments. It's not near my work or apartment, so it's highly doubtful anyone would spot me," I said excitedly.

He shook his head. "No. I'm not letting you near Savannah. I can afford to pay. It won't break me."

"Whether it will or not isn't the point. I can take care of myself. You and the club are doing more than enough for me already. This is too much. I feel like a user. Doing a tiny bit of cleaning, laundry, and cooking is hardly repayment," I protested.

We were on the couch and had been half-watching an action movie when we started talking. When I made the user comment, I was hauled up and over until I was straddling his lap. His hands were on my hips, holding me there. His eyes were narrowed on me.

"I don't want to hear you refer to yourself as a user again, you hear me? You're far from one. I wouldn't begrudge anyone this money if they're in true need, so why would I begrudge it when it's you? Correct me if I'm wrong, but aren't you and I together? You're mine, and I'm yours, right? If our roles were reversed, would you expect me to pay you back?"

"Of course, I wouldn't, but it's not the same."

"Yes, it is. Are you gonna keep arguing with me?" He cocked a brow at me.

"It's a conversation," I said in a sassy tone.

My new sassiness earned me a light swat to my ass then he was devouring my mouth. We kissed until I was dazed, panting, and forgot what we were talking about. When I remembered it the next day, he refused to debate about it, the stubborn man.

All those were stressful, but the biggest thing that had me feeling so insane was the sexual tension between us. It was growing worse every day, heck, every hour. He found reasons to frequently touch me, although not in an overtly sexual way. I did the same. I loved being connected to him, no matter how insignificantly. Kisses were always a must, according to him, and when we did, they heated my blood to a boil and left us both sexually frustrated. I knew he was because he sported raging erections the majority of the time. He wasn't embarrassed to let me see them, either. They tempted me to reach out and cup him. I was on the brink of begging him to take me, which was something I never thought I'd do with a man.

At night, when I went to bed alone, I'd dream of him and the things I wanted him to do to me. I wasn't sure if I'd find them all pleasurable, but the women in the books I read seemed to love men doing those things to them. I was resorting to touching myself and bringing myself to an orgasm over and over. I achieved them, but it wasn't enough. I would still ache and burn after coming.

Lying here in the dark, recollecting all the times I had and even tonight's session, I moaned aloud. God, make it stop. My boobs throbbed and felt swollen and hot. My pussy was aching and so slick. I squeezed my legs together and then rolled onto my side. The movement made me whimper. It was no use. I had to try again. Diablo had gone to bed when I did over an hour ago. He should be sound asleep. No worries that he'd hear me. Earlier, I'd done it in the shower.

Rolling out of bed, I shed my nightgown and

panties. I was too hot to have those on. Lying back down, I closed my eyes and pictured Diablo with me. In my head, I knew what I was doing and was a confident woman. I was standing in front of him as he reclined on the bed. I was naked, and I was enticing him with the sway of my body and how I was touching myself.

He was naked, too, and was watching me intently while his fist encircled his erection and he stroked his long length. His gaze was bright as he scanned my body. This vision had me slipping my hand between my legs and through my folds. Slick heat coated my fingers. The friction over my clit made me cry out. My hips jerked off the bed.

Wanting to come as fast as possible, I pressed harder and rubbed faster. On my downward slide, I thrust my finger inside of my pussy and pumped a few times before moving back up to tease my clit. I continued to imagine him rising from the bed and coming to me. His hands began touching my body, homing in on my chest and between my legs as his mouth skimmed my body. It wasn't enough, so I brought my other hand up to my boobs and ran it back and forth over my taut nipples. More of my cream released on my other hand. I was quickly building to the release. Feeling extra needy, as I kept Diablo firmly in my head, I tweaked my left nipple at the same time I pinched my clit.

The fire and sensation it made streaked through my body and made me utter a small scream. I bit my bottom lip to stifle it before I got loud enough to be heard. Only I was too late. As my outburst died on my lips, the door to my room came crashing open. I screamed for real, this time in panic.

Seeing Diablo standing there in nothing but a pair of shorts, his eyes glued to me and what I was doing, made me freeze. He took a step into my room, then another. I couldn't look away, nor did I remove my hands. He stalked to the bed like a predator coming up on his prey. When he reached the bed, my mind began to work again, and I tried to grab the comforter to cover myself. Mortification had my cheeks burning hot, and I knew they were bright red. I wished the bed would swallow me. His barked command made me freeze.

"Stop! Don't. Don't cover yourself. Please. Jesus, Jauhnna, I'm sorry, but I've got to look at you. Do you know what seeing you like this does to me? Do you?" he asked in a low, husky voice. I saw the erection pressing out against his shorts, and I licked my lips without thinking. He groaned.

"Baby, don't look at my cock tenting my damn shorts and then lick those lips. It makes me want to let you have a taste. The thought of those lips of yours wrapped around my cock, taking me inside that sweet mouth, is torture. Christ, I've got to go. I'm sorry. I shouldn't have barged in here," he said before turning to head for the door.

I knew his departure would hurt. I was scared, but my desire exceeded my fear. Taking a deep breath, I let myself say what I had been dying to say for days.

"Don't leave. Stay with me. Please. I need you."

He halted but kept his back to me. He was shaking his head and had it bowed. "Darlin', if I stay, I'll be on that bed with you, and I'll be begging you to let me touch you, taste you. I know full-out sex is out of the question, but God, the things we could do short of me putting my cock inside of you, the orgasms I can give you. I want to make you scream in ecstasy," he muttered. His words made my temperature rise and my body throb for more.

"I'm scared," I confessed.

He groaned. "Babe, you don't need to be. I'll leave." He took another step.

"No! That's not what I mean or want. I'm scared that I'll chicken out or I won't be what you want or can give you what you need. I've never enjoyed sex with a man, you know that. What if I can't? I want you. Please don't think for a second I don't. I'm just unsure." I tugged the sheet up over me.

"Jauhnna, there's nothing you can do or not do that'll turn me off. I want to explore so much with you, but it will always be your choice. If you say no, then it's no. Believe me, there are plenty of ways to get sexual gratification. I'm scared too, you know."

This surprised me. He still had his back to me. He was too far away. I wanted him next to me, even if all we did was talk.

"Come join me. Tell me why you would be scared. You have no reason to be. I'm the one who's broken, not you."

He swung around and came charging to the bed. He was frowning. He stopped at the edge. "Don't ever call yourself broken. You're not. Have you been damaged? Yes, but you're not broken, and you never will be. I won't allow it. Are you sure you want me to stay? We don't have to do more than talk. I don't want you to be uncomfortable. I know me busting in here did that. I'm sorry. I heard you, and it was like my body took control of my brain."

I reached over, flipped back the corner of the

sheet, and patted the bed. I was tired of letting Galway and what he did to me control my life. I was taking the bull by the horns and running with it.

He watched my face as he lowered himself and slid underneath the sheet. He propped himself up against the headboard, and his hand came out to grab mine closest to him. He gave it a slight squeeze. It reminded me where my hand had been. I flushed and tried to tug it away as I hastily babbled, "I need to go to the bathroom."

"Do you need to go because you need to use it or to wash your hands? Because if it's the latter, don't. I'm not offended at the thought of where you had it. In fact, it's all I can do not to bring it to my nose so I can see what you smell like," he said with a smirk.

I was rendered speechless. Was he serious? Did men like to smell a woman's scent? I knew they did in books, but I thought it was just fiction. He was studying me.

"Serenity, can I smell your spice? You can say no. I won't be mad. It'll just be something I have to continue looking forward to. This is all about getting comfortable and discovering each other. No pressure. Anytime you're done, tell me to leave."

"Do men really like that? I mean, do they want to smell a woman's, you know? I thought it was just in books."

"I can't speak for all men, but for me, hell yeah. I want to smell you, taste you, all of it. It's different based on who the woman is. I've been dying to know, but again, no hurry."

My stomach was fluttering inside as I took the next major step for me. I let him stay and get into bed with me. I could do this. "You may if you want."

As he slowly lifted my hand, I had the inane thought that I was glad I'd just showered. When he had it to his nose, he inhaled deeply. His eyes closed, and he got what I'd call a blissful look, and then he let a small groan out. He inhaled again.

Feeling silly but wanting to know, I asked, "Do I smell alright? The way you thought?"

His eyelids raised. I saw what appeared to be an increase in heat in his eyes. "Jauhnna, you smell so much better than I dreamed. If you mean by alright, do I like it? I fucking love it. You need to be warned. I'll be taking every chance I get to smell your spicy scent. Don't be surprised if I drag you off in private and bury my face between your legs. I promise to control myself and not do it in front of anyone, though it'll be hard."

I laughed, thinking he was joking, but the way he hiked up an eyebrow, I realized he was earnest. "Wait. You mean that?"

"Damn right, I mean it. Your man wants all of you. I love the smell of your hair and your skin when we're close. This only makes it better. I'm a very tactile and sensory-driven man. Touch, smell, taste, and what I can see and even hear are all necessary for me."

"Hear?"

"Yes. Your sighs, moans, and other sounds tell me whether you're happy, enjoying, or hating something." He inhaled a third time. "God, you have no idea how much I want to taste your finger. Distract me," he muttered.

His words made me even slicker. They were turning me on more. Something I would've never thought. I pressed my hand closer to him. He hiked up that eyebrow again. I nodded. I wasn't able to speak. A smile spread across that sexy mouth of his, and then he opened his lips and inserted my finger. I moaned when his mouth closed around it and his tongue wrapped around my digit, then he sucked. It tore a moan from me. He was laving on it like it was his favorite treat. I shivered at the streaks of desire that shot through my body and centered in my core. He reluctantly let go.

"Jauhnna, you taste divine. And one day, when I get to taste from the source, you might have to resuscitate me. Damn woman, you kill me," he said huskily.

The visions those words brought to my mind made me whimper. I pictured him with his head buried between my legs, and I knew it would feel amazing. Having never had a man do that to me, I had only my imagination to go on. I jolted as his hand came up to cup the back of my head, and he drew my mouth to his. I eagerly kissed him. I loved it when our mouths were together, tongues twining and teeth nibbling. The man could kiss and make me forget my name, and my body always caught on fire. I had never known what that remark truly meant until meeting him.

When he lifted his mouth away and began kissing and licking my neck and upper chest, it registered I was on my back, and he was hovering over me. He momentarily lifted up to look at me. "Is this okay? I just need to taste your skin."

"Yes," I whispered. At that moment, I believe I'd say yes to almost anything he asked.

His mouth went back to my neck. He kissed below my ear and then licked before biting down gently. My nipples were hard nubs. Aching for more contact, I pressed them into his chest, hoping the contact would ease the burning there. It didn't. It made it worse. Whimpering, I rubbed them back and forth. He took it as a hint, and the next thing I knew, his fingers were teasing and plucking them. I cried out. He tightened his fingers and did it harder as his mouth traveled down to my breasts.

His hand continued to play with one nipple as he licked the other. The rasp of his tongue made goosebumps pop up on my skin. He swirled his tongue around it a few times before he closed his mouth around the nub and sucked. I moaned and jerked with the little shocks it caused.

I wanted to do more than lie there and take from him. I wanted him to experience gratification as well. Unsure where he liked to be touched, I decided to start touching him and see what he said. If he disliked something, I had no doubt he'd tell me.

Since there was a gap between our bodies, I slid one of my hands around to his front. Starting at the base of his neck, I lightly ran it down to his chest. I moved it along his well-defined muscles, outlining them. When I ran it across his nipple, he inhaled deeply, and I swear I felt it harden instantly. Wondering if it felt as good to him as it did to me, I circled it, then swiped across it again. His second swift inhalation told me it did. Following what he was doing to me, I squeezed his next. His mouth left me, and he groaned.

"Christ, that feels so good."

"Do you like to be touched anywhere else? Or are there places I should avoid?" I asked.

"Serenity, you can touch me anywhere you want, however you want. What about you? Anywhere you don't like?"

It was a difficult question to answer since, before this, no touch had been enjoyable for me. The intention was never to bring me enjoyment, only pain and humiliation. My silence had him rising up and gripping my chin lightly.

"Let me guess. You don't know. That's okay. How about we experiment and find out? I'll touch, and you tell me to stop if you hate it. If you're not sure, then I suggest you let me continue until you do know. Sound reasonable?"

He was so good to me, and his willingness to go at my pace and to let me have ultimate control was thrilling as well as kind of scary. There was no way I'd pass it up, though. "It sounds perfect. May I do the same?"

"Hell yeah," he said with a grin. He placed a quick kiss on my mouth, and then he was back to kissing, nibbling, scraping his teeth, and licking my skin while his hand explored too. I had to fight not to get lost in the sensations and forget to pay attention to him.

Whimpers, shuddering breaths, faint moans, and groans, along with the wet sounds of his mouth on my skin, filled the room. I had no idea how long it went on before he moved down my body. He did it leisurely, allowing me time to object, I had no doubt. I stayed quiet. He had me so inflamed I was dying to have his mouth on my most private part. My pussy was slick and weeping. I needed to know what it felt like. To see if I would enjoy it or not. Something told me I'd adore it.

This moved him out of reach for me. I was left only able to touch his head and shoulders. I rubbed my nails lightly over his scalp. It got a reaction from him. He purred like he was a cat. Wanting to hear him do it more, I flexed my nails a tad deeper. His purring increased. I giggled. He glanced up at me.

"What's that giggle for?" he asked.

"You. You're purring like a cat, Victor."

"It feels good, although I hope you don't see me as a tame old house cat."

"Oh no, you're a big cat for sure. A panther waiting to pounce," I said with a wink.

He laughed, then pounced. I let out a ragged cry as he shoved himself lower, pushed my thighs apart, and slid his hands underneath my ass all in one move. Before I could catch up, he leaned down and swiped his tongue up my slit. The roughness of his tongue set my nerve endings off.

"Oh my God!" I hollered. He chuckled and did it again.

I was melting into the bed. It was beyond anything I'd dreamed. I was beginning to float on the sensations he was causing when he upped it. His mouth closed around my clit, and he lashed it with his tongue, then sucked. My hips tried to levitate off the bed. His body kept me in place. Right after he did that, a finger traced the edge of my entrance. I moaned loudly. The more sounds I made, the more he did. My body was tightening within no time, and I knew I was about to come. I warned him. Although I don't understand why.

"I'm gonna come," I whimpered hoarsely.

A growl came rumbling out of him, which vibrated through my pussy, causing me to tip over. Just as I did, his finger thrust inside. I shouted his name. My body flew apart, and it was unlike any orgasm I'd ever given myself. As I shattered, he hit something inside of me, which made me come even harder and longer. I was frantically pawing at his head as I came. He kept lapping, sucking, and thrusting. I shuddered and moaned harder. I was in an unending loop of ecstasy. I never wanted it to end, but eventually, it was too much, and I had to call it quits.

"No more. It's..." I ended with a whimper.

Diablo: Chapter 11

Listening and watching her come, tasting her in my mouth, and knowing what her cum tasted like and how she smelled had me hard as steel. My cock was trying to burst through my shorts to get to her at the same time as it was attempting to come. I was worried I'd come in my pants like a green kid with his first woman.

I'd been with plenty of women over the years. I'd enjoyed my releases, and there had been plenty of desire involved, but nothing like what I was experiencing with her. I'd never been this aroused, not even with my wife. I pushed that thought away. There was no room for her in this bed with Jauhnna. She was my past, and my Serenity was my future.

I reveled in all five of my senses. As her cries continued, I kept pushing her higher. I wanted her to experience maximum satisfaction. It was her whimpering plea for me to stop that finally caused me to reluctantly pull my mouth and hand away. Not to be wasteful, though, I sucked my fingers clean as I watched her languishing on the bed. The blissed-out expression on her face told me she was drifting in subspace. Pride filled my chest.

Rolling onto my back. I grimaced at the throbbing in my cock. I tried to ease it by adjusting myself, but all it did was make it worse. I was fighting not to kick the sheet off and remove my shorts to get all the stimulation off it. A moan slipped out. This brought her attention to me. She eased onto her side and gave me a smile.

"Are you alright?" she asked.

"Are you? How was that?" I asked, not only because I wanted to hear what she thought but also to help divert my thoughts from my unruly second head.

"You mean you don't know? I thought my screams and moans would tell you."

"I'd still like to hear it from your lips. Was there anything you wanted me to do more of or less of? Or something I didn't do?"

"Victor, you gave me the best orgasm ever. I've never had that before. I didn't know what to really expect. It was mind-shattering. You'd better watch it, or I'll be dragging you off to have you do that all the time."

I chuckled at her threat as if it was one. Feasting on her sweet pussy would become one of many pastimes I knew I'd be indulging in. I reached out and traced my finger around her nipple. She shivered.

"I won't complain. You don't know how happy it makes me to know I gave you such a thing. Your taste is like ambrosia to me. I can feast endlessly on you, so be warned."

"Noted. Now, why did you moan? You didn't say."

"It's because I'm trying to calm the hell down, and a certain part of my anatomy isn't cooperating." I ruefully pointed to the sheet, which was tented. Her eyes widened. The next thing I knew, she had the sheet off me, and she cautiously traced a finger over my cloth-covered bulge. I groaned. My cock jerked underneath her touch. She jumped.

When I didn't reprimand her, she did it again. Jesus, if she kept it up, I'd come. I warned her. "Baby, if you keep doing that, I'll be coming in my shorts. Not something a man my age should be doing. Let me go wash the scent of you off me. It'll help me to settle. Hopefully. Unless you want me to go." I prayed she wouldn't. I wanted to see if I might be able to convince her to sleep with me tonight and every night going forward. If she agreed, I'd be carrying her off to my room. My bed was nicer.

"What if we take off your pants, and then you come? Would that be better?" she asked.

I blinked a couple of times as what she said registered. For a second, I wondered if I had dreamed it, but the way she was studying me and the slight apprehension on her face told me I hadn't.

"Jauhnna, if you truly want that, then yes, but don't feel pressured to do it just because I got you off. It's not tit for tat. Just being here with you is more than enough."

"Victor, I don't want to do it just as repayment. I want to know what gives you enjoyment. On top of that, I don't want you hurting. It hurts, doesn't it? And I want to see you come like you made me."

Seeing she meant what she was saying, I gave up arguing, but not before I added one more thing. "Tell me if it becomes too much."

"I will. Take off your pants, Victor. I want to see you. Is it okay to touch, or should I not?"

"Touch as much as you want. Just know, he might come without warning."

"Warning noted. Please, let me see you."

Not bothering to say more, I kicked the sheet

further down and then eased my shorts off, tossing them on the floor beside the bed. My cock was fully erect and an angry red. The head and my lower stomach were covered in the precum I'd been leaking. As much as I wanted to grab it and jerk off until I got relief, I didn't. Instead, I remained still, letting her look at me and waiting to see what she wanted to do. A swift inhalation from her brought my gaze to hers. She was staring at me, and there was awe mixed with fear in her expression.

"What's wrong?" I asked.

"You're so big."

"Does that scare you?" It wasn't as if I could do anything about my size. I was blessed to have an above-average-sized cock. There were larger men, but a lot more were smaller. She swallowed before answering me.

"A little. What if…" she petered off.

"What if what?"

"What if it won't fit or it hurts too much?"

I rolled onto my side and caressed her face. "Baby, it'll fit. No worries about that. As for hurting, if I do my job, then it won't hurt. The key is making sure you're aroused sufficiently. Believe me, the way you got wet for me shows me you can do that. If you're ready, why don't you get acquainted with him? Do whatever feels right to you."

"Okay," she whispered.

I lay back on my back. She came up on her elbow, so she was hovering over me. She started at my neck and traced a finger down. She traced my tattoos and then teased across my nipples. I knew she was working up her courage, and since I loved her touch regardless, I didn't mind.

"I love your tattoos. They're so gorgeous. I bet they hurt."

"I'm glad you like them. They did hurt, but it wasn't unbearable. I found after the first one, I caught the fever of wanting more. It becomes addictive. Have you ever wanted one?"

"I thought about it but then worried it would hurt too much."

"If you change your mind, we just found a new guy. He did a fabulous tat on Thunder. We're all trying to get in to have him ink the rest of us. However, if you don't want one, I won't complain. I love your perfect skin." I traced a finger down her arm.

"I might," she muttered, but the way she was scanning me, I knew she was more focused on my body, so I shut up. As she ventured closer to my cock, I fought not to grab her hand and force it to me. That was not what she needed. Later, after she was at ease with me and my body, I'd become more insistent.

I was a rather dominant guy, and I'd have to learn to temper that in order not to frighten her. The last thing I wanted was to make her fear sex with me the way she had with that bastard, Radigan. However, something told me that with the right approach, she'd be open to that side of me. I just had to be patient.

Her hand was right above where the head of my cock rested. She had stopped. Holding my breath, I waited to see what she'd do. I let out a deep groan when her finger ran down the length and then across my balls. My cock jumped. She did it again. Gaining confidence, she explored my whole shaft and balls with her delicate fingers. I was about to beg her to either grip me fully or touch the head when she ran a fingertip across the crown. Fire shot through me. I hissed. She snatched back her hand.

I reached out and grabbed it, bringing it back to hover over me. "Don't stop unless you want to. It didn't hurt. It feels so fucking good."

It killed me in a way that for a woman who wasn't a virgin, she seemed to be so unsure and unknowledgeable, but on the other hand, it thrilled me to know she'd experience it all with me. And since I intended to be the last man she was ever with, it made it even sweeter. I let go of her hand.

She ran her finger around the head of my cock, gathering the precum. When she raised it to her mouth and sucked it inside, I moaned. Her hum of approval made me leak even more. I hoped she liked the taste. I had no idea if she had ever tasted cum or not.

Suddenly, she shifted and brought her body lower so her face was level with my cock. I blinked in shock as she lowered her head, and her tongue came out to swirl around the head of my cock. I fisted my hands to keep from gripping her head and forcing her to take me inside her hot, tight mouth. Fuck, this was going to be harder than I thought.

A cry was torn from me when she unexpectedly engulfed me. Shit, she was tight. She was sucking it deeper when her hand moved to the base of my shaft. She gave me a short pump with her fist. Son of a bitch! I knew much of this, and I'd blow. I didn't want her to stop, but I warned her.

"Darlin', you keep that up, I'll be filling your mouth with cum. If you don't want that, you need to stop. I don't have a lot of control right now."

Her answer was to suck harder and hum. My eyes rolled into the back of my head. I gave up resisting. I lay there, letting her work me. She sucked and swirled her tongue while pumping my cock. I groaned when she moved her hand down to cup and massage my balls. She did that a couple of minutes. As the tingling moved from my feet up my body toward my cock, I gave one final warning.

"I'm close."

She took me even deeper and hummed again. That did it. My entire body tensed, and the tingles centered in my balls. Then I was coming. I jerked over and over as my cum flooded her mouth. She choked a little, but she kept swallowing and sucking. She didn't stop until I was finished and lying limp. When she released me, she placed a kiss on the head of my spent cock then glanced up at me. She had a questioning look.

I ran my thumb over her bottom lip to catch the drops of cum there, then pressed it inside. She sucked on it. Goddamn, she was sensual without even knowing it. "Baby, that was fucking amazing. You short-circuited my brain. You didn't have to swallow, I hope you know."

"I know. I wanted to. I wanted to know what you tasted like and how it felt."

This told me she'd never given a blow job. What the fuck did her husband do other than shove his cock in her and force her to take it? *No, stop thinking about him. It's just you two. He's not important.*

"And what did you think?"

"It's not what I thought it would be like. It's kinda sweet and salty. It's not bad."

"That's the way you taste to me. Thank you for that and for trusting me. I have something else to ask you."

"Sure. What?"

"Will you sleep in my bed with me tonight? I don't expect anything more. I just want to hold you." I was expecting her to hesitate, but she surprised me by agreeing immediately.

"I'd like that. Will you give me a few minutes to get cleaned up, and then I'll come to your room?"

"Take your time. I'll be waiting." I placed a quick kiss on her mouth before I got up. If we'd been together longer, she and I would be cleaning each other, but I thought this was enough for one night. It was already more than I thought or hoped to get. As I made my way to my room, I began making more plans. It was time to have a talk with my daughter and let her know I had found someone.

Sitting at my desk at Prep & Restore, I was daydreaming about last night with Jauhnna. It was wonderful. To wake up this morning with her in my bed and arms had been even more amazing. I hated to leave her, but I had a meeting today and other work that had to be done at the office. It took several kisses before I was able to leave.

My meeting was over. I knew what I wanted to do next. Taking out my cell phone, I opened the contacts and brought up the number I wanted. I hit the *call* button and let it ring as I put it on speaker. It rang three times before it was answered.

A breathless Brooklyn said, "Hi, Dad."

"Hello, sweetheart. Did I catch you at a bad time?"

Before she could answer me, I heard Torch yell from the background, "Hell yeah, you did. We were just getting busy, and you had to call and cockblock me."

"Torch!" she hissed at him.

Knowing he hoped to get a rise out of me, regardless of whether they had been fooling around or not, I gave him what he wanted. "Listen, bastard, you'd better keep your hands and other parts of your anatomy off and away from my daughter if you want to keep them," I growled.

He laughed. "I hate to break it to you, Diablo, but if I haven't touched your daughter, how do you explain those two grandsons of yours?"

"Easy. Divine conception," I shot back.

He chuckled louder. "Alright, keep telling yourself that. I think you need to explain the birds and bees to your dad, babe. Hey, I'd love to stick around and make you go grayer, but I gotta run. Talk to you later," he said.

"Later. Go annoy someone else and let me talk to my little girl in peace," I shot back.

"Later, asshole," he said.

"Bye, shithead," I countered.

His laughter grew faint. She sighed. "I swear, the way you two talk, you'd think you hate each other sometimes or you're only out to embarrass me."

"Honey, it'll take more than that to embarrass you. And who says I don't hate him? He steals you away and then keeps you and my grandbabies hostage up there. It's nicer in Florida," I teased her. It was my running comment to them. I knew he'd never leave his club. I didn't blame him.

"Dad, it's not happening."

"I know, but I'll keep saying it anyway. How're you four doing?"

We spent several minutes talking about what the

kids had been doing and what was happening with her and the Warriors. When she was done updating me, she turned the conversation to me.

"What about you? You usually don't call in the middle of the day. Is everything alright?" Concern tinged her voice.

"Honey, nothing is wrong. I just wanted to talk to you. As a matter of fact, on my end, everything is great."

"Really, well, do tell. What is making you sound so happy? Did you get a new bike? Terrified a prospect into wetting himself?"

"Hey, that only happened once, and it's not my fault he couldn't hold on to his piss," I groused. One time, and she never let me forget.

"Dad, you were yelling in his face and scared him to death. He thought you were about to kill him."

"Well, he should've kept his goddamn eyes to himself and not eye fucking my daughter. He's lucky I didn't kill him."

"He didn't eye fuck me, yeesh. He was smiling at me."

"As he licked his lips and pictured all the dirty things he wanted to do to you."

"Okay, enough. We'll have to agree to disagree. Back to you. What happened?"

Taking the plunge, I told her. "I've met someone. Her name is Jauhnna."

The absolute quiet at my announcement made me check to be sure the call hadn't dropped. Nope. It was still connected. I waited to give her time to process before saying anything more. It was a good two minutes before she responded.

"You met someone. How long ago? You haven't

mentioned her. Why didn't you say something at the wedding? Is it serious? Please don't tell me she's one of those women who come prowling around the clubhouse, Dad." Her remarks and questions came rolling out of her. I smiled.

"First, no, she's not one of those women who comes to the clubhouse. Give me more credit than that. And the reason I didn't mention her at the wedding was because I didn't know her then. We met a month ago. And is it serious? Yes, it is."

"You've only known her a month, and you already think it's serious!" she exclaimed incredulously.

"Remind me how long it was after you met Torch that you two were all serious?" I asked her.

"That's different. He and I are soulmates. How do you know you and this woman will be anything more than a short, casual affair? How did you meet her? Has Micro checked her out?"

She knew that anyone associated with the club would automatically be investigated to be sure they weren't a threat. Smoke did the same in Dublin Falls. You couldn't be too careful. I'd learned that the hard way, and I never forgot it.

"It's not different, and just as you knew Torch was meant to be with you, I know the same thing about her. And yes, I know everything I need to know. The rest will come with time. As for how we met, the club and I found her. It's a long story. I'll tell you all about it soon. I just wanted to let you know. I know I said all these years I'd never have another old lady, but you proved me wrong."

"Old lady! Have you claimed her and given her a property cut already?" she exclaimed in disbelief. Why was it so hard for her to believe when she and Torch had moved even faster?

"I haven't given her the cut, but it's coming. As for making her official, the club knows how I feel and that it's coming. We're dealing with some stuff right now."

She was quiet for several heartbeats before she said more. "When do we get to meet her? Are you coming up soon?"

"I'd love to, but we can't right now. I promise, as soon as we get this business wrapped up, I'll bring her to meet you. You're gonna like her, I promise."

I was about to say more when there was a knock on the door before it opened. It was Crash.

"Honey, I hate to cut this short, but Crash just walked in. It looks like he needs me. I'll call you again soon."

"Alright, Dad. Talk soon. I want to hear more about her. Love you."

"Love you too, Brookie. Bye."

As I hung up, I gestured for Crash to come the rest of the way inside. He came over to the desk.

"Sorry to disturb you, but we've got that asshole back again, and he's out there demanding shit. You said if he came in, to let you know. Sorry to cut your call short with Brooklyn. Are they doing good?"

"They're great, and yes, I want to talk to him. Enough of this shit."

Raising to my feet, I let him take the lead as we went out to the main reception area. I geared myself up to make sure this guy never darkened our doorstep again. He was someone we'd done work for, and when it was all said and done, he tried to stiff us for the job. When he refused to pay the second half of his bill, I'd turned it over to collections. I could've easily gone and visited him as a biker, but I tried not to do that. We didn't want to get a bad reputation. Though if he kept acting like a stupid ass, I might reconsider my decision. As I approached the front, I heard him yelling at Carly, my receptionist.

"I want to see that goddamn prick! He sicced the bill collectors on me. I told him I wasn't paying the remaining bill. You bastards didn't finish the job. You should repay me what I paid to begin with."

"Sir, please calm down," she asked calmly. It took a lot to rattle her. She was used to working with loud, big, burly men. Her husband was one, and he was the foreman on one of our crews. If he came in and heard this guy going off on his wife, he'd beat his ass. I almost wanted it to happen, but if it did, the asshole would have him arrested. I couldn't afford not to have Rex working.

When he saw me, he came stomping around the desk toward me. I held up my hand. "Mr. Ackerman, stay where you are. This area is for employees. Do you mind telling me why you're yelling and using foul language in front of Carly? I don't appreciate my employees being berated," I informed him as I widened my stance and crossed my arms over my chest.

I knew what I was doing. I was a big guy, and I had huge biceps. I worked hard to get then maintain them. With my arms folded, they appeared even bigger. With my tats, cut, and the scowl on my face, I was intimidating. I used it to my advantage whenever I could. I'd rather avert fights and unpleasantness if possible, but if not, they knew they were more than likely going to get their asses handed to them. Our security cameras would show he was the aggressor, and I would make sure if punches were thrown, he would do it first. That way, I was merely defending myself and my employees.

"I don't give a fuck what you like, you son of a bitch! I have collections calling my house every day, insisting I pay your goddamn business. I told them, and I'm telling you again, I'm not paying for work you didn't do!" he hollered.

His face was beet red, and there was a vein running down his forehead that looked like it was ready to burst at any moment. If he wasn't careful, he'd either have a heart attack or stroke. Sweat was beading his face. It was a warm day, but he was inside in the air conditioning. He shouldn't be sweating so much. He was breathing hard as if he'd run.

"Why don't you have a seat? Can I get you something to drink?" I asked as concern overcame my irritation with him. I might dislike him, but I didn't wish him to drop dead in my building either.

"I don't want to sit or have a drink! I want you to stop harassing me for money. If you don't, I'll have to sue you."

"Mr. Ackerman, I'm not harassing you. I'm requesting you pay what you owe us. You claim we didn't finish the work, but that's not true. Everything we agreed upon and signed in the contract was done. After the fact, you came back and wanted us to do more but at the original price. I told you that wasn't possible, but if you wanted the additional work done, we'd be glad to do it for additional money. You said no," I reminded him.

He knew very well he was full of shit. He was

trying to cheat us, and no one cheated the Horsemen. I bet he'd done it to others and got away with it, so he thought he would do the same to us. Wrong. Many people, I bet, would pay him back or stop asking him to pay them to stop his outbursts and his acting like a fool in front of customers and others.

"Bullshit! That contract is forged. I never signed it. The original included that work," he blustered.

"No, it didn't. No one forged anything. Now, I'm kindly asking you to leave and not return. I expect the money to be paid within thirty days. If it isn't, then I will take legal action through my lawyer." I was done playing nice, or as nice as I got in situations like this.

His eyes bulged as fury overtook him. I knew what was coming before he ever swung. I could've easily avoided it, but to be able to hit him back, I had to let him hit me. His punch was decent, and it stung when the hit landed on my jaw. Luckily, I didn't have a glass jaw, and I was able to shake it off without too much damage. I might have a bruise, but that would be all. He immediately followed up that punch with another. This time, I didn't let it touch me. The whole time he was throwing punches, he was still yelling at me.

"I'm not afraid of you or your motorcycle gang! I have friends who'll chew you up and spit you out if your gang tries anything. Call off the collection agency and forget the money, and we'll call it even."

I laughed at his audacity. He thought I was scared of his so-called friends and would let him cheat us out of the cash we earned. He was delusional.

"Mr. Ackerman, your attempt to cheat us out of the payment we earned isn't happening. I don't know who your friends are, and I don't care. I'll get my money one way or another."

He threw another punch. I stopped this one with the palm of my hand. I squeezed his fist until he cried out and grimaced. I let go of it, but I wanted to keep going until I broke every damn bone in his hand. He took a step back and shook it out, flexing his fingers.

While this was happening, Carly and Crash were watching avidly. They knew not to interfere unless I got into trouble or asked them to. I knew by the expression on Crash's face he wanted to get a few licks in against Ackerman, too. The man had bawled him out a few times, too. In fact, there was no one at Prep & Restore who hadn't been on the receiving end of his tirades at least once.

"Is that a threat?" he yelled.

"Nope. Just a promise. Now, you can leave of your own free will, or I can call the cops and have them remove you. If I call them, I'll be forced to show them the security tapes of you bursting in here and throwing punches first. Then I'd have to file assault charges, and you'd be arrested and a whole lot more. I'm really too tired to go that route unless you force me. I want to go home to my woman, not piss around with a man like you. What is it gonna be?"

There must've been the ever-so-tiniest drop of common sense buried deep because he scanned the room as if looking for the cameras. I had news for him. He wouldn't find them all. We had the obvious ones and then others disguised.

"I've got an appointment, but don't forget what I said. I'm not paying," he reiterated.

"And don't forget what I said. I'll get the money you owe us for our work. Expect to be contacted by my lawyer," I said offhandedly.

Scowling, he stomped his way to the door and then outside. As soon as the door fully closed, Carly sighed. "God, Diablo, that man is a few fries short of a meal. If he comes again, do you just want me to call the police?"

"If neither Crash nor I are here, then absolutely. Don't engage. If he is acting the way he was today, get in the back and lock yourself and everyone else in there. You don't need to deal with his bullshit. You getting hurt isn't worth it to us."

She nodded and gave me a smile. "Enough about him. Let's talk about the important thing."

I gave her a puzzled look. What was she talking about? "I have no idea what you mean."

Her smile grew. "I'm referring to your comment about wanting to go home to your woman. Is there something you've been hiding from me? Or is he lying?" She directed the last question to Crash.

I was fighting not to smile. Carly loved to be in the know. She'd been after me for the past five years to date and find myself a woman.

"He's not lying," Crash told her with a smirk.

She narrowed her eyes at me, placed her hands on her hips, and began to tap her toe as she stared at me. "Diablo, why would you keep something so important from me? How long has this been going on? When do I get to meet her? You know I have to make sure she passes muster. What if she's bad news and only out to use you? You can't be too careful."

I had to grin hearing her say those things. As if I needed a little thing like her taking care of me. However, it warmed my heart to know she meant it. And she knew I would do the same for her. Deciding to come clean, I waved to her chair.

"Have a seat, and I'll tell you about her."

She almost ran to her chair. Crash walked over to lean against the small counter in the reception area. He crossed his ankles and arms.

"What do you want to know?" I inquired.

She rolled her eyes. "Everything, duh. Who is she? Where did you meet her? What's her name? Is it serious? Everything."

I didn't want to announce to everyone, not even her, that Jauhnna had been found bloody in a trunk. It would raise questions I didn't want answered.

"Her name is Jauhnna. I met her a month ago, although it seems much longer. She has some things going on that we have to resolve before she can come to meet you. I met her when the club was out on a ride." I paused. I noticed Crash had turned his face, so Carly wasn't able to see it, nor the smirk that came over him when I said we met on a ride. Well, it was technically true.

"Does she live here in St. Augustine? What's she like? Do you have a picture of her?" she eagerly responded.

I did have a picture. She'd tried to hide when I insisted she let me take pictures of her, but I wouldn't take no for an answer.

As I took out my phone, Crash piped in, "She's gorgeous and way too good for this old dog. He's robbing the cradle, Carly," he teased, giving me a sly glance.

"She is gorgeous and too good for me, but I'm not giving her up. As for robbing the cradle, I am older than her, but it's not like she's eighteen."

"There's nothing wrong with a nice older man. It's better if the man is older."

"Why?" Crash asked her.

"Because it takes men so much longer to mature. A woman of twenty is like a man of thirty-five when it comes to maturity. How old is she?"

"Thirty-two," I confessed. It did bother me slightly that she was only six years older than my daughter.

"See, she's the same age as you, maybe a tiny bit older than you in maturity years. You're good. Does she have family here? You never said if she was from St. Aug."

"She's not from St. Augustine. She has no family, and she's just moved here. Here she is," I said to her, handing her my phone.

She scanned it and then gave me a pleased smile. "She's gorgeous. Better keep a close watch on her, or someone might steal her away."

"If they try, I'll tear them limb by limb. She's mine, and no one is taking her from me," I told her with a tiny growl. She nodded with a pleased look on her face as she handed me my phone. As I took it, she hit me with one more question.

"Does Brooklyn know about her?"

"She does. I told her right before Ackerman showed up. She was shocked, I think, and wanted to know when she could meet her and all that. I said soon," I explained.

"And she accepted that?" she asked.

"Yeah, why wouldn't she?"

"I just don't see Brooklyn being that laid back about her dad finally finding someone after all these years. She has to be dying of curiosity and wants to know everything about her, plus know she's not out to hurt or use you," Carly explained.

"I'm an adult. I can look out for myself."

"No, you're a man, and that means you need a woman to look out for you while letting you think you can do it yourself. Believe me, if one didn't, you'd be screwed. I've been doing it for years for Rex," she said smugly.

I might've not been in a relationship in decades, but I knew better than to argue. My life was worth more than the aggravation it most likely would cause, so I didn't touch it. Unfortunately, Crash wasn't that smart.

"You're full of it, Carly."

I wisely beat a hasty retreat and left them to battle it out. I didn't need to stay. I knew who would win, the five-foot-three dynamo. Poor bastard didn't know what he unleashed. I entered my office, chuckling. At least my bad mood was lifting. Time to get the last few things wound up, then to go home. It was a good forty-five minutes before I saw Crash walk by dejectedly. I laughed. All he did was give me the finger and kept walking.

Jauhnna: Chapter 12

Another boring day. I'd already gone to see the horses and spent time feeding and grooming them. The house was clean. I was trying to read a book, but my attention kept wandering. Instead, I was sitting here daydreaming about Diablo.

Yesterday, after he got home from work, he filled me in on his day. He told me about the annoying asshole customer who didn't want to pay his bill. It was nice to be able to just relax and talk to someone about mundane things. I'd never had that with Galway or even when I lived at home. My mom sure never did it with my dad.

When it was time to go to bed, I was back in his bed with him. He refused to allow me in mine. There had been another intense round of mutual gratification, which made me sleep like a baby. This morning, I sent him off after kissing the hell out of him. He tried to stay, but I knew he had to make the rounds on the other businesses, so I pushed him out the door. It was cute to see such a powerful man pouting.

Glancing at the clock, I saw it was one in the afternoon. Just four more hours, and he should be home. I was making a huge pot of vegetable soup and homemade bread. He'd told me it was one of the things he enjoyed. I made enough to last for a few days. When I was growing up, my mom and the family chef taught me how to cook. Hopefully, mine would be to his taste.

So far, anything I'd made, he praised. Speaking of soup, I recalled it was time to stir it again.

In the kitchen, I gave it a stir and then tasted it. It needed a pinch of salt. I was adding it when I heard the front door open. Smiling, I whirled around to greet him. My words died on my tongue. Coming into the living room slash kitchen was a man. The only thing that kept me from screaming and running was one, we were within the compound, and two, he was holding a toddler. Right behind him was a young woman carrying a baby. I gulped. I recognized them. There were pictures of them all over the house. It was Diablo's daughter and her family. What were they doing here? They were eyeing me as I stared back at them. What broke the silence was the oldest boy.

"Down. Where's Pop-pop?" he demanded. His father, Torch, I recalled was his name, set him on his feet. He immediately ran over to me.

"Who you?" My heart melted seeing his little face and hearing the demand in it along with curiosity. Shit, what did I say? Did they know about me? Had he told them? If he had, why hadn't he warned me or told me they were coming?

Thane was a carbon copy of his daddy with his dark brown hair, piercing light blue eyes, and handsome face. Not knowing what else to do, I crouched down so I was closer to eye level with him. I smiled. "Hi, my name is Jauhnna. You must be Thane."

He nodded and smiled as he pointed to himself and proudly said, "Tane." I guess "th" was hard for him to say. God, he was so adorable I wanted to squeeze him. Seeing him made my heart hurt. I'd always wanted kids. Knowing I would never have any like him was a knife through me. Standing back up, I gave the others a strained smile.

"Hello, I'm Jauhnna. I know who you are. I recognize you from your pictures. Uhm, your dad isn't home yet from work. Does he know you're coming?" If they said yes, I'd have to kill him for not warning me. I was standing there barefoot, in a plain t-shirt and shorts without a scrap of makeup on and my hair up in a sloppy ponytail. Not how I wanted to look when meeting his daughter for the first time.

It was Torch who answered me. He gave me what I thought was a sympathetic smile. "Hello, Jauhnna. I'm Torch, and you've met Thane. This is my old lady, Brooklyn, and our son Jai, just to make it official. No, Diablo doesn't know we're coming. Something I didn't know until we got here." He frowned at Brooklyn before continuing. "Although, I have no doubt he's on his way. The prospect at the gate was scrambling when we passed him. Sorry for descending on you this way."

"Why are you apologizing to her? This is my dad's house, not hers. This place has been my home all my life. I have the right to visit whenever I want, and I've never had to wait to be invited or approved before. What're you doing here alone while my dad is at work? Shouldn't you be at the clubhouse waiting or wherever you live until he calls for you?"

Her tone made it clear she was putting me in the same category as the club sluts and hangers-on. Anger flickered within me. She didn't know me. What gave her the right to make assumptions or to treat me as if I were beneath her?

"Tornado," Torch said in a warning tone.

"Don't. We don't know this woman. Dad has

barely known her for a month, and she's all comfortable in his house, cooking and God knows what else. I'm not about to let some gold-digger user come in and take advantage of him because he's lonely. Look at her! She's my age. You need to get your stuff and leave," she ordered me.

The old me would have avoided confrontation. The new me didn't. I straightened to my full height, and I let her know she had no say over me. "I'm sorry this is a surprise for you, but that doesn't give you the right to come in here, insult me, and issue orders. This is Diablo's house and club. He's the only one who can ask me to leave. If he does, then I will. Why don't we get comfortable while we wait for him to get home? Can I get you something to drink?"

She huffed, and then, as she passed Torch, she handed Jai to him. She stomped to the fridge as she glared at me. "I don't need you to get me anything in my dad's house. Why delay the inevitable? When Dad gets here, you'll be gone." She gave me a smirk. Torch rolled his eyes at me.

I wasn't sure of their dynamic. I doubted Diablo would let me act this way. Why did Torch? Deciding to hell with it, I shrugged and then walked over to the living room. I took a seat in Diablo's favorite chair. It made me feel secure surrounded by his scent. I wished I had a cell phone right now so I could text him and see what he wanted me to do. But if he had been told they were here, he was probably on his bike. I didn't want to distract him while he was riding.

An uneasy silence surrounded us. Well, it did the adults. Thane didn't appear to notice. He went to one of the built-in cabinets along the wall. He opened it and grunted as he pulled out a box. I watched as he began to dig through it, tossing toys left and right. He was so cute doing it. I smiled. He let out a triumphant yell as he held up a toy truck. He got down on his hands and knees and started to push the truck around, making engine noises.

"So, are you just gonna sit there, or are you gonna tell me how you got your hooks into my dad? I've got to admit, there've been a lot of sluts who've tried over the years, but none have ever done it. What's your story? Where did he meet you? Why are you staying here? I wouldn't get comfortable if I were you."

"Listen, I don't know what I did to have you acting so hateful, but I won't argue with you. Your dad will explain when he gets here. Although, I don't think he'll be happy that his daughter is acting this way with someone he cares about," I admonished her. In reality, I wanted to slap her.

She laughed. "Cares about? Please, just because he's screwing you doesn't mean he cares. You're just where he puts his—" she paused and glanced at Thane.

Fury flowed through me. In order not to punch her in the face, I turned my attention to Torch. He was sitting on the couch next to her, holding Jai, who was asleep. "How was your trip? How long of a drive is it?"

"It wasn't bad. The drive is eight-and-a-half hours, but with the kids, we had to stop a couple of times, so closer to ten. Gotta admit, the temperature down here is warmer than at home right now, although it's not bad. It would've been good riding weather."

"Are you like Diablo and ride everywhere, no matter the time of year?"

"If I can, although it's harder to do with the family. Haven't figured out how to get two car seats and all their junk on the bike with us," he joked. I laughed. He grinned.

"Why are you being so nice to her?" Brooklyn snapped.

"Because until we talk to your dad, I'm not making any judgments."

She snorted. Ignoring her, he and I spent several minutes chatting about the weather, the drive, and bikes. I didn't know a lot about bikes, but I was learning from Diablo.

Suddenly, she shot to her feet and glared at me. "Don't think you can charm my old man. He's not into women like you, either. Why don't you save yourself the humiliation and leave before Dad gets here? He'll be kicking you to the curb with the rest of the trash."

I'd had enough. I came to my feet. "I don't know what your problem is other than you're a spoiled brat who he should've spanked more growing up. I can't believe you. Diablo will be ashamed of your attitude."

"You don't know jack about me, my upbringing, or my dad!" she snarled back.

"Ladies, cool it," Torch interjected.

Jai woke up crying, and Thane was yelling now due to the loud voices. It was a crazy mess.

I flinched when a sharp whistle split the air, and a voice I recognized bellowed, "What the hell is going on in here?"

Whipping around, I saw Diablo standing at the entrance to the living room. He was scowling. Needing his comfort, I reacted by rushing to him. He opened his arms and tugged me against his chest when I got to him. His lips landed on the top of my head as he gave me a gentle squeeze.

"Pop-pop," Thane yelled. The next thing I knew, he was bouncing into our legs as he tried to hug his granddad's legs around mine, and then he clamored for him to pick him up. I eased back to let him. Diablo bent down and picked him up, then placed an arm back around me.

"Dad, you have to get rid of this woman," Brooklyn demanded. Jai was screaming, and Torch was trying to be heard over it all. Thane was babbling about his trip. It was utter chaos. If I wasn't upset over how she'd been treating me, I would've laughed.

"Everyone needs to quiet down. I can't get a word in, and my head is pounding!" he hollered over the din. He whispered something to Thane, kissed him, then set him on his feet. He happily went back to his toys. Diablo held out his free arm to Torch, who came over to us and placed a crying Jai in his granddad's arm. Instantly, he stopped bawling and beamed up at him. Brooklyn was standing there wearing a mutinous expression.

Thinking it might be better to leave them alone to talk as a family, I suggested, "Why don't I let you talk to them? I'll be upstairs unless you want me to go to the clubhouse," I said softly.

"Yes, leave," Brooklyn said.

At the same time Diablo answered, "No, you stay right here. This is your home. I'm not kicking you out."

"Her home? Since when? Dad, what is going on here? I swear, I know you've been lonely for a long time, but she isn't the answer. Is this a mid-life crisis?"

"Brooklyn, enough! You're being a brat. Let's sit down, and then you can start by telling me why you're here. When I spoke to you yesterday, you didn't mention you were coming."

He eased us toward his chair. He sat down, tugging me to come with him. I ended up on his lap with Jai lying on his chest, drifting off. The man must be some kind of child whisperer or something. Brooklyn and Torch sat on the couch. She was watching me. I wasn't able to decipher the look on her face. It almost appeared satisfied, though why that would be, I had no clue. This wasn't the way I pictured my first meeting with her and her family to go or the reaction I hoped for.

"Diablo, I've got to apologize. I had no idea you didn't know we were coming. Brooklyn led me to believe you invited us to come and meet Jauhnna as soon as possible. It wasn't until we got here that I found out you hadn't." He gave her a censorious look, which she ignored.

"Why doesn't that surprise me? Brooklyn, care to explain yourself? Why not call?"

"Because I wanted her not to have advance warning. I needed to see who you've brought into your life. You told me you had her checked out, but how deeply? What makes you think she didn't engineer a meeting so she could wiggle her way into the club and your life? There are countless women who want to be an old lady. You've always eluded them. Why not her?"

"That's enough of that talk! Jauhnna didn't engineer anything. She isn't playing a game to get a property cut. She's nothing like those women. I won't have you saying she is or making her uncomfortable. And yes, this is her home."

Brooklyn crossed her arms over her chest, and her gaze drilled into me. "Okay, then tell us about yourself. Who are you? Where do you come from? Family? How did you meet my dad?"

"Darlin', you don't have to tell her anything," Diablo informed me.

"No, I think I do. Obviously, she came here to run me off, and she has no desire to know me, but I'll tell her what she wants to know. First, let me say I was really hoping you and I could be friends. Diablo has told me nothing but good things about you. He adores you and your family. Anyway, let's see. You know my name. I'm thirty-two. I'm originally from Nevada, the Las Vegas area. I have no family worth speaking of. For the past three years, I've lived in Savannah, Georgia. What else do you want to know?"

"If you live in Georgia, how did you and Dad meet?"

I glanced at him. I wasn't thrilled to share my pain with her, especially with her attitude. Did he want me to say anything? I was learning about what he referred to as club business. Did this fall under that?

"Why are you looking at my dad? Is there something you don't want me to know? Why the mystery?" she snapped.

"Brook, if you can't be civil, this is done. You can cart your ass to the clubhouse," Diablo warned her. Thinking of what I should say, I shivered. This caused him to hug me closer and kiss me gently on the lips. It was a quick one, but it gave me comfort.

"Want me to tell them?" he asked.

"No, I can do it. I met your dad when he and the club returned from a ride. They stopped and helped me. Actually, they saved my life..." I paused before continuing. There was a lump in my throat. Just thinking about it made me sick. How close I came to dying.

"How did they save you?" Torch asked kindly.

"There was a car abandoned alongside the road. They stopped to check it out when they noted it remained there for several hours. Diablo saw clothing sticking out of the trunk, so he opened it. He found me inside, unconscious and bloody. He brought me here since the ambulances were tied up in town with a major accident, and Wolverine doctored me."

I noted the shock overcoming Brooklyn's face and the speculation on Torch's. He glanced at Diablo, who I saw nod. They were silently communicating over something. My attention was diverted back to Brooklyn when she spoke.

"You were in a trunk. Why were you in it? What happened? What does that mean for the club, Dad?" She wore a worried frown.

"I was in it because when I was leaving my home to go to work, I was jumped by two men. There was an altercation, which ultimately they won, and I was rendered unconscious and thrown in the trunk. I have no idea why they brought me to Florida. We speculate they left me in the car when it broke down because they panicked, thinking I was dead. I've been here ever since. The club and your dad have been wonderful about ensuring I'm safe." I left it at that. If he wanted to tell her more about what the club was doing, he could.

"They just jumped you? Surely, you have an idea why," was her comeback.

"We suspect we know why. You asked what it means for the club. Simple. It means we're working to prove who did it and why. Once all the pieces are verified and in place, we plan to go after them and ensure they never bother her or anyone else again. There's a slight chance it was human traffickers who happened upon her, but I don't believe it was. We're working with the Dark Patriots right now," Diablo explained.

"Have you spoken to Terror about us helping?" Torch asked.

"I haven't. I didn't want to drag anyone else into it unless it became necessary. The Patriots have men watching the suspected culprits behind it while Micro and their people do the investigating. It's taking time, which is frustrating. Hence, why Jauhnna has to remain on the compound. We don't know who did it, so we have no idea if they might be hanging around and are still a threat."

Brook scooted closer to the edge of the couch cushion. "So this is really all an act. You're pretending to be involved so you can use it to draw out these people when the time comes. Why didn't you just say so? I know how protective you and the guys are when it comes to those in need. You're just like the Warriors," she said with a smile.

"We are protective, but this is no act. Jauhnna is mine. I'm claiming her as my old lady. The club is aware and in agreement. It's my duty and privilege to protect her. The ones behind this will pay. Even if the men who took her aren't connected to the others, they'll still feel our wrath," he growled.

"Why would anyone want to hurt her? What did she do?" she asked.

"I didn't do anything! Why does it have to be that I did or didn't do something? Do you think I deserve to be hurt, humiliated, and traumatized for years?" I asked angrily. I was trying to get to my feet, but Diablo's arm kept me in place.

"Let me up," I demanded.

"Stay here. You're not going anywhere. Brooklyn, you've been told enough. All I want is for you to treat her with courtesy. If you plan to stay for a couple of days, you won't attack her, make her want to leave her home, or anything else. This is her home. I won't have you or anyone running her off. Don't test me," Diablo warned.

"Do you love her?" she asked suddenly.

"I do. She's the one I want to spend the rest of my life with. You knew when you met Torch that he was for you. Well, it's the same for me." He said it without missing a beat. He was staring into my eyes.

My insides turned to goo. I knew he was growing to care for me more every day, hence claiming me, but he hadn't said he was in love with me. Was he just saying it to appease her?

"My Serenity, I'm not saying that to make Brooklyn settle. I mean it. Not the way I wanted to tell you, but it's the damn truth. I love you." He gave me an apologetic smirk.

Unable to resist and not caring who was watching us, I leaned into him and grasped the back of his head to bring his mouth to mine. I kissed him, pouring everything I felt into it. I took my time, and when I pulled away, we were both flushed and slightly breathless.

"I love you too, and I didn't intend to tell you like this either," I said with a grin. He laughed.

"Well, that's sweet. So are you planning to marry her or just have her be your old lady?" his daughter asked. I didn't hear any animosity in her tone, which surprised me.

"Babe," Torch said.

"Well, I want to know."

"Marriage is a discussion between her and I. If she doesn't want that, then we won't. Regardless, it's a moot point at the moment. We can't do it."

I was back to feeling anxious for two reasons. One was his declaration that he was thinking of marriage, and the other was his reminder that I was already married.

"Honey, you know I won't be free unless…"

"Unless?" Torch asked.

I glanced over at them. They were watching us avidly. I saw they were holding hands. "Unless my husband dies. There's no way as long as he's alive that I'll be free. He'll never let me go."

Astonishment turned to upset on her face. Torch's face was strangely blank. "You're hooked up with a married woman! Dad, I never thought you'd do that." There was censure in her voice.

"She's not married to him in her heart. She never has been. I wouldn't have crossed that line if this was a typical situation."

I hated her having a bad opinion of him, which was what made me spill the details. "I was forced at twenty by my father to marry my husband. It was a business deal. He was an awful man by reputation. I begged my father not to allow it, but he refused to listen. See, it benefited his yearning for more power and wealth. I was merely a tool to get it. From the day I wed until three years ago when I ran, I was verbally abused, physically abused, terrorized, and humiliated. When I got free, I swore I would never go back. We think the men who grabbed me are after the reward my husband

and brother have put up for my return. Lucky for me, it's only to be paid if I'm alive. Undoubtedly, Galway wants to continue to torture me. As long as he's alive, he will never grant me a divorce. He'll always be a threat to me and anyone who helps me.

"I begged your dad and the club not to get involved, but they wouldn't listen. They keep promising me they can remove his loathsome self and that of my brother and their criminal organizations forever. All I have to do is let them work, get the information they need, and get their people into place. I swear, hand to God, that I'm not here using your dad or the club. I'm not a gold digger. I have money. I never thought I'd end up in a biker compound, falling for the head biker, but I did. I love him and want to spend the rest of my life with him. If I was free and he asked, I'd say yes to being his wife in an instant, which for me is big. I swore if given the chance, I'd never marry again. I didn't want anyone having that kind of control over me."

My chest was aching when I finished. Suddenly, she was on her feet and charging toward us. I jerked back and then steeled myself. If she took a swing at me, I'd defend myself regardless of whether she was his daughter or not. No one hit me anymore. Imagine my shock when she didn't hit me. Instead, she flung her arms around me and hugged me as she talked.

"You poor thing. I'm so sorry you went through so much. Trust Dad and his guys will get you free of them. I know our club will help, too. I can't tell you how happy it makes me to see him finally have someone and to be in love. He deserves it. I've been trying for years to get him to find someone. Thank you."

I was confused. Did she have split personalities? I

patted her back hesitantly. When she stepped away, she giggled.

"No, I'm not crazy. Sorry, I had to know for sure you and he were serious. That this wasn't some phase. Forgive me."

"A phase? I don't understand," I muttered.

"Maybe I can explain. Forgive me, too. I went along with her plan. She filled me in on her call with Diablo yesterday. She insisted we had to get here ASAP to make sure he wasn't being used and he wasn't making a mistake. Brooklyn, being the devious woman she is, devised the plan to come at you and see how you reacted and what you'd say. She knew her dad would be called the instant we entered the compound. She needed to see how he'd react and interact with you," Torch explained.

"You're fucking kidding me," Diablo grumbled.

"It was all an act?" I asked, trying hard to be sure I understood.

"It was. I love Dad, but he's been alone a long time. I never once heard or saw him get close to a woman. When he told me about you, I knew I had to meet you and see for myself. You can never be too careful, so I acted the bitch. I have to say, you showed considerable restraint. I would've punched me in the mouth and kicked my ass a few times if I was you. You were strong yet controlled about it. That's good. As the old lady of the president, you'll be looked to by other women when these idiots start settling down, as well as outsiders to the club who will depend on you. You'll be the queen to his king." She gestured to Diablo, who was studying us. There was a faint smile on his face.

I gulped. My mouth was dry. I'd be a leader?

Queen to his king? Oh my God. "Nope, sorry, but all bets are off. You never told me I'd have to be a leader," I told him in a panic. I liked to stay in the background where it was safe.

Brooklyn took a sleeping Jai away from her dad. This left him with two arms to encircle me with. "Baby, calm down. You've got this. You're a strong-ass woman, which is what a man like me needs. Yes, others will look up to you as mine. However, you always have me to help you if you need it. It's true as other old ladies are added, they'll look to you to guide them, but I'll be here to guide you."

"And you can always ask me. I'm not the queen bee in Dublin Falls. That's Harlow at home, but I know the majority of the job. Although, I do have one question."

I was beginning to calm down enough to speak to her. "What's that?"

"Do I need to call you mom because that just feels weird when you're only a few years older than me? Dad, I never knew you'd be such a cradle robber, you dirty old man," she said with a giggle and wink.

A growl came rumbling out of him. "I'll show you an old man. I still have a lot of years of fight in me. And I'm not a goddamn cradle robber."

I couldn't help but laugh. "No, please don't call me mom. Imagine people's faces if you did."

This made her laugh harder. "Oh God, yes. That's it. I'll have to do it occasionally, just for the shock factor."

And just like that, the tension of the past hour melted away. It was as if a whole different person inhabited her body as she chatted with me, and I got to know them.

Diablo: Chapter 13

After the surprise visit from Brooklyn and the gang and the subsequent interrogation, or whatever you wanted to call it, things mellowed out. I admit when I came in and found her basically attacking Jauhnna, I wanted to spank my daughter and send her to her room like she was a naughty teenager. Finding out it was all a ploy to gauge both our feelings and level of commitment had me wondering at her deviousness, on top of being proud of her. She had moved from a club princess to an old lady and owned her role. Thank God Torch was a strong man who could handle her.

We spent hours just talking. They learned about Jauhnna, and she got to learn about them. It had been heartbreaking at one point when Thane crawled on her lap and was showing her his toys. The yearning I saw on her face gutted me. It was so goddamn unfair she could never have children. She'd make a wonderful mother. You could see it in the way she interacted with him.

When he played around the room, she kept an eye on him to be sure he didn't get into anything he shouldn't or would hurt him. As for Jai, eventually, he ended up in her arms. The same hunger was there. Later, when I was coming from the bathroom, Brooklyn cornered me outside the room.

"Dad, you'd better watch out."

"For what?"

"From the way Jauhnna was eyeing Thane and holding Jai, she might want kids. Are you prepared to start over from scratch? Will I get some siblings, finally?" There was a teasing quality to the question, but I still heard the question underneath.

"Brookie, for her, yes, I would. I've always wanted more kids, but I never thought I'd get the chance. Seeing how Bull and Bear are with their children later in life, I know I can do it, but it's not possible."

"Why not?"

"Honey, she's not able to have children. It's one of the things which made her time with that fucker Galway even worse. You have no idea what that man did to her."

"Oh, Dad, I'm sorry. Poor thing. Well, you could adopt or foster kids. She seems really good with mine."

"We haven't discussed it, but if she wants that, then yes, I'll gladly do it. Just don't ask her right now about it, okay?"

"I promise I won't. I like her. I think she'll be good for you. Sorry I pulled that trick, but I had to be sure."

"You're a brat. If you do anything like that again, I'll spank your ass," I groused.

She laughed, and we were still grinning when we rejoined the others. The hours had flown by. We'd enjoyed a rowdy family dinner earlier. The soup and homemade bread Jauhnna made was devoured and praised. She had made dessert, apple pie, my favorite. Afterward, some of the club members dropped in to say hello and spend time with them. They always loved Brooklyn's visits.

When it was time for bed, they retired to their usual rooms. Torch and Brooklyn had a room next to another where the boys slept. They were on the opposite end of the house from my room. I loved them, but I didn't want them right on top of me. When Jauhnna tried to say her sleeping with me wasn't a good idea with my daughter and grandkids in the house, I put my foot down. No damn way I was sleeping alone. They were adults. The kids wouldn't care or know. She eventually gave in.

We showered and were in bed. She was wiggling as if she wasn't able to get comfortable. Snagging her around the waist, I moved her closer until I spooned her.

"Why are you so restless, baby?"

"I just don't want to ruin how Brooklyn and I are getting along after that start. What if she's upset that I'm sleeping with her dad in the house with her kids? I mean, I'm technically married, and we're not. Do you think that matters to her and Torch? People can be touchy about exposing their kids to situations," she fretted.

"Serenity, if she was offended or had an issue with it, believe me, she would've spoken up. It's not a big deal. The kids have no clue what marriage is anyway."

I felt the tension begin to ease from her body, but not enough. Knowing what would get her to completely relax and her mind off my family, I slid my hand around to cup her tit. I gave it a squeeze and then tugged on her nipple. It hardened instantly, and a whimper slipped out of her. I kissed from her neck to her ear. Between nibbles and blowing air into it, I whispered in it.

"You need to unwind, and I know the perfect way to do that."

"Victor, we can't," she muttered, although it wasn't very convincing. Her body was rubbing against mine, making my semi-erect cock go totally erect and rock hard.

"We can do anything we want," I was kissing her bare shoulder.

"They'll hear us," she hissed.

"No, they won't. This room is soundproof. I made sure of it along with the office when I built this house. I got the idea from some of the other guys at the different clubs' compounds. Do you think Torch and Brookie don't fool around when they're here? Fuck yeah, they do, although I prefer to pretend they don't. I sure as hell don't want to hear it. No one will know what we're doing. Baby, I'm so hungry for you. Please, let me taste you," I pleaded.

My mouth was watering at the thought of tasting her sweet cum. I loved eating her pussy, just like I loved having her go down on me and give me the best blowjobs of my life. When she was into something, she gave it her all. Her next wiggle made me groan out loud. The next thing I knew, she was turning in my arms to face me. I saw the heat in her eyes a moment before her hand moved and cupped my cock and balls. She gave them a squeeze. I groaned louder, and my cock jerked in her hand. When she slowly licked her bottom lip, it was too much.

Thrusting my cock harder into her palm, I rolled so she was underneath me and I was hovering over her. Her fingers were teasing up and down my shaft and then tracing my balls.

"Jauhnna, you keep that up, and I'll be coming in that hand. While I love anything you do to me, the thought of wasting it rather than feeling your tight mouth sucking me dry makes me want to cry. Plus, I'm dying to taste that pussy that belongs to me. I haven't had my daily taste."

She moaned. "Victor, God, you make me crazy. Just a few words and touches, and I'm so turned on. Yes, I'd love for you to go down on me, and I want to do the same to you. It would be an utter shame to waste your cum."

I placed a hard kiss on her mouth. Before I got lost in kissing her, I tore away. I had a mission to complete. I'd come back and kiss her afterward. Rising up more, I rolled off her and onto my back. Tugging on her waist, I got her up and turned so she was straddling me, and we were in the classic sixty-nine position. Her lovely pussy was right above my hungry mouth. The tantalizing scent of her hit my nose. Not waiting to be told, I licked up her slit and got my first taste. I hummed. Yes, this was what I needed.

I moaned as she swiped her tongue down my length, circled my balls, and then went back up. It took concentration to focus on pleasuring her when she was driving me insane. The way she sucked cock was like someone savoring the best meal of their lives. She sucked, licked, nibbled, stroked and kissed all over. She'd work me in her mouth until I was on the edge of shooting my load, and then she'd back off and lick or kiss or fondle my balls.

Not to be outdone, I employed all my skills in doing those same things to her, plus finger fucking her while targeting her G-spot. She confessed after our first time doing this that she had no idea a G-spot was real until I found hers.

Wanting her to lose focus, I edged her to an orgasm and held her there for several minutes, making whimpering and whining sounds before I gave her what she wanted. Her cry of relief as she came was music to my ears.

I didn't want her to come down yet, so I kept her excited enough that when she was done, I pushed her straight toward the next one. It was unfair a woman could orgasm as many times as she wanted, but a man had to have recovery time. It was a cruel cosmic joke.

She must've taken my actions as a challenge because she intensified her efforts. By the time I had her ready to tip over a second time, she was pushing me to come, but I fought it. When she came, I lapped up all the creamy goodness she flooded my mouth with.

She was sagging into me spent afterward, and I was enjoying the satisfaction of making my woman come hard and more than once when abruptly she was gone. She moved to hover next to me. She was staring hard at me. I saw the passion still consuming her.

"What's wr—" I didn't finish asking her what was wrong because she was kissing me. Our tongues and teeth clashed a little as we consumed each other. When she lifted away, we were both panting.

"Christ, that was amazing. Shit, Serenity, I need to come. Will you help me?" I asked gruffly.

She caressed my jaw. There was a tender, loving expression on her beautiful, flushed face. "Yes, I'd love to help you. Can I do it my way?" she asked hesitantly.

I had no idea what she meant, but I didn't give a damn how she did it as long as I shot my load. My whole body was tense and edgy.

"Darlin', you can do it however you want. I'm yours."

She gave me a slight smile, and then she leaned her upper body more fully over my chest as she concentrated on my eyes for some reason.

"Then I need to know. Which position do you prefer?"

"Prefer? Do you mean to come? I don't care. It's whatever you prefer."

"I don't want to suck you off, Victor, as much as I love doing that. I want you inside of me. I need you to come inside of me."

Her words penetrated my lust-fogged brain. When they did, I wanted to shout, but I held back. I had to be one hundred percent sure I understood her correctly and make sure she was fully onboard with it. I didn't want her doing it because she knew I wanted it. My cock, though if it could speak, would be shouting, *shut up, you dumb fuck!*

"Jauhnna, are you sure? I want you, don't doubt that, but are you ready for us to do this?"

"I've been thinking of nothing else when it comes to us. I'm scared, but that'll be there no matter what. I need to know, Victor. Can I be with you fully? Will it give me satisfaction like you give me with your hands and mouth? What if I freak out?"

"If you freak, then we'll stop, talk, and then you'll decide where we go. We can stop for good, take it slow, or change something up. There's a host of things, but you need to know you ultimately are in control. It doesn't matter if I'm ordering you to do or not do something. You always have the choice to stop it. That's my promise to you. I want you so badly it hurts, but it has to be right for you."

She took a few moments before she answered me. "I'm ready. Please, make love to me. Show me how it's supposed to be between a man and a woman. Teach me what you like. I'm yours."

Pride and desire streaked through me. Rising up, I gave her my first order. I'd start out the way I wanted to proceed and see how she did. I was a demanding man in bed and out. I'd temper it to make it work for both of us, but I wanted to see how far I might be able to go.

"Get on your back, I want you to spread those sexy legs and make room for your man."

She shakily did as I ordered. I moved so I was hovering over her. I ran my eyes from her face to her pussy, then back. I reached out and petted her wet folds, teasing back and forth over her clit. She moaned. Her hips arched.

"Do you want me to slide my big cock into that tight pussy and fuck you until you scream Serenity? You were worried I wouldn't fit. Do you want us to find out if you were wrong? To let me take you and make you scream for me until you feel insane? Let me fill you full of my cum as we both explode?"

The words were meant to excite her, but they were doing the same to me. I was anticipating how she'd feel and what she'd do. Needing something, I reached down to tug on my cock a few times. She watched, and then her hand was pushing mine away. Her soft, smaller one wrapped around me and began pumping it. God. I tugged on my balls to keep them from contracting up in preparation to come. I wanted to make this last. Her strokes became more insistent.

"Victor, I need you. Now. Do it. Let me feel my man's cock in my pussy. Fuck me," she begged huskily. Her chest was flushed, and her breathing had become faster.

Not wanting to delay but knowing she needed

to know, I grounded out two things for her. "It won't just be fucking. I'm making love to you. And I know you can't get pregnant, so I want you without anything between us. I'm clean, in case you were wondering. I bet you are, too. Can I take you without a barrier?" If she said no, I'd wear one, but I prayed she'd say go for it.

I guess God was listening because she gave me that. "I'm clean, and yes, you may go without a condom. We're lucky we don't have to deal with those."

She was still looking a bit apprehensive, so I leaned down and kissed her. She returned it just as eagerly. With her distracted somewhat, I removed her hand from my aching cock, gripped the base, then rubbed the head up and down her folds. We both groaned. Our kiss stopped. Rubbing the head in circles on her clit, she moaned, and her hips jerked. Taking it as a sign she was ready for the next step, I notched the crown at her entrance. Pushing inward, I breached her with my cock for the first time. The tightness encircling the knob of my cock was unbelievably tight. She was slick and hot. I fought not to sink all the way in, in one hard thrust, and to say the hell with whether she was ready or not.

I eased deeper. She moaned and made a slight hissing sound. I froze. "Are you alright?"

"Yes, you're just big. I feel stretched to my limit."

"Does it hurt?" I didn't want to hurt her. She needed no reminder of that fucker Galway.

"It burns a little, but it's not bad. Don't stop. I'm… God, it feels good, too. Hurry, Victor, Hurry."

It was her pleas that made me continue. Watching her face closely for bad emotions I didn't want her to have, I inched in more. Each forward movement pushed another inch or more of my cock inside utter heaven. Jesus Christ, I'd never felt anyone this tight. She was strangling my cock. The desire to bury myself and then pound her into the mattress until we both came was overwhelming, but I fought it.

I hissed when her nails bit into my lower back before sliding down to do it again on both ass cheeks. The unexpectedness of it made me pull my hips away from her nails. The other outcome, besides evading her nails, was it sank my cock to the hilt inside of her. She cried out my name as her head went back, and she arched her neck as her mouth fell open. I gave her a few moments to adjust.

When she opened her eyes, they appeared dreamy. She smiled at me. "More. Don't stop. Show me what makes you the most excited."

"I won't stop unless you tell me. Ready?"

She nodded. Drawing back my hips slowly, I didn't stop until the head of my cock was barely still inside. I gazed down. Seeing her slickness coating me and the feel of her surrounding the head of my cock was too much. I swore. "Goddamn, look at that," then I thrust hard back to the hilt. She shivered and tossed her head from side to side.

Wanting her lost in an overload of sensations, I made sure my pubic bone would hit her clit then I would circle my hips. I used one of my hands to caress her breasts and then tweak her taut nipples. She responded beautifully. Building my thrusts until they were in a hard, deep rhythm, I pushed her to come for me. I needed to feel her strangling me.

"Jauhnna, baby, shit, you're tight., You feel incredible."

"Oh God, oh Victor. It's incredible. It feels so good. Please, make me come," she pleaded. Her hands gripped my ass cheeks minus the nails. Truthfully, I missed them.

"Make me feel those nails, baby," I demanded.

She gave me a surprised look, then it turned to a smug one right before she began running those nails all over my ass. She sank them in, then let up. As she did, she would grip my cheeks in her hands and try to push me forward. I resisted. I'd fuck her at my pace. She whimpered.

Deciding I'd toy with her more next time, I gave in to my burning urges. I started thrusting harder. I brought her ass up off the bed with my hands, and I went to town. I got lost in hearing her pleas and moans. Minutes later, when she came, she came hard, and I swear I saw stars, but I gritted my teeth and kept going. I held back my nut somehow.

One orgasm kicked off the climb to the next. She was dripping wet. The slickness made it possible to be inside of her. If she hadn't been excited, there was no way I would be able to fit in her. The heat surrounding me, along with the cum, had me chasing the ultimate orgasm for both of us. As we got close, I let go of her ass and raised my hands to pin her wrists to the mattress. I stared hard at her.

"Come for me, Serenity. Give me your cum. Make me give you mine. Come on. Scream for me. Take it," I snarled. My vision was darkening. Tingling and heat were rushing from all over my body to my cock. My sac pulled up tight.

"I'm gonna come," I warned her.

It seemed to push her. She threw back her head,

her pussy cinched down on me like a vice. I fought to continue thrusting, and then she screamed so loud my ears hurt as she came. It was nothing like her previous ones. The amount of cum she produced was unbelievable. She gushed and soaked me and the bed. It was perfection. I thrust one more time, halted, and then shouted her name as sheer bliss filled me as I came. I never remember an orgasm lasting that long or me coming so hard. It felt like the cum was being torn from deep in my balls and pelvis.

When we both stopped orgasming, I was weak. Not ready to be parted from her, I cradled her to me as I rolled onto my side. My spent cock was slowly deflating, content in its new home. She cuddled close. We were both working to regulate our breathing. Her hand came up to caress my cheek. She lightly scratched my beard. I sighed. It felt amazing.

"How was it? Was it what you expected? Wanted?" I asked.

I wasn't one to so openly question a woman about her satisfaction, but in her case, I wanted to know. I was willing to adjust my approach to make it good for her.

"It's nothing like I thought it would be. I never knew you could feel like that. You're amazing. I'm so lucky to have found you."

I rubbed her cheek and then traced her lips. Dropping a quick kiss on them, I shared how this experience affected me.

"Darlin', lord, where do I start? You were incredible. I'm warning you. I'll want you over and over again. You've created a monster," I let out a deep growl.

This set her to laughing, which made her jiggle and then squeeze around me. It shot streaks through me. To my absolute astonishment, I began to harden again. It had been years since I rebounded that fast. I wiggled my hips experimentally. The streaks increased along with my hardness. I raised my eyebrow.

"I want you again. Are you ready, or do you want to rest? I don't want you to end up too sore."

"I won't. Yes, please. Again." she clenched her inner muscles around me. I groaned loudly and deeply.

I needed a new position. I reluctantly withdrew. She cried out and tried to hold me to her,

"Jauhnna, baby, I'm just changing it up. I want you to come here," I guided her to the edge of the bed, then over and up onto her hands and knees. Recognizing what I wanted, she helped me.

I stood up and admired her round, plump ass, and her arched back. Her tits hung full and swayed with the movement of her body. Pushing my hands between her legs, I parted them so I could see her pussy peeking at me. It was glistening with the combination of our cum. Fierce pride filled me.

Growling, I dropped my head and latched onto her folds. I lapped up our cum. Some men, make that a lot, shied away from tasting their own cum. I hadn't done it since Amy, but with Jauhnna, it didn't bother me.

"Victor! You can't do that," she said in a shocked tone.

"Like hell, I can't. This is us. We taste so good together, baby. You wanna taste?" I swiped a couple of fingers through the cum escaping.

She was shaking her head no, but her eyes were latched onto my shining fingers. I moved them right outside my mouth. I was about to clean them myself when she grasped my wrist, and her tongue came out to wrap around my digits. The feel of her tongue lapping at our cum turned me on.

So much so as soon as she was done, I withdrew my hand, gripped both her hips with mine and thrust into her. It was still slow progress even after just having been inside her. It was the same fantastic feeling, though.

Feeling even more animalistic than the first time, I let go of most of my control as I set up an almost punishing pace. I waited to hear her ask me to stop or slow down. Her cries and moans, mixed with mine, invigorated me. The room was filled with the sounds of skin slapping into skin. The wet sound of her pussy trying to hold on to my cock. All the pants and sounds, plus the smell and the taste of us still on my tongue, made me let go even more.

Her screams when she came vibrated her body, but I was still chasing mine. She came hard and then slowly began to regain her senses. I drove into her harder until blinding pleasure washed through me. I froze and then shouted, "Fuck," before I began to erupt. I was shocked at the amount I still had to give her. This time, when we both were finished, we collapsed on the bed. I rolled at the last second so as not to crush her. I held her glued to me. I wanted the contact of her soft, warm skin with my skin.

She smiled. She knew what I wanted. She rubbed her body against mine and purred like a little kitten. Like I said, she was perfect. Now, to make sure I kept her. Her enemies would soon know what the wrath of the Horsemen felt like.

Jauhnna: Chapter 14

Brooklyn, Torch, and the kids stayed almost three full days. We spent lots of family time with them, getting to know them and vice versa. I learned a ton about Dublin Falls. It sounded like a great place. I wanted to see it for myself one day. We spent a decent amount of time at the clubhouse with the rest of the members as well. They were all thrilled to see them, and they paid attention to the kiddos. It was fun to watch these big, tattooed men play with Thane. He loved it, and it was obvious he did it at home. He had zero fear of the hulking men.

While they were here, I found out Diablo ordered that no club sluts or hangers were allowed at the clubhouse until it was after midnight. They had to be cleared out by six before the kids got up and there was the risk of Thane seeing any of them. I was surprised none of the guys voiced objections, but it seems to me they were used to it. It pleased me. I'd seen the women the one time, and since then I'd avoided being there when they were, I knew it wouldn't last. I had to conquer the feelings of insecurity when I thought of or saw them.

We saw the little family off early yesterday. They wanted to be back before today, which was Halloween. Apparently, the Dublin Falls gang had a big party planned. Early in the evening, they'd celebrate by going trick or treating with the kids in town, and then it was back to their clubhouse for games, food, and fun. Thane was old enough this year to enjoy dressing up to get candy and then to play.

A part of me wished I could see it. Being with them for these few days had set up that yearning again. The one where I wanted kids desperately. I tried to be logical and remind myself it wasn't possible, but it didn't make a difference. I swear, when I held Jai, my ovaries twinged.

Today, it was back to the normal routine, which was me sitting at the compound bored and Diablo off to work. I hated begrudging him the freedom to leave since I knew it was to work, but I needed something to do. Restlessness was growing. If they didn't do something soon about Galway and Janus, I'd have to demand I be allowed to leave the compound and explore the town. It seemed I would be staying here, so there was my apartment in Georgia to sort out and a job here to find. There were things to do if they'd allow me.

The thought of a job led me to be on the computer in Diablo's office, researching local animal shelters or any business that dealt with animals. I'd always wanted to go to college and be a veterinarian. Of course, Father refused to allow it. Why did I need an education or job when my value was to be a bargaining chip only? That's why when I was finally free of Galway, I ended up finding work with animals. I couldn't be a vet, but I could still help them in some tiny way.

I was more than excited to see St. Augustine had more than a couple of places that rescued or sheltered animals. Even better, a few were looking for people. I grew excited. Could I apply and see if they would even interview me? If I got a job, wouldn't Diablo have to let me go to work? I knew why he was so protective, but I was about to lose my mind.

Determination filled me. I wasn't a prisoner. Diablo wasn't my warden. This thinking was what pushed me to apply to a few of them. I hit a snag, though, when I didn't know the address of the compound to put on the applications. I almost gave up until I saw mail on his desk with the address. From there, I just supplied my regular information. I was feeling good when I was done. I would tell Diablo what I did when he got home.

With that out of the way, I spent the remainder of the day with the horses. Cowboy had told me I was a natural, and he now left me to do whatever I wanted with them. He trusted me, which was amazing. I knew how protective he was of his horses. They were like his children. If I ran into anything worrisome, I had his number to call him.

I got so caught up in the horses I was caught off guard to note it was after five o'clock when I walked back into the house. Diablo would be home any minute. I hurried to the bathroom to take a shower. I smelled of horses and hay. Stripping off my clothes, I barely let the water get hot before jumping in. Wetting then soaping my hair, I scrubbed it thoroughly. I was rinsing out the conditioner when I felt a draft, and then hands touched me.

In the past, I would've screamed and instantly gone into fighting mode, but I was secure here, so I knew it had to be Diablo, but I decided to mess with him.

"Whoever you are, I don't think my man will like you being in here with me."

"Whoever I am? Woman, there better not be anyone getting in the shower with you but me. I'm the only one allowed to see or touch this body. Understand?" He finished his lecture with a sharp, stinging slap to my ass.

I cried out, partially in shock at the unexpectedness of it and partially because of the electrical shock it sent through my body. It went to my pussy and breasts. My nipples hardened, and my pussy began to get slick.

"Shit, I'm sorry, baby. I didn't mean to do that," he said hurriedly. His hand rubbed the spot gently.

I didn't want him to stifle who he was out of fear he'd trigger something in me. I loved that he wanted to do it, but I needed the real Diablo. His being someone else wouldn't make either of us happy in the long run. I wanted us to last. I reached back and grabbed his hand in mine.

"Do that again. I don't know if I fully understood you," I told him. I made sure my tone was sultry.

A groan came from him. "Are you sure?"

I let go of his hand, pushed my ass back toward him, and wiggled it. His hand left my cheek, then I yelped and jumped when a second smack landed. I moaned, which made him swat me a few more times. Each one was harder than the last and was sending my body into a frenzy of need. Who knew spanking could do that to me? Suddenly, I was moved toward the built-in seat, and my back was pressed on, making me bend forward.

"Put your hands on that and stick your ass out. Fuck, I can't wait, Jauhnna. Please tell me you're ready for me," he muttered.

His fingers probed my pussy, and I knew he found I was more than a little wet for him. A groan followed then I felt the hard head of his cock pushing against my entrance a moment before he thrust hard, parting me and filling me to the max. I moaned loudly and gripped the seat.

His pelvis barely kissed mine before he pulled back and slammed into me. He set up a hard pace, but I had no objections. I was consumed with desire. I wanted to come. These past few nights, especially last night, had set off intense sexual yearnings in me. Ones I never imagined I would experience.

"Christ, I could live inside of you, Serenity. You have no idea how wonderful you feel or how you make my body react."

I wasn't able to answer him because I was just on the edge of an orgasm, and it was going to be a big one, so all I did was whimper. He was pounding in and out, and I loved it. What sent me tumbling over the figurative cliff was the two slaps he gave me on the same ass cheek he'd spanked before. It sparked me, and I detonated. I clamped down on him and screamed as I came. He was swearing and frantically stroking in and out. I was still in the throes of my release when he froze, bellowed, then began to come. His warmth flooded my pussy. I felt his cock jerking inside of me.

When I was done, I was barely able to hold myself up. All I wanted to do was melt into a puddle on the floor of the shower. He was slumped over my back, breathing heavily on my neck. I was about to suggest we get out and move to the bed when he stood, withdrew, and then stormed out of the shower and disappeared. What the hell was that about?

"Victor, come back," I yelled. I got no answer. I tried again.

"Victor, where are you?" Again, nothing.

I hastily shut off the shower and got out. I barely dried my skin before wrapping a towel around my wet hair and rushing out to the bedroom. He wasn't there. Desperately, I ran out of our bedroom and started to search the other bedrooms. As I did, I called for him, but he never answered. I was about to panic when I found him. He was in his office, staring down at his desk with his head bowed.

"Victor, what the hell is going on? Why did you leave the shower? And you wouldn't answer me. What did I do wrong?" I asked. My voice was funny because I was trying not to cry.

He shook his head. He didn't look at me as he answered. His voice was tight and gruff. "You didn't do anything wrong. I did."

"What did you do wrong? I don't understand. I thought you were into it."

"I was. It wasn't that, believe me. God, I didn't even give you a choice. I just ordered you to bend over. Hell, I pushed you over, then I took you. When we came, I realized something." He stopped and took a deep breath.

"What did you realize?" I prompted. I needed to understand where his head was and why. This Diablo I hated to see. He appeared and sounded defeated in a way.

"That I'm no better than Galway. He gave you no choice every time he took you, and I just did the same. I might've half asked if it you were ready, but I didn't wait for an answer. You had to have thought that.

Christ, I'm sorry, baby, so sorry. I never want you to accept me out of fear. I'm demanding, I know that, but you don't have to submit. I won't hurt you or get angry. I swear, I'm working to curb those dominant tendencies. Please, tell me I didn't just fuck us up." His tone was pleading, and he was looking at me now. There was fear on his face and tears in his eyes. He was truly torn up and concerned.

I moved over to stand next to him. He turned enough to face me completely. I slid my arms around him and hugged him to me. His hands came up hesitantly to grip me close.

"Victor Tate, I want you to listen very closely to me. Are you listening?"

He nodded as he said, "Yeah, I'm listening."

"You are nothing like Galway, not even a smidge. I don't ever want to hear you say such a thing again. It's blasphemy to say that. What you did in that shower was nothing like him. You were dominant, I agree, but I know if I said no, you would've stopped. He wouldn't have. You were forceful when you took me. He would've been violent, trying to hurt me. You only wanted me to experience pleasure, which, in case you missed it, I did in a spectacular way."

His chest rumbled as he silently laughed. I kept going.

"Those spankings made me hot. I loved those. The way you took me was hot and amazing. You acted like you were dying to have me. That's a huge turn-on for me and makes me want you even more. I've never felt I was wanted for a good reason. Sex was always used as a punishment. You make me see what it should be. We can be frantic and desperate and crazy to have each other, but I know it will always be with our mutual satisfaction as the goal, not my humiliation or pain. I don't want you to suppress your dominant side, Victor. I want the real you, and I want all of you. Can you give me that? I won't live with half a man or half of a life. I've already lost too many years to bullshit."

He let out a groan, and then I was lifted and swung around. He sat me on the desk and then kissed me. It was a hot kiss filled with yearning and promise, I thought. I returned it just as eagerly. We kissed for a long time before he broke it. When he did, I saw the passion and love on his face. As we kissed, I felt him grow hard. Reaching out, I grasped him, and then I leaned back on my free arm and spread my legs. The towel gaped open. His eyes went straight to my exposed pussy. That kiss had reignited my passion for him.

"Take me, Victor. Take me on your desk and make sure I know you're my man, and you will always see to my every need, just as I will yours."

He growled before pressing me flat. His hands yanked my ass to the edge of the desk then he was sliding into me. We both moaned together at how wonderful it felt. I expected him to take me hard and fast. Instead, he stared into my eyes as he stroked in and out slowly.

"I love you, Jauhnna. I love you so goddamn much. I never want to lose you. I wouldn't be able to stand it. I'd take out the world and then join you. Do you understand? You're my life. I love you. If I ever want something you don't, please tell me."

"I will tell you, Victor. I love you, too. I had no idea that feeling like this was possible. I'm yours."

He slowly drove me out of my mind. I never knew

slow and easy could be as hot and mind-altering as fast and hard. When I came, he was right there with me, and we both smiled and then kissed as our orgasms ebbed away. I sighed and closed my eyes in contentment.

"Baby, it's time to wake up, or we'll miss it," Victor's voice jerked me awake. As I surfaced, I thought back to how I got in bed. The last thing I recalled was being on his desk after he'd made love to me. I opened my eyes and sat up. He was across the bedroom putting on his cut.

"Did I fall asleep?"

He grinned. "Yep, I must've worn you out. I hate to wake you up. You looked so peaceful, but we don't want to miss this."

"Miss what?"

"Trick or Treat. It starts in just over an hour. We need to get to the senior community center."

"Why?" I felt muddled. What was he talking about?

"Each year, the club does a Trick or Treat after-party at the senior center. They serve hot chocolate, coffee, and goodies to the kids after they get done gathering their candy. The seniors love to see the kids in costumes and interact with them. We help with the cost of the chocolate, coffee, and other items for the event. It's become a pretty big thing. We all go and help out."

I jumped out of bed and ran to the bathroom. He followed. I saw myself in the mirror. My hair was wild from sleeping with it wet. I grabbed my brush and attacked it. As I did, I gave him hell.

"Why didn't you tell me this ahead of time? I would've been ready. And how can I go? You said I have to stay hidden here at the compound."

"You don't want to go?"

"Yes, I want to go. I'm dying to get out and do something. I just don't understand how this is all alright tonight but not any other time. Or why you sprung it on me?"

"We'll be in an enclosed environment, and the whole club will be there. Also, I know how crazy being cooped up is driving you. I wanted to surprise you, so I didn't tell you. My intention was to tell you as soon as I got home, but I was sidetracked by the sexy goddess in my shower, and you know what happened. I'm sorry. My surprise could've been timed better."

I put down my brush and moved over to hug him. I raised up on my toes, and he leaned down so I was able to kiss him. When I was done, I smacked his chest. "Stop distracting me. I need to get ready. How long do I have before we leave?"

"Half an hour. We're meeting the guys at the clubhouse and riding in together."

"Well then, get." I waved him away.

He chuckled as he left the bathroom. I got to work. I made his deadline and had my hair braided, makeup on, and dressed to be on his bike with two minutes to spare. I was pumped to go for a ride with him. He'd taken me around the compound on it when I confessed I'd never ridden. I enjoyed it, but I wanted to feel what it was like out on the road. When I walked into the kitchen, he was waiting. He scanned me up and down before giving me a nod and smile.

"Perfect. You ready?"

"I am. I'm not sure which I'm more excited about —getting out or riding your bike."

"Well, then, let's get your sweet ass on that bike and see. We need to meet the guys at the clubhouse first, then we'll go."

I happily went with him. We walked over to the clubhouse, holding hands. He must've left his bike there rather than riding it to the house when he got off work. Coming up the hallway to the common room, you could hear the roar of the guys talking and laughing. They were in a good mood. When we entered, they all turned to face us. They were smiling, although I had no idea why. Greetings were called out, and I returned them. We went over to stand by Scorpion. He whistled.

"That's it. You look almost like a biker's old lady dressed like that. Good. Hey, Pres, she's missing something, don't you think? Without it, she's not totally pulling off the old lady vibe."

I glanced down at myself, trying to figure out what he meant.

"You're right, VP, but I think I have a solution for that," Diablo said confidently.

I glanced over at him to find him smiling at me. Butcher came from somewhere and placed a box in his outstretched hand. Diablo handed it to me. Putting it on the table next to us, I scolded him.

"Diablo, you don't need to keep buying me things. What is it?"

"Open it and find out. As for buying you things, you'd better get used to it because I have no intention of stopping."

I rolled my eyes, but I did smile. He was so sweet yet obstinate. I undid the bow on top and lifted the lid. Everyone had gotten surprisingly quiet. I gasped as the content appeared. I was afraid to pick it up in case it wasn't what I thought it was. Diablo must've read my mind because he did it for me. I got teary-eyed as I examined it.

It was a property cut like the one Brooklyn had worn while she was here. Her cut was the first one I'd seen up close. I'd been envious of it, if the truth be told. Seeing the double horse logo of the Horsemen was wonderful, but it didn't compare to seeing *Property of Diablo* written on it. He slowly turned it so I was able to see the front. Stitched on the upper left side, over my heart, was the word *Serenity*.

Unable to wait any longer, I let out a squeal and held out my arms to the side. This caused the room to laugh. Diablo chuckled as he slid it on. I hugged it to myself.

"I hope it's alright that I bought it. Or do you want me to return it?" he teased.

"Try to, and I'll cut your ass or smother you in your sleep," I threatened.

Hoots and hollers rang out.

"Hot damn, she's converted to an old lady, alright. Let's get this show on the road so we can get back and have a drink to celebrate our queen," Scorpion yelled out.

The others all shouted their agreement. This broke up the group, and the guys began to head for the parking lot. Diablo hugged me close and gave me a quick kiss before we followed them.

"Now you can't get away. It's official. You're my old lady."

"I wasn't planning to get away. You're stuck with me."

He smiled as he led us outside to the line of

bikes. When we got to his, he had another surprise for me. Sitting on the passenger seat was a helmet. It had the words *Diablo's Serenity* in flowing script on it in glittering red. It popped on the matte black helmet. I had to give him another kiss, which was interrupted by the guys calling out we'd be late if the two of us didn't stop all the sucking faces. I gave them the finger, which they found hilarious.

Diablo helped me get the helmet on, and then he handed me a leather jacket. It was in my size. On the back, it had the same thing as my property cut. The man wanted me covered in him. I didn't mind at all. I proudly put it on, then let him help me straddle the bike behind him. In no time, the bikes came alive, and the roar of the engines made my body vibrate. As a unit, we swept out of the compound gates and got on the road into town. I was psyched to finally see it.

The ride into town wasn't as long as I hoped. I found I enjoyed the vibrating ride along with the wind in my face. It was refreshing and freeing at the same time. At one point, it felt so amazing I spread both arms and yelled out my delight. This made all the guys honk their horns. The cars passing us slowed down and stared at us. I waved at them.

When we got within the city limits, the club slowed down. It was dark. Kids were running everywhere, trick or treating. You couldn't be too careful in case one darted out in the road. They made their way through town until they came to a parking lot. They all pulled in and ran their bikes up into the grass. I assumed that was to leave room for cars to park later. I worried for a moment the center wouldn't like it, then I saw the sign, *Horsemen Parking*. I guess not.

As we shut down and everyone got off, I had to ask. “How did you guys get hooked up with the center? Don’t take this wrong, but it doesn’t seem like something a bunch of bikers would do.”

“It isn’t in a lot of cases, but unlike the outlaw, one-percenter clubs, we do things to benefit others by holding poker runs, charity events, and fundraisers for the things we believe in. This senior community center is filled with elderly who have served our country and done other vital things. Now they’re older, and people tend to forget about them. We got involved in a Christmas charity event for kids, and this brought us into contact with this group. One of the members got us involved. It grew from that.”

It pleased me to know what they did for others. I was anxious as we entered a couple of minutes later. The room was more than half full, mostly of older people. They looked up when we came in. Smiles spread, and suddenly, different ones were calling out the guys’ names. They knew them by sight. The men returned their greetings, and they used their names. Diablo hadn’t been exaggerating. They did know them rather well.

I was garnering lots of curious stares. I guess being the only woman among a horde of bikers would attract attention. Diablo had his arm around me as he led me to a table right in the middle of the main room. Sitting at it were several men and a couple of ladies. He stopped next to one of the men. The man was tattooed like my man, with a long white beard and hair pulled back in a ponytail. He sat erect and had a watchful look about him. He ran his eyes up and down me before he looked at Diablo.

"You gonna introduce me, boy? It seems you have something to tell me." His voice was deep and powerful despite his age.

"I was about to do that. Hold your horses. So damn impatient. I'd like to introduce my old lady, Jauhnna. Baby, this is Sledge. He's a retired member of the club. He and my dad, Fiend, were best friends. He tries to keep this unruly bunch in line." He said the last part louder. The seniors around the room all chuckled and heckled him. It was fun to see and hear.

"It's a pleasure to meet you, sir," I said to Sledge as I held out my hand. I wasn't sure what to do when meeting a former Horseman. Heck, I didn't know there were any, but it did raise the question of how many there were and why they left. Was there an age limit?

His stern expression turned to a smile as he took my hand, but he didn't shake it. Instead, he raised it to his mouth and kissed it. He tongued my knuckles. I was shocked. Diablo growled at him.

"Stop trying to flirt with her and keep your mouth and tongue to yourself, you old bastard. Babe, I'll take you to wash your hand when he lets go."

Sledge just laughed, placed a second kiss, then let go. "You can't blame me for trying. She's beautiful. I'm not dead. Honey, if you drop his ass and become mine, I'll die way sooner and leave you all my money and possessions. You'll be a young widow and can choose any man you want after I'm gone. I'll be your sugar daddy."

I had to laugh at his wiggling eyebrows. "I'm sorry, Sledge, but I can't. See, I love this growly man beside me, and I have to stick with him. I hope you understand. Your offer, while having some appeal, just can't compare to being his."

He nodded. "Good goddamn answer. She'll do. Now, why am I just hearing about her? How long have you been hiding her?"

"We met just over a month ago. We've been busy," Diablo explained.

I was surprised when an older woman walked over and handed me a wet wipe. She rolled her eyes as she tapped Sledge on the shoulder and shook her head before walking off. I guess this wasn't unusual for him. It made me wonder how many of the ladies in here he romanced. He was still a fine-looking man. I guessed him to be in his early seventies.

"A month? And how long has she had the property cut?"

"I gave her that tonight, but she was claimed before that."

"Why so long? You had to take that long to know?"

I thought he'd question him on how fast it was, but no, he thought Diablo was slow.

"Sledge, I knew almost the instant I saw her, but there were some extenuating circumstances. I'll explain later. This isn't the place for it."

Sledge perked up as a knowing look spread over his face. "Got it. Well, welcome, Jauhnna. Make yourself at home. If you need anything, just ask. The kids should start filtering in within the hour."

"Thank you. Can I help get anything ready? I hate to just sit and watch others work."

He rose to his feet. "She'll make an excellent old lady. Come with me, and I'll introduce you to the ladies in the kitchen. They'll be able to tell you if anything needs to be done."

And that was how I was slowly introduced to a crowd of seniors. As time passed, Diablo and the guys made the rounds. They did some heavy lifting and set up more tables and chairs. The ladies in the kitchen were busy getting drinks and desserts ready. I helped wherever they pointed. They were full of curiosity about who I was, where I came from, and how I'd captured the elusive, sexy Diablo, their words. More than one ogled him unrepentantly in front of me. I answered what I could and was vague only on my past. They let me get away with it.

In no time, it felt like the first kids had come in. Most were with adults. Their costumes were adorable, and I got a kick out of seeing all of them. They came to the counter between the kitchen and the main room to get drinks and food. They were polite, and I chatted to as many as I could about their costumes and how they did on their candy hauls. I was working to refill the desserts when a little girl came up to the counter. She was maybe four years old and the most beautiful thing dressed as a fairy. Her big blue eyes and blond hair made her look like an angel. I smiled at her as I spoke to her.

"Do you want some hot chocolate?"

She didn't answer me, just stared. I went to ask again when the older woman behind her answered for her.

"I'm sorry. She can't hear you. Jaycee is deaf and still learning to read lips. Here, I'll ask her in sign language."

Before she could, I leaned down to get closer to Jaycee's level. "Hello, Jaycee. My name is Jauhnna. Would you like some hot cocoa?" It had been a while since I signed, but I thought I got it all right. The way her face lit up and she smiled told me she understood.

She quickly signed back. *Yes, please. How do you know how to sign?*

I replied. *I learned it growing up. I had a friend in school who was deaf. It's been a long time since I did it, so forgive me if I mess up. Would you like a cookie or brownie to go with your cocoa?*

A cookie, please.

Her mom, or maybe it was her grandma, watched us closely. She smiled at me.

"It's great to meet someone who can communicate with her. It's such a fight to find anyone who can. That's why she's still placed with me."

As I got the requested cocoa and cookie, I chatted with her. "Placed?"

"Yes, she's my temporary foster child. We're trying to find her a permanent home, but it's tough. No one seems to know how to sign, and she needs it. She's not old enough to read yet, and if they can't sign, she'd be isolated in a world of nothing. There are families who could take her, but they don't want to learn ASL. She's been with me six months, the poor thing."

I handed over the cocoa and the cookie. Turning to Mabelle beside me, I asked, "Would you be okay if I took a short break? I'd like to talk to this nice lady and this sweetheart."

"Sweetie, take your time. We've got plenty of hands. Go." She waved me away.

Having her permission, I stepped out from behind the counter. I wanted to talk to this woman longer. I led them to a table with open seats. We sat down. I held out my hand. "I'm Jauhnna. It's nice to meet you."

She shook it as she introduced herself: "Hi, I'm Susanna. It's very nice to meet you. Do you do this every year? It's incredible. I'm glad I brought her. She was so excited to get to go trick or treating this year. It was her first time."

"This is my first time too. My man and his club help with this and other events here."

I think that was the moment my cut registered with her. Her eyes rounded. "You're part of the motorcycle gang, the Horsemen of Wrath? I've seen them around town."

"They're not a gang but a club. I got it wrong my first time, too. Yes, they do a lot of things. I was told they help with charities and such. Actually, see that man over there?" I pointed to Sledge. She nodded. "He was a Horseman, but now he's retired. He seems to run things around here. I'm new to this club thing, so I'm still learning. May I ask something personal?"

Susanna nodded, so I asked, "What happened to Jaycee's parents, or is that confidential?"

Jaycee was happily eating her cookie and drinking her cocoa as she watched all the kids around us. I saw yearning there. She wanted to go play with them, but how would she communicate? The poor thing was so isolated. It tore at my heart. I wanted to wrap her up in hugs and kisses and tell her it would all be okay.

"No, I can tell you. They were killed over a year ago. There was a house fire. Her dad got her out and then went back for his wife. They weren't able to get out in time, and the firefighters hadn't gotten there yet."

"Oh my God! The poor girl. What about other

family? She has no one?" I asked in shock.

"There were distant cousins, but they didn't want the responsibility of caring for a special needs child. Some have their own children, and others don't want kids. It's a shame because she's the sweetest thing. She was born deaf. They started teaching her sign language as an infant, so she's fluent. She needs a family who can communicate with her. Until we find one, she'll stay with me. I can't let her go to someone who won't even try to be a part of her world."

"I don't blame you. You're a good person to do it. May I ask how you know it?"

"I learned it in college. I had to take a foreign language, and the usual ones didn't interest me, so I took ASL. How about you? I caught you signing something about a friend."

"I had a friend growing up who was deaf, so I learned for her. It's been a while, though."

"You did great."

I was about to ask more about Jaycee when Diablo walked up. He bent down and kissed me. It was quick, but I saw Jaycee. She was staring at him as if mesmerized. When he stood back up, he smiled at Susanna.

"Sorry to interrupt. I had to have a kiss. Are you doing alright, babe?"

"I'm fine. You?"

"Great. Who are your new friends? I'm Diablo, by the way." He held out his hand to Susanna as he introduced himself.

"This is Susanna and Jaycee. Susanna, this is my man, Diablo. He's the president of the Horsemen. We were talking about Jaycee."

"Really? What about her?" He was smiling at her. She was still staring at him. When he smiled, she inched closer and traced a finger over one of his tattoos on his arm, then jerked her hand back.

"Jaycee, it's okay. Diablo won't bite. He's mine. Do you like his tattoo?" I signed and spoke it aloud so Diablo would know what I said. His eyebrows rose in surprise at seeing me signing. Jaycee immediately signed back.

He's your husband? He has pictures like my daddy did. They're pretty.

Knowing she was too young to understand boyfriend versus husband, I left it alone. Her mentioning her daddy made me sad.

"He is. They are pretty pictures. Do you want to see them up close? I bet he'd let you. I want to get one, I think."

As soon as he heard me ask if she wanted to look closer, he grabbed a chair from the table behind us and brought it over. He sat between her and me and laid his arms out on the table for her to inspect. She shyly inched her finger out again and touched a different one.

"Darlin', will you translate what I say? I don't know sign language, unfortunately. I want to tell her about some of them," he asked quietly.

"I will."

"Thank you. First, tell her I love her costume. She's a beautiful fairy."

I did as he asked. Her smile became radiant. She signed back that she thought he was beautiful. This made him laugh. Soon, they were deep into a conversation. I had to work hard to keep up with the two of them. Occasionally, I got to throw in a few comments of my own. I lost track of time. Susanna sat there quietly, watching us. It was a good hour, at least, before she broke up their lovefest.

"I hate to break this up, but I need to get her home and to bed. I can't tell you how great this was for her. She's so lonely. That smile on her face is a gift. I'm thankful I came to this. You two aren't by any chance approved to be foster parents, are you?" She sounded so hopeful.

"No, we're not," I said dejectedly, hating the fact we weren't.

"Too bad. You're exactly the kind of parents she needs. Oh well, if you ever want to do it, let me know. I can help you navigate the process."

This led to us exchanging numbers. She thanked Diablo. As Jaycee left, she was waving and signing goodbye. I did the same back while Diablo grinned and waved at her. She had a sad look on her face as she went out the door. As the door closed behind them, tears fell.

Diablo wrapped me in his arms. "Shh, why are you crying, baby?"

"It's Jaycee. She's so alone with no one other than Susanna to talk to. Her parents were killed in a fire. The family they had didn't want her. Foster families don't want to learn to sign, and if they don't, she'll be stuck in a world of silence. It makes me sick. Just because she's not what they see as normal, they aren't willing to adapt to help her. She's never going to be adopted. What is her life going to be like, Diablo? Will she ever be happy and loved?" I was outright bawling at this point. I hid my face in his shirt. My heart was aching. He bundled me up, and it wasn't long before he hustled me outside to take me home. I didn't care where we went. I was too miserable to pay attention.

Diablo: Chapter 15

Jauhnna still wasn't herself. Ever since Trick or Treat and meeting Jaycee, she'd been depressed and withdrawn. I tried to cheer her up, but she couldn't seem to shake it. I felt for the little girl, but it seemed she and Jauhnna had bonded. Hell, I felt like I had bonded with her, too. I knew part of it was probably her desire to be a mom. It killed me that she would never have children of her own. You could see she was meant to be a mother.

Those thoughts reminded me of the conversation I had with Brooklyn about starting a second family. After seeing what Bear and Bull were like with theirs, I knew I'd be willing to do it if she desired it. Since having kids of our own was out of the question, that left fostering or adopting. Fostering, I didn't see happening. She'd get too attached and wouldn't be able to let go. Damn it, I wouldn't either. If we ever fostered, it would only be a temporary thing until we were able to officially adopt.

It was with that in mind and her unhappiness that I did what I did today. I called Susanna to question her on the foster parent requirements. They were extensive, and she sent over the paperwork to me. She told me everything we'd have to have and do to qualify. It would take months to get clearance if the State deemed us foster parent worthy. There was concern that they might think the head of a motorcycle club wasn't appropriate. On top of it, she said they tended to grant it to couples who were married. They saw it as more stable than just boyfriend and girlfriend relationships, even though it wasn't hard to get a divorce these days.

I thanked her and told her I might be calling to ask more questions. She was agreeable. I did ask her not to tell Jauhnna about our conversation if they happened to talk. I explained about her not being able to have kids and how I didn't want to get her hopes up only to dash them. She was sympathetic and said she understood. Mum was the word. When I was done with her, I went straight to Micro. Surely, there was a way to speed this up and eliminate any obstacles.

I caught him working in his office at Vintage Rummages. When I knocked on his open door, he gave me a surprised look but waved for me to enter. I came in, closing the door behind me, which raised his brows. I sat in front of his desk.

"What can I do for you, Pres? If this is about Galway and Janus, I'm just waiting for the Patriots to give us the green light. I don't think there's anything more I can dig up on the bastards."

I knew everything he'd found, and there was a lot. It made it complicated to take them out. If I had my way, I'd find them and kill the bastards and get rid of the bodies and be done with them. However, their organizations were into some ugly stuff. None of us wanted to leave them standing. Hence, there was a delay as we got everything in place and had a solid plan that would eliminate everyone who needed to go in order to have the two organizations fold. The six men who'd touched her against her will, in addition to Galway, were his personal guards and enforcers. Not decision makers, but they'd die too. I itched to have it done and over with so she could get on with life, free of that worry. Soon. This was what I kept telling myself and her.

"I know. That's not why I'm here. I wondered if you might be able to do some work and find me some answers on something totally different."

"I probably can. What is it?"

"I want to know if there's a shortcut to applying and getting approved to be foster parents. I don't want to wait months. I don't want them to come back and not approve us due to me being a biker. It's bullshit, but you know how people are."

I saw I'd surprised him. "Damn, Diablo, I have to say, I wasn't expecting that. It's wonderful that you and Jauhnna want to do it. I think she'll make a great mom, and I know you'll do the same as a dad. All you have to do is see you with Jai and Thane. You're taking a leaf out of Bull and Bear's book."

"Yeah, it seems like it. I know she's always wanted kids. Not being able to have any hurts her. She bonded the other night at the senior center with that little girl, Jaycee. You saw her crying." He nodded. The whole club had. I excused us right away so I could take her home. The others stayed, with the exception of Butcher. He escorted us home.

"We did. Let me see what I can find out and do. If I need more help, are you alright if I reach out to the others?"

I knew he meant the computer guys in the other clubs when he said the others. "I am, but all of you need to keep it on the down low. Jauhnna has no idea I'm working on this. I don't want to disappoint her if the State says no. If they say yes, I want to be able to surprise her. Fostering will only be a stepping stone to adoption for us. There's no way she can take a child in and then let them go. Hell, I don't think I can do it."

"Adoption is great. My parents are one of the best things to ever happen to me. I hate to think how I would've turned out without them."

I knew he'd understand. Micro had been in the foster system until he was adopted at five years old. He was lucky and ended up with wonderful parents. He was close to them and his siblings. They came to the compound for family occasions and holidays. They didn't live too far from St. Augustine.

I stood up and held out my hand. He took it, and we shook. "Thanks, brother. I know you're busy with everything else. I appreciate this more than you know. Don't hesitate to ask some of the others to help. Hell, if he's not too busy, or she isn't, I bet Smoke and Everly know shit we can only dream of."

He grinned. "They probably do. I swear, one day when I grow up, I want to be like them. They're scary good. I feel I know my stuff until I go up against them, and then I feel like a first grader just finding the on button on my laptop," he admitted ruefully.

"You're much better than that, but I get it. Okay, I'll get out of the way. If you need something, let me know."

"I sure will. Later, and Pres, this is fantastic."

Giving him a chin lift to acknowledge what he said, I opened the door and was gone. I had to get back to Prep & Restore to finish off some things, so I was free to go home. I was looking forward to spending more time with my woman.

My phone went off as I was riding there. I didn't have my earpiece on to answer it, so I let it go to voicemail. I'd be at the shop in less than ten minutes. It could wait. As I got to our street, I thought I knew what the call was about. There were two police cars parked outside Prep & Restore.

There were people standing on the sidewalk, and I saw a few bikes I recognized parked close by. I didn't waste time finding a parking spot and then getting my ass to the shop. As I walked up, a couple of cops tried to tell me I couldn't enter. Lucky for them, Crash saw me and told them I was the owner. Moving past them, I saw what the commotion was all about. One of the big front windows had been busted out. Glass was all over the sidewalk and, no doubt, the front reception area. My first concern was Carly.

"Is Carly alright? Did the glass cut her? Was anyone else up front when it happened?" I asked Crash, who'd come sauntering up to me.

"No, she's fine, and no one was up there but her. She sat far enough back that it didn't get to her, plus the desk and counter shielded her, too. She's a little pissed but unhurt."

"Thank God. Okay, do you have any idea who did it? I doubt whatever was the cause was accidental."

"You'd be right, and yes, we know who did it. Carly watched it happen. It was Ackerman. He stood out on the sidewalk, screaming we weren't getting away with this, then he hurled a brick through the window," Crash snarled. We'd been joined by Thunder, Turbo, Cowboy, and Punk, as he explained.

"Christ, is that man mental? Did he honestly think he'd get away with it? I hope the cops have gone to arrest his ass," I snapped.

"Oh, they didn't need to. The idiot stood there ranting after he did it. Rex was here visiting Carly in between jobs. He went out and restrained him until the police could arrive. Carly called them as soon as he showed up outside and began yelling. They were dispatched before he threw the brick. They have him in the back of a squad car over there. I figure the cops will want your statement about the issues you've been having with him. Carly told them, but you know how they are," Thunder added as he waved in the general area of the cop cars.

"I can do that. Why are you guys here? Not that I mind, just curious."

"We'd taken a late lunch and were on our way back to our places when we rode by and saw the commotion, so we stopped. Carly tried to call you, but she said you didn't pick up, so she left a voicemail," Turbo told me.

"I didn't have my earpiece in, and I was close, so I planned to get it after I got here. Well, shit, there goes my plan to get home early. Point me to whoever is in charge so I can get this farce on the road. Maybe arresting him will wake the stupid fuck up," I grumbled. My earlier good mood was quickly evaporating.

As a group, they led me over to an officer. He was slightly older looking than the others. He scanned me from head to toe when I stopped in front of him. His gaze stopped on the word *President* on my cut.

"You must be the Diablo these guys have been talking about."

"I am. And you are?"

"Officer Merritt. Mind telling me what the deal is with you and Mr. Ackerman?"

"Well, I believe Carly, my receptionist, filled you in, but if you need to hear it twice, here goes. The long and short of it is we did a job for Mr. Ackerman several months back. A contract was signed and agreed to. We completed that work and asked for the remainder of our fee. We get half up front and the other half when the job is done. At that time, he asked to have additional work done. I informed him it would cost extra, but we could amend the contract and do it. He wanted it done but at the original price, which wasn't possible. It was extensive work he was asking for. When he refused, we left it as it was. However, he refuses to pay us the remainder of our money. He says the job isn't done. He claims we forged the document with his signature on it. I got tired of fighting with him every week to pay, so I handed it over to collections to deal with him. He was here not long ago, contesting it again, and I informed him if he didn't pay, it would go to our lawyer next, and then I had him leave. That brings us to today."

"He claims you and your club have been harassing him. That you came to his home and tried to intimidate him. He claims the incident today was him showing you he wouldn't be pushed around by you. He did say you cheated him out of work and are demanding payment for work you didn't finish," Merritt informed me. He was watching me closely as he did.

I couldn't help it. I laughed. He gave me a puzzled look. "What's funny?"

"The idea that if we had visited him at his home, he'd be able to come here today and do this. Believe me, if I had been inclined to do that, his ass would be in the hospital."

"Sir, that's a threat. You shouldn't be telling an officer of the law this."

"Whatever. He doesn't have a mark on him, and if he does, it wasn't put there by me or any of my brothers. Personally, I think the guy has a screw or two loose. What are you gonna do with him? Can I expect him to get some jail time out of this, or will he post bail and be back out causing trouble before the day is over?"

He sighed. "Truthfully, he'll post bail and probably get a fine. It depends if he has a history of priors. If he does, then a magistrate may do more. If he's been adamant about not paying and that you cheated him, then I'm not sure he'll quit. As for you getting paid, that's not likely either."

I liked how forthcoming he was. He didn't automatically side with Ackerman just because we were an MC. Usually, the police did.

"I'm afraid you're right. We're a business, Officer. We have a great reputation. I won't have him messing with it. If he doesn't pay, I'll seek legal recourse. It's in his best interests to pay us and move on. Maybe you or one of your people can talk some sense into him and make him see that."

"We'll try. Okay, I need your legal name, phone number, and address for my report."

Taking out my wallet, I removed one of the business cards I carried with me. I rarely gave them out, but they had everything on them he needed. He took it and then gave me one of his. In a matter of minutes, he rounded up his people, and they headed out with Ackerman. As they drove off, I saw the crazy bastard staring at me from the back of the squad car. His eyes told me this wasn't over. Knowing I could do nothing about him at the moment, I got to the important things I could.

"I need to call our glass company and get them over here as soon as possible to replace this. In the meantime, get Zax and Liam over here with some plywood and nails to cover this up. I'll get the brooms. This glass needs to be swept up so no one gets hurt."

"I've called the prospects already to get their asses here. Rex said he'd call the glass company. We'll get the glass out here and in reception swept up. Why don't you go talk to Carly and Rex? We've got this," Thunder offered.

"Thanks, I will." I gave them all a chin lift of thanks, then headed inside to question Carly and Rex.

As I passed through the lobby area, I noted the glass had already been swept up. Leave it to those two to be on the job no matter what. I found them in the employee breakroom. Carly was sitting at a table drinking coffee, and Rex was up pacing the room. The fierce expression he wore told me he wasn't happy, and if he had the option, Ackerman's neck would be between his hands. I gave him a nod of understanding as I went straight to Carly. I gave her a one-armed squeeze.

"How're you holding up, Carly? You didn't get cut, did you?"

"I'm fine, Diablo. Just pissed. That man needs his head examined. He was out there ranting like a lunatic about harassment, cheating, and how we wouldn't get paid a dime more. I called the police like you told me to do. We were waiting for them to come when, out of nowhere, he hefted up a brick and threw it. I have no idea where he got it. I didn't see it until he threw it," she said.

"You should've let me go out there and deal with the bastard. Then we wouldn't have a broken window," Rex groused.

"If you went out there, it would be you in the cop car headed to the jail, not him. You know he was hoping someone would lay hands on him," she chided him.

He scowled harder, but he didn't argue with her. I slapped his shoulder. "I feel ya. If I'd been here, it would've been my first reaction, but she's right. We have to play it cool and by the law with this one. Until we get this resolved, one way or another, I'm having one of the prospects here during work hours. I don't want you alone, in case, when he gets out on bail, he comes back."

I saw some of the tension leave Rex, and Carly smiled. I knew it had to have been preying on their minds. Like Rex, I would be the same if it was Jauhnna or Brooklyn in Carly's situation.

"Thank you. I would feel better," she admitted.

"No need to thank me."

"I already called, and the glass company will be over before the end of the day to take a look. They may have to order a pane, but they'll put a rush on it. I can board it up until they can replace it," Rex offered.

"Thanks for calling them. The prospects are on their way to board it up. All I want is for you to make sure you give Carly the comfort she needs. If you need something, I'll be in my office."

I stayed and chatted a couple of minutes more about nothing too serious. I mostly talked about how the current jobs were going, then went to my office. As soon as I got there, I placed a call.

"Hello," Jauhnna answered on the house phone. Yeah, I was one of those people. No matter the technology, I still kept a landline at home. I told people it was so I could have a fax machine, which was true, but the real reason was I didn't fully trust cell phones to work when you needed them, even if I did have one. Now that I thought of it, she needed one. I jotted it down on a notepad as I answered her.

"Hello, Serenity. How's your day going?"

"It's okay. The usual. Is everything alright? You don't usually call me this time of day."

"I wanted to let you know I won't be home early like I said. There was a problem at work. I'll tell you about it when I get home. I wanted you to know."

"Did anyone get hurt?" Her worry came through.

"No, baby, no one is hurt. I should be home by six. If I get delayed longer, I'll call."

"Okay, just take care. I'll see you when you get here. Ride safe."

"I will. Love you."

"Love you, too."

We both said bye at the same time. I reluctantly hung up. The urge to say the hell with it and go home was strong, but I had responsibilities to see to. Buckling down, I got to work so I could get out of there as soon as possible.

It was closer to six-thirty when I rolled into my garage at the house. I'd called and let her know I was running a tad behind my six o'clock estimate. When I left the shop, I had to make a pit stop. The item I got was in my cut pocket. Shutting the garage door, I entered the house through the door that connected it to the garage. It brought me in through the laundry room slash mudroom, which was a short distance from the kitchen and living room. The scent of food led me to the kitchen first.

I was right to check there. She stood in the kitchen stirring something. She looked up and gave me a blinding smile. My whole body felt lighter just seeing her. It was amazing what a change she'd already brought to my life in such a short time. I went straight to her. I opened my arms, and she slid into them. I hugged her close as I devoured her sweet mouth. She moaned and gave as good as she got. It was with great reluctance I stopped, but if I didn't, she'd find herself over the counter or on the dinner table as my supper. Just the kiss had gotten me hard.

The damn temptress knew it, too, because as we parted, she rubbed her hand up and down my bulge. I growled and gave her a stern look. "Darlin', you keep that up, and your fantastic-smelling supper will get cold."

She smirked at me. "And it would be worth it. However, I know how hungry you are when you get home. How about we say it'll be continued later? Now, go wash your hands and get comfortable. Dinner will be served in ten minutes."

Giving her a quick peck on the lips, I patted her ass and then left the kitchen to go to our bedroom. I didn't waste time changing into a clean shirt and a pair of shorts and washing my hands. I put her gift on my nightstand to give her later, then went back to see if there was anything I could do. She let me set the table. It was a big thing for her. She wanted dinner to be at least a sit-down meal at an actual table. I hadn't done it in years, but I didn't mind.

I helped her carry the bowls and platter to it. Tonight's menu included fried chicken, mashed potatoes, gravy, roasted asparagus, and hot rolls. My stomach growled. I'd had to up my workouts since she started cooking for me. After pulling out her chair and seating her, I took my seat.

"Babe, this all looks and smells so good. Did you know fried chicken is a favorite of mine?" I asked as I placed food on her plate. I would always serve her first. Once I thought I had enough on hers, I began to work on mine.

She gave me a secretive smile. "I might've had a little birdie who told me."

"Really? A birdie. And which of the guys would tell you that?"

"It wasn't one of your brothers. This birdie lives further away."

"Brooklyn? When did you talk to her?"

"Today. She called to see how I was doing. We got to talking about food, and she gave me the lowdown on what her dad loves. She hinted the way to your heart might actually be through your stomach, so cliché," she was grinning as she said it.

"Babe, you already have my heart, so no need to win it. You know, I love anything you make, but you don't have to cook for me."

"I know I don't. I enjoy it. It's nice to have someone appreciate it. Okay, enough talking. Let's eat. I hope you like it. It's a recipe I haven't made in ages."

Liking it ended up being way too tame of a description. I loved it. The combination of spices she put in the coating on the chicken was amazing. It was hands down the best fried chicken I'd ever had. The potatoes were creamy, with the right amount of butter and a hint of garlic to them. The gravy just added to the flavor explosion, and the asparagus, not something I ate much of before, was great. She made it al dente, and it had hints of garlic to it. The rolls were warm and tasted wonderful. I sat back, groaning when I was done. She finished before me but sat there, keeping me company. I patted my stomach.

"Woman, you're gonna make me fat and lazy if you keep cooking like this. My workouts will need to double just to stay ahead of the pot belly."

"I doubt that. You don't have any fat on you, which disgusts me, I hope you know."

"Why's that?"

"Because I have to watch everything I eat, and I still gain. I have excess weight, which pops up on my ass, hips, thighs, and my stomach. Men have it easy."

Shoving back my chair, I stood and moved to stand next to hers. I tugged it away from the table, and then I lifted her up. I grabbed her ass and hoisted her onto the table. I shoved the plates to the side. Pressing my groin between the V of her legs, I rubbed my growing erection against her pussy. Only the thin fabric of our shorts separated us.

"That body you're talking trash about is mine. I happen to love every inch and pound of it. These thighs, that ass, your hips, stomach, and tits drive me wild. I don't want you to lose any of it. I want you soft, not a hard, bony stick. When I make love to you, this gives me something to hold on to and softness to cushion us when I'm pounding this pussy." I rubbed my cock up and down her V. She moaned and shivered. Desire had her pupils dilating slightly.

"Victor, don't talk like that."

"Why not?" I had my hand underneath her shirt, pushing her bra cup out of the way so I was able to tweak her nipple.

"Because if you don't stop, I'll strip naked right here and beg you to take me on the table," she said breathlessly.

"Good. I need some dessert. Strip. You have two minutes to be bare and spread out on the table for me. I want you on your back with your legs spread wide," I ordered gruffly.

My cock was throbbing at the images her words and mine put in my head. I backed off. She was on her feet, hastily shedding her clothes. I did the same. As soon as I had mine off, I moved the plates to the counter. I didn't want to break them or create a mess, and I knew I was about to get vigorous.

The sight of her soft, creamy skin and all the things she'd been disparaging made me lick my lips. I fisted my cock and stroked it. She watched and whimpered when she saw me do it. Her hand crept toward her pussy. I had to stop her.

"Don't you dare touch yourself. Your orgasms are mine to give or take. You'll get them when I say you can. Lie back."

She pouted but did as I told her. I was beyond happy that my demanding attitude didn't turn her off. She assured me it was different from Radigan's when I asked. As she got in position, I pulled a chair up to the table and sat down. I slid my hands underneath her ass and slid her to the edge so her legs hung over. Bending forward, I put her legs over my shoulders and inhaled.

Her scent made my cock throb more. Not wasting time, since I was ravenous for her, I took my first taste. Her flavor on my tongue sent me into a wild frenzy.

I licked, sucked, and nibbled as I growled. I ate her from top to bottom. She was panting and crying out for me to make her come. I teased her to the brink, then backed off a couple of times. She was spilling her cream, and I was lapping it up. The third time, when she got to the brink, I let her come. She wailed my name as she gushed and fed me more of her delicious cum.

When she came down from her orgasm, I knew I wasn't able to wait a minute longer to have her. Lowering her legs, I stood, placed the head of my cock against her entrance, then slid in hard. She moaned and gripped the edge of the table. She was so warm, wet, and tight that I groaned the entire thrust. She was clasping me in a hard grip.

My plan was to take her slowly. She ruined that when she panted out to me, "Victor, baby, please. Fuck me hard. I need to come again. I want you to take me. Claim me. God, do it!" she sobbed.

She was trying to ride my length, but I had my hands on her hips, holding her still. When she wasn't able to do it, she clenched her inner muscles around me. I broke. I slid my hips back and then snapped them forward, impaling her. She moaned.

Setting a hard, fast pace, I pounded in and out of her. As I did, I whispered to her. "Is this what you want? You want me wild and out of control. Desperate to have you? If so, you got it. I want you to scream and beg me. Fuck! You have no idea how good you feel. Or the things I think about doing to you."

"Tell me. What would you want to do that you

haven't?" she whispered back hoarsely.

I hesitated. I hadn't planned to introduce her to all my fantasies until she was more comfortable with me and sex. So far, nothing I'd done triggered her, but I was afraid one day I would.

"Victor, tell me, please."

"They're just fantasies. You don't have to ever let them happen. Alright? I dream of taking you while you're tied to the bed and totally at my mercy. There are so many toys I could introduce you to. I've pictured you dressed in sexy outfits, begging me to take you. Taking you in every way possible." I explained as I thrust over and over. I'd slowed down a little as we talked. Her pussy contracted around me as I told her each of them.

"In every way possible? Do you mean you'd want to have anal sex, too?" she asked cautiously.

I had no clue if Radigan or those other bastards had forced that on her as well. If they had, I doubted they'd properly prepared her, and if not, they'd definitely traumatized her. She might never want to even let me play with her ass, let alone fuck it. Even women who hadn't been raped didn't want anything to do with anal. I'd experimented with it after my wife died, but it wasn't something I had to have or desired all the time. Missionary sex had never been my preferred position, but as the years passed, I explored more and found things I enjoyed more.

"Baby, we can talk about this later. Right now, I want you to come for me. Show me you need me as much as I need you," I diverted her attention.

She didn't say more. As she tried to thrust back into me, I forgot our discussion and went for it. I pounded into her so vigorously that the table scooted across the floor. She gripped the edge until her knuckles were white, but her expressions and the sounds she made told me she wasn't in pain or hating it. It was absolute pleasure coursing through both of us.

Rubbing her distended clit, she came hard. I was able, by some miracle, to hold back mine. I kept thrusting through hers. When she came out of it, I drove her right up toward the next one. Needing her on her belly, I withdrew long enough to roll her over then I re-entered her. It allowed me to go deeper. She whimpered.

As I hammered into her, I worked myself closer to coming. When I knew it would be impossible to hold back, I raised her upper body off the table and pressed her back against my chest. As I thrust up into her, I grasped her tits and kneaded them, then plucked hard at her nipples as I gently bit her shoulders and the back of her neck. She screamed and then came in a gush of her cum. I growled and latched onto her shoulder with my teeth and rubbed her clit with one hand and twisted a nipple with the other. She squeezed my cock so fucking hard, I saw stars, then I was exploding and shooting my load deep. It went on and on as she continued to grip me and cry out her ongoing orgasm.

As I came down from my mind-numbing release, I wasn't able to stop myself from wishing she was able to get pregnant. The thought that this time would create a baby filled me with hope. I knew it was impossible, but if things turned out the way I hoped, we'd start a family in a different way.

Exhausted, I slumped over her, pressing her into the table. I had enough sense not to crush her. I kissed her sweaty neck. She was breathing hard like I was.

"You undo me, Jauhnna. That was incredible."

"I can't move, Victor. I can't feel my legs. It was incredible. You'll have to leave me to sleep here tonight."

Chuckling, I raised up and reluctantly slid out of her. I caressed her ass cheek.

"Babe, you'll never sleep on something like this. I'll carry you to bed," I promised.

"No, I'll walk. Give me a few minutes. Why don't you go upstairs, and I'll be up after I clean up from dinner."

"Nope. I'll help you do it tomorrow. It can wait. Getting you cleaned up and comfortable in our bed can't. As amazing as that was, I have the feeling it won't be the last time tonight."

She whimpered, but not in a bad way. She tried to argue that she would walk, but I wasn't having it. As soon as my legs were stable, I scooped her up and carried her to the bedroom. First stop, a bath. Then we'd snuggle in bed and see where it led. Yeah, it was early, but I only needed to be with her. Creating memories was what I wanted. You never knew how long you might have to do it. I'd learned that the hard way.

Jauhnna: Chapter 16

I was curled up in bed with Diablo after a warm bath. He'd joined me and insisted on washing me. Even though he did nothing on purpose, his touch still aroused me. Lying beside him, I was barely controlling my need to touch him and see where it led us. I was tracing his tats on his chest, which was something I loved to do. As I did, our unanswered question from earlier when he had me on the kitchen table popped into my head.

"Victor, can I ask you something, and you promise to answer truthfully?"

He moved so he was able to see my face. He was slightly frowning. "Of course you can. I will always tell you the truth. What is it you want to know?"

"Earlier, I asked if you were interested in anal sex, and you didn't answer me. You kinda blew me off. Why?"

He sighed, then reached up to run his thumb along my cheekbone. "I wasn't trying to blow you off. I thought it was something we needed to talk about more fully, and in the middle of me being inside of you, close to coming, wasn't the time. I'm sorry you thought I was avoiding it."

"No, I'm sorry I took it that way. You're right. That wasn't the time to discuss it. Will you talk to me about it now? I just have this fear." I paused after saying more to think about how I wanted to broach this topic. It had been nagging at me for a while.

"Baby, I'll talk about anything you want. What do you fear?"

"That you'll hold yourself back because you fear doing something that'll remind me of the things Galway and those other men did to me. I don't want you to suppress who you are and what you sexually desire because you're afraid I'll freak out or something. If you do, you won't be satisfied, and then what? What's to keep you from…" I let it peter off. I didn't want to say it.

"Keep me from what?" he asked gruffly.

I didn't answer. I was running out of courage. What if I angered him? As much as he had already changed how I viewed men, there was still a part of me scared of ruining what we had.

"Were you about to say what would keep me from seeking sexual gratification elsewhere, with other women?"

Swallowing the lump in my throat, I nodded. I was watching his face as I did. Anger came only to be swiftly replaced with sadness. I hurried to try and soften it. "I'm sorry. Forget I said anything," I pleaded.

"No, I won't. I'm upset you'd think me capable of cheating on you. It pissed me off, then I remembered what you have been through, and it makes me sad that you would ever believe it. A man who's in love with you won't cheat on you, Jauhnna. You'll fulfill all his needs. Yes, there are things I like, and I told you some of them. It doesn't mean in order to be satisfied with you, we have to do them. As for your question about anal sex, yes, I've had it. Have I enjoyed it? Yes. Would I like to do it with you? Only if you agree. I want to because I need to find every way possible I can give you pleasure. Your initiation into sex and the first decade of it was a travesty. I don't want to scare you or make you do something you're not ready or willing to do."

His sincerity and how he continued to caress my face and arms settled much of my anxiety. I knew I had to voice my concerns and wants to him.

"Until you, sex was horrible. It was degrading, it hurt, and I hated everything about it. I had hoped that with someone else, it might be different, but I didn't know for sure. Like a lot of women, I read romance novels. What they describe in them seems so impossible. We might wish a man was like those fictional men, and we'd enjoy all the things done to and with us, but it's fiction. Maybe it was just authors pouring out their secret yearnings as if they were real. I know after being with you, it's not a lie, or at least what we've done so far isn't. It makes me wonder if the other stuff is enjoyable, too.

"A lot of them do describe more intense sexual practices and desires. Anal is one of those. In a lot of those books, women seem to end up liking it, and they want it again. Yes, they say it hurts, but that changes into something very enjoyable. I don't want to be afraid to try different things, and I don't want you not to ask for what you want due to fear of triggering me. I hope that makes sense."

"Serenity, it does make sense. How about this? If you want to try something, you tell me. If I want to change it up, I'll tell you. We decide together if we do it, and we'll take it as slow as we need to. If you change your mind, then tell me, and we'll stop. I haven't lied about the fact you have given me more fulfillment than anyone I've ever been with."

I wondered if that included his wife, but I didn't ask.

"And that includes Amy," he added.

"How did you know I was wondering that?"

"Your expressions tend to give you away, baby."

"Is it weird that I wonder about her and what she'd think of us? I know you'll always love her, and I'm alright with that. She gave you Brooklyn, and you loved her enough to marry her. That doesn't just go away because she died or you found me. I hope you know you can talk about her. Have her picture up in the house. When Brooklyn comes, I bet she'd like to see a picture of her mom."

I gasped as I was pressed onto my back, and his mouth took mine. I responded like I always did. Our kiss was passionate and long. When he finally let up, I was dazed and scrambling to remember what we'd been talking about.

"Do you know what it does to me to hear you say those things? You have the biggest heart of anyone I know. I'll always love Amy, but it's different from the love I have for you. She was my first love. We were young. Had she lived, would I still be with her? I'd like to think I would, but it wasn't in the cards. As much as it hurt, maybe God knew you were out there, and one day I'd meet you. I love you so much. And your offer to talk about her and have pictures in the house is just damn beautiful. Thank you. I'll see if Brook would like that. I never want you to think you mean less to me. And I believe Amy would've really liked you. She'd be happy that we've found each other." His answer made me happy.

I hugged him. “Good.”

“It is. Now, what would you say to your man making slow, passionate love to you? Would you be willing to let him do that?”

“I think I could be persuaded.”

This answer led me to being tortured by him for close to an hour. He wrung orgasm after orgasm out of me before he succumbed and came himself. I was so exhausted afterward that I drifted off without even bothering to clean myself up.

Sitting at the desk in Diablo’s office, trying to be productive while daydreaming about last night hadn’t gotten me far. I closed the browser and sat back in his chair. Last night, our talk about Amy had been good. I didn’t want to pretend she hadn’t existed and had no part of Diablo because it wasn’t realistic. I was coming to terms with the fact she wasn’t truly a ghost I had to compete with. He was making sure of it. However, she was a part of our lives and would remain so because of Brooklyn and her children. Amy was their actual grandmother, regardless of whether they ever met her. They should know her and not just from their mom.

Some people would think I was crazy to want her picture up in the house or to talk about her. Those people didn’t know what it was like to have a family who did nothing but betray and hurt you. Amy was the opposite, and her love for her family should be celebrated. She saved her daughter’s life at the risk of her own. That was love.

A chime brought my attention back to the

computer. It was my email alerting me that I had mail. Clicking on it, I was excited to see one of the applications I'd put in had gotten a response. I knew it was probably just a thank you for submitting one, but at least they acknowledged me. Opening it, I scanned the words. My breath hitched. It wasn't a form letter. It was an actual response, and they were interested in meeting me. They asked if I could come in for an interview the day after tomorrow.

I didn't know what to say. I hadn't told Diablo I'd applied anywhere. I wasn't exactly hiding it. I just kept letting other things divert my attention. Okay, yeah, I was procrastinating. I knew he wouldn't be happy with me doing it. However, if I didn't get out and be productive soon, I'd lose my mind.

I debated for a good half hour before I made my decision. I'd promised myself when I got away from Galway that I would never let someone control me. As much as I loved Diablo, I wouldn't allow him to do it, either. No matter that he was doing it out of love and the desire to protect me.

I quickly sent back a reply agreeing to the time and place and thanking them. Once I sent it, I got up. I had to steel myself to tell Diablo about it tonight. I needed someone to go with me the day after tomorrow. There was no way I could sneak and do it. I would be escorted, possibly by Zax or Liam. I headed upstairs to go through my things to see what was appropriate to wear for an interview. It didn't need to be a suit. I wasn't applying for a management job, but it still had to be nice.

I was lucky that the clothing Diablo kept insisting I buy, or he bought for me, wasn't all casual, everyday clothes. There were lovely dresses and a few nice pairs of slacks with pretty tops. There were even heels. I laid them out on the bed and studied them. I played around with accessories and combos. I even stripped and tried the ones I liked best on. I was removing another one when I heard the door downstairs slam. I jumped. I hadn't heard his bike. Had he left it at the clubhouse for some reason? I tried to gather my clothes and hide them. I wasn't ready to tell him yet. I needed to gather more courage for the argument that was to come. Why was he home this soon? He typically called me when he decided to come home early.

I wasn't fast enough. When he entered the bedroom, I knew immediately by the look on his face that he knew what I had done. How? I had no idea, but he did. He appeared angry. His gaze zeroed in on the clothes in my arms. His mouth tightened.

"Victor, I can—" he cut me off after three words.

"Don't. I don't want to hear your excuse. What I want is for you to put those goddamn clothes down and go contact that place. Tell them you're no longer interested in the position. And you'll follow up with the others you applied to and tell them the same."

His barking orders at me without regard for what I wanted or needed, only his opinion mattering, reminded me so much of Galway, my father, and my brother that fury instantly took hold of me. I threw the clothes on the bed and stormed over to him. I had to look up, but I didn't give a damn. I poked him in the chest with my finger. It hurt, which only pissed me off more.

"How dare you cut me off and demand anything of me! I'm not your fucking slave, Diablo. I'm not here to do as I'm told and to be forced to submit to your every whim and have no say in my life. If that's what you want in an old lady, then you can take your goddamn property cut back, and I'll be on the road by nightfall. I lived with one tyrant. I won't live with another," I shouted.

His face went slack. I thought I saw remorse there, but I didn't care. I was too hurt and upset to give a shit. His hand came up. I flinched and took a step back automatically.

"Serenity, baby, I'm sorry. Please, don't move away like you think I'm gonna hit you. I would never do that. I think we need to sit down and talk about this." His tone was calmer. Unfortunately, I wasn't.

"Oh, you want to talk now after jumping down my throat and telling me you didn't want to hear my excuses. Well, guess what? I'm not in the mood to talk to you. Get out of my way," I snapped. I tried to go around him, but he shifted, so he remained in front of me.

"Jauhnna, don't. This is important. We have to talk about it. I'm sorry I jumped you. Let's go downstairs to the couch, where we can relax."

"And if I say no? What will you do? Forcefully restrain me and make me? If I refuse to agree to do what you ordered me to do, what happens then? Will you lock me in a dark room and starve me? Beat me? Force yourself on me? Turn me over to your brothers so they can help discipline me?" I shouted.

I knew what I was saying wasn't him, but his attitude triggered something deep inside me. All my anger and pain over the years of Galway's abuse and that of my family before that was seeping out. I tried to hold it in, but I couldn't. Horror filled his expression. He was the one to step back this time. He looked sick.

"Darlin', I swear to God in the heavens and on my daughter, grandkids, and this club that I would never do any of those horrible things to you. Jesus, tell me you don't actually believe I'm capable of those things." There was pleading in his tone, and it was all over his face.

My anger began to ebb as his pain hit me. I wasn't quite able to answer him, but I did shake my head. I hoped he took it as my answer. The way he hung his head told me he didn't. I took several calming breaths before I walked to him. I placed a hand on his chest.

"I'm sorry. No, I know you wouldn't. You triggered my buried feelings. Ordering me the way you did was too close to what he always did," I whispered brokenly. Tears were on the verge of overflowing.

His arms slowly raised up, and then he placed them around me, tugging me gently toward him until I was plastered to his chest. I lay my head on it and closed my eyes. His chin rested on my head. He guided us to the bed. He sat down, bringing me with him. His body shuddered as he took a breath before he spoke.

"I hate that I made you think of him. It's the last thing I ever want to do. Let's talk about this. I approached it wrong, I admit, but it still remains that you exposed yourself by applying for jobs, Jauhnna."

"How did you find out? And what do you mean, I exposed myself?"

"Micro told me. He was searching for anything that might mention you on the internet. While he was doing it, he thought of what you did in Savannah. Why he got the idea you might be applying to places here that are similar, I don't know. It's how his mind works but thank God it does. He looked up places and placed a call. He somehow convinced them he was someone checking into a prior employee, you, and asked if you worked there. They got worried, and the ones you'd applied to admitted they had your resume. One of them added they were set to interview you. He called me right away."

I sat up so I could see his face. "They had no right to share that information with him! And what did he say to them? Are they going to cancel my interview because he spooked them? Did he badmouth me?"

"He didn't say anything bad, just that he was searching for you due to an issue that came up that he needed to talk to you about, but you can't do the interview. You've already exposed yourself enough. Hell, if Radigan or your brother's people get their hands on your resumes, they'll know exactly where you are. You used our address."

"Surely those places won't give anyone that information. Victor, I can't remain hidden behind this fence forever. I need to work, to be productive. You said your friends were setting everything up to rid me of Galway, Janus, and the others. I've been here six weeks. How much more time do they need?"

"I know it's hard to stay put, but it won't be much longer, I promise."

"Is it you need more information on who to take down with them or on the method you want to use?"

"We have the dirt. The thing we're working on now is how to draw the ones we need out together. If we hit them individually, the others might get wind of it and go underground. It may be years before we find them all. It has to be done in one big operation."

I was quiet as I thought over what he'd said. It was clear to me what they needed to do. Why hadn't any of them hit upon it? Or had they, and it was vetoed? The way I saw it, it was the only way, and by applying for those jobs, I'd provided them with a perfect opportunity.

"You know what you have to do, Victor. I can't believe none of you haven't thought of it."

He began shaking his head emphatically. "No, don't say it. We're not doing it."

"We have to. You know it. If they somehow figure out I've applied for jobs at those places and they get my address, it'll help us. They won't suspect a thing. They'll believe they can sneak up on us and take me. All we have to do is be ready. Hell, maybe Micro can leak that information someway on the internet so we make sure they find it."

He let a growl loose, slid off the bed, and then started to pace the bedroom. His face looked like a thundercloud. It was dark. His eyes were snapping with fire. Standing there was a bigger glimpse of why he was called Diablo. I'd asked him once how he got the name. He said I didn't want to know. I chose to let it go until a later time. I think he thought there were parts of him he had to keep hidden because they were too dark. What he needed to understand is I knew dark. I'd lived with it. There was the kind that was pure evil and then the kind that was only dangerous when unleashed on those who earned it. Diablo fell into the second category.

He rubbed his hand over his jaw and squeezed the back of his neck. He was staring at the floor as he paced. I let him think. I knew getting him to agree would take convincing, but I saw no other way. After a solid five minutes of utter silence, I had to say something.

"Honey, look at me."

He was now at the window staring outside. He didn't turn around. I got off the bed and went to him. I slid my hand up his back. He was so tense. He felt like a slab of concrete. Reaching up to his shoulders, I kneaded them. There was barely any give, but he groaned. Gradually, the tension eased. Finally, he swung around to face me.

"My beautiful Serenity. You have no idea what doing something like this might do to me, do you? You still don't get it," he said hoarsely.

"What don't I get, my love?"

"What would happen if anything were to happen to you? If they were to get their hands on you and harm you in any way, a monster would be unleashed. Blood would be shed, and more than the bosses, plus those who touched you, would be slaughtered."

"Victor, I don't believe your friends and brothers would get that out of control."

"I'm not talking about them. I mean me. I told you when Amy was murdered, I searched for the men responsible for months. I had no idea who did it. It wasn't until Brooklyn talked after six long months that we found out who was responsible. With the help of my club, I hunted them down. My brothers got their hands dirty, but nothing like I did. I was covered in blood, figuratively and literally. I made every one of those motherfuckers bleed and suffer, but nothing like what I did to Piranha. I made him suffer and linger for days. There's a reason I'm called Diablo. The devil has nothing on me when it comes to serving justice and getting vengeance. It's my dad in me. I love you more than I care for myself, and as bad as it sounds, more than my brothers' lives.

"I went crazy and into an extreme protective mode after her death. I think with you, it would be worse. You've suffered so much. I wouldn't be able to let you out of my sight. I'd have to live with you not only hating me for allowing you to be taken and hurt but for smothering you afterward if you'd even stay with me. I'd lose my mind without you. I've got a second chance, and I can't risk losing you," he said gutturally.

Emotions flooded me. His love was stark and harsh but so real at the same time. He would no doubt kill and die for me. What he didn't know was I would do the same for him.

"And I can't lose you, either. I would do anything to make sure you're safe. too. I understand having to get them all at once. It's far safer. If we work together, I'll be much safer than if we're at odds. I don't want to go against you. However, I need to live. Please, baby, help me do this so we can be together, free of threats, and get on with the rest of our lives." As I finished saying it, I circled to the front of him and tugged his head down so I was able to take his mouth in a heated kiss.

Instantly, I went up in flames. Desire rushed through me. He groaned, then hands were underneath my ass, lifting me up. I wrapped my legs around his waist and my arms around his neck. He held my ass in both hands as he walked to the bed. I was laid down carefully. It barely registered that he shoved all my clothes onto the floor. He came down on top of me and resumed our kiss.

As much as I loved kissing him and the drugged sensation it gave me, I needed more. I pushed on his chest. He reluctantly lifted up. He gave me a concerned look. "What's wrong, Serenity?"

"Nothing is wrong. We need to finish this conversation and make a plan, but I can't think about that right now. I need you, Victor. I want you to show me more of you."

"More of me?"

"Yes. You spoke of things you'd like to do to and with me. Show me. Spank me, tie me up, show me what fun toys can be, play with my ass. I don't care. Just let me know all of you. Your darkness is part of you. Don't hide it. I want the whole Victor slash Diablo, not pieces."

"Jesus Christ, Jauhnna. You can't say shit like that," he muttered.

"Yes, I can. Show me!" I demanded.

"What if I do and I scare you!?" he partially shouted back.

"As long as it's you, I know I'm safe even if I'm scared. Claim me fully, my love. Help me banish the demons that haunt me."

He studied me for a good minute or more before I saw the surrender in his gaze. A huge thrill went through me. I was apprehensive and excited all rolled into one. His hand came to the front of my tank. The next thing I knew I felt tugging and then heard a tearing sound. He tore it down the front as if it was made of tissue paper. My heart leaped. He was staring into my eyes.

Next, he rose up and lifted me enough to be able to remove the ruined tank. I thought he'd throw it on the floor. Wrong. He held onto it and laid me back down. As soon as my back hit the mattress, my wrists were captured in his hands. They were tugged above my head, and then the torn tank was wrapped around them a few times before it was knotted around one of the metal slats that made up the headboard.

"Is that too tight?" he asked.

I jerked on it. It was snug but not too tight. I was able to wiggle and feel my fingers. I shook my head. Being restrained was a little alarming for me. Galway had done it more than a few times when he wanted to punish me. My breathing kicked up a notch, recalling it. Maybe this wasn't such a good idea. Panic was beginning to filter in when he grabbed my attention.

"Jauhnna, look at me," he ordered. I did.

He smiled. "You're safe. It's me. I'll never hurt you. We're exploring, remember? If it becomes too much, tell me. If I can't help you past it, we'll stop," he promised. His tone and the loving way he looked at me calmed me down.

I smiled back and nodded as I said, "Alright."

I hadn't bothered to put on a bra when I got dressed this morning. My bare breasts were in full view and begging him to touch them if the hard nubs were any indication. He didn't ignore them. His hands massaged and teased them, then he lowered his head and sucked my left nipple into his hot mouth. He licked and sucked on it intensely while the other was teased and tweaked by his hand. The jolts of electricity he was creating in them traveled straight to my clit, making it throb and my pussy weep. I moaned and rubbed my thighs together, trying to get some relief from the terrible aching he was already creating.

I floated in the haze of hunger he created. I had no idea how long he loved on my breasts before he left them to kiss, lick, and bite his way down my body to the waist of my shorts. When he reached them, he sat up. His hands impatiently undid the snap and lowered my zipper before tugging them down to my ankles and then off. His hands came back up to land on my panties.

I lifted my ass to help him get them off, only he didn't lower them. Instead, he yanked on both sides until the seams parted. He flung the ruined panties on the floor to join my shorts. I moaned. I found it incredibly sexy the way he was undressing me. Like I was at his mercy, and he was a wild beast ready to consume me.

I shivered as another moan of desire escaped me. He smirked. "Is my baby liking this? Is that little pussy all wet and tingly? I should see," he said a second before he yanked my thighs apart and exposed my pussy to his gaze. I knew what he saw. I was dripping wet. It would take very little to make me come.

He licked his lips before moving to lie on his belly between my legs. He was at eye level with my pussy. He inhaled like he did every time he was near it. A rumble of appreciation rolled out of his chest. He ran a finger from my clit through my folds to my entrance, where it paused before thrusting inside of me. I cried out, and my ass came off the bed. Or it tried to, but he held me in place.

He released a growl, then fell on me and began to lap at me. He was consuming my cum as he licked, then nibbled and sucked on my clit and my pussy lips. He'd bite gently and tug on them while his finger thrust in and out of me, simulating a cock. I was climbing toward an orgasm as soon as he started. He wasn't gentle with his thrusts, and he worked in more fingers as he went until I was stretched wide and burning to come.

I was so into the quest to orgasm it took a second or two for it to register that something wet was running over and over the opening to my ass. I tensed and then tried to relax. I'd told him I wanted to know.

When I didn't say anything, I guess he took it as consent because the next thing I knew, as he sucked hard on my clit and thrusted in and out of my aching pussy, that wet fingertip of his pushed the ever slightest inside my ass.

It burned, but I knew it would. I'd had fingers roughly shoved into my ass before without lube, and this was nothing like that. The one thing I hadn't had to bear was anyone actually putting their cock in there. Why, I had no idea unless they didn't like the idea. As mean and hateful as Galway was, he kinda was a prude, I now thought. *Forget him! This is you and Victor. Enjoy,* I scolded myself. I shoved thoughts of that bastard and the others behind a closed door in my mind.

I jumped as his tongue flicked around the finger in my ass, giving him more lubrication. He pushed it further inside. "How does this feel, babe? Do you like it? Want me to stop?"

"It's, oh God, it burns, but I don't want you to stop. Victor, please. I need more," I whined. My body was vibrating with the need to come and to do it hard.

He sped up his thrusts and sucked on my clit harder. I was just about there when he eased a second finger into my ass. That did it. I let out a scream and came hard and long. As I did, he kept up the fast pace of his thrusting along with the sucking and licking he was doing, interspersed with the occasional bite. I fought to get my hands loose, but I couldn't.

When I was almost done orgasming, he abruptly

sat up and removed his fingers. I moaned in denial. Then I understood why. He was practically growling. He stood and tore off his shirt, followed by his jeans, underwear, and socks. He must've taken off his cut and boots when he came inside downstairs.

I admired his naked glory as he stood by the bed, watching me as he aggressively stroked his cock, which was dark red, the head covered in precum, and the veins running the length were more than evident. He only did it a few strokes, then he was on the bed, straddling my chest. His cock was pressed against my lips.

"Suck it. I want you to take me as deep as you can. Choke on it," he gritted out.

His words should've terrified me, but they made me hotter. I wanted to please him and make him lose his mind the way he made me. Teasing him, I flicked out my tongue to swipe across the head, then back in. My mouth remained closed. He growled and pressed harder. His hand slid under my head to grip my hair, and then he gently shook it.

"I said suck it. Taste that precum. It's all for you. Suck me good, and I'll fuck your pussy until you scream and come so goddamn hard," he promised.

That promise had me opening wide to take him. He pushed in aggressively. I fought to take his length. He moaned, then began to thrust in and out, going deeper every few strokes. Without my hands, plus being on the bottom, I was at his mercy. He could literally choke me to death with his big cock. I fought to lick and suck him as hard as I could.

His groans and growls grew louder and more frequent. "Fuck, baby, you don't know what it does to me to see you taking my cock like this. So beautiful. So hot. One of these days, if you let me, I'm going to fuck this pretty mouth, fill it with cum, then I'll fuck your pussy until we both come before I finish up by taking your ass and filling it up too. God," he groaned. I swore I felt his cock swell. I was prepared to swallow down his cum, but somehow he held back.

He withdrew. He was breathing raggedly. I spread my legs. "Give me that big cock in my pussy, baby. Fuck me, nice and hard. And one day, soon, I'll let you have that fantasy you just told me," I offered wildly. I was desperate to come and have him inside of me when I did.

I jumped as he let out what sounded like a howl, and then he was on me. He ripped the knots, holding my hands above my head undone. He threw the ruined tank away, then had himself on his back with me straddling him but facing his toes.

"Lift up," he demanded.

I did it. When I felt the head of his cock pressing against my opening, I moaned. I was about to start lowering myself down on it when his hands grabbed my hips. He yanked me down. He filled me in that one hard thrust. I wailed and shook. It was like a restraint gave, and I went crazy. Gripping his legs to give me leverage, I lifted up and slammed back down. I rode his cock frantically. He swore.

As I worked both of us toward a spectacular orgasm, I froze for a moment when a wet digit probed my ass then slid in. I thought it felt good before. But as I slid up and down his cock, I was now doing the same on his finger. He pushed in another. I knew what it must feel like to have two cocks inside of me at once. It was so damn incredible. The sensations coursing through me were too much. I came whimpering and sobbing. He grunted, but to my shock, he didn't come. He kept pounding away. As he did, he muttered.

"That's it. Squeeze my cock. Flood me with all that cream of yours. Christ, your pussy and ass are so fucking tight. I'm gonna blow soon. The thought of someday taking your ass is so hot. Jesus Christ! Fucking ride me harder!" he yelled.

As spent as I was, I wanted him to come like he had never come before. I found the strength to ride him harder and faster, working my inner muscles to squeeze his cock and fingers. It lasted maybe a couple of minutes, and then he bowed his hips off the bed, buried himself to the hilt, and bellowed. His warm cum bathed my insides. It swirled into a huge ball of desire coursing throughout my whole body. I came with him. I swear even my toes came. When I was done, I collapsed on his legs. I was feeling faint and shaky. As I lay there, his hands rubbed soothingly up and down my lower back and over my ass.

"Jauhnna, that was unbelievable. Thank you for trusting me."

"Victor, I'll always trust you, and yes, it was unbelievable. You may have just created a monster. I hope you're prepared," I warned him as I nipped his leg with my teeth. He laughed, which made me moan since he was still inside of me. I lay there dreaming of the future and this man until I was able to move.

Diablo: Chapter 17

I still wasn't thrilled with Jauhnna's idea to use herself as bait, but she wasn't wrong and the Patriots had already gently brought it up, and then I shot it down. However, I now had to broach the topic again. My gut clenched at the thought. I hadn't lied to her when I told her it would release a monster if anything were to happen to her.

It was Friday, not our usual day to hold church, but we couldn't wait until Monday to do it. Everyone wanted to get this over with, although none as much as she and I did. We had Undertaker, Sean, Griffin, and Gabe on the speakerphone in the middle of the conference table in church. My guys were gathered around it. Tension was rising as we listened to the Patriots go through their plans. I didn't have any real issues with them, except for the last piece they shared.

"Mind saying that again?" I asked.

"Yeah. It seems that Vierra and Radigan have gotten on the wrong side of the O'Sheeran family. You know them. They're right there in St. Augustine with you guys. Have you had any interactions or problems with them?" Undertaker asked.

"Yes, they're here. No, we have not. What do you mean they're on the wrong side of them?" I asked.

"Apparently, those two families have been trying to run their illegal businesses in the O'Sheeran's territories. Florida is one of them, and they've gotten wind of the human trafficking they've been involved in. The head of the O'Sheeran family, Patrick, and his brothers, Sean and Cormac, don't hold to that shit. Not even back in the day when they were less respectable. They have some morals, and not hurting innocent people is one of them. Hell, they never dealt in prostitution back in the day.

"They had their suspicion it's been happening, but after Maverick's Rylan said something to Donal O'Sheeran, a lawyer friend of hers, about finding a woman that we think was to be sold, they put all their focus on discovering their whole operation. Radigan and Vierra haven't only been dealing with human trafficking, either. The O'Sheerans helped us find it all," Sean added cheerfully.

"Are you sure getting in bed with the Irish Mafia is the thing to do? I know the rumor is they're legal these days, but are they? What will they expect from you and my club for accepting their help?" I asked. I'd worked hard not to get on their radar.

"Nothing. Bull verified that when they helped with Rylan's problem, they asked nothing in return. They've had no issues with them. It's been two years since that all went down. Everything we have found and we've dug up, believe me, indicates they're a Mafia family with a conscience. Smoke and Everly got involved with the research into them, too. Patrick offered to help, and we're confident they won't ask for anything we wouldn't be willing to give if they ask for anything at all," Griffin added.

"But is there really such a thing as good Mafia?" Scorpion asked.

A throat was cleared on the other end. "They're not all bad. Everything I heard growing up and since I've been an adult indicates the O'Sheerans stick to their word. As long as you don't fuck with them, they won't fuck with you," Gabe added.

Hearing this come from him did add weight to it. We'd known the Patriots for three years. A little over a year ago, while undercover on an assignment, those of us who were friends with Gabe discovered he grew up under a different name. Imagine our shock to find out his family was a hardcore Italian Mafia family. He hadn't wanted that life, although he had been thoroughly trained in it, so he was given a way out. His assurance settled more of my anxiety.

"If you're all confident in their word, then we'll take a vote. How many of you believe we should allow the O'Sheerans to assist in eliminating Radigan and Vierra along with their key people and businesses?" I asked those around the table.

This would be a club vote. The majority would determine our course. Gabe and the other Dark Patriots remained quiet as I went around the table. In the end, to my surprise, all of my guys voted to work with the Mafia.

"Alright, you heard them. Were you clear with them that the actual torture and killing of the eight names I gave you rests with me and my men? There's no negotiating on that. They will die by our hands and no one else's," I reiterated.

"We were, and Patrick, Cormac, and Sean had no objections. We explained you had a personal score to settle. As long as these two families are removed as annoyances in their territories, they don't care. They offered the use of one of their ships. They suggested it might be better to carry out the actual hands-on lessons and the subsequent disposal at sea in International Waters," Sean chimed in.

It would help make sure nothing came back on us, hopefully. The ocean was vast. The odds of them being found would be damn slim to none. My brothers were all nodding and murmuring in agreement.

"Okay, that sounds good to us. If that's all, then there's another item I want to discuss. We know everything is on hold due to trying to figure out how to get all the main ones in one fell swoop so they don't run and hide. You suggested we use Jauhnna to bring them out in the open together." I paused.

"We did, and we know why that's not something you're willing to do, Diablo. We get it. Believe us, we understand. We think we're close to finding a different way," Griffin assured me.

"Well, there's been some reconsideration of your suggestion," I told them around the lump in my throat. Astonishment spread over every single one of my brothers' faces. They muttered under their breaths. I held up a hand to quiet them.

"Diablo, are you sure?" Undertaker asked cautiously.

"Hell no, I'm not, but it seems my woman thinks it's the way to go. She's tired of living caged. And since she decided to apply for jobs without telling anyone, there's a slim chance they might find her if they're smart and have a Micro. Jauhnna suggested he could find a way to leak her location on the internet in a way that wouldn't make them suspicious. They would believe they had the upper hand and the element of surprise. In reality, we'd be waiting for them. She thinks the eight of them will want to be present for her capture and return."

"Wow, I wasn't expecting that. Okay. Umm, question, why would all of them want to be there? I mean, I understand her husband and brother, but those other six are merely bodyguards and their enforcers, from what we understand," Sean asked.

I hadn't shared the exact details of what happened to her with any of the Patriots. They knew what Radigan had done to her, but not the rest. She'd given me permission to share it if it was needed to end this whole affair. My brothers were watching me closely.

"Radigan wasn't the only one to abuse her during those nine years. Later, after he discovered the reason she never conceived was due to her not being able to have children, he continued to try to get her pregnant. When she didn't, he came up with a new way to punish her when he was feeling especially ugly and hateful. He not only beat and raped her, but he allowed those men to do it as well. They're all gonna die, and I'll be the one to end every single one of those motherfuckers," I snarled.

I heard swearing from the other end of the line. There was what sounded like a loud crash. There were muttered conversations and more swearing. It went on for a good couple of minutes before anyone actually said anything intelligible. It came from Gabe.

"Sorry for that. Undertaker had to take a break. Fuck, we're sorry, Diablo. We had no idea. We don't blame you for wanting to be the one to take those motherfuckers out. We'll do everything we can to make sure it happens. Have you had her talk to someone?

You know, another woman who has experienced it or a counselor?"

"I haven't, but it's not a bad idea. I'll suggest it to her. She's a strong-ass woman. Most would've buckled long before she escaped," I said.

"I don't know if you know anyone, but I've heard the woman, Jade, who helped Aria in Hunters Creek, is great. And you know Aria, Rylan, and a few others in the clubs have histories similar to hers. I bet they wouldn't mind talking to her," Sean added.

"I think so too. She hasn't gotten to meet any of them yet, but once this is over, I plan to take her to visit Brooklyn and the others. I'll see what I can arrange."

They dropped the subject after that. The remainder of the call was spent determining when to set the trap. It was decided we'd wait and do it the following weekend. It would give everyone involved time to be ready. With it being a weekend, no one would notice if we weren't at our various businesses since we tended not to work on Saturday and Sunday if at all possible. We could put out this coming week that we planned to go on a ride over the weekend and would be gone both days. Finishing up and saying our goodbyes took a matter of a couple of minutes, and then we were done. Now it was time to tell my woman that by the end of next week, she would be free.

As soon as we hung up, I dismissed my brothers. I was standing up when Wolverine came over to me. Since I staked a claim to Jauhnna, he'd avoided me. I didn't really blame him, so it surprised me that he approached me.

"Can I help you?" I asked. I wasn't in the mood to spar with him if that was what he wanted to do. She was mine. It wasn't up for debate. For God's sake, she had my name on her fucking back, and she lived with me.

"I want to apologize for how I acted after Jauhnna came. I was a jerk. I won't lie. I did kinda hope there was a chance she'd be the one for me. She's a beautiful woman, and her strength and vulnerability attract me. I guess I now know I have a type if you want to call it that. Anyway, I wanted you to know I won't be acting like an asshole anymore, nor do you have to worry I'm lusting after your woman. She's moved into the hot sister category," he said the last part with a slight grin.

I hauled off and punched him in the arm. I didn't do it as hard as I could've, but it would hurt. I accepted his apology, but it would be a reminder that I wouldn't hold back if he didn't keep his word.

"Fucker, you'd better put her in the ugly sister category and forget she's a woman, period," I growled.

"Hey, I'm not blind or totally brain dead." he paused and then got serious. "I'm so damn sorry she suffered all that. If she wants to talk to someone local–a professional, I have contacts I can ask to get her the best. Just let me know."

This time, I gave his shoulder a friendly squeeze. We were moving toward the door and the common room. Everyone else had already left. "Thanks. I'll let you know. Right now, we have to get this over with so she can truly live."

"Sure thing. I think someone is anxious to speak to you," he said as he gestured to the right of us.

Glancing over, I saw she was standing there, twisting her hands and looking anxious. Giving him a nod, I left him and went to her. I knew what she needed. I enveloped her in a hug as I gave her a tender kiss.

Tension lessened in her body. I felt it. When I let go of that luscious mouth of hers, she started questioning me.

"What did they say? Is everything in place? Will they do it? Am I helping?"

"Whoa, slow down. Let's have a seat, and then I'll tell you. I could use a drink. How about you?" I guided her toward the bar.

Liam was behind it dispensing drinks to the brothers. It was standard for one of the prospects to man it after church. We didn't have enough of them to have someone there all the time. They had too many other duties to perform for it to be feasible. Besides, it didn't hurt anyone to get their own drinks. Making the prospects wait on us was more of our initiation ritual than anything. We gave them the dirty and boring, sometimes disgusting jobs to see what they were made of. If they complained, balked, or outright refused, they weren't worth spending time on to determine if they had the more important characteristics we wanted in brothers.

"What can I get you, Pres, Jauhnna?" Liam asked with a smile.

"I'll have a shot of my whiskey. Baby, what do you want?" I asked.

"I'll take the same and a Coke, please."

I was taken aback by her order. I hadn't seen her drink alcohol since I met her. As he got them, I softly whispered to her, "Are you alright? You don't usually drink."

"I like wine and drink it sometimes. As for the whiskey, it seemed like one of those occasions to me. Don't worry, I'm not a secret lush," she teased.

"I'm not afraid you are. I hate to think this is driving you to drink."

"It won't. Believe me, if it could, I would've been an alcoholic years ago to escape my hell."

The truth of her claim had me dropping a kiss on her temple. I was interrupted from saying more by Liam bringing us our drinks. I gave him a chin lift. Jauhnna gave him a blinding smile and a sweet, "Thank you, Liam."

He turned pink and stuttered, "Y-you're welcome. Let me know if you need anything else."

I made sure to give him a warning glare just for the hell of it before steering her to an empty table. After seating her, I sat next to her. I picked up my whiskey and held it up in the air. She copied me. "Here's to getting your life back, Serenity. It's almost done." I toasted before I shot it in one swallow. I was stunned when she did the same and didn't even sputter. Most women didn't like whiskey or shoot it.

"I see this isn't your first shot. You said you like wine. Tell me what to get. I'll have the prospects make sure there's some at the bar and at home. I'm not much of a wine drinker, but you and guests, especially other ladies, might want it."

"I'd like that. I'll write the names and types down at home. Okay, hit me with it. What did they say? What's the plan?" she asked in a nervous tone.

"They agreed with your idea. I still hate it, but we voted, and it's a go. We're having Micro leak the information you're here, but we've decided to move the fight away from the compound. When he leaks it, he'll also let it be known you are going on a ride with the club next weekend. It'll be too tempting for them to pass up, to catch you outside the fence. Plus, don't you think they want to get their hands on the men who've been helping hide you? They'll underestimate us. We'll lead them to where we want them. When they strike, the Dark Patriots and others will be there to help us end this."

"End it how? What others? God, please tell me you can do this without getting caught. Away from here, the chance someone will see or hear something they shouldn't increase."

She wasn't wrong, but Undertaker and the others assured us they'd have it covered.

"Darlin', we've got this."

"I need something," she said firmly.

"Anything."

"I know you. You plan to tuck me away somewhere safe once they make a move. I love you for it, but I have to be there when you end them. I have to watch them pay for everything they did to me. I want to watch them suffer," she said fiercely.

I wasn't expecting that. The protective man in me said fuck no. The man who wanted to give her anything and everything she wanted and needed said to give it to her. She needed it to heal. I groaned.

"Jauhnna, baby, you don't know what you're asking. I don't want you anywhere near them or to have those images seared into your brain. They won't die easy. And I don't want you to see me as Diablo. If you ended up fearing me, it would kill me. Ask me for something else."

The plan was to let her be seen so she could be identified, then make a switch out and have an operative of the Patriots take her place. I wasn't thrilled to have another woman on the back of my bike, but it was extenuating circumstances. When the switch occurred, Jauhnna would be whisked away to safety and kept there until I came for her. I quickly explained it to her, hoping it would change her mind. When I was done, she was shaking her head.

"I can't. Please. You have no idea how I've dreamed of this day and thought it would never come. I have to face them, or they'll haunt me for the rest of my life, I'm afraid."

I let out a growl. After hearing her say that, I knew I had no choice. "Alright, we'll change the plan, but you will stick to me or the brothers like glue. You will do what we say, no matter what it is. No arguing or hesitating. This is dangerous. We're used to working together, but you're not. Don't make me regret this. If it looks like it's going south, I will pull you out, and the hell with them. I'll find a way to get them later," I warned her.

"I'll do exactly what you say when you say it."

Not wasting time, I yelled out, "Huddle," as loud as I could to be heard over the chatter. My brothers immediately came to attention and converged on our table. They were staring intently at me.

"There's been an adjustment to the plans for next weekend."

"What?" Scorpion asked.

"Instead of an operative taking Jauhnna's place once we hook them, she'll remain with me."

"Is that wise?" Butcher asked. He cast her a concerned look. He, more than anyone, knew what I was like when I let my inner beast loose. He'd been with me over most of those bloody years.

"She needs this in order to heal. She's aware," I told him.

He was quiet along with the others for several tense moments, and then he nodded. "Okay. We'll adjust. We'll have to notify the Patriots tonight. Jauhnna, I know he told you this already, but you must do everything we say exactly and immediately. We all want to come out of this alive," he warned.

"He did, and I will. Thank you. I hate to do this to all of you, but I can't stay behind. You said you were going to do it somewhere else, and you had others, besides the Patriots, helping. Who?"

Typically, this wouldn't be shared with an old lady or family members since it was considered club business, but she was fully in the middle of it. She knew we were going to kill them. What could it hurt? I addressed Butcher's remark about telling the Patriots first.

"I'll call Sean tonight and explain. As for your questions, there has been a development. Someone who isn't happy with your brother and Radigan running their illegal shit through their territories has offered to assist. They especially hate human trafficking, which we now know was your fate after he got you back." I stopped. I hadn't shared this with her. She caught onto my slip.

"How do you know they were going to sell me?"

Micro was the one to answer. "I found it when I was doing my research. If you know how to find them on the dark web, there are sites where you can buy or sell anything, including people. I got the wild idea to set up a program to continually scan for mentions of women being sought who matched your description.

You know, height, hair, eyes, body type, that sort of thing. Anyway, it paid off. I got an alert one day. When I backtraced it through what they thought was an encrypted, secure IP, it led me to Radigan. He had every intention to sell you, Jauhnna. I'm sorry."

She sighed. "I'm not surprised. There's nothing that bastard won't do if it serves him. Why didn't you tell me?" She directed this question at me.

"Because you had enough worries without knowing for sure what his intention was. It was need-to-know."

"You and I need to talk about need-to-know, honey. Alright, so he wants to sell me. Who are the ones who are opposed to it?"

"You lived in Vegas, so I know you're familiar with the Mafia in some form or another." She nodded. I continued. "There are Mafia families all over the US. We have one here in Florida. In fact, they're home-based here in St. Augustine, of all places. It's them who want nothing to do with this happening. They're Irish, and though they're still seen as Mafia, they're supposedly legitimate these days. They offered to help us clean up both men and their businesses."

Her face was screwed up in what appeared to be concentration. "You said they're Irish. Are you talking about the O'Sheerans?"

"How do you know that? Do you know them?" I asked. I saw the rest of the club, and they were just as surprised as I was.

"I know of them, but I never met any of them. Galway talked about them a few times. He was disgusted that they had everything they could ever want, yet they threw it away to become law-abiding citizens. He envied their power, wealth, and businesses. He said they were ideally located to do so many things. He and Janus would rant about them from time to time. I tried to ignore them when they did, but the name stuck."

"Yes, it's the O'Sheerans. Everything the Patriots and others have found indicates they're out of the life. They helped out someone in one of our allied clubs. They're offering us the use of a ship. Everything will be carried out in International Waters."

"And that means no one has jurisdiction. Plus, the likelihood of finding them is almost nil. Can we trust them? Will they want something in return? If they do, is it something you're willing to do?"

Her questions made me realize she knew more about the seedy side of business than she let on. It made me wonder what else she knew about Radigan and Vierra's businesses. "Babe, I should've asked this from the beginning, but what do you know about what Radigan and your brother are involved in?"

"I know enough that if you give me the details you have, I can tell you if you missed anything. I've heard names and can possibly help you find connections you need to be sure to take out. Dismantling their little kingdoms won't be done in a day. It'll take time, even after you cut off the heads of the snakes. I can help you make sure you get all the little snakes."

There was satisfaction written all over her face. Micro groaned and smacked his forehead with his palm. "Christ, we're idiots. Why the hell didn't we think to ask her? We have a fountain of knowledge right here, and we totally overlooked her. I'm so stupid," he muttered.

"If you are, then you're in good company because the rest of us didn't think of it either. Goddamn, wait until we tell the Patriots. They'll laugh their asses off telling the others about it," Scorpion grumbled.

"I'm sorry. I didn't think to tell you," she apologized.

"Honey, you had other shit on your mind. Recovering, staying hidden, falling for this big, ugly bastard. We forgive you," Cowboy assured her with a grin.

"I'd watch who you're calling ugly, fuckhead," I shot back.

Just like that, tension eased, and we were laughing. Rather than continuing the discussion about our plans, I decided to let it be for tonight and just be immersed in our family. We had time to adjust the plan and share what we knew. It was looking like a busy week ahead, but I was looking forward to the conclusion. I could almost feel their throats in my hands and me squeezing the life out of them.

Jauhnna: Chapter 18

The weekend passed slower than I would've liked. I usually loved them since Diablo would be home with me for two entire days. This time, I was wishing the hours away despite enjoying every moment with him and the club. Part of it was spent preparing me for what was to come and going over the plan in detail.

Diablo called the Dark Patriots and explained the change. I wasn't part of the call, but when he was done, he told me it was a go. It was now Monday. The guys were working at the various businesses and spreading the tale about how we were going on a weekend-long ride. At least I had something to keep me busy other than to spend time with the horses and cleaning. I got the information compiled by Micro about Janus and Galway. I was reviewing it and making notes of people and things he missed. I wanted nothing to remain of their horrible kingdoms when we were done.

Just as I finished reading and taking notes, my cell phone rang. It startled me, and I wasn't expecting it. Picking it up off the table, I saw an unknown number. I cautiously answered it. "Hello?"

"Hello, may I speak to Jauhnna Carter?" a woman's voice asked briskly. She sounded all business.

"Speaking. How may I help you?"

"Ms. Carter, my name is Gail Kerr from Furever Caring. We got your message last week that you were unable to make your interview."

"Yes, I'm so sorry. I was looking forward to it, but a family emergency came up." I hated to cancel it, knowing they'd hire someone else, but I couldn't do it with this takedown deal happening. Diablo made me see that. I used the excuse of a family emergency because it was all I could think of.

"We understand, and I'm calling to see if we can reschedule it. Has your emergency been resolved?"

"It hasn't, but it should be back to normal after this weekend."

"Good. Would you then be willing to come in the following Wednesday and interview with us?"

I wanted to squeal with delight. There was still a chance. This was the place that I wanted to work at the most. The things they did for animals were similar to what I wanted to do for them.

"Really? I thought for sure I missed my opportunity, but yes, I'd love to interview. Thank you. What time should I be there?"

"Please be here at ten a.m. You'll be meeting with Mr. Tuckerman. He's the founder of our organization. Please make sure to bring your references. We're looking forward to meeting you next week. Have a good day."

"Thank you, Ms. Kerr. I'm looking forward to it too. Have a good week," I rushed to say before she hung up.

I jumped to my feet and did a happy dance. A chuckle had me whirling around and gasping. There stood Micro grinning.

"You scared me to death!"

"Sorry. I knocked, and you told me to come back

at eleven. It's eleven. What's got you so excited? No, wait, don't tell me if you just got done having phone sex with Diablo. I don't need to know that." He pretended to gag.

Grabbing a scrunched-up piece of paper I had on the table, I threw it at him. Of course, he was coordinated, something I wasn't. He caught it and chucked it back, smacking me in the middle of my chest.

"Do you have siblings?" I asked him, picking it up off the floor where it landed.

"I do. A brother and a sister, why?"

"Because you have that annoying kid brother vibe down pat," I teased.

He laughed. "I'm the middle child. My sister is the baby."

"That explains it even better. And no, it wasn't me having phone sex with Diablo. It was from that place I was to interview with last week, Furever Caring. They still want to interview me next week. I said yes. This better be over by then. I need to be able to contribute to society again."

"It will be. Think positive. Did you get a chance to look over that stuff, or do you need more time?"

"I think I got most of it, at least the crucial stuff. I made notes. If I think of anything else, I'll let you know," I told him as I handed over the papers. He skimmed them and whistled.

"Damn, you did remember a lot. This is great. Thanks. I'm gonna get out of your hair so you can go back to dancing." he smarted off, then chuckled as he hurried away.

It was a letdown to have him leave. I didn't have anything to do. I wandered the house for half an hour, searching for something to occupy myself with. Nothing. I knew I could visit the horses, but it wouldn't keep me busy until the end of the day. Finally, I settled on reading. I got my e-book reader and scanned the selection to see if any of my favorite authors had released a new one. I was excited when I noticed there was one. Downloading it, I curled up in the sunroom in my favorite chair and got to reading. She was one of those steamy romance authors.

I was lost in the intrigue and hot sex happening between the main characters when a hand slipping over my shoulder and down underneath the front of my top to grasp my breast made me jump, but I knew that touch. Expert fingers teased my nipple as a mouth nibbled and sucked on my neck. I moaned and closed my eyes.

"Oh, Gregory, that feels so good. More," I whispered. I knew I was asking for it, but the book had me hot and bothered, and I wanted my man to go all caveman on me. A deep growl came out of him, making me shiver.

"Who the fuck is Gregory?" he snarled in my ear.

"Oh, it's you, Victor. I'm sorry. I was so caught up in what Gregory was doing in my book that I thought it was him," I teased.

In the next instant, my reader was torn from my hand and tossed on the couch, and then I was scooped up out of my chair. I giggled and peeked up at him through my lashes. He was giving me a scowl, but instead of scaring me, it made me hotter.

"You think ole Gregory is hot, do you? Well, let's see if you still think that when I'm done with you. Get your shoes, and cut on, then get your ass out to the garage. I'll be there in a minute."

He gave me a hot kiss before setting me back on my feet and slapping my ass. I raced to get my shoes and cut on and out there. I was dying to know what he had in store. I didn't have to wait long. When he came out, he went straight to his bike and started it. He gestured for me to get on behind him.

"What about helmets and stuff?" I asked.

"We don't need them. We're not leaving the compound. Get on."

I swung up behind him, wrapping my arms around him. He revved the engine, and then we were off. He rode down the main road that ran from the gate, past the clubhouse and the houses, back toward what I assumed was the rear of the property. I'd explored some, but all that was back there was open ground and trees as far as I could see, so I hadn't gone all the way. He stayed on the road for a few miles before he abruptly turned onto a dirt path leading into a bunch of trees. In the center of them, when we got there, I saw there was what I would call a rundown shack or cabin. He stopped and shut off his bike. I hopped off. I had no idea what we were doing here, but I was excited to find out.

"Victor, what is this place? Why did you bring me here?"

"How adventurous are you feeling, Jauhnna? How much do you trust me?" he asked gruffly.

My pulse sped up, and my body went wild at those words. It was his tone and the way he was watching me as he said it that did it. It was as if I was prey and he was the predator. When Galway made me feel that way, I'd been terrified. Diablo only made me eager for more. I trusted him completely, which was insane after such a short period of time, but it was true.

"I trust you with my life. I'm willing to try whatever you want, Victor."

A slight smirk twisted his lips before he hit me with a bomb. "Then, if you trust me, you'll strip naked. I want you to stand there and let me inspect you. You're not to move after you get undressed, and you're not to say a word unless I say you can. Understand?"

I gulped as I nodded yes.

"I need words right now. You can speak."

"Y-yes, I understand."

"Good, strip," he ordered.

With shaking hands and legs, I peeled off my property cut. I didn't know what he wanted me to do with my clothes. I glanced around for somewhere to put them.

"Put your clothes on the railing. Make sure your cut doesn't touch the ground," he told me.

I moved to the rail he was indicating on the porch to the cabin. I carefully placed it so I was sure it wouldn't slip off. Once it was safe, I worked on the rest of my clothing. He leaned against his bike and watched me without saying a word. It was nerve-racking. Next, I took off my shoes, top, and then my pants. This left me in my bra and panties. It felt weird to be exposed outside where anyone could possibly come along and see me, even if it was unlikely back here. Why would anyone have a reason to be this far out? I paused to gather my courage.

"You're not done. Take off the rest. Then, I want you to walk to the railing, turn your back to me, and bend forward with your hands on the rail. Eyes on the ground," he ordered.

What was he planning to do? I trembled as I removed them, leaving myself exposed completely to him. I went to the railing and assumed the position. My heart was beating like crazy.

I heard rustling sounds next. It was so hard not to turn to see what he was doing, but I didn't. I was determined to do whatever he told me. The sounds went on for a couple of minutes before they got silent—well, all except for the sounds of nature surrounding us.

I jumped when a hand landed on my back. A soft growl of displeasure caused me to freeze. His hot, rough hand ran down my back to my ass cheek. He squeezed it once before moving to do the same to the other. His other hand joined the one on my ass. They began to skim down my legs slowly until they reached my ankles. They gripped them, and then they were being tugged on. I automatically spread my legs. He hummed in approval.

"Mmm, look at that. All this soft skin and a dripping wet pussy. I like this. I wonder what else she can do. I've always wondered what it would be like to have a sex doll. One that I can do anything I want to. One I can touch anywhere. Taste all over. Play with any way I want. The best part is I can fuck her every way I want, as much as I want," he growled.

Hearing him refer to me as a sex doll should've made me feel cheap and degraded. It didn't. It made me feel sexy and turned me on. I knew my pussy just got wetter. I felt it. A small moan escaped.

"Ah, it seems I have the deluxe model—one who can make sounds. I might just like that. I wonder how many sounds I can get her to make and how loud—maybe loud enough for someone to hear and come to investigate."

A whimper left me. I wasn't sure I wanted anyone to see me, but the thought of it in the hypothetical sense made me shiver. In my books, I'd read about women who got turned on by having people watch them have sex. In some cases, other men would join. I didn't want anyone but Diablo, but in the pretend world, it was sexy to wonder and fantasize about it happening to me.

The whole time I was thinking these things, his hands were rubbing all over my lower body. The one place he avoided, though, was my pussy. He'd get right up to it, then bypass it. I was growing frustrated. I wanted his touch there desperately.

Suddenly, his hands were running up my stomach and then beyond to my breasts. He began kneading them while twisting my nipples. This pulled a moan out of me.

"Hmm, it seems I need to do more to get her to make sounds for me. Ah, I know what'll help."

He was acting as if he was talking to himself. There was more rustling, and then I yelped when my legs were shoved even further apart. His hot mouth was on my pussy. I sighed in relief. I wasn't relieved for long. He was determined to push me to make noise. The aggressive way he was eating my pussy told me that.

I was holding back not because I didn't want to give him what he desired. It was fear of someone hearing us. It made me hot at the same time as it made me nervous. I was fighting not to cry out when, out of nowhere, I felt my entrance probed. Next, something long and hard was pushing inside me. It wasn't his cock, but it kinda felt like one, only not as thick, and it was harder. It barely got inside before it began to buzz. This made me cry out.

He zeroed in on my clit with his mouth at the same time. He was sucking and lashing it with his tongue as the vibrator was worked in and out of my pussy. The combination had me soaked. I was climbing so close to coming in a matter of a minute or two. Whimpers, moans, and sighs were coming out of me despite trying not to make a sound.

A growl vibrated through my clit. At the same time, the vibrator kicked up a notch as my asshole was breached by a finger. I broke and screamed as I came. I orgasmed until my legs were weak, and I thought I might fall. I was trying to stay upright and catch my breath while trying not to pass out. I wasn't given the chance. The next thing I knew, I was being picked up and moved over to the bike. I was then lying front first over the seat with my ass in the air, pointing toward him.

"Yeah, that looks so pretty. I loved those sounds, but I need more. Let's see if I fuck my toy on my bike if she makes more noise. I gotta see if this pussy can squeeze my cock the way I like it," he whispered in my ear.

He hardly got the words out before the vibrator was removed. His cock was sliding into me to take its place. I cried out at the feeling. His cock stretched me so much more than the toy. I was stretched so wide and full. I loved it. I moaned, then gasped as he drew back. He held still, making the anticipation rise before he snapped his hips forward, burying himself balls deep. I cried out.

"That's it. Scream for me, my little fuck toy. I want everyone to hear how good I make you feel. How much you love my cock. I wish you could talk. Just enough to beg and tell me what you want me to do to you. God, that would be so hot," he muttered. The whole time he was talking, he was sliding in and out of me, but he was doing it in a slow glide, not the hard, deep way I wanted it.

I was feeling wild inside. I wanted him to be wild with me. Deciding to see how far I could push him, I let loose. "Oh, oh, yeah, oh, that feels good, but it would feel so much better if..." I stopped short.

"If what? Talk to me, doll. Tell me, what'll make this sweet pussy gush, and you scream? What will make you clench down on my cock like a vice and pull the cum out of me?"

Feeling daring, I told him. "Something in my ass would feel good." I wiggled my ass as much as I could with him inside of me. This earned a groan out of him. I smiled. I liked having his fingers in my ass.

Only he had a surprise for me. He reached into the small bag on the side of his bike. When he pulled out his hand, it had a bottle in it. I recognized the lube. I waited breathlessly to see why he needed it. A minute later, I knew why. It wasn't his finger that slid into my ass. It was the small vibrator he'd used on me minutes ago. I moaned long and loudly at how full it felt with his cock in my pussy and it in my ass. It burned, but he was gently inserting it, so the burn wasn't too much, and it began to ease not long after he got it all the way in.

With it in place, he began to stroke both the vibrator, which he set to low and his cock in and out in sync. When he pulled back his cock, he did the same to the vibrator. Tension was coiling tighter and tighter inside of me. My pussy was soaked, and my cum was running down on my thighs.

"Fuck, you feel so motherfucking good, doll. Can I fuck you harder? Do you want me to really hammer this pussy and your ass and make you come for me? Do you wanna come?" he snarled.

I shoved my ass back to meet his dual thrusts as I cried out, "Yes! Fuck me. Use your little fuck toy and fill it with your cum," I hollered. I was shocked at the things he had me saying, but I didn't care.

He let out a growl then I was being fucked harder. It didn't take but a couple of minutes of him pounding into me for me to detonate and scream. I jerked so hard I shook the bike. I vaguely was waiting to feel him come inside of me, but to my utter astonishment, he didn't. He kept thrusting enough to prolong my orgasm, but not to come. When I finally stopped, I lay limp over the seat of the bike.

I moaned when he removed the vibrator from my ass. He was back to thrusting slow and easy. I jumped when he bit my shoulder. I shivered when he whispered in my ear.

"Do you know what I want, my little fuck toy?"

"W-what?" I asked hoarsely.

"I want to know what that sexy ass feels like clamped around my cock as I fuck it. I want to fill your backdoor full of my cum, then watch it drip out of you."

"Do it then. I'm your little sex toy, aren't I? You can fuck me anywhere you want," I told him boldly. My courage was at a high. I could take anything he had to give me right now.

"Are you sure?" he asked hoarsely.

"Yes, yes, hurry. Fuck me. Fuck my ass!" I moaned. He was ramping me back up. The thought of him doing it was driving me crazy. I was so horny despite just coming. I felt insane.

He groaned, then slipped out. I glanced back and watched him slick up his cock with the lube. I knew I had plenty still inside from the vibrator. He was looking rather feral as he stared at my ass and stroked his cock, which was dark red. When he had it covered, he wiped his hand on his hip.

"Spread those cheeks for me, baby. Let me see that little hole."

I reached back and did it. As I held myself open, he gripped the base of his cock and pressed it to my opening. I fought not to tense up. As he pressed inward, I remembered to breathe. The pain was much worse than with his fingers or the vibrator. I almost told him to stop, but as he got past the two rings of muscles inside, it eased somewhat. I held on and let him work himself in and out. Each thrust took him deeper. As he did, he praised me.

"Oh, look at that. Yeah, you're doing so good, baby. Taking that big cock in your little ass. You feel out of this world. I'm so proud of you. So brave. Oh, fuck," he moaned. When he had me impaled fully on him, he held still and let me get used to the stretch and burn. As it began to ease, I wiggled my ass.

"More," I whispered.

"Don't move. I'm on the edge. I don't want to hurt you."

"It feels too good. I need you to move," I panted as I squeezed down on him.

That was the last straw. He let out a loud roar, and then he was thrusting. He started out easy, but each stroke ramped up just a little harder. Soon he was pounding my ass with abandon. The sensations were mostly intensely pleasurable ones, so any discomfort was forgotten. It wasn't long before I was screaming and then coming. I didn't care who heard me or even if someone was watching. I sobbed and wailed as I kept working his cock to join me. When he froze and bellowed my name, then jerked over and over, coming in my ass, everything went gray and hazy. I slumped boneless on the bike. The next thing I knew, I was in his arms. He was staring down at me in alarm.

"What's wrong?" I croaked. I felt weak and exhausted. My ass was sore, but I'd never felt more sated sexually. I was floating in utter bliss.

"You scared the hell out of me, that's what. You passed out on me. Christ, I need to get you back to the house. I'm sorry I let things go too far. God, tell me you'll forgive me. It won't happen again," he rambled.

"Victor, stop. Look at me. Listen. You did nothing wrong. It wasn't too far. It was amazing. It was just sensory overload, honey. You should be beating your chest, actually." I said with a smile.

"Why the hell would I do that?"

"Because you made your woman come so hard, so good, you made her pass the hell out. You're a stud. Now, if you don't mind, I'd like to stay in this floaty state I'm in for a while longer."

His astonishment turned to relief, then to amusement. He began to laugh. Moments later, he was sitting on his shirt on the ground with me cuddled in his arms. I snuggled up against him, placing kisses all over his chest. I knew a couple of things for sure, he would always be able to satisfy me, and things would never be dull with him.

We sat there and gave each other sweet kisses and talked about the things we'd do once we eliminated my demons. Eventually, we knew we had to make our way back to the house. He stood and helped me get dressed, and then he put on enough of his clothes to ride back. I clung to him, inhaling his scent and running my hands over his bare abs and chest the whole way back. He'd put his shirt in the bags after using it to wipe us clean. We both needed a shower. I was sticky but so satisfied.

As we pulled into the garage, I briefly wondered if anyone saw us return and wondered what we'd been doing. Then I shrugged. Who cared? We were adults, and so were they. I wouldn't hide how much I desired and loved him, and I didn't want him to hide his love and desire for me. My life was finally complete. Or as complete as it could be without children, but that wasn't meant to be, and I had to give up that impossible dream. Diablo, Brooklyn, her family, and the club would be enough.

Diablo: Chapter 19

I was sitting at my desk remembering yesterday's mind-blowing sex with my woman. Going home early to find Jauhnna reading one of her hot romances had led to a sexual encounter that I never anticipated. I knew she read some spicy stuff, but to have her pretend I was the guy in the book had set something off inside of me. I don't know why I thought of the whole sex doll idea, but when it came out of my mouth, and she went along with it, I committed to the role-play. And role-playing had never been one of my things, but after yesterday, it would be.

The things she said and let me do had blown my mind. I was hoping to play with her ass more, but actually, to have anal sex with her when she offered it, I was scared that she'd regret it. It was the last thing I wanted to happen, but her insistence made me ignore my fear. Thankfully, I did. It led both of us to have an out-of-body experience. Although her passing out had scared the shit out of me until she assured me it was due to pleasure overload, not me hurting her. We'd gone back to the house and bathed, spent the rest of the afternoon and night together talking, having supper, and later making love in our bed.

Now, it was back to the less-than-pleasant stuff. The anticipation for the weekend to come and our preparations for it should be enough for anyone to deal with, but God or maybe the Devil decided we didn't have enough on our plates. I knew this when there was a loud knock on my office door at Prep & Restore. Carly came rushing in without waiting for me to tell her to enter. I knew something was wrong when she did that. Despite our friendship, she observed certain professional boundaries.

I came to my feet while I asked, "What's wrong, Carly?"

"That crazy man is back. I'm afraid he's here to cause more trouble. He's demanding to speak to you."

"Did you call the police?" I asked as I rounded my desk and went to her. I put what I hoped was a calming hand on her arm.

"No, not yet. I wanted to tell you first. He's calm, which scares me more. I'll call them now." She went to turn around, but I gripped her arm and stopped her. She gave me a questioning look.

"Call them from here. When you're done, stay here until someone from the club or I come to get you. I don't want you exposed to him. I have no idea what he might do." My gut was clenching, and I had a sick feeling. When I got like this, it was typically not a good situation.

"Okay. Be careful."

"I will. Close and lock the door behind me," I ordered.

She nodded to let me know she understood. When I exited my office, I paused to listen. I smiled when the door closed, and I heard her lock it. With her safe, I headed to the front. I wondered if anyone was up there with him or if she had left him alone. The latter wasn't something I would've done, but he rattled her.

Arriving in the reception area, I saw it was empty. My first thought was he'd grown impatient and left, but I rejected that immediately. That wasn't his personality. I went on high alert. Locking the front door so no one could enter and get caught up in this, I pulled my gun from my holster in the back of my pants. I kidney-carried mine. I had a permit to carry, but even if I didn't, there was no way in hell I'd go unarmed.

Leaving the reception area, I began to cautiously check the other rooms we had. There were storage and offices as well as the breakroom, bathroom, and the large workshop to clear. I got through a couple before I got to Crash's office. The door was closed. He should be here. As far as I knew, he hadn't gone to a worksite today. I knocked softly. I heard him call out for me to enter. Keeping an eye on the hallway, I eased it open. A swift glance at him showed he was coming to his feet.

"Ackerman is somewhere loose in the building. Carly is locked in my office and calling the cops, but we've got to find and contain him until they get here. My gut is churning. He was calm, she said. Not good."

He was pulling his weapon, as I explained. He joined me at the door and gave me a chin lift. Just like that, we fell into warrior mode. As a club, we practiced how to search a building for an enemy. We might not have all served in the military, but we used their tactics. My dad had taught me those and a lot more growing up. He covered the right, and I covered the left.

We quickly discovered he wasn't in the other rooms, which left the main workshop and assembly area. Some of the things we built we did onsite, then transported to the location where we finished assembling them there. There were stacks of lumber, pallets, boxes, and a slew of other stuff in there. All of them were potential hiding places. Fuck, who knew how long the cops would take to get here. Pausing, I signaled for Crash to wait, then I took out my phone. I sent a group text to the guys.

Me: 911. Potential hostile at Prep & Restore. Use caution. Cops called. CIS.

I knew they would understand, CIS was one of our standard abbreviations. It meant "come in silent." Quickly, I sent another to Carly.

Me: Front door locked. Club 911. Active hostile. Shutdown protocol.

She would know to alert all staff not in the building to remain away, and those who were here would get a mass text warning them. Those who were able would lock themselves in the offices. We trained all our employees for this and practiced it routinely. You never knew what could happen in this crazy world. Sliding my phone back in my cut, I nodded to him.

We entered the workshop low and went in opposite directions. We'd work our way along the perimeter, then inward. Or that was what we would've done, but only this time there was no need. Standing in the middle of the large room in the open assembly and loading area stood Ackerman, bold as brass. To my dismay, he wasn't alone. He had three of our employees huddled on the floor. He had a gun trained on them.

Wanting to have him focus on me and hopefully get his gun trained off Kurt, Morris, and Robin. It was pure bad luck they happened to be in the shop. They were usually on job sites working. I slid my gun under my cut in my waistband so I could get to it fast. With it out of sight, I stood tall and moved out so Ackerman could see me. He spotted me within seconds. A satisfied smile spread across his face.

"Ackerman, what is the meaning of this? Your issue is with me, not my employees. They just do as they're told. They have no say in whether we do more work for you or if I do it for free," I said loudly.

He hadn't spotted Crash, who was sneaking to get in a better position to cover me and, if the opportunity arose, to take him out as a threat. If it meant shooting him, we'd do it to save the others. They were terrified. I saw it in their faces. They gave me pleading looks.

"Ah, there's the boss. About time you showed your face. You should be ashamed of yourself. Hiding behind your employees. Did you expect them to protect you? If so, sorry to disappoint you," he said gleefully. The man was a certified nutcase. I had to get them out of here before he went over the edge. His eyes were bright with excitement and insanity.

"I don't need to hide behind anyone. Holding onto innocent people is a new low for you, Ackerman. A real man would keep this between the two of us. You want to talk, then let them go, and we can talk," I demanded.

I wanted him not only to focus on me but to turn his anger only on me. His smile slipped a tad.

"Did you keep it between us when you sicced those collection people on me or called the cops?"

"First of all, I didn't call the cops. I wasn't here when you busted the window. As for collections, you kept refusing to pay your bill. I had to do something to get you to understand I was serious."

"I shouldn't have a bill! You didn't finish the job you were hired to do," he shouted.

It was the same old shit he spouted every damn

time. I was tired of hearing it. I knew that in order to change the dynamic, I had to take a risk. I turned my back on him before I took a couple of steps toward the way I came. It appeared that I was walking out on him, which was what I wanted him to think.

"Come back here!" he screamed, sounding almost hysterical. I stopped and then glanced back at him without turning back. He was staring at me wide-eyed. He'd turned his back on Morris, Kurt, and Robin. His gun was pointed solidly at me. Good.

"You want to talk, let them go. That's the deal."

"You don't tell me what to do! I'm in control here, not you. You think you're a badass with your leather vest and motorcycle. Well, I'm not afraid of you or your gang. It's time people around here stood up to you and stopped letting you push them around."

I was riding the line of pushing him far enough he'd focus on me without pushing him too far and having him go after my people to get back at me. I was a bundle of nerves inside, but on the outside, I knew I appeared unconcerned and calm. I'd perfected it over the years. In this life, especially when we were an outlaw club, you didn't survive long showing fear.

"If you were smart, you would be. Are you letting them go? Or are we done? I have things to do," I said offhandedly.

I kept my eyes on him, although I wasn't fully turned around. I made sure not to shift them to watch Crash, who was in my peripheral vision, make his way closer to him. He'd signaled to the guys on the floor not to make a sound. I needed to get Ackerman to come toward me. If he did, Crash might be able to sneak them away. Christ! Where the hell were the cops?

Ackerman was staring even more wildly at me. I took two more steps away from him. He ran toward me about a half-dozen steps and raised the gun higher. "Get back here!" he shouted.

I didn't move, but I kept my body angled so only the side of me was facing him. It made me a smaller target if he decided to shoot, but it had another advantage. My side, where I had my gun, was facing away from him. I had my hand on it and was easing it out of my pants. My gut told me he was going to shoot, regardless of whether I pushed him or not. If he did, I'd do what I had to in order to protect everyone.

"Let's go to my office, where we can sit and talk."

He shook his head. "No, we can talk right here. I want your people to hear what a dirty dealer you are. They need to know the kind of person they're working for. After this, I bet you won't have anyone to do your work. Good. It means you won't be able to rip people off."

"Do you do this to everyone?" I asked abruptly.

He gave me a confused look, which was what I wanted. Time to throw him off kilter. "What do you mean, do this to everyone?"

"You know. Do you accuse every company that does work for you or who you buy things from of not holding up their part of the contract or whatever? Is it your way of causing trouble for the fun of it? If so, I'm surprised you haven't been dealt with."

"I don't do this for fun! Only when there are people and companies like yours. However, you've been the worst. You're so stubborn. Refusing to do the right thing. At least the others have."

Well, that answered my big question of whether

he'd done this to others. He took a couple more steps toward me. My three guys were now totally hidden from his view. Crash was frantically gesturing for them to come to him. Wanting to cover any noise they might make, I began to shout.

"I can't believe others have given in to you and your outrageous demands! We did the work in full and in good faith for you. It's not my fault you decided you wanted to tack on more, and then you were too cheap to pay for it. Your lies about me altering the contract and forging your signature are such utter bullshit. I thought the cops hauling your stupid ass in would knock some sense into you, but obviously it didn't. They should cart your stupid ass to the loony bin for a long stay. Maybe some shock therapy and drugs would put you right," I yelled as loud as I could.

Fury overtook him, but it served my purpose. He was so focused on me that he had no idea Crash had our three men safely hidden. On the far side of the room, I saw a couple of my brothers creeping in. It was time to put an end to this. I was about to signal one of them to make a noise to get his attention so I could charge him when a voice boomed through what I assumed was a bullhorn.

"This is the St. Augustine police department. Mr. Ackerman, we can resolve this peacefully, and no one has to get hurt. If you have a weapon, throw it down and come out with your hands up."

I saw the second he decided he was going to take me out. His gun hand had lowered while I was yelling. As he was beginning to bring it back up to chest level, I swung and fired. I heard the retort of not only my gun but another. I felt a burning sting along my upper bicep.

I fired again. He was down, but I wasn't taking any chances.

He was on the ground moaning and writhing in pain. The large roll-up door to the workroom came flying open, and in poured several cops with their guns drawn. Immediately, I placed mine on the ground and lifted my hands in the air. The left one didn't want to go far. I could feel warm blood running down it.

Scorpion and Butcher were at my side in a blink. Their concern was evident. Butcher was wrapping a bandanna around my arm.

"You alright, Pres?" Scorpion asked.

The cops split up. Some went to Ackerman, and the others went to me.

"Get down on the ground and put your hands behind your back," one barked.

"You two, get back," another yelled. They had their guns trained on us.

"Can't you see he's unarmed, and so are we? He's bleeding. I'm trying to stop it. Maybe instead of shouting stupid shit, you can help us. He's the victim here," Butcher snarled.

"Butch, it's fine. Step away. We don't want any accidents. Officers, I don't think I can get on the ground and then back up. And cuffing my arms behind my back is gonna hurt like a bitch. How about you cuff them in front of me?"

"We tell you what to do, not the other way around," the first one snapped.

"Why don't you two go make sure no one else is hurt? I've got this," a voice I recognized told them. It was Officer Merritt. The two younger ones didn't look happy, but they did it. He must have authority or seniority over them. As they walked off, he grimaced.

"Sorry about that. They're green. This is their first shooting. They got an adrenaline burst from this. Let's get your arm looked at. We got a call from your receptionist stating Mr. Ackerman had returned, and he was armed."

"What took you so damn long? I was trying to wait, but he had my people at gunpoint. I had to get his focus on me."

"I was on another call. As for the others and why it took them so long, I have no idea. Shit, Chief Tremblay isn't gonna be happy."

He took me outside. There were pedestrians, cops, and emergency personnel crawling all over the place. I was taken to a paramedic, I assumed. He was dressed in one of their uniforms. While he was working on my arm, I watched two others bringing Ackerman out on a gurney. He was carrying on.

"I'm dying! He shot me. Arrest him. See what he did. He tried to kill me. Oh my God, give me pain medicine. Why are my hands cuffed to this thing!" he shouted.

He rattled the cuffs on the rail of the gurney. They stopped outside the ambulance to work on him. The way he was yelling made me think he wasn't too badly hurt. When I fired, I tried not to hit him anywhere vital. As much as I might want to kill him, it would've been bad for me and the club. At least the security cameras in the building would show him taking my people hostage and that he was the one to decide to shoot first. All I was doing was defending myself.

I hissed as pressure and something that burned pressed into my wound. Merritt waited until the paramedic declared I wasn't in danger of bleeding out before he got to questioning me. By the time he was done and Crash, Carly, and Zax gave their statements, along with Morris, Robin, and Kurt, I was exhausted and ready to go home. Ackerman had been transported to the hospital. Officers followed him there. He was under arrest, at least.

It was mid-afternoon before I was told they were finished, and I was free to go about my day. Thankfully, after conferring with someone, I was informed by Merritt that they weren't pressing charges against me. My gun was legal, and I had the required permit to carry it. My guys had hidden theirs before the cops came in to simplify things. It was Butcher who'd opened the door for them. Micro arrived at some point. He handed off to the police a copy of the security tape showing the whole thing. I was beyond ready to get rid of the cops and spectators and go home. I grimaced, thinking how Jauhnna would react to this.

"Did anyone tell Jauhnna about this?" I asked Butcher.

"Not as far as I know. You know she's gonna lose her shit when she finds out you were shot, and no one told her," he warned me.

I groaned. "I know. Fuck. I need to check and make sure Carly and everyone is good to go, then I'll go home and tell her."

"Everyone is good. I already talked to them. We're closing it down for the day. I told Liam to bring a vehicle to pick you up. He'll haul your bike home," Scorpion stated.

"I don't need anyone to pick me up. I can ride. My arm isn't that bad," I protested.

This led to a ten-minute debate until I pulled rank. I told them I was riding. They weren't happy, but Liam was called off.

"Speaking of Zax, he was supposed to be on guard duty today. Where the hell was he when Carly came to find me?" I asked.

"He was on a food run. It's not his fault, Diablo, it's mine. I sent him to get it. I was guarding Carly while he was gone, and then I got a call from the one inspector we've been trying to pin down. I ran to my office to get the information he was asking for out of the file. Just my rotten luck. That was when Ackerman showed up. It was my fuck up," Crash admitted.

I could tear into him, but it could've happened to any of us. I would've probably done the same thing. "Don't worry about it. Hell, knowing him, he probably timed it. If he's been watching us, he has to have seen a prospect here every day since he was arrested. Okay, let's get out of here before someone else decides today is the day to mess with the Horsemen," I grumbled.

Discovering the others had already left, I locked up. I wasn't amused to see several of my brothers were escorting me home. I wanted to tell them I wasn't a damn baby, but I held my tongue.

When we came through the gate of the compound, I was ready to get off my bike. I would never admit it to them, but the vibration and movement had my arm throbbing. Scorpion and Butcher, the hovering hens, followed me right up to my house and watched me park my bike before they left. I gave them the finger as they did. They just laughed at me.

Walking into the house, Jauhnna caught me in the mudroom slash laundry room. I sat down on the bench built in there to remove my boots. She was smiling.

"Honey, I didn't expect you to be home early. What—" she stopped abruptly.

Her gaze was zeroed in on the stark white bandage wrapped around my upper arm. I was pissed all over again seeing it. The bullet not only gouged a line across my arm, which fucked up my tattoo there, but it had put a hole in one of my favorite shirts.

"Victor, what happened!?" she cried as she rushed over and dropped down next to me.

"Baby, it's nothing. Just a flesh wound. It's a little sore, that's all."

I was trying to tug off my boots as I said it. Unfortunately, a hiss of pain escaped. The next thing I knew, she was pushing my hands out of the way and removing my boots as she interrogated me.

"A flesh wound? What kind? How did it happen?"

I waited to answer. I rose up after she got my boots off. I went to shrug off my cut. She grabbed it and eased it down my arms, then hung it up. "Come in the kitchen, and I'll tell you. I need a cold drink."

She came with me, but she had her arm wrapped around my waist on my good side. Since I loved having her touch me no matter the reason, I didn't object. She gently pushed me toward one of the stools at the counter. I sat down as she went to the fridge.

"What do you want to drink?"

Thinking over what we had, I decided I needed caffeine and sugar. "I'll take one of those Cokes."

She came out with two of them in her hands. Of course, she had to get glasses of ice and open them, as well as pour mine for me, before she handed it over and poured hers. She was casting me concerned looks.

"Babe, stop it. I'm fine. Thank you. I'll tell you what happened, but first, I want you to promise you won't get upset because you can see I'm fine." Maybe if I said that, it would help. Not. Knowing I'd procrastinated long enough, I launched into an abbreviated explanation. I tried to downplay the danger of it. When I got to the part where we shot each other, she turned pale. Right after she did, she let out a loud bellow. I didn't know that someone as small as her could be that loud.

"YOU WERE SHOT AND NO ONE CALLED ME!"

I flinched. Damn, my ears hurt. I held up my hand. "It's just a scratch, Serenity. Things were hectic, and we were dealing with the police, staff, and Ackerman."

"I understand in the heat of the moment and immediately afterward, but you rode all the way home. You didn't think that sometime between the time it happened and you walked through the door, I should've known? You sent out a text to your brothers. Why couldn't someone send me one? Something. What if you were seriously injured or killed? Would they just let me wait and not say anything for hours?"

"Baby, calm down. You're getting upset over nothing," I tried.

"Oh, really, nothing. Okay, let's see if I'm the only one who thinks it's nothing," she snapped before yanking her cell phone out of her back pocket. She was pressing a couple of buttons. I wondered which of my guys she was calling to chew out. She hit the speaker button. We listen to it ring. When it was answered, my heart sank.

"Hi Jauhnna, what's up?" My daughter's cheerful

voice came over the phone. I tried to snatch it off her, but my woman slapped my hands away and gave me a death glare.

"Hello, Brooklyn. I'm sitting here with your dad trying not to smack the crap out of him. I called you to get a second opinion."

"What about?" she asked curiously at the same time I tried to head off a second explosion.

"Brookie, it's not as bad as it sounds."

"What sounds?"

"An irrational customer he's been having issues with ended up coming to the shop today, holding a few employees at gunpoint. Your dad faced off with him and ended up being shot in the arm, and no one thought to call and tell me."

"WHAT THE FUCK!?" Brooklyn shouted.

Jauhnna was giving me a self-satisfied smirk. "Exactly. And he's been trying to tell me it wasn't a big deal and they were busy, so no one told me. I found out when he walked into the house with a bandage around his arm. Hours after it happened."

"Dad, what the hell were you thinking? You faced off with this nut, and then when you got shot, you didn't think me and Jauhnna needed to be notified? What if it had been serious, or you were killed? How bad is it? Where's the fucker who did it? Is he dead?"

"Christ, you two act like I'm helpless. I had to get him away from my guys and keep him from killing anyone. I planned on telling her when I got home and then calling you to tell you. If it had been serious, or God forbid I was killed, of course, you would've been told right after things were contained. As for Ackerman, I shot him twice. The last I heard, he was in surgery and expected to live. He'll be going to jail for a while."

"Yeah, bet the whole club was there, though, weren't they?" Brooklyn muttered.

"They were or at least they were all texted when it was happening," Jauhnna happily narced me out. This got another curse word out of my daughter. I hoped the kids weren't around.

"Jauhnna, have you seen it? How does it look?"

"I haven't, but I'm about to look. You, stay right there and don't move. I'm getting a pair of scissors and more bandages to rewrap it. Or better yet, Wolverine can come do it up. Was he there?" she asked as she went to the block holding the knives. There was a pair of scissors in it. I thought better of telling her they were for cutting meat. She might just stab me with them.

"I'm texting Wolverine to get his butt over to the house and fix him back up," Brooklyn said.

I wisely remained quiet. Jauhnna had the dressing off in no time. There wasn't really any way to stitch it, so a three-inch furrow ran across my bicep. It was angry-looking. Jauhnna snatched up her phone, snapped a picture, and then tapped on the buttons. I knew what she was doing. It was confirmed when Brooklyn hissed.

A sharp knock on the front door was followed by footsteps. Wolverine came around the corner. He appeared resigned. He'd been there but let the paramedics take care of my arm. Lucky for me, I had a tetanus shot a couple of years ago.

"Hi Jauhnna. Brook, I'm here," he said.

"Good. Dad, that looks like it hurts. Did you get a tetanus shot?"

"I don't need one. My last one is still good. It's

sore. It'll heal. I'm just pissed he ruined my tattoo," I bitched.

"He could've killed you, but you're worried about it messing up your ink? I swear to God, I'm gonna brain you," Jauhnna threatened.

I heard Brooklyn giggle. Wolverine tried not to smile, but I saw his lips twitch. It was time to take control. I noticed he was carrying a first aid kit with him.

"Mind fixing this up for me so they won't worry? Sorry about dragging you over here."

"It's alright. I kinda expected it, though I didn't think Brooklyn would be the one texting or calling me to do it."

While he worked, I watched as Jauhnna took her phone and went to the far end of the living room. She was talking to my daughter, but she was speaking too low for me to hear what she was saying.

"Damn, they're upset. I'd hate to be in your shoes," Wolverine said as he wrapped new gauze around the non-stick pad he had placed over the wound after cleaning it and applying some kind of ointment.

"I'll have to figure out how to get them off this subject and onto something else. Hell, it's a scratch."

"It's a little more than that, but you should feel good about the way they're acting."

"Why?"

"Because it shows how much they love you. We're not used to having to think about looping in anyone else other than each other. That's gotta stop now that you've claimed Jauhnna. She's the only old lady, but if things follow the way it's happened in the other clubs, she's just the start. More old ladies will be joining the club.

None of them will be happy to find things like this out hours later."

He had a point. I pondered it as he finished up. When he was done, he patted my shoulder and then announced across the room. "He's good to go. Watch it for drainage, and redness, if the pain increases, or he spikes a fever. If any of that happens, call me. I'll leave this here. If you want me to change it daily, I can."

"Thank you, Wolverine. I'll keep an eye on it, and I can take care of it," she told him nicely.

"You're welcome. Later, Brook," he called out.

"Later, Wolverine. Thank you," she shouted through the phone. A chin lift in my direction, and then he evaporated.

I settled in to continue the ass-chewing with my ladies. I doubted I was off the hook yet. As annoying as it was on one hand, on the other, it did make me feel warm inside. I was loved. I had adjustments to make, but they were worth it.

Jauhnna: Chapter 20

I was nervous as we left the compound further and further behind us. The past few days have been stressful not only due to worrying about today and how the plan for Galway and Janus would go but also because I had fretted over Diablo and his bullet wound. The man still thought Brooklyn and I were overly concerned about what he called a scratch, but he had admitted he understood why we were upset about not finding out until hours after it occurred. That was the conclusion after our drawn-out discussion with Brooklyn on the phone the day it happened.

I'd been accused of hovering too much in the following days, but I couldn't help it. The thought of losing him terrified me. He went along with most of my pampering until I suggested we postpone the takedown until he was healed if he wouldn't agree to stay home and let the club, the Dark Patriots, and the O'Sheerans take care of them. I got to see my man laying down the law to me. I found it hot, though I didn't tell him that.

He threatened to spank my ass if I dared to suggest he stay behind or wait again. I was tempted to do it just so he would, but I didn't want to cause issues with his healing if he used his bad arm, and knowing him, he would to prove a point. Last night, we had a call with the Patriots to run through the plan one more time.

Today, we were taking a roundabout way to the southernmost part of St. Augustine to an area called Rattlesnake Island. Since I wasn't familiar with Florida, I had no idea about what it was or why it would be a good place to spring our trap. I got a tourist overview and a history lesson from the guys explaining why. I found out the island was a popular picnic destination for area boaters. There were trails all over it. People loved to go there to enjoy the birds, butterflies, plants, and wildflowers as they picnicked. The section we were concerned with was Fort Matanzas. That was where the history lesson came in.

Matanzas was a fortified watchtower built in the mid-eighteenth century. Its purpose was to defend the southern approach to St. Augustine, which was then a Spanish military settlement. People came there to see not only the tower but the three hundred acres of Florida coast that were the home of dunes, marshland, forest, and various endangered and threatened species of flora and fauna.

That was where we were hoping to lead my brother, Galway, and their main flunkies, as I referred to them. The Horsemen and Patriots would be waiting for them. They'd spring their trap, capture them, and then smuggle the lot of them onto a small waiting boat. The boat would then work its way from the Matanzas River to the Atlantic Ocean, where it would rendezvous with a larger ship owned by the O'Sheerans. It would then transport everyone out into International Waters, where the real work would begin. I was shocked to learn International Water was only twelve miles off the coast.

Before we left, Micro was able to confirm that my brother and former husband, as I now refer to Galway in my head, along with a contingency of their men, were seen entering Florida the day before yesterday. They'd taken up residence in a rental not far outside of St. Augustine. Of those with them, the six who'd hurt me along with Galway were part of their entourage. The rest were personal guards of my brother.

I wished I could enjoy the ride more, but I was too anxious, which was a shame. The weather was sunny and warm. There was so much to see and enjoy if I'd let myself. They made sure to take their time. We stopped to eat and even browsed a couple of shops in town before heading out. They took a circular route rather than riding straight to the Fort. I would've rather just gone straight there, but I get why they didn't. It was hard not to keep looking behind us to see if we were being followed, but they'd stressed how important it was for us not to indicate we knew we had eyes on us. If they did this all the time, they had nerves of steel. No one seeing them would ever get a hint they were aware or worried in any way.

I did enjoy seeing more of my new home a little. It was different from Georgia and drastically different from Nevada. I was beginning to love it here. Lucky for me, I'd become used to humidity over the last three years. It had been a huge shock for me at first, coming from Nevada's dry desert heat to the raging humidity in Georgia.

Diablo and I had talked a couple of nights ago about St. Augustine being my new home. We discussed packing up my things in Savannah and moving them after this nightmare was taken care of. I hated that he was still paying my rent, so the sooner, the better, as far as I was concerned. While I'd miss the people I worked with, I hadn't really ever allowed myself to get super close to people, just in case I had to up and leave. I wasn't leaving behind anyone I was extremely attached to. I couldn't wait to get my possessions here and have that chapter of my life over.

Stopping outside the Fort, we parked together. There were other people and vehicles around, so we made sure to park away from them. Getting off the bikes, everyone huddled together as if talking about the ride and scenery before going into the watchtower. A few of the guys were pointing out things around us to help sell the lie. In reality, we were getting an update from Micro.

"Sean said we've definitely got tails. They've been with us since right after we left the compound. I spotted them. They're good, but not that good. The Patriots' crew confirmed Radigan, Vierra, and the six others we want are in the vehicles following us. They're in three SUVs. It looks like some of your brother's guards stayed behind. Are you ready to do this, Jauhnna? We're going to split off and let you, Diablo, Butcher, and Scorpion take off to explore the marsh area while the rest of us go to look at other areas. Here's the camera to make it more realistic. Once you're out far enough, they'll make their move to acquire you. When they do, the rest of us and the Patriots' hidden operatives will converge on them. Any questions?"

"Wait. If we're all going on the ship, won't it look suspicious to leave your bikes here?" I asked. I hadn't even thought of that until now.

"Don't worry. Liam and Zax are staying behind. Sean and his guys have a transporter coming in later. They'll load and transport the bikes to another location a few miles down the coast. When we return, we'll be dropped off there to get our bikes and resume our ride. The beauty of this location is there are no CCTV cameras recording everything. Even if we're suspected of having something to do with their disappearances, which, why should we, there won't be any proof," he said with a wink.

Diablo squeezed my hand. I knew he felt how clammy it was, and I had a slight tremor. "You can do this. I know you can. Just stick to me and remember, do what we say without hesitation. I won't let anything happen to you."

"I'm not concerned about me. What if they shoot you guys to get to me? I don't want any of you dead because of me. If they take me, I'll take care of removing myself from the equation."

An angry growl rumbled out of him. He scowled. The Horsemen didn't look any happier. "I don't want to hear you say another word about killing yourself. It won't happen. If by some ungodly chance they did get their hands on you, remember, we can find you. We'll come for you. Hell, even if we're dead, someone will rescue you. All you have to do is hang on."

I nodded because I wasn't able to say anything. I knew he was referring to the shot I was given last night by Wolverine. They explained it was some kind of tracking device. I didn't fully understand how it worked, but they assured me all their friends and their old ladies had them. I asked if they did. Their hesitation told me they didn't. I balked at getting it, but in the end, to appease me, they got the shot as well. It was some super-secret thing the government had. I figured they got their hands on it because of the Dark Patriots. I'd learned they still did work for our government at times. I was looking forward to meeting them in person, just as I was the other clubs.

"Alright, let's do this. Everyone, good luck, watch your sixes and keep your heads on swivels. Roll out," Diablo ordered.

And just like that, we were separating and walking off in different directions. I remained glued to his side. They were able to talk and joke easily. I couldn't speak, but I did remember to raise the camera and take pictures of the scenery around us. I'd have to come back here again and do this for real. It was fascinating to see the various plants, birds, and butterflies.

I worked to keep myself from glancing over my shoulder every two seconds. I knew the guys were all armed. I was, too, sorta. They wouldn't let me have a gun, but they did give me a knife and a taser. Tasers were the weapon of choice for this part of the plan. They didn't want to kill them, nor did they want to make noise to raise suspicion, so they were going to knock them out with tasers and then inject them with a drug that Wolverine had brought to keep them unconscious until we were out at sea.

I'd always wanted to see a taser in action. I hoped I might get a chance to use mine. It would be deeply satisfying to shock the shit out of one or more of those monsters. The problem would be not doing it until I fried one of them to death. Along with my nerves, my hate was steadily coming out. I wanted them to suffer and die in terror and pain. When I confessed this to Diablo last night as he held me in bed, he swore to me they would.

We'd walked a good distance away from anyone

else. Scorpion was pointing off in the distance, calling my attention to a bird when it happened. Moments before a hated voice spoke, I heard the whisper of footsteps behind us. It was Diablo's hand on my waist that kept me from turning.

"Well, well, look who we have here. My whore of a wife and her whore masters. You guys hooked up with the wrong bitch," Galway said acidly, with underlying glee in his voice. Those with him chuckled.

Turning slowly with my guys, I met his gaze. His hate poured out of him. I let mine show, too. The days of me cowering from this man were long gone. When I left him, I'd promised myself never to be a victim again, and I worked to make it so I wouldn't be. Even Diablo and the Horsemen had no full understanding of just what I did to make myself strong. It might not be enough against numerous ones, but one-on-one, I'd take my chances.

"Look what crawled out of the sewer. I bet you guys have never seen pieces of shit this big, have you?" I asked the Horsemen. I knew my job. I was to keep their attention on me so the others could take them out. Thankfully, we were far enough out that no innocent bystanders would get hurt. My guys snorted and then laughed.

I watched Galway, Janus, and my six other worst enemies flush with anger. The smirks slid right off their faces as I smirked at them. Now that it was happening, my anxiety was settling, and my bravado was growing.

"Shut your mouth, bitch. No one wants to hear you talk. You know what that mouth is good for. I bet these guys know it too," Alfie said suggestively.

He was Galway's main enforcer and the one out of the six I feared the most. He'd hurt me more than anyone except Galway. In the past, I avoided him if I could and never spoke to him.

"At least they don't have to force a woman to have sex with them. They don't rape and beat women, either. They're real men," I told him.

"Wait until I get my hands on you, slut. I'll make you wish you were dead," he promised.

While all this was being said back and forth, my brother stood there impassively. There wasn't an ounce of remorse or brotherly love showing. I always knew he didn't have a heart. Diablo, Scorpion, and Butcher had remained quiet. I knew they ached to say stuff, but this was part of the plan, to make them seem less of a threat. Their time would come soon enough.

"I'm not afraid of any of you. You're no longer a problem," I said casually.

"Oh yeah, how do you figure that, Joanne?" Ezra piped up to ask.

"My name is Jauhnna now. And the eight of you and your whole evil lives and businesses are about to be wiped off the face of the earth. I hope you can swim," I said with a grin. Galway was opening his mouth to say something, but he never got the chance. Gio and Aryan, two other men I knew were Patriots, plus Thunder, Wolverine, Punk, and Turbo, struck from behind.

It was a thing of beauty to see my eight worst enemies jerk and fall to the ground as the electrical shocks went through them. They lay there twitching. I laughed as I noted Galway had pissed himself. I knew that would humiliate him when he recovered his senses. Without missing a beat, Wolverine went to each of them and injected them in the neck.

"Good job. Let's get these guys out of here," Gio

said as he winked at me. A large panel truck pulled up. I glanced around to see if we'd gotten anyone's attention. I didn't see anyone. We were out of view of the watchtower. They quickly and none too gently loaded them in the back of it. They threw them on top of each other. Three got in the front while the rest of us climbed into the back with the cargo.

Diablo hugged me. "You did great, my sweet Serenity."

"Hell yeah, she did. You kept them right where we wanted them. They never knew what hit 'em," Butcher said with a grin.

"Thanks. All I can think about is their faces when they finally realize what's in store for them."

"Babe, it's still not too late to let us do this alone. One of the Patriots can take you to the meeting place," Diablo offered. I'd been expecting it. I shook my head and squeezed his hand resting on my thigh.

"No, thank you. I've got to do this."

He sighed as he nodded. I sat back and listened to them talk as the truck took us to the first boat. I was reserving my energy for what was to come.

I stood on the deck of a boat, eyeing the ocean surrounding us. There was no land in sight. The transition of our captives from the truck to the boat on the river and then to this one had gone off without a hitch. We were now in International Waters. The real work could begin. I was taking in the salty sea air as the Patriots and Horsemen finished preparing for the fun to come. I called it fun only because they did. Yeah, they were dark, but nothing like the eight men they had below.

A hand sliding around me made me jump. I knew his touch, though, so I relaxed instantly. He held me close. "Are you ready to do this?" he asked softly.

"I am. Let's go."

He turned me to face him. He stared intently into my eyes. "If at any time you want to step away, tell me. There's no shame in it. No one will think any less of you. To torture and kill someone is life-altering, Jauhnna. I'm giving you this because you said you need it. However, the last thing I want is for you to be haunted by it. If I see you're being too adversely affected by it, I'll have you removed."

"I swear I'll tell you. Don't remove me just to prevent me from seeing you at your worst, though. I have to know the whole you, Victor."

"I know. Okay, give me a kiss, and then let's get this done." Our lips met. Our kiss was long, hot, and intoxicating. When we were done, I felt like I was floating. He winked at me before leading me below.

It was stuffy down there in the hold area, I guess you'd call it. In the middle of the empty space, the eight men were lined up in a row. They were bound to chairs by their wrists and ankles. They were awake and had gags in their mouths. They were shooting hateful looks at the men surrounding them. That hatred only worsened when they spotted me and Diablo. He walked me over to stand right in front of them. The Horsemen and the Patriots, who were not with the crew of the boat, all nodded or gave us chin lifts in acknowledgment.

"Before we get this party started, let me introduce myself and my guys. My name is Diablo. I'm the president of the Horsemen of Wrath MC. These are my men, and those not wearing a cut are friends of ours from the Dark Patriots. Let me be clear in case you think there's a chance you'll be walking out of here. There's not a snowball's chance in hell of that happening. Your recent activities in the human trafficking market were enough to guarantee that fate." He paused before continuing.

"However, what guaranteed that you'd die hard and only after being thoroughly tortured was you laying hands on this woman. See, if you hadn't done that, we would've probably just whacked your asses and been done with it. But you didn't do that. You forced her into a marriage she never wanted, then humiliated, beat, and raped her for years. Then, when she escaped, you couldn't let her go. I'm gonna fucking enjoy making you scream and beg. My friends and brothers will too, but no matter what, I'll be the one to end each of you," Diablo snarled.

He gestured to the men to our right. They must've known what he wanted without him saying a word because they walked over and began removing the gags. As they did, the prisoners started swearing. It wasn't until Galway was ungagged that a question was asked.

"You're a motorcycle club. Why the hell do you give a fuck if we sell people or what we do or did to her? She's nothing. A means to an end. There are plenty of women to replace her. I doubt she's that good of a lay that you can't give her up. She never was for me." Galway smirked.

To my surprise, Diablo laughed. I expected him to explode in anger. "If you think by pissing me off, you'll die sooner and easier, forget it. As much as I'd love to do it, I won't. As for your questions, first, we hate anyone harming others the way you do by selling them. Secondly, there's no one who can replace her. She's priceless, and she's my old lady. Do you know what that means? It means in my world, she's my wife, and you just insulted her." He growled the last words before hauling back his fist and slamming it into Galway's jaw. The wimp cried out in pain.

Diablo's revelation caused the others to make disbelieving sounds and exchange glances. My brother was the next one to speak. "Joanne, I'm your brother. I had no say in you marrying him. That was all Father's doing. I admit, I had no idea he did those things to you or that he planned to sell you. I would've never gone along with it. You have to believe me."

I moved a couple of steps closer to him. I saw what I thought was hope flare in his eyes. He thought I was stupid. I smiled at him. He smiled back, but it soon disappeared when I responded.

"Janus, you can't lie to me. I know you. You're as heartless and cruel, maybe more so than our father. You knew exactly what Galway was doing, and it was all to solidify your needs for power, standing, and money, just like it was Galway's. You knew what I'd suffer at his hands. There were enough rumors about how he treated women to know. And selling me isn't a surprise either. I have no sisterly feelings for you to prey upon to save you. You're dying along with the rest of this scum."

"You fucking cunt! You were always useless. All you had to do was marry him and give him a couple of heirs, and you couldn't even do that! What did you expect? You're a woman. You're only worth is your womb and connections," Janus hollered. I was shocked when he was hit not by my man but by Butcher.

"Cocksucker, you don't talk to our queen that way. She's the president's old lady and our queen bee. You'll keep a civil tongue, or I'll fucking remove it. Jesus Christ, what's missing in your twisted psyche to be like this period, let alone toward your sister?" he asked. Blood was running down Janus' chin. Butcher had hit him right in the mouth and busted his lips on his teeth.

"Thanks, brother. Baby, is there anything you want to say before we get this show started?" Diablo asked.

"There is, honey. I want you to know that I told them everything you did to me. I'm gonna enjoy watching every second of your torture. When you leave this world, I want you to know that I'll go on to live happily ever after with this wonderful man. I've gained a family in the Horsemen and their many friends. Your entire evil kingdoms will be systematically torn down. I'll help them find every single person they can to make sure of it. You'll be forgotten. However, there is one thing I am thankful to you for. If it wasn't for what you did, I would've never left Nevada and ended up in Florida to meet Diablo. I think that's all I have. If I think of more, I'll let you know, babe," I told Diablo as I backed away.

"I want them up against the wall. Remove everything but their underwear. Faces to the wall," he ordered.

Everyone was quick to do as he asked. The eight men tried to fight, but they were no match for the men with me. In short order, they were stripped, secured, and facing away from us. There were manacles attached to the wall and floor as if the O'Sheerans knew we'd need them. I had no idea if Diablo had told them what he'd need or if the boat was already equipped for it. If it was the latter, I wondered how many others had been dealt with in a similar way. Time to punish these bastards. I stood back to see what the first thing would be done to them. I knew whatever it was, it would hurt.

Diablo: Chapter 21

Seeing them shackled to the wall with their backs to me made me happy. Over the years, ever since I was a teenager, I'd been schooled and then perfected my skills in breaking men and, if needed, eliminating them. My dad, Fiend, had gained his road name for a reason. His years in the military and what he'd seen overseas in the war had shaped him. He knew how to take a man apart not only physically but mentally. He never wanted those he loved or under his protection to suffer what he'd seen, so he ensured not only his fellow Horsemen were well versed in torture and interrogation techniques but also his only son.

My mom hadn't been thrilled that I was taught those things, but she understood the need and supported him while working to instill humanity in me. She never wanted me to become one of the monsters I hunted. The closest I'd come to becoming one of them was when I found and killed Piranha and his brothers for what they did to Amy. Today just might be on par with that.

In a way, to me, they deserved as bad or more even though Jauhnna was alive. Amy had been hurt, and no doubt suffered, but it was over with rather quickly. Jauhnna had suffered for years. In my mind, it made it close to being as bad. The various techniques taught to me by Fiend and those I learned for myself would be put to good use today.

My brothers were eager to assist in the torture. I promised they could for a while. I'd been approached by Gio and Aryan after bringing the prisoners on the second boat. They asked if they could assist as well. I guess their prior meeting with Jauhnna had her firmly in the category of a friend in their books. I agreed.

There were so many things we had to choose from to inflict pain on them. If I had days, there were ones I would love to use, but I didn't plan to prolong it that long. It wasn't because they didn't deserve it. Rather, I didn't want to drag it out for her. This horrible chapter of her life needed to be closed, and us moving on. I had plans as soon as we got home.

I'd gone over what I wanted to do to them over the days leading up to this. When I went to the table we had set aside with most of our personal toys on it, and I opened my leather case, which contained my knives, those assisting me on this one did the same. Lucky, Punk, and Micro lined up beside me behind the first four. Galway was first in line, with her brother on the opposite end and the guards and enforcers in the middle.

A common pastime we enjoyed was working on our knife work and target practicing with them. Regular knives weren't suited for throwing, although we did that, too. These knives happened to be the right kind.

Our captives were twisting their necks, trying to see what we were doing. As one, we moved closer and began the first opening move. I had Galway. No one would touch him but me. I sliced a cut from his shoulder diagonally to the opposite hip. It laid his skin open. Blood began to flow. We kept them shallow enough to prevent them from bleeding to death. It was more painful and shocking than anything. My three brothers had copied my move. The four men cried out in pain. We waited before placing the corresponding slash, creating an X on their backs. As they yelled louder, I glanced back to see how Jauhnna was doing. Butcher had her next to him. She was waiting impassively.

As the blood flowed, we walked over to a cast iron container. There was a fire built underneath it in a shallow bowl. Sticking out of the container were several pieces of metal with handles on them. Removing them from it, we revealed the glowing hot branding irons. They were ones I'd requisitioned personally. Gio and the other Patriots had brought them.

Walking back to the first four, we pressed the hot brands into the middle of their slashes. They screamed as the flesh was burned. The sickening smell of burned flesh filled the space. The ones not being mutilated were crying out and begging us not to do it to them. When we were done, we handed off the brands to other brothers so we could move on to the other four. Visible on the first four's backs were the word *rapist* over and over. I heard Jauhnna inhale deeply. Checking, I saw she was holding up fine. Once we were through marking all eight of them, we let them stand there and anticipate what was next. This was part of the psychological torment.

Next, we used them as target practice for those same knives. We drew a bullseye on each ass cheek of their underwear. Standing back, we threw three knives each. These went much deeper but weren't at risk of piercing anything vital. When we removed them, we made sure to wiggle them back and forth. Their cries were loud. This time, when we went to get the brands, Jauhnna moved up to me.

"Do you want to leave?" I asked.

"No, I don't. I'd like to close up a few holes if you're alright with that."

Gauging her mood, I saw she was steady. I took the brand Scorpion handed me. I gave it to her. "Who do you want to cauterize?"

"I want to do one of each of them. They all enjoyed raping me, and I have no doubt Janus has done it to someone." A satisfied murmur came from my guys and the Patriots.

I waved toward the prisoners. "Go for it. Guys, let her get her turn first."

Micro, Lucky, and Punk stood back. She went to Galway first.

"Don't you dare," he shouted.

She jabbed the brand onto one of his punctures. He screamed and swore at her. She went down the line doing the same to the others. My guys were on hand to give her a fresh brand when the one she held grew too cool. When she was done, she moved back to allow us to finish off. By then, the smell was almost unbearable, but luckily for us, the boat had good ventilation. A central fan system kicked on, and the odor began to dissipate.

The three knife wielders moved back to be replaced by Cowboy, Turbo, and Crash for the next treat. This one was an oldie and might not seem to most to be bad, but it hurt like a bitch. I was handed a pair of pliers. Together, we started on the opposite end of the line. Nails were yanked out of their fingers one at a time. They were sobbing by the time we were done. Blood dripped from their fingertips, but it wasn't enough to worry about. Besides the cauterizing we were doing, their blood was clotting faster than usual due to the additive Wolverine put in the shot that knocked them out.

After that, we decided to change it up. All of us, including the four Patriots, slipped on brass knuckles. I laughed when Butcher withdrew a pair of pink ones from his cut and handed them to Jauhnna.

"Just in case you feel like pounding some. If not, no problem. You can keep those. You might need them one day to get through his hard head," he told her as he grinned and pointed at me.

"What a buddy, fucker," I muttered, but I was grinning. The smile those knuckles and his words put on her face was great. She slipped them on her right hand. That's when I saw spelled across the brass knuckles the word *Queen*. The rest of us had two pairs since we were used to punching with both fists.

It was satisfying to pound on their flesh. I kept her with me. She surprised me with how hard she was hitting. When she hauled off and kicked Galway, I knew she had more than a passing familiarity with fighting.

As we rested, I had to ask. "Baby, where did you learn to throw punches and kicks that way?"

She was breathing hard, but she answered me. "After I got away, I knew I never wanted to be at the mercy of someone again. I took whatever self-defense classes I could find. I might not be able to fight a bunch at once, but one-on-one, I felt I had a chance."

I gave her a squeeze and then a kiss. The guys were all cheering for her. When we stopped kissing, one of the men, the one who had mouthed off to her earlier, Alfie, spoke again. I knew all their names. I'd memorized them along with their faces when Micro got the information on them after she confessed what they did to her.

"You stupid bitch, you could've had it all. He was gonna keep you even if you couldn't give him an heir. You would've still lived in the lap of luxury. And we would've had you all to ourselves. Do you honestly think these bikers are keeping you? They'll sell you as soon as they're sick of you, and you'll be the plaything of countless men," he sneered.

I charged up behind him, grabbed the back of his head, and pounded his face repeatedly into the metal haul until my shirt was tugged on. I looked around to find it was her.

"Diablo, don't. He wants you to kill him. He's a pussy. He's not to die yet. I want him and Galway to be last. They were the ones to hurt me the worst."

This was news to me. She hadn't told me one was worse than the other when it came to the six men. Her confession had more than me growling low. Fury was climbing. I wanted them to hurt more.

"Then they'll be last, my love."

Glancing back at my men, I gave the next order. "Bring out the nines."

Delighted smiles spread over their faces as they did as I asked. From a bag, several cat 'o nine tail whips were removed. Before handing one to me, bottles were removed next. The contents were poured over the leather tails.

"What's that?" she asked curiously.

"Lemon juice. It'll help them remember the lashes," Butcher told her.

Her eyebrows raised. This time, I went first, landing the first lashes on the backs and buttocks of each man. It caused the cauterized wounds to reopen. Then, the juice penetrated not only the lash cuts but the stab and cut wounds. This set them off crying for mercy and pleading for us to just get it over with and kill them.

We took time between the different punishments and interspersed them with more beatings. They vomited vile words when they could. The entire time, I kept a close watch on her for signs that it was becoming too much for her. So far, she was standing strong.

"She's a warrior woman. She can handle it," Beau whispered to me. He and Ben were the other two Patriots there.

"She is. I just don't want her to push herself to prove she is."

"I get it, but she needs this. It's been a few hours. You want to take a break and come back and finish them off?"

I was torn. I decided to leave it up to her. Going over to Jauhnna, I gave her the option. "My Serenity, I need to know what you want. Do we let them wallow in their pain for a while, and we take a break? Or do we continue and get this over with sooner? It's entirely up to you. I could do this for days, but I'm not. We have our life to get back to."

She took her time thinking before giving me an answer. As she contemplated it, she studied them. They were worse for wear and sagging in their shackles. After five solid minutes of silence, she answered.

"I think we should take a break. They're not going anywhere. When you're ready, we'll come back to finish this. I'm anxious to get home. We have to plan our trip to Dublin Falls and to Savannah to get my things."

"We do, and there are a few other things we need to do."

"Oh, really. Do tell."

"Nope. They're surprises," I teased her.

Leaving them to hang there, we exited with my brothers and friends. We went to another area of the boat, which the O'Sheerans' men had told us was at our disposal when we came onboard. None of us had been there yet. I was pleased to find there were sandwiches and snacks awaiting us. Washing our hands, we sat down to eat. Most people would think this was awful, but we knew to eat when we could. Jauhnna sat with me, but she barely picked at her food.

"Darlin', are you alright?" I asked.

"I'm just a tad queasy. And before you ask if it's due to what we're doing to them, the answer is no. I've been feeling this way since we got on the boat. I think it might be mild seasickness. I'll be fine. Eat."

I took her at her word. It didn't take us long to devour the food. We sat around talking for a while afterward. It was a good hour and a half before we decided to go back and see how they were doing. Reentering the hold, I saw they looked even worse than when we left. Groans of misery filled the space.

This last bit of torture was the part I worried the most about. I'd informed my guys ahead of time what I planned and that I was the one to do it on each one of them. They hadn't argued. They knew it would do them no good. The reason I was worried was because Jauhnna would get to see what a sick bastard I was.

"Jauhnna, I want you to stay back. This is about to get messy, and I don't want any of their blood to get on you. I love you."

"I love you too," she said before giving me a kiss. I poured all the love I had for her into it and prayed she'd still want me after this was over.

Turning to look at the pieces of meat on the wall, I gave my last order to my guys. "Turn them around and remove their underwear."

This got reactions out of the fuckers. They whimpered, and I heard some of them praying. As my brothers and the others wrestled them loose, turned them, and then shackled them again, they made weak attempts to fight. When they were secured, my guys backed off and gathered in a semicircle to watch the show.

I went to my pack and removed my sheathed knife. It wasn't a small throwing one like before. It was longer and had a serrated edge on one side of the blade. It was razor sharp. I took it out of the sheath. Walking over to them, I started with Janus. I sliced off both his nipples before he could blink. He screamed as the blood poured out of him. I made sure before moving to the next guy to brand his wounds closed. As I worked on them, more than one had pissed himself or passed out. When the latter happened, water was thrown on them to wake them up. As I went down the line, treating the others to the same treatment, a couple had to be woken back up. I left Alfie and Galway for last. I took my time slicing theirs off. When I was done, I dumped their severed nipples in a pile in front of them. All of them were staring in horror with dazed expressions.

I laid my bloody knife on the table to be cleaned afterward and grabbed the final tool I needed, which was in the same container over the flames as the brands had been. I placed a fireproof glove on my hand before removing it. It was an odd-looking pair of shears. I'd discovered them years ago in an antique store. When I asked the owner what they were for, he'd avidly told me they were called crocodile shears and they were from medieval times. I could see where they got the name.

The blades were shaped to resemble a crocodile with sharp teeth. The man had detailed what they were used for. The devil in me loved his story, so I bought them. I hadn't used them since the night I killed those responsible for murdering Amy. I'd kept them in perfect working order, though, just in case I ever felt the need to use them again.

I marched up and down the line, holding them up. Their eyes widened, and utter fear was evident. Only Butcher knew what these were. I hadn't told anyone else about this part or shown them. He'd seen me use them the first time.

"These are called crocodile shears. They were what some of our ancestors in medieval times were fond of. Can any of you guess what they're for?"

"Please, dear God, don't," Mickie cried out. He was shaking.

"God can't hear you, but the devil can, and I don't give a damn what you want. I want you to suffer like Jauhnna and all those other people you've hurt and sold have. You motherfuckers think it's alright to rape. Well, how does this feel?"

I rushed up to Mickie and placed the shears around his flaccid cock. I closed the blades, but not all the way. I didn't want to cut it off. Instead, I used them to help me tear his cock from his body. His screams were unworldly. Blood flew and poured. Knowing he wouldn't last long with those arteries I'd severed pumping blood everywhere, I added the final insult. I grabbed his lower jaw and forced it open. When it was open, I shoved his severed cock inside and to the back of his throat. He tried to breathe, but it was no use. He thrashed and made muffled screaming sounds as he bled out and choked to death on his own cock.

The cries of astonishment and horror from the witnesses were loud but nothing compared to the seven remaining men. I refused to look at her. I didn't want to see how she was reacting or looking at me. I'd do it after I was done to see if I'd lost her forever or not.

The prayers, screams, begging, and puking were deafening as I worked my way through them. It took time since I had to reheat the shears. I left Janus, Galway, and Alfie for last. I faced a sobbing Janus. He had his eyes closed.

"Look at me!" I shouted. "Come on, be a man!" He shook his head. Shrugging in disgust, I rendered him a eunuch and then suffocated him. He wasn't the one I wanted to look at me anyway.

I moved to face Alfie. He gave me a pitiful face. "She's not worth this," he blubbered. His earlier bravado was all gone.

"She's worth everything to me," I hissed. I lowered the shears and removed the offensive appendage, then shoved it down his throat. I stood there and watched him choke and bleed until he went limp, and his eyes lost all life.

When I moved to Galway, I was more than ready for this to be over. He was shivering and had vomited down his front and shit himself. I curled my upper lip in disgust. "Any last words?" I asked.

"You're a monster. She'll never stay with you after this."

"I am, and maybe she won't, but she'll be safe and free from you and them."

I took my time not only lowering and applying the shears to his pathetic excuse for a cock, but I slowly wrenched it from his body, making sure to twist and tug without too much force for a long time. Finally, after I removed it, I shoved it down his throat and watched him choke to death. That completed my numb state. I dropped the shears on the floor and hung my head. It was quiet behind me. I didn't want to look, but I knew I had to. I might as well get the pain over with. Taking a deep breath, I turned and looked up.

I rocked back on my heels as I was crashed into by a flying object. My arms automatically wrapped around it, holding her to me. She was sobbing and shaking, but she was placing kisses all over my face and mouth. She was rambling about how much she loved me. I sagged and almost hit the floor in relief.

I don't know how long I simply held her before she led me out of the room. My brothers and the Patriots stood there in utter silence. She was carrying a small bag with her. I had no idea where it came from. I was in a daze. The next thing I knew, I was being stripped of my bloody clothes and then shoved into a hot shower. She removed her now bloody clothes and joined me. She washed me from head to toe twice before cleaning herself. Finally, I began to snap out of it when she began to dry me off. I took the towel away and dried her tenderly.

I stayed quiet until we were both dry. As she handed me a set of clothes and shoes out of the bag and took out a set for herself, I had to say it. "How can you do it?"

"Do what?"

"Stand to be near me or touch me. I mutilated and slaughtered those men. Yes, they were animals, but I'm no better."

"You did do those things and more to them. But there's a reason I don't see you in the same light as I did them. The reason why you're not an unforgivable animal who I can't stand to touch or be near. Are you ready to hear why?"

I nodded.

"It's because you turn into a blood-thirsty avenger in the name of vengeance, but not just any vengeance. Yours is the kind to take out the true monsters in the world who prey on the innocent and those in need of saviors. You don't do it for pleasure, petty revenge, or money. That Diablo, I can stand by every damn day of the week. You're not getting rid of me that easily, Victor. I love you."

I dropped to my knees at her feet, clasped her to me, and sobbed into her belly. She held my head and let me weep like a baby. She held me until I was all cried out, then helped me to my feet.

"Jauhnna, you are one in a billion. I will never forget this. I love you so damn much, baby."

She smiled and then took my arm. "Don't forget you said that when I argue with you or piss you off."

I chuckled. I knew there was nothing she could do to make me ever stop loving her. We left the bathroom to find the others. We were met by Gio, waiting outside the bathroom. "I've been delegated to tell you two to get some rest. We're cleaning up the mess, then we'll be headed back to Florida. There's a room you can relax in. It's the Captain's berthing, but he said to tell you to please use it." He led us down the passageway to another door.

"Thank you, Gio."

"It's my pleasure. Go. Relax."

He smiled as he walked off. Opening the door, I took her inside. It was a nice room. Much nicer than I expected on a boat. I took her straight to the bed. I was exhausted. I knew she had to be too. I curled up on the bed with her. She snuggled into me and sighed. I rubbed my hand up and down her back. In no time, my eyes grew heavy. I drifted off with my Serenity in my arms and my soul filled with light and happiness.

Jauhnna:

We'd been home for a week. Our time on the ship seemed like a bad dream. I wasn't remorseful at all for what we did to those eight, not even my brother. They didn't deserve my pity. The person I was concerned about was Diablo. The way he'd been after he finished them off had scared me. Then, to have him break down and cry had torn my heart. All because he was terrified I would hate him and no longer love or want him. Since our return, we have been kept updated by the Patriots' leaders on what was happening to Janus and Galway's two mini kingdoms. They were being torn apart, and those who were at the top or were key members were systematically disappearing or arrested.

We were all gathered in the clubhouse this evening. Torch, Brooklyn, and the kids had come for a visit. They planned to stay the week and spend Thanksgiving with us. I was excited. She and I had a whole feast planned for the club. They'd gotten here several hours ago. We'd spent time at the house, just the six of us, before coming over to hang out with the club.

I was enjoying watching Thane running around the room and having a ball. Brooklyn and I were sitting together. Torch was talking to some of the guys with a sleeping Jai in his arms over at the bar. Diablo had excused himself a couple of minutes ago to go take care of something. He told me he'd be back in a few minutes.

I was laughing at Brooklyn's story about how she met Torch when Diablo returned to the table. I glanced up, smiling at him. It quickly turned into a gasp as he hit the floor. He was down on one knee, and in his hand was a ring. There was no doubt, seeing it, that it was an engagement ring. My mouth dropped open.

"Jauhnna, my Serenity, my love, I can't wait any longer. Our whole family is here. Will you do me the greatest honor of saying yes to becoming my wife? I will love you until the end of my days and beyond," he said sweetly.

I was speechless. His words and the ring took my breath away. It was a heart-shaped diamond with alternating blue sapphires and white diamonds along the band. There were intricate borders made of tiny beads of metal. The gems were set in silver. Blinking back tears, I whispered the one thing that would prevent me from saying yes.

"We can't get married. I'm still married to Galway, and it'll take seven years for him to be declared legally dead," I moaned. Even dead, the bastard was still messing up my life.

"Is that your only reason for not letting me put this ring on your finger?"

"Of course it is! I love you. I want nothing more than to marry you."

His smile took me by surprise. Then he slid the ring on my finger. It was so beautiful. I loved it. "But—"

"But nothing. I have a way to make it happen."

He rose to his feet and held up my hand. The guys all began cheering along with Brooklyn. Thane cheered, although he had no idea why. He made me laugh. Diablo sat back next to me. We received everyone's congratulations. Brooklyn admired the ring before it got quiet enough for him to explain how we could possibly pull this off.

"We can be married as soon as you want."

"How?"

"Well, we have Micro and Smoke to thank for that. It seems they didn't want us to have to wait seven years. They knew I'd want to make you my wife, so they worked their combined computer magic. Lo-and-behold, we have official paperwork filed in Nevada, it seems, signed by Galway Radigan, dated three months ago. It seems he filed for divorce, and since you didn't contest it, it was finally reviewed by a judge, and he signed off on it three days ago. You're no longer Joanne Radigan. At the same time, the judge authorized your name change request. Joanne Radigan nor Joanne Vierra exist anymore. You're legally Jauhnna Carter, soon-to-be Tate."

I squealed, then launched myself into his arms. He chuckled as I kissed him. He slipped his tongue into my mouth and kissed me deeply. We kept going until Brooklyn made us break apart laughing.

"Ewww, come on, Dad, stop kissing Mom and giving her tongue. My poor eyes," she said with a crinkled-up nose and laughing eyes.

"Keep that up, and you'll be sent to your room, young lady," I teased back. I then thanked Micro, who waved it off as if it was nothing. Everyone was talking and teasing when Diablo held up his hand. They got quiet.

"I've got an engagement present for you. Well, it's actually for both of us. I can't claim sole responsibility for it either. Again, Smoke and Micro and probably

Everly had a hand in this, too. Here," he handed me an envelope.

"Honey, I don't need anything else," I protested.

"You'll want this," Micro said with a grin.

Opening it, I read the paper inside. My heart leaped, and I had a hard time catching my breath. As the words sank in, I dropped the paper and lifted a shaky hand to my mouth. I stared at Diablo in utter disbelief.

"Is this for real? Are you sure?" I whispered.

"It's very real, and I'm one hundred percent sure."

"Well, what did he give you?" Brooklyn asked impatiently.

"A child," I said hoarsely.

"A what?" she asked.

"A child. Remember I told you about Jaycee, the little deaf girl at the Halloween party? This says that official paperwork has been submitted to adopt her. It was backdated to six months ago. How? There's no way they'll do this."

"Actually, they will. According to their records, you and I have completed all the required background checks and other requirements. Having a judge sign off on it is the final thing. As long as we're married before the final paperwork is filed, it's a done deal. It seems the Patriots have connections. And if that doesn't seal the deal, I've been told the O'Sheerans have some judges who owe them favors as well. In the meantime, since we've also been approved as foster parents, Jaycee can be brought home with us as early as tomorrow if we want. She should be with her family for Thanksgiving," Diablo told us softly.

As Brooklyn began to scream excitedly about finally having a sibling and the guys were congratulating us a second time, I burst into tears and fell into my man's arms. Never in a million years had I thought I'd be this happy or have everything I dreamed of.

Diablo: Epilogue-Christmas Day-Five Weeks Later

Watching Jaycee playing in the common room with Thane and the new toys Santa had brought them for Christmas made me smile. She'd settled into her new home with us effortlessly. The entire club, as well as Brooklyn, Torch, and even Thane, were learning sign language so we could communicate with her. She was learning to read lips, which helped.

She was a happy little girl who smiled constantly. She adored her room and loved picking out all the furniture and colors with her new mommy. Every time she signed Mommy to Jauhnna, my woman's eyes would mist up, and she'd smile. Brooklyn adored her baby sister and teased me about making her wait so long to give her one. I joked back, telling her I had to wait for my woman to grow up.

The age difference between us didn't truly bother me, although I knew some people might have an issue with Jauhnna being so close in age to Brooklyn. Those individuals could go fuck themselves. I was happy and content.

Next month, the judge was to sign off on Jaycee's adoption. We could hardly wait. In order to be ready for it, the week after I asked Jauhnna to marry me, we went to the courthouse and got hitched. We were planning to have a celebration after Jaycee became ours to celebrate our wedding and her adoption together. Invitations had already been sent out to our friends in the various clubs and the Patriots. It was going to be a huge affair. I offered to do a large fancy wedding after the courthouse one, but my wife said it wasn't necessary. We had photos of us dressed up for it, and that, along with the marriage certificate, was all she wanted.

Everyone was in the best of moods after a fantastic Christmas dinner cooked by the ladies. I offered to have it catered since they did Thanksgiving, too, but they got mad and told me no way. They'd made a massive feast. We'd be eating leftovers for a couple of days. I loved holiday leftovers.

I was relaxed back in my chair, talking to Torch, Butcher, and Scorpion, when Jauhnna came over to me. She was giving me a tender look. I returned it as I held out my hand to her. She let me draw her down onto my lap. As she settled, she surprised me by handing me an envelope. I took it.

"What's this, baby?"

"One final Christmas present."

"Serenity, I don't need anything else. You, Jaycee, and Brooklyn spoiled me this year. Enough." I tried to hand it back. I had no idea what it was but I didn't need it.

She shook her head. "No, you need to open it. If you don't want it after you do, then we'll talk."

The others gathered around to see what it was, the nosy shits. I opened it, withdrawing the single paper inside. Unfolding it, I read it. I stopped breathing. I gulped and re-read it. Reading the same thing as the first time, I glanced up at her. I knew disbelief was written all over my face.

"Is this for real?" I asked hoarsely.

"What is it, Pres?" Turbo asked. Others were asking the same question.

"It's very real. Do you want to return it?" she asked huskily.

"Fuck no!" I shouted as I came to my feet with her in my arms. I swung her around as I latched onto her mouth. I consumed her. As I did, the others were all shouting, asking what it was. I took my time answering. When I let go of her mouth, I faced them with the biggest grin on my face.

"Well, what is it?" Brooklyn asked impatiently.

"It seems my beautiful wife had to one-up me and make me even happier. She got me a baby for Christmas." Silence greeted that announcement. Pandemonium broke out seconds after my announcement.

"A baby?" Brooklyn shrieked.

"How?"

"What do you mean?"

"You're adopting another one?"

Those questions came from my brothers. I waited for them to settle down. Once they did, I asked her, "How is this possible? You can't get pregnant."

"Well, it seems Galway was a liar in a lot of ways. He took me to the doctor and had us both undergo testing. I was told by the doctor I was barren, as you know. It seems it was a lie. He must've paid the doctor to tell me that instead of the truth, which was he was the one who was sterile. Seems Micro is very thorough in his research. I asked him to check it out for me because I couldn't believe the results either. He was able to access my actual record and results. And yes, it's been confirmed by an actual doctor. We're going to be parents in mid-July. It seems we've been playing with fire all this time. I hope you're ready to expand our family. I know it's sooner than we talked."

We'd talked about adopting another child in a few years after Jaycee was in school and fully settled.

"Serenity, I'm more than ready."

It was deafening as everyone shouted their amazement. I let them hug her and shake my hand, but as soon as they were through, I was done.

"Thank you, but I need to have some alone time with my old lady. We have some private celebrating to do. Brookie, watch your sister."

"Eww, Dad," she said as the others laughed. Jauhnna giggled as I lifted her higher in my arms and headed for the door. It was time to take her home and make love to her. Who knew a stop along the road to investigate a car would lead me to a second chance at absolute happiness and a second family? Fate took away with one hand and gave with the other.

The End Until Book 2: Title TBD

Note: For those who read my O'Sheeran Mafia series, you may be confused by me referring to Patrick as the head of that family and not his oldest son, Darragh. The reason is, Diablo's book occurs almost eight years prior to Darragh's Dilemma, the first O'Sheeran book.

Printed in Dunstable, United Kingdom

80185140R00208